Triple Layer

Kingston High, Volume 3

Sundae Leighton

Published by Sullen Press, 2022.

Triple Layer (Kingston High Book Three)
Available in these formats:
978-1-7376181-5-7 (Paperback)
978-1-7376181-6-4 (Ebook AZW)
978-1-7376181-7-1 (Ebook EPUB)

Beta Reader: Stephanie Cooper

Cover: E. Leighton – inspired by Books and Moods 'Piece of Cake' cover

Editor: Kay Kemp Book Polishing

Playlist

One Too Many— Keith Urban/Pink
  1 Kissed a Girl— Katy Perry
  Then He Kissed Me— The Crystals
  betty— Taylor Swift
  Heathens— Twenty One Pilots
  Burning— Alien Ant Farm
  Wrecked— Imagine Dragons
  Easy On Me— Adele
  Way Down We Go— Kaleo
  Here With You— Sick Puppies
  Bang, Bang— Ariana Grande, Nicki Minaj
  Shivers— Ed Sheeran

To the people who are never afraid to be themselves, this book is for you.

A note about Triple Layer

This book takes place after *Cakewalk*, but before the epilogue. The Knights have not yet graduated high school, which also means Brett and Easton are not married. If you have not read the first two books in the Kingston High series, *Piece of Cake* or *Cakewalk*, and wish to avoid any spoilers, I highly suggest reading them both before going any further. If not, proceed at your own risk.

As with all of my books, this is intended for mature readers over the age of eighteen. It contains violence, sexual nature, dark themes, and suicidal tendencies that may cause triggers for some readers. Proceed at your own risk.

Welcome back to the madness of Kingston High. The Knights have been waiting for you.

Prologue

Jonathan

I was so drunk that I could hardly see straight. Oz Maxwell had insisted on throwing a party because he could, because it was Christmas break, we didn't have school, and—I think, but don't quote me on this part—because he wanted to try to get drunk enough to get Palmer Wilson out of his head. He was going about things all goddamn wrong, but I was one to talk, wasn't I? I knew nothing about love or relationships.

There was a strange girl rubbing up on me right now, tits pressed against my chest, and her arms wrapped around my body. And even though I thought I was strictly into dudes until this very moment, I was certainly enjoying myself.

This girl... She was anything but ugly. I glanced down to find her watching me from beneath long, dark lashes, her eyes bright and green. Her cheeks flushed pink when our eyes made contact, but she didn't look away. Instead, she slid her hand up to my neck, and then this strange girl was kissing me, and I was kissing her back with a force that I had never used before. Her tongue was everywhere inside my mouth, twisting and turning around mine; and my dick, well, it was responding—as it should. God, I was rock fucking hard for her.

"You're an amazing kisser, Jon." Her breath was hot against my mouth. She slid her hands down my chest before she dragged them back up and into my hair. "Confession," she murmured. "I've had an eye on you for a while now, but—and please don't take offense—I thought you might be into guys." Her soft giggled made my stomach clench.

She nipped hard at my bottom lip before she spoke again. "Maybe we can take this somewhere a little more private?" She pulled back as her green eyes darted around the overcrowded party.

It wasn't like girls hadn't come on to me before—I was a Kingston Knight—but I usually made out with them for a bit, let them fondle my cock, and then made up a lame excuse that they seemed to buy. I had no idea who this gorgeous girl was—which meant Easton and Oz would have my balls tomorrow—but I realized as I searched her face that I really wanted her.

She had long, almost white hair that fell straight to her hips, plush, plump lips that turned up into a beautiful smile, and big emerald eyes, filled with lust and heat, that seemed to watch me.

I nodded, reached for her hand, and began to lead her upstairs to my room.

It felt normal to be doing this. Some of the other guys did this shit all the time, but I wasn't like them. I was the quiet, shy loner, who didn't hook up with random girls only because I was gay, or maybe I just hadn't found the *right* girl. At this moment, I had a beautiful one who couldn't seem to keep her hands off of me. We stopped so that I could unlock the door to my room, and before I had a chance to shut it, she pressed her frame against mine, her hands wrapped around my waist. I kicked the door closed behind me.

"Kiss me again, Jonathan," she whispered, and I did just that.

The moment our lips met, 'heat began to build all over my body. Her scent was intoxicating. Her hand slid under my shirt against my skin, and I felt like I might die if I didn't get inside her. I started to drag her toward the bed, then eased onto the mattress.

I pulled back to stare down at her. "Who the fuck are you?" I hissed, drinking her in.

Her chest heaved as she sucked in air, and the tight yellow dress she wore highlighted every curve of her perfect body.

"Does it matter?" she purred, trying to lean back in to kiss me again.

When I held up a hand to stop her, she rolled her eyes.

"Ellie," was all she gave me before her hands started to wander again. This time, they traveled down to my dick, and it was anything but flaccid. "Looks like you like girls after all, Jonathan." Ellie reached for the button on my jeans before she moved to rest her lips against my ear. "Or maybe it's the boy in the corner who's doing it for you," she whispered. "I don't blame you; he's a looker, that's for sure." Her breath was hot against my skin, and desire pulsed through my veins.

Wait, the who in the what? It wasn't completely dark in my room, and as I let my eyes move around, I noticed the figure sitting in the chair in the corner.

"Who the hell is he? How the hell did he get in here?" I resisted the urge to push Ellie from my lap. Then I realized he was naked and stroking his dick, his pants pooled down around his ankles. My own cock jerked inside my pants.

"Relax, that's my boyfriend. He picked the lock on your door." Ellie's tongue rolled against my skin, causing the blood in my veins to pulse. "He likes to watch." She nibbled my earlobe. "And maybe if you're a good boy, he'll join us when the mood hits," she purred.

I should not be doing this right now. Easton would fucking freak if he knew I was having sex with two random fucking people in the house, but Jesus Christ, Ellie had her hand wrapped around the width of my cock, and her boyfriend was jerking himself off. What if he wanted to join in? Did he want to fuck me, too? My eyes rolled back as Ellie fondled my balls, and I thought about what it would be like to have someone inside me, fucking my ass as I fucked her pussy. One of my fantasies coming to life.

"You like that, don't you, dirty boy," Ellie whispered into my ear, and I groaned as her hand moved up to wrap around my length again. "What if I sat on your dick instead? Bet you would like that, too." She sank her teeth into my neck, biting softly, and I didn't hold back the groan that rumbled through my body. This was wrong in every way imaginable, but I liked it.

"Fuck him, baby," her boyfriend ordered from the corner. "Ride his cock so I can watch."

My eyes flew open to meet his hooded brown ones, and a sly smirk spread across his handsome face. I noticed how tightly his hand was wrapped around his own length. It looked almost painful, but I couldn't look away.

He was, without a doubt, the most attractive guy I had ever seen. Dirty blonde hair, dark brown eyes, and broad ass shoulders that looked like they were meant to be held on to. His chest looked massive, as if he spent hours in the gym, and I was mesmerized as his bicep flexed with each movement. He didn't shy away from my stare, never broke eye contact, and neither did I, even as my brain screamed at me to run. Run as far away from this situation as possible before it was too late.

Ellie planted wet kisses against my neck and up my jawline before she sat back on her feet. "Is that what you want?" She glanced over her shoulder to look at her man before she met my eyes again. Her hand came up to graze my chin. "We're not going to hurt you, Jon." The pads of her fingers danced across my face, and it was like little shocks of electricity hitting my skin. "Unless you're into that sort of thing." Ellie winked.

Hurt me, I screamed inside my head, but instead I swallowed the lump in my throat. It felt so dry I could hardly breathe.

"Yes." I croaked. "I want that." I sounded so fucking lame, but I couldn't help myself. I was finally about to lose my virginity.

"Good." Ellie dragged her thumb over my bottom lip before she climbed from my lap and then the bed, keeping her back to me. "Be a sweetie and unzip my dress?" she asked.

My hands shook nervously as I reached out to pull down the silver zipper. When I did, she turned back around to slip the yellow straps down over her shoulders, and the fabric dropped to the floor. Ellie wore no bra underneath, only a simple yellow thong that matched her dress.

"Thanks." The smile she flashed lit up her face, and I realized just how beautiful she was.

Dimples appeared in her cheeks, and her skin was a creamy porcelain. I suddenly had the urge to grab her so that I could kiss her until one of us had to come up for air.

Ellie pointed at my crotch with a manicured nail. "You want to take off your clothes or just stay like that?" The teasing in her voice made my dick twitch.

"Take them off," her boyfriend demanded, causing my eyes to move back to him. I noticed a few pieces of ink dotted across his chest that I couldn't make out from where I was. "Stare later, sweetness. Take off your clothes," he growled, and again my cock jerked against my pants.

I could fight him. He was in my house, my bedroom, and I was, after all, a fucking Kingston Knight. But when it came to sex? I was a novice. I also had this need to be dominated that I couldn't explain, and as I climbed from my bed to tug off my shirt, remove my boots, and shed my jeans, I couldn't help the thrill that ran through my body. I knew the rest of the guys weren't virgins, nor had they been for a long, long damn time. I wasn't like the rest of them, and I had been waiting what felt like a lifetime for this moment.

"That's much better." Ellie's hands suddenly danced across my chest, over my pecs, and grazed my nipples, causing me to hiss as she hooked them around my neck. She was smaller than I had realized, hardly coming up to my shoulders. "You're a ballplayer, right?" She tilted her head up to meet my eyes. When I nodded, Ellie's plump lips landed against my chest, her tongue flicking against my skin. "Nice," she cooed. "Sit back down, Jonathan."

I did as she asked. "Condom," I blurted out just as Ellie started to straddle my waist. "It's the only thing I'll ask of you." I glanced over at her boyfriend, who gave a curt nod. "In the top drawer of my dresser," I told her.

Ellie pressed her lips against mine. "You're prepared," she murmured before she slipped from my lap. "I like that in a man."

She quickly found the never-opened package of condoms, ripped open the box, and then tore the wrapper off as she turned back to me. I groaned softly as her hand gripped my thick length so she could slowly slide the rubber down to the base.

"There you go, baby, all safe and protected." Ellie climbed back up onto my lap. "You're going to fucking love this, I promise." Her eyes glittered with need before she slammed her lips over mine.

My eyes went wide the moment Ellie's wet entrance made contact with my dick, and even her mouth couldn't hide the sound I made when she ground herself down my length. I gripped her hips, my nails digging into her skin, and Ellie moaned softly as she wiggled against me. She lifted her hips back up, and I saw stars as she began to slowly move above me.

"You like that?" she murmured, her hands in my hair as she slowly bounced on top of me.

All I could think about was not blowing my load, because I was seconds away from doing that. My balls twitched as Ellie yanked on my hair, her lips never leaving mine. Her soft little moans only made it harder to concentrate. I tried to think about things that wouldn't turn me on. My twin brother Jameson having sex, my grandmother having sex—hell, anyone else in my group of friends having sex—but it wasn't working. I pinched my eyes together as liquid fire rolled through my body and tried to enjoy my first time, but it was going to be over soon if I didn't rein it in.

"You look so sexy, baby." His voice was closer now. *Too close.* "You're so fucking beautiful," he whispered.

My eyes popped open to find Ellie's boyfriend right behind her, his hands cupping her tits, rolling her nipples between his fingers. She turned her head back to kiss him, their tongues tangling together before she turned back to face me.

"You good, Jon?" Ellie panted, but my eyes were no longer focused on her.

It was him I was watching now. His dark, smoldering brown eyes drew me in as Ellie rolled her hips over mine. Her little mews of delight filled our ears, her tight cunt working me over.

He leaned forward, bringing his lips closer to my ear. "You like her fucking you, Jon, or is it me you wish was fucking you instead?"

I couldn't stop the groan that escaped my throat. He chuckled softly.

"That's what I thought, sweetness." His hand suddenly gripped my throat, his lips found mine, and his tongue invaded my mouth in a violent kiss just as my orgasm hit me.

I gripped the nape of his neck, pulling him closer, biting and sucking on his tongue while he tightened the grip he had on me. He captured my cries as I came, his teeth biting at my lips. The bitter taste of copper filled my mouth as I poured myself into the condom.

Ellie rode me, flicking my nipples with her fingers, and my body jerked and trembled until I had nothing left inside me. Her pussy clenched around me as her orgasm hit her, and then hot cum splattered against my chest as Ellie's boyfriend's own release hit me. It only made me want more.

He pulled back with a proud smirk on his face, his fingers releasing my throat and trailing down my chest.

"Fuck, that was hot," he commented. "Babe, wouldn't you agree?" He turned to look at Ellie, who was still sitting on my lap, her hair plastered to her face with beads of sweat.

"Fucking hot," she agreed. "We should do that again, but I need a minute to gather myself." Her face was flushed as she eased up off me to lie on the bed.

I looked up at her boyfriend, whose name I still didn't know, just as he leaned forward to slide his lips over mine, catching me off guard.

"Mind if I use your bathroom?" He tilted his head toward the door. When I nodded, he disappeared, and I brought my attention back to Ellie.

"He likes you."

"How can you tell?"

Ellie brushed the hair from her face. "He doesn't normally kiss the first time. Just me." She touched my face. "Are you all right with all of this? I mean, honestly? You were a little drunk when we burst in on you." She seemed different now that the booze was wearing off, but I couldn't let my guard down.

"It's fucking. Of course I'm all right with it." However, my heart was beating so loud in my chest I was pretty sure the entire house could hear it over the music. I carefully removed the condom from my dick, tied it up and tossed it into the garbage can by my bed, trying to calm myself down.

She twisted her lips up into a half smile. "Right." Ellie's eyes moved to where the bathroom was before she spoke again. "He won't fuck you this time." She sat up to twist her long hair up into a ponytail and yanked a yellow elastic from her wrist to keep it there. "Maybe next time, though."

"What about next time?" He came strolling from the bathroom, a smile on his handsome face, and my dick was instantly hard again. "We're already planning a next time?" He winked at me. "Get on all fours, baby." He playfully slapped her ass as she did.

Ellie grinned at me as she wiggled her behind. "You ready again?" Her green eyes blazed with need as I watched her boyfriend raise her hips before he sank inside her pussy. "Fuck, that's it." She moaned and reached out her hand. "Let me suck your cock, Jon."

I glanced up at him, waiting for his instruction, and when he nodded, I moved closer so that Ellie could wrap her red lips around my dick.

But my eyes never left his face.

Chapter One

Jonathan

My brain was literally vibrating in my head. Jesus Christ, I had way too much booze last night, not to mention the MJ that Ellie had been passing around between her boyfriend and me while we caught our breath before going at it again. He never touched me other than that kiss we shared and to wrap his hand around my throat, but I was more than happy to suck him off while I fucked his girlfriend the second time around.

I sat straight up in my bed, not caring that the room was spinning and I felt like I might pass out. Ellie was gone. Her boyfriend was gone, too, and I was alone. Shit, they left without even saying goodbye or exchanging numbers.

Idiot, I thought to myself. That was a onetime three-way with a gorgeous girl, and her hot as hell boyfriend, who let me suck his dick, kissed the shit out of me, but didn't tell me his name or fuck me. Damn. What a waste of a first time.

I managed to climb from my bed and move to the bathroom to take a piss and freshen up a bit, before I noticed the message scrawled across the mirror in bright red lipstick.

That was fun. If you're interested in doing it again sometime, you can text me. Xo Ellie

She had left her number, too. As I stared up at the red mess, I felt a smile stretch across my face. They hadn't snuck out doing the walk of shame after all. I ran my hand through my messy hair and thought about texting her. It was a terrible idea, but since she had left her number, it couldn't hurt.

I moved to grab my cell from where I had left it charging on the corner of the dresser, added Ellie's number, and then quickly cleaned off the message before I turned off the bathroom light. I dug around for a clean pair of sweats in my dresser and skipped down the stairs into the kitchen to find the rest of the Knights, sitting around the kitchen table.

"Someone got some last night." Cash Donovan snickered while his blue eyes danced with laughter. "Could you at least put a shirt on and cover up the evidence?" He jutted his chin at me.

When I glanced down, I noticed the hickeys and claw marks all over my chest. How had I missed that in the mirror?

My eyes went wide. "Shit, I didn't even realize." I folded my arms over my chest, trying to remain cool about the situation, but my insides felt like jelly.

"Who was the lucky girl?" Oswald Maxwell grunted without looking up from his phone. Bastard was meaner than hell lately since Palmer Wilson had broken his heart. Not that any of us ever thought he had one in the first place.

"Was it that cute blonde-haired girl I saw leaving this morning, because, dude? She was fine as hell. Nice little ass." Jameson, my twin, wiggled his brows at Oz, and I tried not to look guilty as I looked to Lennox Maxwell, Oz's cousin, for help. Shit, the cameras were everywhere outside.

Lennox smacked the back of Jameson's head. "One, you have a girlfriend, or did you forget?" She stood up to wash out her cereal bowl, knocking into Cash on the way. There was no love lost between those two. "And, two, you saw a girl leaving. Maybe she was with Jon." She was the only one other than Brett and Jam, who knew I was into guys. She flipped on the water to drown out the noise.

"Not with me. I never let them stay overnight," Oz announced. "But can someone tell me what the fuck Spencer Pearson was doing leaving here last night?" His near black eyes met mine. "Because that prick isn't allowed anywhere near my property, even if he's making a booty call." His nostrils flared as he waited for an answer, looking around the table before they landed on Len.

"Why are you looking at me?" she demanded.

Oz narrowed his eyes into angry slits. "Because you're the only single female in this house, cousin. So unless Spencer was sleeping with Cash or Jon, then you need to explain yourself," he growled.

I swallowed. "Spencer Pearson?" I couldn't breathe as I tried to remember why that name sounded so familiar.

Cash cackled like a hyena. "Yeah, Spencer Pearson Kissed my sister, tried to steal Easton's girl. *That* Spencer Pearson. Goes to Weston High, big, dumb asshole of a football player." He tilted his head. "You feeling okay, Jon? You look a little peaked." He pursed his lips. "Wait, Len, did you fuck Pearson?" Cash suddenly realized what Oz was talking about as he sprang from his chair. "Lennox, I swear to fucking God, I will kill that motherfucker if he even touched one hair on your gorgeous head," he warned.

Lennox rolled her eyes. "Calm down, caveman." She placed a hand against his chest before she smacked the back of his head with the other.

"What the fuck, Len?" he shouted as her hand made contact.

"Oops, my bad." She batted her lashes at him. "Come on, Jon, let's go upstairs. I have to talk to you for a second, bestie to bestie." Len flashed a smile at her ex. "And, no, Cash, I didn't fuck anyone last night except my vibrator, which, if you must know, is the only action I'm seeing these days." She started to guide me around the back of the table and up the stairs to my room, where she shut and locked it behind her.

"Seriously?" she hissed. "You slept with Spencer Pearson?" Her jaw was clenched so tight I thought she might break her teeth.

I shook my head. "No, I... not exactly." I grabbed a shirt to cover up the hickeys all over my chest. "I wanted to, though. He kissed me." I left out the part about me getting him off with my mouth.

"Jonathan, what were you thinking?" Lennox sat down on my bed but quickly jumped back up and brushed off her behind. "What about Ellie? Her, too?"

"We had sex."

"Jesus Christ."

I shook my head. "No, not him." I tried to make a joke, but Len didn't even crack a smile. "I didn't know who they were!" I exclaimed, and then clamped my hand over my mouth. "I was drunk, high, and stupid. Ellie came onto me. We kissed, fucked, and then Spencer kissed me." God, did he kiss me. My eyes must have given me away, because Len's face softened. "It was amazing. I did suck him off, though," I admitted.

She smiled. "Tell me about it," she said, sitting back down again. "Come on, come on, and don't leave out the details because I know how big of a deal this was for you." She patted the spot next to her.

It felt good to have my best friend here with me. I missed having Lennox in my life, and as I eased myself onto the mattress next to her, I couldn't help but spill everything that had happened.

Once, when we were little, Lennox and I were close. Best friends close, and when she stepped back into Kingston months ago, I had hoped it would be that way again. It took a little while, but Len was starting to open up to me again. Little moments like this were what helped.

I chewed on my bottom lip. "I always thought my first time would be with a boy," I admitted. "Not that it wasn't amazing, because Ellie felt perfect." My stomach clenched at the memory of her wrapped around my dick, and I felt desire stir within me.

Lennox grasped my hand and laced our fingers together. "You're still a virgin where it counts." She teased. "You know that you can't see either one of them again, though, right?" Her eyes were serious as she ducked her head to meet my eyes.

"Don't talk to me like I'm a still a kid, Len." I yanked my hand away. "It was a stupid mistake."

Lennox dragged her teeth across her bottom lip. "Promise me."

I gritted my teeth. "I don't have to promise you shit." I grunted. "I need you to leave so I can take a shower." I stood up.

"Jon, please, I'm your best friend. I'm only looking out for you. If Oz or Easton—"

I saw red. "Best friend? Really? Because the way I remember it, you decided to get into a shitload of fucking trouble, and I didn't hear from you for nearly two years. What kind of a best friend does that, huh?" I roared, not caring who heard me. "Get out." I pointed at my door. "Now, before I physically remove you. We wouldn't want to explain that to the rest of the Knights now, would we?" My lip curled up over my teeth.

I saw how Lennox wanted to push back. How her eyes went round at the anger in my voice, the fight in my words, but she simply stood up and moved to leave like I demanded. She unlocked the door and twisted the knob, but before leaving, she turned to glance at me over her shoulder.

"I'm sorry, Jon, for hurting you the way I did. You know that. It hurt me more than you know. I missed having you in my life," she whispered before quietly shutting the door behind her.

"Fuck!" I cried, and before I realized it, I had reached for the lamp next to my bed, tossing it against the door. I watched it smash against the wood and break into pieces on the floor. I dropped back onto the bed, cursing myself for my sexuality, my friends, everything. Then I remembered Ellie had given me her number. I yanked my phone from my pocket, knowing this text was going to seal my fate.

Jon: *You should have told me who your boyfriend was.*

Ellie: *Who is this?*

Jon: *Let me refresh your memory. You rode my dick while your boyfriend kissed me, then came all over my chest. Sound familiar?*

Ellie: *Jon, how are you?*

Jon: *Very fucking funny. Spencer does know how much the Knights want to kill him, right?*

Ellie: *Not you?*

Jon: *We can't do that again, do you understand?*

Ellie: **sad face emoji**

Jon: *I'm serious, Ellie. My friends will castrate me, kill your boyfriend, and Oz will do God only knows what to you.*

Ellie: *That sounds like it might be fun. Is Oz into anal?*

This girl was fucking sick, and I'd be lying if my dick didn't like it because it was so hard right now it hurt.

Jon: *You can be cute all you like, but I shouldn't even be having this conversation with you right now.*

Ellie: *Aw, you think I'm cute?*

Jon: *You know you're gorgeous.*

Ellie: *Thanks, Jonathan. You're not too bad yourself, handsome.*

I needed to stop texting her. I needed to delete her number, block her, and forget about everything that happened last night before this got out of fucking control.

Ellie: *Are you still there or did you block me already?*

Jon: *You know I can't keep doing this.*

Ellie: *Doing what?*

Jon: *This, whatever it is.*

Ellie: *It was fun, right?*

Jon: *It was fucking amazing.*

Ellie: **water emoji* You should come over tonight. Spencer's parents are away.*

Jon: *I can't do that.*

Ellie: *Right, the Knights. It's too bad you let them make all the rules for you, handsome. Oh, wasn't your brother dating*

Easton's ex-fiancé or something like that? How did that play into the situation? Didn't Josie try to kill Brett, who turned out to be her sister? Or did I get that all wrong? News travels fast. Even to Weston.

I stared at my phone, debating on whether I should respond. I could hear my friends laughing downstairs, Cash hollering at Oz about being a dickface because he drank the last bottle of Gatorade, Easton screaming at everyone to shut the fuck up because he and Brett were still sleeping, and Jameson was saying something about leaving—he was off to see Josie. I sighed as I felt that familiar feeling of being alone settle over me. I already knew what I had to do.

I quickly deleted Ellie's message, then blocked her before I jumped into the shower. I guess I would just have to get used to being alone.

Chapter Two

I heard about what happened to Cash Donovan and the rest of the Knights through the grapevine. News traveled fast, especially stuff like that, and even though Spencer and I knew getting involved with the one of the Knights was a horrible idea, we didn't care. I was glad to hear that Cash was okay, though. I had left Jonathan my number the morning before we left, scrawled across his bathroom mirror, and I had never expected to hear from him. After all, he was from Kingston, I lived in Weston, and my boyfriend was Spencer Pearson.

I was more than surprised to hear from him the next morning, only to have him block me minutes later. I guess we should have told him the truth. But if we had? Jon never would have taken it as far as he had.

I had always thought he was cute, handsome even, and that was the reason we had crashed the party in the first place that night. Spencer had gone to their Christmas party—not for Diana Monaco, but to try to talk to Easton about what had happened with Brett—only to be shoved into something he never expected. He had told me to stay home, afraid I would get hurt or worse.

Turned out he was right about that. Easton had threatened to kill him for showing up after what had happened when he'd kissed Brett, and luckily, Spencer had been able to escape while no one was watching, but we knew we couldn't go back there. *Ever.* Anything we thought we might have felt with Jonathan wasn't something we could act on. He would need to come to us, and that didn't seem like it was going to happen any time soon.

I looked up at the sound of the bell over the door announcing a new customer. I plastered on a fake smile, raised my chin, and felt my stomach drop when I saw his brown eyes. I knew it wasn't Jameson, his twin brother, because Jonathan was different. Handsomer, kinder, and the hickey I left on his neck was a dead giveaway. I could see the surprise on his face, too, when he saw me.

"You." He seethed, taking a step forward. "What...?" He glanced over his shoulder toward the window. That only meant he wasn't by himself.

I licked my lips. "Welcome to Gerry's Donuts." My voice shook as I spoke. "Can I interest you in one of our holiday flavors? Get them before they disappear. Peppermint Glaze is one of most popular this time of year." I watched as Jonathan's hands flexed into fists at his side. "Or maybe you'd like to try our Eggnog Surprise."

"I don't give two fucking shits about your stupid holiday donuts, Ellie," he hissed between clenched teeth. "You could have told me your boyfriend was Spencer Pearson." A darkness I didn't like had spread over his face. His brown eyes were now black, and his lips pinched into a thin line.

I opened my mouth to tell him we were just trying to protect him. To keep him safe from the rest of the Knights, from people at Weston. But the look on Jon's face told me that he had already made up his mind about us.

"I'm sorry," I whispered.

"Sorry?" Jonathan's eyebrows shot up. "You're sorry? Do you know what would happen to you, to Spencer, *to me*, if Easton finds out about *any* of this?" He took several steps closer. "He'll kill you both and banish me from Kingston forever."

His nostrils flared, and I couldn't help but want to reach up and touch his face. Drag my fingers across his strong jawline, over the scruff that wasn't there the last time I had seen him. I couldn't help but remember what it had felt like when I had kissed those lips while I was above him, riding his thick, long cock until I came undone.

Heat stirred in my belly, and even though I knew he hated me for lying, I wanted Jonathan to touch me just like he did that night. He had grown so hard when Spencer had kissed him. Spencer and I'd had plenty of threesomes before, but none of them had compared to what we had felt with Jonathan. He was different.

We stared at one another for what felt like forever until someone laid on a horn outside, causing us both to jump. I laughed nervously, but Jonathan only bared his teeth, spun on his heel, and stalked away from the counter as the door opened again.

"Dude, what in the fucking... hello." Cash Donovan grinned at me with surprise on his face. "Is this what's taking you so long?"

He didn't try to hide the fact that he was checking me out. His blue eyes moved from my face, down to my breasts, and over my hips before they met my eyes again. "Wait, you're her." He pointed a finger at me as he nodded his head approvingly.

My pulse started to speed up. "Her?" I glanced over at Jonathan, who looked like he was ready to rip Cash's head from his neck. Had he told his friends about me? About what had happened? That was impossible, because after Jon texted me, he blocked my number. He wouldn't have. Would he?

"Forget it, man." He slammed his hand against the glass display case. "A dozen of whatever. I don't care."

Cash shook his head. "No, she's the girl from the party. The one that you fuck—uh, slept with." A sly smile the size of the Grand Canyon spread across his gorgeous face.

Say what you want about the Knights, they were all beautiful in their own way. Cash had those boy-next-door good looks with his blonde hair and blue eyes, but I could see something brewing beneath the surface that told me not to mess with him.

"That's what was taking so long. Where you trying to get her number or something?" He wiggled his eyebrows at me. "Make sure there are at least four chocolate frosted in that mix. Those are Brett's favorite," he added as I began to pick out donuts. "Make it two dozen. I'm buying. Add in some strawberry frosted, too, if you can. Len likes those."

"The fuck are you doing?" Jon grunted. "You shouldn't even be out of the truck. Brett will kill me when she finds out." His eyes felt like they were burning right into my soul as I boxed up the first dozen and started on the next.

I glanced over at Cash, who winked at me. "I, uh, heard what happened," I muttered, making sure to grab the best-looking frosted donuts. "How are you feeling?" I tried to make conversation.

"Don't talk to him." Jonathan sneered.

Cash's brows dipped. "Dude, rude." He shook his head. "You heard, huh?" He gave me a flirty wink. "I'm healing. Thank you for asking." He leaned casually against the glass case. "You should come hang with us sometime. Come to the house and meet the rest of the fam."

"Cash," Jonathan warned. "Shut your fucking trap."

That was never going to happen, but I appreciated Cash trying to include me. He clearly was the nicest one of the Knights, but if he knew who I was? He would haul my ass back to Easton so fast I'd never see the light of day again.

I closed up the second box, slapped a Christmas sticker on top, and placed it on the counter. "Thanks for the offer, but I'll have to pass." I rang up the two dozen. "That will be eighteen forty-six," I announced, not making eye contact with Jonathan.

I could feel the anger radiating from his body, and I knew that if I looked at him, I would unleash my own hell. He had no reason to take out his aggression on me. We never agreed to anything other than a good time. Even if what we shared was mind-blowing.

"He has my number." I shifted my attention to the friendly Knight, whose jaw dropped at my admission.

"He hasn't called you?" He gasped.

If looks could kill? Yeah, I'd be dead. Jonathan's eyes were narrowed into angry slits as he stared at me while he shoved his credit card into the machine before Cash did.

"Ellie, maybe you could shut your goddamn fucking mouth, too," he warned.

Cash looked between the two of us, tilted his head, and smirked. "You know, I thought for the longest time that my man, Jon, here might be batting for the other team. Not there is anything wrong with that, because there are some fine ass men out there. Myself, included." He slapped Jon on the shoulder. "Fix this shit because she seems too good for you." He grunted. "I'll be outside. Nice to meet you, Ellie, and maybe I'll see you at the house sometime." He wiggled his fingers at me before he disappeared from the store, taking the donuts with him.

"What in the actual fuck, Ellie," Jonathan growled, and I'd be lying if this alpha version of him wasn't doing all kinds of things to my lady parts. "Cash is going to tell all the Knights about you. I'm going to have to explain to them who you are, what happened, and why I didn't call you. Or why I blocked your number on my damn phone. You just made this an even bigger mess than it already was." His eyes flashed with anger.

He started to stomp toward the door, and I didn't even realize I was chasing after him until I touched his arm. He spun around and caged me in against the newspaper display.

"I thought..." I couldn't breathe. He was too close, his scent invading my senses, and I just needed him to understand what I was thinking.

"You fucking thought wrong." Jonathan's lips were inches from mine. "You, me, and Spencer?" His lips twitched. "Are nothing more than a onetime mistake that will never happen again. Do you understand?" He pushed away. "Tell your boyfriend if he ever comes back to the house, I'll kill him myself," he warned.

I watched in horror as Jonathan left me standing there, shaking with fear, as he climbed up into the black SUV. Cash said something to him, and Jonathan shook his head, then they looked back at me before I hurried back to the register to grab my phone so I could text Spencer.

***

"I can't believe he said that to you." Spencer had his arms wrapped around me as I sobbed against his chest once I got home. "I'm going over there."

I shook my head. "No, baby, you can't," I warned, pulling back to look at him. "The Knights hate you," I reminded him.

"Fuck the Knights," he snarled, catching a tear that fell from my eye with his thumb. "He made you cry. No one makes my girl cry." He crushed me against his strong chest again. "I don't care what Jonathan Hamden said. I'm going to have strong words with that prick, whether he likes it or not," he promised.

I loved this man. We had met when he was dating someone else—a girl who couldn't handle his sexual tendencies. When she'd gotten jealous because of me, Spencer broke up with her and started dating me instead.

She had been the one to invite me into their bedroom, teasing me about how exciting it would be to have the three of us together, but the moment Spencer put his lips on mine, that was it for her. Me? I wasn't the jealous type. I knew he enjoyed having others in our bed, male and female, but I also knew that Spencer would always come back to me. It had been nearly four years since we'd met, and we were still together.

"I don't want anything to happen to you, Spence."

I couldn't bear the thought of being without him. He was my entire world, taking me in when my mother and stepfather kicked me out when I was fourteen years old. His parents were amazing, too, never asking questions, only wanting to make sure I was safe with a roof over my head. I counted my blessings every single day that I'd found him.

He pressed a kiss against my hair. "I know that you had planned to cook dinner tonight, but why don't we order a pizza, cuddle up on the couch, and find something good to watch on Netflix instead?" Spencer cupped my face with his hands. "We can turn off all the lights except for the Christmas tree, since we'll be taking it down soon." His brown eyes searched my face.

"That sounds perfect."

It warmed my heart how much Spencer cared for me when he could have his pick of any girl he wanted. They were constantly throwing themselves at his feet, stuffing notes in his locker, and, literally, pushing me out of the way. More than once I had been shoved aside when some jealous bitch had tried to get Spencer's attention, batting her eyes, and pressing her body against his. He was quick to put them in their place, making sure to remind them *I* was his one and only.

Spencer slid his mouth over mine. "You never know what might happen, baby," He murmured, his hands reaching down to grip my hips. "A little vodka mixed into my hot chocolate, and I might start to get a little handsy, remove your clothes, and..." He wiggled his brows at me just as the notification on his phone went off making his body grow tense.

I knew what the sound meant because I had the same one on mine. Someone was outside who hadn't been invited.

Spencer's hands landed on my shoulders. "Upstairs, baby." He gave me a gentle push. Just enough to warn me he was serious', and I quickly hurried upstairs.

Chapter Three

Spencer

The second I heard Ellie slam the door to our room upstairs, I hurried outside to the front porch to greet whoever had decided to show up at our house unannounced. Technically, it was my parents' place, but they were hardly ever home. Both were nurses, traveling all over the world and saving lives. I had been taking care of myself since I was twelve years old. There had been nannies, of course, but once Senior and Holly Pearson realized I wasn't going to burn the house down, they let me be.

I reached for the Glock in my waistband as I watched the black, shiny SUV slowly pull into the driveway while fear and desire curled inside my body.

He would never bring his friends with him. Jonathan would come alone, settle whatever beef he had with us once and for all, before he made sure we never said a word about this to anyone else. That, or the Knights were waiting outside the gate. But something told me that wasn't the case. Not with the way he kissed me, the way he touched me, or the way he looked at me with hooded eyes, desire so strong that it made me realize he wanted this as much as I did.

"The fuck, Pearson?" Jonathan didn't even wait until he was out of the truck before he started shouting at me. "You could have fucking warned me." He dragged his hand through his dark hair, and I noticed the exhaustion in his eyes.

What was Jon so scared of? That his friends would find out that he was into me or how much he liked it?

I shifted my weight on to my right foot as I folded my arms over my chest. "Not my fault you didn't recognize me." I tried to play it off as not caring, like I didn't want to shove Jonathan against the SUV, slam my mouth against his, and kiss him until I couldn't see straight.

I noticed the way his jeans hugged his muscular legs, his winter coat hiding any evidence of his thick, chiseled chest, but I remembered. Broad shoulders, the eight pack you could bounce a quarter off, and the perfect v shape that pointed to his thick cock that I wanted to taste with my own damn lips.

"I was drunk."

"Likely excuse, man."

Jon's body trembled with anger, his lip curling up into a snarl. "This can't get out, do you understand? Easton and the guys... will...it just can't." His hands pulled into tight fists at his side as he glared up at me with heated eyes.

I liked that he was shorter than I was, but not too short. I was a solid six three, so I pegged Jon to be around six feet even.

"Wouldn't dream of telling anyone, sweetness. Your secret is safe with me." I smirked.

Either I pushed Jonathan too far or he was already too revved up when he showed up at my house, but his hands shot out from his side to slam against me, and I stumbled, caught off guard. I instantly pushed him back, a growl escaping my throat, and Jon's foot went up, sweeping my leg.

I landed on the hard asphalt beneath me. That was going to leave a mark, but instead of giving up, I reached up, grabbed his ankle, yanked him down, and flipped him beneath me so I could pin him to the cold ground.

"Is that why you showed up at my place announced?" I could see Jonathan grinding his molars so hard that I thought they might snap. "So that you could hit me, push me around. To make sure I wouldn't say anything to the Knights? I'm pretty sure any conversation I have with them is going to start with Easton threatening to castrate me for touching his woman and me running as fast as possible before he makes good on his word."

I watched the way Jon's eyes darkened, the way his Adam's apple bobbed, and then I felt his erection beneath me. "Well, well." I brought my face closer. "You're not just worried about them finding out about me and you." I ran my tongue over his top lip, and the moan he let out had my cock hard as steel. "You're worried they're going to find out how much you want to do it again." I leaned down to drag my tongue over his neck and licked my way across the exposed skin.

"Get off of me." Jonathan struggled, but I pressed all of my weight down. He was a big guy, but I was bigger. Football worked wonders on me that way. His dark eyes flashed with heat, and I knew mine matched his.

"Tell me I'm wrong, sweetness." I felt the way Jon trembled when I called him that. "Tell me I'm wrong, about *all* of it, and I'll never bother you again. I'll take your secret to the grave." When he didn't say anything, I let out a small chuckle. "That's what I thought," I said softly. "Your secret's still safe with me, don't worry." I started to climb up off him, but this time, Jon grabbed me around the waist and slammed me back down so hard that when my head hit the blacktop, I saw stars.

He gritted his teeth. "You don't fucking know shit, asshole." He glared at me with fury all over his face.

"You want to hit me, tough guy? Go for it. I can't defend myself like this, but just know if you do? I'll come after you ten times harder," I warned.

Jonathan raised his fist, and I widened my eyes to prepare for the hit.

Only, it wasn't his hand that it hit my face. His mouth landed on mine, wild, fast, and hard. He tore at my lips, his hands digging into my hair with a growl so deep it vibrated through his chest. I opened my mouth and sucked his tongue. Raw need made Jonathan brutal with desire. He wasn't alone. Our tongues fought for control, our hands everywhere we could grip one another until just as suddenly as it started, Jonathan was up and on his feet, staring at me with wild eyes.

"I didn't. I shouldn't..." His hair stuck up in every single direction. "Shit!" he shouted before his eyes zoomed in on something behind me.

I slowly moved myself up into a sitting position and knew instantly, without turning around, that Ellie was there. "Baby, want to see if our guest wants to come inside? Fix him some of the hot chocolate that we like?" I kept my gaze fixed on Jonathan.

Ellie walked around me. "Would you like that, Jon?" She didn't try to touch him, but I could smell her soft perfume as the wind picked up. "We were going to relax by the Christmas tree. You're welcome to stay for as long as you like." Her voice was soft, sweet, and alluring. Ellie always had a way about her. Jon might have been mean to her earlier, but she would forgive him the second he stepped into the house.

Jon licked his lips nervously, and for a split second, I thought he was going to say no. Instead, he nodded his head before he followed her up the steps into the house. I would give her hell for dressing in nothing but a bathrobe later, but right now, I needed to put some ice on the knot that was forming on the back of my head.

I slowly climbed to my feet to walk inside and did a double take when I saw Ellie leaning against the doorframe, watching me. "Where is he?" I whispered, embracing her.

"Sitting in the kitchen, staring at the hot chocolate. I think that he might be worried it's laced with something."

"Baby, it is. There's vodka in it."

She swatted playfully at my chest. "I meant something worse." Ellie giggled before we walked inside the house. I locked the door and set the alarm behind me. When I got to the kitchen, Jonathan had a ring of chocolate around his mouth. Clearly, he wasn't worried about dying tonight.

"Um..." I pointed to my lips. "You have a little..." I leaned forward to reach for the napkin in front of him, only to have Jon slap my hand away.

"I'm an adult, Pearson. There's no need for you to clean me up," he assured me.

I held up my hands. "Fine, sure, you got it." My eyes slid down his exposed arms, the way his biceps flexed with each movement, only to have Ellie elbow my side. "Right, you're welcome to stay. We're ordering pizza." I moved toward the walk-in pantry to grab a plastic bag before I opened up the freezer, dug out some ice, and placed it against the back of my head. Fuck, that hurt.

When I walked back to the table, Ellie was holding Jon's hand in hers, talking softly to him. "He'll stay." She glanced over her shoulder at me. "Said he doesn't want to drive home now that he's had a little alcohol."

"Trying to get me drunk now." Jonathan rolled his eyes. "Pizza sounds good, too," he added, making sure to keep his gaze on Ellie. "If the offer still stands."

Ellie jumped up. "Of course." She grabbed her phone. "We usually order half cheese, half pepperoni, but since there's two of you the size of Texas, how about we get two large of each?"

"Sounds good, baby." I hooked an arm around her waist, dropped a kiss against her cheek, and then sat in the seat she just vacated. "You're not going to stay here, eat my food, and drink my booze, only to ignore me." I placed the bag of ice on the table. "You can act like I exist." I grabbed Jonathan's hand when he tried to stand up. "I mean, dude, if you're not interested, fine, but don't pretend I'm not here," I snarled.

Jonathan looked down at my hand before he dragged his eyes up to mine. Fire flared behind his chocolate browns, and that's when I realized what the actual problem was.

"It's not that I'm not interested, Spencer," he assured me. "They don't know."

"My brother knows. Brett and Lennox, too, but the rest of them have no idea."

"Dude, it's not like this is 1776 or something. Times have changed. You really think that the Knights would hate you because you're into guys?" I felt my stomach sink when I realized the actual problem. "It's me they would hate you for."

Jonathan nodded, but then surprised us both by lacing his fingers through mine. "Answer me something," he said, his thumb rolling against my palm and stirring my cock again. "Why did you go after Brett?" He looked up at me from under his lashes, which were thick and longer than a man should have.

I cupped Jon's cheek with my free hand before I could stop myself. "Because I was after you, idiot," I told him. "There are rumors about you. How you're the only Knight who doesn't have a girlfriend or doesn't have a different chick on his arm wherever you go. Kissing Brett was not what I had planned. It was an accident, and it was fucking stupid. Ellie and I have shared girls before, but she's the only one I want." I stroked his cheek with my thumb, watching the way his pupils dilated. "You're going to go back to hating me after tonight, aren't you?"

"I don't have a choice, Spencer." Jonathan sighed. "Up until that night, with the two of you, I had never been with anyone. Male or female." His voice was soft when he spoke.

I tried to keep the shock out of my face, but it was hard. The famous Knight, Jonathan Hamden, had never fucked anyone? "Are you lying?" I whispered, pulling his face closer, wanting his mouth on mine, his lips, his tongue, his *everything*.

"Not to you." Jonathan untangled our hands to run his fingers through my hair. "I don't think I could do that."

I stared at him, and he stared right back, looking at my lips as if they were his dinner instead of the pizza that Ellie had just ordered.

"Why?" I pushed.

"I hate myself."

That did it. Our lips collided when he admitted that, and I could hardly keep myself from ripping off his pants to wrap my mouth around his dick. I wanted to make Jonathan see that he didn't have to hate who he was, that he could be gay, straight, bi, or anything he wanted in this world. People would love him for him, and if the Knights couldn't love Jon the way he was? He could find people who would. His hands yanked on my hair, his breath came faster, and I reached down to cup his junk, only to have him groan at my touch.

"I'm starting to feel like you two only like each other." Ellie's teasing voice came from beside us. When I held out my hand, she took it so I could yank her closer and pull her into the embrace I was sharing.

"You two are so hot when you eat one another's faces like that," she murmured. When her tongue slipped in with ours, blood roared in my ears, and my dick strained against my jeans like it wanted to punch its way out.

Soft little moans, harsh growls, hands everywhere, grabbing and gripping as the three of us tried to keep from losing ourselves all over again. I was seconds away from pushing Ellie and Jon away so that I could take control. Order them to both strip off their clothes, take turns licking one another before I got my hands on Jonathan. I might have, too, if the pizza hadn't shown up.

It didn't matter. The night was young, the three of us were already revved up, and I planned on having my way with Jonathan before he left my house tonight.

Chapter Four

Ellie

I stared at Jonathan as he slept in the guestroom. He had one arm flung over his eyes, his mouth slightly open, and even though he wasn't snoring, I imagined it would only make him more adorable if he were. He had drunk way too much vodka with his hot chocolate last night to drive home, and even though Jon had insisted he was fine, Spencer and I convinced him to stay the night.

Spencer had parked his SUV in the garage so it wouldn't be seen, put his boots, keys, and cell right next to the bed in case he needed them, then left him alone so he wouldn't feel like we were trying to take advantage of the situation. I don't think Jon felt that way about us, not anymore, but we still wanted to make sure.

"What time is it?" Jonathan grumbled from the bed. "How long have you been watching me?" He rolled onto his side to reach for his phone, and I caught a glimpse of his toned side as his shirt lifted. "Shit, I should go. I never texted anyone to tell them I wasn't coming home." He sat up. "Fuck." Jon combed his hand through his hair as he turned his cell back on.

I dragged my teeth over my bottom lip. "Couldn't you tell them you're with me?" His head spun around to meet my gaze. "Cash already saw me yesterday; saw how you acted around me." I shrugged my shoulders. "Wouldn't that be a good cover?" I saw the wheels in his brain starting to move.

"Maybe." His voice sounded like he was a million miles away. He stared down at his cell as a bunch of messages started to come in, not saying anything. He finally looked back up at me. "Where's Spencer?" Jon let his gaze travel down my body, taking in my oversized Weston Eagles sweatshirt and skinny jeans I'd thrown on after my shower.

I took a step into the room. "Is that what this is? You prefer him over me?" That had happened once before. A football player from another town had hooked up with us, but really, he'd wanted Spence, and when he'd tried to push me out of the picture? Spencer had set his ass straight. I ran my hand over my ponytail, twisted the hair around my wrist, and waited for Jonathan to answer.

He didn't respond at first. Then he stood up, so that he towered over my five foot six frame, and stalked toward me. "Did I fucking say that, Ellie?" Jonathan growled, pushing me back against the doorframe, and slid his hand up to my neck. "I'd kiss you, but my breath is—"

I rose to my toes so I could kiss him, not caring about Jonathan's morning breath nor the aftertaste of the alcohol from last night. Just a soft brush of my lips over his to watch the way his eyes darkened, feel his grip on me tighten, and feel Jon press his body closer against mine.

"Spencer had something to do with the football team this morning," I whispered.

And, just like that, Jonathan took a step back.

"What's wrong?"

"I should go."

I shook my head. "Jon, you don't have to leave." I watched as he yanked his keys from his boots before shoving his feet inside. "Talk to me first," I insisted, wanting to touch him, but afraid of what might happen if I did.

"It's so easy for you, isn't it?" He grunted, sitting down to tie his laces before he looked at me with anger in his eyes. "You can be with Spencer, or whoever, and no one cares. But me?" Jon stood up. "I can't be that guy." He stabbed himself in the chest with his index finger.

I swallowed nervously. "No one is saying you have to be *that* guy," I whispered. "We like you. That doesn't mean you have to have sex with us. Just hang out."

Jon's nostrils flared as he stared at me, his face stone. "I. Can't," he hissed and brushed past me on the way out the door.

I couldn't just let him leave like that. Already, Spencer and I felt a connection to Jonathan Hamden. One we knew he felt, too, and if he left now? He would never come back. I watched his back, his broad shoulders, as he retreated down the hallway, and my heart stuttered in my chest.

"Jonny!" I called out to him. The nickname wasn't something I had ever thought someone would use on him, but somehow it felt fitting at this exact moment.

He came to a complete stop. "Why... why would you call me that?" Jonathan's voice was low as he slowly turned back around. "My dad used to call me that when I was kid, said my mom called me Jonny when she was pregnant..." His voice caught in his throat, and I rushed to him without thinking.

"Come sit back down." I wrapped my arms around Jon's waist. "Just for a second." I tried to tug him back down the hallway, but he felt like he was made of bricks. His arms landed around my body, and that felt like a step in the right direction.

"Ellie, I can't stay here," he warned.

I rested my chin against Jonathan's chest. "I didn't say stay, did I?" I huffed and saw the corner of his mouth twitch.

He moved with me this time when I started to walk and sat down on the bed with me. I released him to crawl up onto the guest bed and stretched out my legs. "My parents kicked me out when I was fourteen," I announced. "Well, my mother and stepfather," I corrected myself.

Jonathan's head spun around to look at me. "Why?" he demanded. "Did you do something that got you in trouble?" He twisted his frame slightly. "Other than the liking to have sex with multiple partners at once, you seem like a good girl," he teased.

I lifted my arms up to rest them behind my head. "I do, don't I?" I pursed my lips. "I got into some trouble at the school I was in before." I crossed my feet at the ankles, waiting for him to put two and two together, but when he didn't, I glanced at the empty spot next to me. "Lie down, and I'll tell you a story, Jon." When he did as I asked, even copying my pose, I giggled and shook my head. "Can I ask you a question first?"

"Not if it has to do with my parents," he answered, keeping his stare fixed on the ceiling above us.

Fair enough.

I sighed, turned onto my side, and flattened my hands onto the pillow. "Fine, I'll just tell you why my parents kicked me out instead," I said. "They left me home alone a lot, and I was bored." I waited to see if Jonathan would interrupt or interject, but when he didn't, I continued. "I started throwing parties for the kids in school. I charged a few bucks a head to pay for the booze, the food, and stuff like that. Which isn't really a big deal until one of the older kids I was hanging out with suggested we start having orgies."

That got Jon's attention. His head turned ever so slowly, his eyes wide, and mouth slightly agape. "Say what?" He blinked at me.

"Teenagers get horny. You know that."

"You're telling me that you threw fucking sex parties. At fourteen years old." I could hear the astonishment in his voice.

I nodded. "Until someone caught the clap and started to pass it around the entire school," I admitted, sitting up and wrapping my arms around my legs. "I'm not proud of that." I told him, seeing the look on his face.

Jonathan stared at me until he threw his head back and laughed. Not just any laugh, a full-on body-laugh that made my lady parts tingle with a need so strong that I wanted to beg him to eat my pussy until I came shouting his name. It was nice to see him let go and relax. Clearly, he didn't do that enough.

"I was suspended from school once they found out." I flopped back onto the bed once he had stopped laughing. "Then my parents kicked me out. My stepfather said something about me being a bad influence on my younger brother and sister, or something like that. I had met Spencer at one of the parties, so I wasn't participating in them anymore, and when I told him, he invited me to come live here with his parents, no questions asked."

Jonathan reached for my hand. "He seems like a good guy." He applied a little pressure.

"He's the best," I assured him.

"My mother died after giving birth to Jam and me." Jonathan's eyes were sad as he spoke. "My dad tries, he does, but he's never around. I can't tell you the last time he was home, and sometimes I think he has a family somewhere else. He called us on Christmas, but we never saw him." He closed his eyes for a moment.

"Is that why you live with Oz?" I pushed, and when he nodded, I leaned forward to brush my lips against his. "The Knights are your family." I understood now why Jon was so afraid to tell them. He had no one else.

"Fuck." He sat up and grabbed his phone from where he had dropped it. He shot off several texts and then glanced at me. "Hope you don't mind that you're my new girlfriend." A blush creeped up his neck. "Um." Jonathan ran his hand up through his hair and then down to grip the nape of his neck. "Lennox knows about us, all of three of us. She's the only one."

I tilted my head. "Who?" The name sounded familiar, but for some reason I couldn't place her.

"Lennox is Oz's cousin." Spencer announced from the door, his arms folded over his chest. "How does she know?" He looked pissed about something, and I bet it had something to do with the football team. They hadn't been having the most spectacular year.

Jonathan popped his jaw. "I told her," he admitted. "She and I were—*are*—close. Why you two ever came to that party is beyond me." His eyes darkened, and I'm sure his memory was flashing back to that night, just like mine was. "There are cameras all over the place. Outside, inside, just not in our rooms. Oz fucking saw you, Spencer, but not at the party, only leaving." His nostrils flared angrily. "I told Len about what happened, and she won't tell anyone. She's trustworthy."

"Not even Cash?" Spencer moved to sit on the edge of the bed. "They were together once, correct?"

I looked between the two of them. "Wait, Cash? Cash had a girlfriend?" Why couldn't I remember her? I thought I knew everyone from Kingston High.

"I really have to go now." Jonathan's phone was blinking like crazy as he climbed to his feet. "Thank you," he blurted. "For letting me stay here last night, and everything." He dropped his gaze until Spencer gripped his chin. "This has to stay quiet for now."

Spencer nodded. "You need to tell them. I don't care what they do to me."

"I fucking care, and I won't let them hurt you or Ellie. Just because she's a girl doesn't mean they won't hurt her," Jonathan snapped. "Please, just let me do this my way." He nearly begged.

Spencer leaned forward. "For now," he whispered.

Chapter Five

Jonathan

Jameson: *Dude, where are you? It's nearly midnight. Not that I'm your babysitter or anything.*

Oz: *Take me out of your stupid group texts. I'm fucking serious. I hate this shit.*

Lennox: *Jon, are you okay?*

Cash: *Bet he's with Ellie.*

Brett: *Who's Ellie?*

Cash: *The girl he met at the party. She works at Gerry's. Seems she gave him her number, and he never called.*

Easton: *You really need to get laid, don't you, Cash?*

Lennox: *Um, you do remember I'm in this group, right?*

Easton: *Who do you think I was talking about when I said he needed to get laid?*

Oz: *Dude, gross. That's my cousin you're talking about. I hate it here. I am blocking every single one of you sick fucks.*

Cash: *Eat a dick, Easton.*

Easton: *That's what I have your sister for, asshole.*

Brett: *Easton!*

Easton: *Sorry, babe.*

Jameson: *Is that why you're not texting us back? Because you're balls deep in that blonde?*

Cash: *Len, you know where to find me.*

Oz: *I'm turning off my phone now. Forever. Don't knock on my door or I'll murder you all.*

Jameson: *This keeps getting better and better. Is someone making popcorn?*

Jonathan: *Sorry, guys, I was busy with my girlfriend. I should have texted sooner. I'll bring her over for dinner tonight. Can you at least try to be respectable adults when you meet her? Yes, Cash, that was directed at you!*

***

I took a deep breath, climbed from the SUV, and headed inside the house, only to have Cash nearly knocked me over as I made it into the kitchen.

"Get the fuck off of me!" I tried to push him off, but he wouldn't budge.

"Jon has a girlfriend!" he sang out to the entire house. "Did you all hear that?" He slung arm my shoulders with a big grin across his face. "When do we get to meet her?"

I rolled my eyes. "You met her already, asshole," I reminded him. "Shouldn't you be, I don't know, resting instead of tackling me like that? You were fucking shot." I met Lennox's gaze as we walked into the finished basement.

"Is it the girl who was here the other night?" Len asked casually. I could already see the questions in her eyes, and the fact that I had ignored the separate texts she had sent me. I had been busy, a little hungover, and scared as fuck. I still was.

Brett looked up from where she sat on Easton's lap. "Welcome home, Jon."

She had her purple hair pulled up into a messy bun on her head, her face clear of makeup, and a sweater that matched her hair, curtesy of Cash. At one point, we all thought he had the hots for her, before we found out they were twins, but that was a story for another time. She unfolded her legs to stand up. "Are you really bringing her over tonight?" She flashed a smile at me, but I could already see her mind working. It was why we all loved Brett so much.

She was one of us—a Knight—even before we realized it. She knew my secret, but there was nothing on her face or in her eyes that even gave it away.

"Easy, babe, give the guy a break." Easton tugged on her hand and pulled her back into his lap. He was territorial all the time with Brett, growling and grunting at anyone who dared look in her direction even though it was clear she only ever had eyes for him.

I squared my shoulders. "Her name is Ellie, but you already know that." Holy shit, I didn't even know her last name. "And, she's coming over tonight so you can all meet her. Mostly because I want this guy to leave me alone." I hooked a thumb behind me at Cash, who was leaning against the banister of the stairs with a wicked grin on his face.

We had planned that before I left. Ellie would come over around seven, we could have dinner with the Knights, and then she could go home. Easy peasy. I knew Spencer was worried about how the guys would grill her, but with the girls here, it wouldn't be too bad.

"You're inviting strangers over without asking me first? You know how much that thrills the crap out of me." Oz grunted from the floor where he had paused his Xbox game. "Do you pay the bills now, too?" He grabbed for the cigarette behind his ear and stuck it in his mouth without lighting it. Geez, he was more miserable than ever.

I took a step forward. "I'm cooking. I already picked up the food, so you don't have to worry about paying for that, dick, and I'll clean up any mess, like I always do," I reminded him. I glanced up as I heard footsteps overhead.

"That's probably Jameson and Josie." I had texted my brother to tell him I expected him to be there and to bring his girlfriend, no matter how awkward it might get for everyone.

"Josie?" Easton growled from the sofa. "You think maybe you could have run that by *me* first?" His eyes blazed with anger. "We sort of, I don't know, were kind of engaged—ow, Brett, what the hell?" He winced when she pinched his side.

Brett flashed me a smile before she twisted around on her fiancé's lap. It was still weird to me to think of them as engaged at eighteen, but I guess when you know, you know, and they were obsessively in love with one another.

"Tin Man, we talked about Josie, did we not?" she whispered, but not low enough because we all heard. "She's my sister, and I want to try to get to know her despite everything." Brett cupped his face in her hands.

"Fine, whatever." Easton rolled his eyes, but I saw the smile on his face as he leaned down to kiss his girl.

Oz snorted. "Pussy whipped." He coughed, and Easton shoved his middle finger up in the air to show him how much he cared what Oz thought.

"Sounds like I'm missing all the fun," Jameson called out as he came down the stairs. "Little brother, where's this mystery girl?" He held up his fist, and I gave him a quick bump, but the room grew eerily quiet when his girlfriend—Easton's ex—slowly appeared behind him.

Her red hair was strategically styled over the right side of her face to cover the burns she had suffered from the fire at Brett, Cash, and her father's house last fall, but it didn't hide her beauty. One green eye peered out at me as she gave a quick nod, before she looked around the room.

Josie had changed dramatically since that night. Instead of being dressed in her usual tight, hardly-there dresses, she wore an oversized Knights sweatshirt that I assumed belong to Jam and baggy sweats that did nothing to hide her curvy figure. She looked more than nervous as she hid behind my twin, and I actually felt a little sorry for Josie, even though I shouldn't. She had tried to kill Brett, beat the hell out of her, and used Jameson, who somehow still cared for her; all because she was convinced Easton wanted her. It was messed up.

Wasn't love grand?

"She'll be here soon enough," I told him. "I told her to be here at seven." You could cut the tension with a knife in this room, and it made my skin crawl.

Jameson slipped his arm around his girlfriend's waist. "See, I told you it was cool." He pressed a kiss to Josie's head. "Everyone is cool with this, right?" He seemed like he was daring someone to say something when he was the one who needed to be reminded that he stuck his dick in Josie while she was technically someone else's. Even though Easton did the same thing until he met Brett.

"I'm going to go wash up and get dinner." I didn't want to be here when all hell broke loose, so I headed up the stairs to the kitchen, and then to my room. "Seven o'clock!" I reminded them.

***

I was pleasantly surprised that there was no blood shed when I came out of my room a couple of hours later. I showered, changed into a fresh pair of briefs, jeans, and a white Henley before I came downstairs to start cooking. I stuck my head in the basement to find the boys watching football, while the girls, even Josie, sat around comparing Instagram accounts.

"No, this one." Brett pointed to the cell in Josie's hand. "That would look great on you." She nodded at her half-sister. "You have such beautiful hair," she added.

Wonders never ceased.

I smiled at myself before I went back into the kitchen to take out the food I had picked up on my way home from Spencer and Ellie's house. I loved cooking, always had. It was something I had started doing to relax, to ease the tension when I was younger, and for some reason, everyone seemed to think that I was good at it. So I tried to make dinner on most week nights when we didn't have baseball practice or games, and breakfast on the weekends if we weren't too hungover.

My phone buzzed in my pocket as I was turning the oven on to preheat. I grabbed the apron Jameson had bought me for our birthdays a couple of summers ago, pulled it around my neck, and tied it around my back before I checked the message.

Ellie: *Should I bring something?*

I glanced around the room and nearly dropped my phone to find Lennox standing there, her hip pressed against the counter, arms crossed, and a pissed off look on her face.

"What?" I ignored the message and shoved my phone back into my pocket.

"What are you up to?" Lennox stalked across the room. "Are you seriously inviting that girl into this house? Are you setting her up? She's dead meat if they find out." She narrowed her eyes as she flipped her dark hair behind her shoulder.

We stared at one another as my phone buzzed once, twice, and then it started to ring. "I know what I'm doing." I really had no clue other than what my dick wanted.

"Someone wants to talk to you." She reached down to grab my cell from my back pocket, but I smacked her hand away. "What? Afraid I'll ruin your little game?" She rolled her eyes. "I'm your friend, Jon, not them. They're—."

"Hey," Brett dropped into one of the empty chairs, followed by Josie. "We're bored with the baseball shit. Do you need any... what's going on here?" She waved her finger between Lennox and me. "You two talking secrets or something?" Brett leaned forward. "I love secrets. Spill the tea besties, because I really need some good gossip." She smiled.

I opened the fridge. "No secrets." I yanked out the chicken, potatoes, and veggies I had bought from the store. "No secrets at all." I assured the girls as I dropped everything onto the counter.

My cell buzzed again, and I knew that Ellie's nerves were probably just getting the best of her, but I didn't want to whip my phone out right now. Not with those three girls just sitting there watching me like that.

"Jonathan," Lennox purred, running her nails up my back before she gripped my shoulders. "Don't you think you should check your phone?" I was going to rip her a new one the next time we were alone. Some best friend.

I spun around. "Len." I flashed my fakest smile. "What I really need is for you to stop riding my ass so I can start dinner." I gritted my teeth.

Josie nudged Brett's shoulder with her own and mouthed, *"What's their deal?"* But I saw it. I had never really gotten to know Josie all that well, given that fact that she was forced into our group. Easton never used her more than a warm place to stick his dick in, and I never trusted her.

"Good question." Brett nodded. "What's really going on?" She leaned back in her chair. "I'm not leaving until one of you talks. So..." She brought her finger up to pursed lips and tapped her chin. "Who is this girl?"

I reached into the cabinet to take out the cutting board I needed, gently placed it on the counter, and turned to the half-sisters. Brett and Lennox knew the truth about me, but I wasn't ready to let Josie in on my life. But what choice did I have? She might talk to Jameson, but she wasn't about to run off to spill her guts to the other Knights.

"Ellie is from Weston." It wasn't a complete lie, but not exactly the full truth either. I watched Brett's brows dip, and then reached for my phone when it went off again.

Ellie: *Should I bring wine?*

Ellie: *What about dessert?*

Ellie: *I could make something.*

Ellie: *Are you ignoring me?*

Ellie: *Do you still have me blocked?*

Ellie: *Jonny, what the hell?*

A warm feeling creeped over my entire body at the nickname she had given me. I glanced up to find Brett watching me with a smile on her face.

"What?" I needed to text Ellie back before she thought I'd ghosted her completely.

"You need to tell them before they find out at dinner. If it comes out then? It might get ugly." She stood up. "Come on, girls, let's go upstairs and figure out what we're wearing." Brett wiggled her index finger at Lennox. "You're coming, too, Len, so you can leave Jon alone. He looks frazzled."

Lennox snorted. "I bet he does." She blew me a kiss as she walked off.

Jonathan: *Don't bring anything, and I'm not ignoring you. I've been busy.*

Jonathan: *Sorry, btw. It's crazy here. Fielding lots of questions. Most of which are coming from Lennox.*

I quickly got to work with the chicken, cleaning it out, and stuffing it with the veggies so I could get it into the oven so it would be ready on time. It wasn't until I had it in the oven that I realized Ellie hadn't texted me back. I hoped she wasn't mad at me or changed her mind about coming over tonight. All sorts of scenarios began to run through my mind until I my cell buzzed yet again.

Ellie: *Too late. Spence helped me pick out the perfect wine from his parents' wine cellar. I also baked a pie for dessert because it's sort of what I do. Baking, I mean. See you soon.*

Chapter Six

Ellie

My stomach twisted into knots the moment I pulled my ancient Chevy up in front of the sprawling Maxwell house that had every single light lit up inside. Spencer had offered me one of his parent's' cars, but I couldn't take the chance of one of the Knights running the plate and seeing who it was registered to. Not to mention, I didn't actually want to drive a shiny new Ferrari or BMW when there was always that chance it could snow. They loved me as if I were their own daughter, but that could change if I crashed up one of their fancy, expensive cars.

I unhooked the seatbelt from my shoulder and opened the door so I could climb from the car, admiring all the shiny Christmas lights that lit up the Maxwell house, only to come face to face with Oswald Maxwell himself. His black eyes moved over me as if he were trying to decide if he wanted to have me for dinner, and not in a good way.

A cigarette hung from his lips, the smoke trailing out into the cool night air, and he tilted his head as he continued to watch me as if he were daring me to make a move. He was handsome, if you were into the serial killer type, with midnight black hair, broody dark eyes, and a sneer on his face that told me he already had made up his mind that he didn't like me. He wore no coat in the frigid December weather, and even though I was freezing with one on, Oz looked perfectly comfortable in his short-sleeved Red Sox shirt that stretched across his thick chest.

"Hell... hello." I stuttered over my words as I tried to maintain eye contact. I knew he was trying to rattle me, and I could feel it all the way down to my toes. "We haven't officially met, I'm—"

"Stop." Oz help up a hand, talking with the cancer stick in his mouth. "I know who you are." He ground his back teeth together as he continued to glare at me. "What exactly do you want, anyway?"

I blinked at him in surprise. "What do I want?" I felt the cold steel of my car against my back as I moved away from him.

"Cut the crap, Ellie. If that's even your real name." His nostrils flared as his dark eyes dug into me. He dropped the cigarette to the ground and crushed it with the bottom of his shoe. "You show up out of nowhere, sleep with my boy, and now you're his girlfriend? Smells like bullshit to me."

"Oswald Sidney Maxwell!" The sound of a female voice caused us both to turn to find a petite, lavender-haired girl standing there with her hands on her slim hips. I had never been this close to Brett Cake before, but I could see what all the fuss was about right now. She was stunningly beautiful with her big blue eyes, plump red lips, and curves everywhere. If Spencer had actually been interested in her? I would not have had an issue having Brett in our bed.

"Just what do you think are you doing?" She tilted her head.

"Introducing myself." Oz gave her the side eye as his lip curled up over his teeth.

I turned back to look at the so-called "Iceman" to find him with a sheepish look on his handsome face, but his eyes were still cold.

"That's how you introduce yourself?" I blurted out. "You didn't say hello or even tell me your name. It felt more like the third degree."

Brett stifled a laugh and covered her mouth.

"You didn't let me finish, *Ellie*." The way he said my name made bile crawl up my throat. A sinister grin spread across his face, and goosebumps broke out over my skin. "I'm Oz, but I think you knew that already. Welcome to my home." Oz stuck out his hand. I thought about ignoring it, only to realize I would probably regret it if I did.

Oz's cold hand swallowed mine.

"Ellie Young." I felt way he tightened his grip, a simple warning that he didn't trust me. Well, that made two of us.

"Enough." Brett grabbed Oz's wrist. "Go inside, find Jonathan, and tell him his date is here." She winked at me. "Now. Before I kick your ass for being so rude to your guest." She swatted at his arm as he strolled back toward his house as if he didn't have a care in the world. "Sorry about that, Ellie." Brett shook her head, and I watched as her lavender hair moved against her shoulders. "Oz is... different from the rest of the Knights. I promise you, the rest of them will be much more approachable." She chose her words carefully because he was her friend, and I wasn't.

"He listens to you." I was curious about that. How one woman could do that to them. I knew about the Knights—everyone did—but before Brett came along, they listened to no one but one another. "I understand. He's looking out for his friend." I smiled at her, grateful to have someone in my corner.

Brett shrugged. "I'll let you in on a secret." She moved a little closer. "Oz scares the shit out of me, and we've been friends for a few months now." She giggled nervously. "Did I even introduce myself?" Brett exclaimed, as she realized she hadn't.

"It's fine. I know who you are." I pointed to my head. "Your hair gives you away," I admitted.

Brett ran a hand through her mane. "My hair? Girl, yours is gorgeous. Is it natural?" When I nodded, she sighed. "I'm totally jealous."

"Really?" I wrinkled my nose. My hair was a birth defect that even hair dye couldn't fix, no matter how hard I tried to cover it.

She nodded. "Come on, let's get inside. It is freezing out here." Brett ran her hands over her arms.

"Let me just grab a couple of things." I moved around to the passenger side of the car for the wine and pie so that I could follow Brett inside. "So, you live here, too?" I tried to make conversation as we walked toward the house.

Brett nodded. "Yep, uh, it's a story I'll share another time, but I do. It's crazy at times, but I love it. Growing up, it was just my mom and me, so at first it was hard to live with the craziness. But it grew on me." She reached over to snag the pie from my hands. "Mornings before school are a total shit show, which makes me super happy Easton and I have our own bathroom. Could you imagine if seven people had to share just one?" Her blue eyes widened at the thought.

"Everyone lives here? In one big communal house?" I rather liked that idea. Most of the time it was just Spencer and me in his parents' big, quiet house.

"There you are!" Easton Kennedy slammed the front door against the side of the house to reach for his girlfriend—wait, Jon said they were engaged if I had heard correctly—and lifted her off her feet as he wrapped his arm around her waist. He didn't hesitate to crush his lips against hers, his eyes suddenly zoning in on me. Easton pulled back to take me in.

"This must be Ellie." His voice was low, and I got the same feeling I got when Oz was watching me.

That Easton did not like me, nor did he trust me one bit.

I swallowed nervously as I tilted my head to look up at the giant of a man who held Brett in his arms. His thick, muscled body was covered in colorful ink, his hair a dark brown, and his green eyes the color of perfectly cut grass. I noticed the way his eyes moved as he watched me, the way he sucked on his lip ring while Brett smiled happily up at him.

"Yes, it's nice to meet you." I felt like a pig being sent to slaughter the closer I stepped into this. The chemistry I felt with Spencer and Jon had better be worth it, because if the Knights figured us out? I shivered, and it wasn't because of the cold.

"Welcome." Easton's eyes did not match his happy-sounding voice as he held the door for me to come inside the house, where mass chaos seemed to be going on inside the kitchen.

Cash was running around in nothing but his boxers, while a long-legged, raven-haired girl covered in tattoos sat on the counter, tossing what appeared to be marshmallows at him every time he passed her and laughing when she made contact. Jon was standing there with a shocked look on his face, holding a plate of cooked chicken, his eyes wide, and his jaw pinched so tight I could feel it.

"What in the actual..." Easton muttered under his breath just as Cash came flying by again before he was beamed with another marshmallow.

I skirted past the dozen or so sugary treats all over the floor, placed the wine on the counter next to the brunette, and touched Jonathan's arm.

"Hey," I whispered as his eyes focused on me. "You need some help?" I asked softly.

I started to take the plate from him, but he eased it onto the giant wooden table in the middle of the room. I snapped my fingers at Cash, who looked so startled that he skidded to a stop in front of me. "Go get dressed and come back downstairs to clean this mess up," I ordered. He blinked at me with surprise in his eyes. I turned to look at the girl. Lennox, I guessed by the way she was now sizing me up.

I hated mean girls, but I had seen *Heathers* more than once, and I could be Veronica Sawyer if I needed to be.

Lennox hopped off the counter, and I would be lying if I wasn't a little intimated. She was tall, probably nearly five foot ten and the tattoos didn't help, but again, I was a tough girl who never backed down from a fight. Lennox was beautiful, with brown eyes that matched her cousin's, raven hair that she had up in a high tight ponytail, and curves that went on for days. Dressed in a pair of black jeans that had rips in the knees, and a plan white shirt, Lennox was probably used to people being afraid of her, but I wasn't just anyone.

She stared at me for what like forever until she finally broke into a smile. "Did you talk to Oz like that? Because if you did, I might want to date you myself," Lennox exclaimed before she pulled me into a full body hug.

I chuckled softly as I hugged her back before I felt someone pulling me away, and Jonathan wrapped his arms around me. "Thank you." His voice sent shivers down my spine and over my body, while heat flared between my legs. It scared me just a little because the only other boy who had evoked that response was Spencer, and even though we had his blessing, I wished he were here with us.

"I knew that I liked you," Cash announced as he made his reentry into the kitchen, fully dressed in a pair of jeans and a Pearl Jam shirt. "Did Oz give you the old growl and grit when he went outside to greet you?" He reached for the wine, only to have Lennox slap his hand away. "What?" He blinked.

"That's not for you, dumbass, that's for them." She pointed between Jonathan and me.

I shook my head. "Actually, that's a gift for everyone. I made pie, too." I turned around to where Brett was standing with Easton. "It's lemon meringue."

Cash brought his hand up to his heart. "I am in so love right now." He rushed toward his sister, and Easton growled at him. "What, dude?" He mocked surprise. "I want the pie, not your girl. She's my sister, or did you forget that part?"

"I want the pie, too, and you're not going to get your fat grubby fingers on it until after we eat." Easton lifted the dessert from Brett's hands, marched it over to the refrigerator, and plopped it inside. "Do not touch this or I will hurt you," he warned, but I saw a smile tug at his lips.

I liked the feeling of this house. The Knights really loved one another.

Jonathan still had his arms around me, and they tightened just slightly. "I think they like you," he whispered.

"Damn straight, we like her. She brought booze *and* dessert," Cash answered.

Lennox rolled her eyes. "I think that was directed toward Ellie, not you." She sighed, sitting down on one of the kitchen chairs and crossing her right leg over her left. "But please, make it all about you, nutsack." She flicked her fingers at Cash.

"Let's not do this now, kids." Oz grunted, appearing out of nowhere. He made sure to pin his black eyes in my direction before sitting down at the head of the table. "I'm starving, that chicken smells amazing, and I'm going to eat the entire thing myself if you all don't sit down."

Jonathan unwrapped himself from me and grabbed my hand. "Sit next to me, Ellie." He steered me to an empty chair, which happened to be next to Cash, just as Jameson and a red-haired girl walked in. She looked nervous as she looked around the room.

"You must be Ellie." Jameson leaned over to tap my shoulder. "I'm clearly the better-looking brother, but we can't all be so lucky, and this is my Josie." He indicated the girl next to him.

Holy shit, I thought Josie Silver was supposed to be dead. She nodded at me, her red hair covering half of her face, but it was impossible to miss the burns there and on her hands.

"It's nice to meet you both." I smiled brightly at them with so many questions running through my head. "Thank you all for allowing me into your home and to have dinner with you," I added, looking around the now-crowded table. Cash to my left, Jon at my right, with Brett across from me, and Easton on her left. Jameson was on Cash's right with Josie next to him.

"Any friend of Jon's is a friend of ours, Ellie." Cash stood up. "I'm going to open the wine while Jon starts cutting up that chicken," he announced.

Jon nudged my knee with his, and I hoped that everything after meeting Easton and Oz went smoothly as my nerves began to settle.

Chapter Seven

Ellie

After eating the most amazing chicken I had ever tasted, and then the pie I had made, I felt like I wasn't going to be able to move for a week. My stomach was full, my brain was a bit foggy from the wine, and I had to admit, I was having a much better time than I thought I would. Either the Knights weren't as bad as people thought they were, or they were behaving around me. I had to think it was the latter.

"Ellie, this pie is—" Lennox brought her fingers up to her mouth in a chef's kiss. "You two are a match made in heaven. Jon cooks, you bake, it was destiny." She grinned and licked the rest of the lemon from the fork.

I felt myself grow warm. "Thanks. It's just something I enjoy doing," I admitted. Jon's fingers laced through mine, and my stomach clenched as he squeezed lightly. Was it because I felt like I was cheating on Spencer, or something else?

"It was good," Oz mumbled next to me. The room grew silent at his admission until he looked around at everyone. "Oh, sorry, I paid the girl a compliment." He stood up. "Guess I should go eat shit and die now." He placed his empty plate in the sink before he turned to look at me. "Still not one hundred percent convinced you're not up to something, Ellie, but thanks for the wine, or whatever." Oz disappeared down into the basement as the rest of the Knights burst out laughing.

Easton dropped his arm around Brett's shoulders. "Ignore him; he's just a little dramatic right now." He nuzzled her neck before turning his emerald eyes back on me.

"Right now?" Jonathan snorted. "He's worse than ever." He ran his thumb over the back of my hand. "He'll come around. We don't call him the Iceman for nothing," he added. "You want to hang out a little while I wash the dishes, or do you need to head home?"

Jameson groaned. "Code for do you want to stay and have sex with me tonight?" He stood up. "Which is our cue to leave so we can go to my room." He held out his hand for Josie, who hadn't said two words the entire night.

They weren't too happy when they found out I was from Weston, but they got over it soon enough. Spencer's name was never mentioned, and the only person they asked about was Diana Monaco. I was more than happy to dish about what a cow she was because that bitch was always trying to dig her claws into my man.

The other thing that came up was Cash wanting to know if I got free donuts from Gerry's. He didn't even care if they were more than a day old because—and these were his words—*"Gerry's Donuts are a gift from God."*

I told him I'd see what I could do and had already made a mental note to bring some by the next time I came over. If there was a next time.

I stifled a yawn with my palm. "Let me help you with the dishes," I said to Jon, who only shook his head. "What, is that not allowed?"

"You're my guest." Jonathan squeezed my hand again. "This night was about everyone getting to know the girl I'm seeing. But next time—"

"There's going to be a next time?" Easton butted in. "No offense, but since when do you date? You've never even shown interested in the opposite sex before until two days ago, dude. And again, Ellie, you seem like a nice girl, but we don't really do nice."

Brett swatted his chest as she stood up. "I'm nice." She flashed him a smile, picking up her plate, and then his.

"Bullshit you're nice." Easton grabbed a handful of her backside as she turned her back on him, then roared with laughter when she slapped him away.

"I was waiting to find the right girl, that's all," Jon answered as anxiety began to pull at my insides.

Did Easton know or was he just stating the obvious? Everything had gone much smoother than I had expected up until this point. I was silently waiting for this night to explode in my face. Maybe Oz was downstairs plotting something right now.

Brett wrapped her arms around Easton. "Can't you be happy for them, Tin Man?" She winked at me as her hand slid down his chest.

Easton grunted. "Keep touching me like, babe, and I'll show you just how happy I am," he warned.

"Well"—Cash patted his flat stomach—"This is fun and all, but I'm going to bed since this is turning into a couples thing. Sweetheart?" He held out his hand to Lennox, who wrinkled her nose at him before flipping him the bird without saying a word.

"I have a better idea." She grinned. "Ellie, let me show you to Jonathan's room, where you can rest while he cleans up." Lennox pushed back from her chair. "Not that you don't already know where his room is. You shouldn't be driving after the wine you've had." She teased and made sure to squeeze Jon's arm as we walked by. I clearly had no choice but to follow her.

Neither one of us said anything as we walked upstairs. The house was quieter than the last time I was here since that there was no party going on. I wasn't sure if I should try to make conversation with Lennox or if she was going to use this chance to give me the don't-hurt-Jonathan-or-else talk. She stopped at Jonathan's door, unlocked it, and motioned for me to go inside, but followed right behind me.

"So," Lennox sat down on the same chase lounge that Spencer had been on that fateful night. "You probably know that I know." She leaned forward, planting her feet on the floor. "Where is Spencer right now?" she whispered, pursing her lips.

I swallowed nervously. "Home." I twisted my hands together. "I'm not sure what you think is going on, but we like Jonathan. We care for him, and we want this to work, Lennox. We're not going to hurt him," I assured her.

She leaned back, bringing her left leg up to rest it on her right knee. "So, maybe you shouldn't be doing this? If you really do care about him."

I smoothed the front of my dress down as my hands began to sweat. "I don't understand," I admitted.

"It's simple, Ellie. If you care about Jon the way you say you do, *you don't do this*. You don't date him, you don't see him, and the two of you don't fuck him." Lennox stood up with fire in her eyes. "When the Knights find out who you are—and believe me, it's only a matter of time before they do—they will kill Spencer, torture you, and banish Jonathan from here without a second thought. They won't make it easy on Spencer either, because of what happened with Brett, and when he just happened to show up at the party we had to try to get Diana Monaco to show up. She fucked with us, she put her hands on Easton without his consent, and now she's hiding. They want her, and they will do *everything* they can to find her."

She tilted her head. "Do yourself a favor. End this tonight and walk away." She patted my arm as she walked past me. "I do like you, which is a shame, and feel like you could fit nicely in our group, but Spencer Pearson?" Lennox shook her head. "He will never be welcome here." She shut the door behind her leaving me alone.

I sat down on the edge of the bed as tears filled my eyes. I couldn't let anything happen to Spencer. He was the love of my life. We had big plans to get out of here when we graduated in June. We both felt a connection with Jon, but we weren't sure if it was enough to risk our lives. Or Jon's.

I had never liked Diana very much, even if she was the queen of Weston High. She didn't pay much attention to me, even though I was Spencer's girlfriend, and made it a point to exclude me from parties even though Spencer always brought me whether she liked it or not. She tried to get into his pants more than once but gave up after she realized he wasn't going to dump me.

"Knock, knock," Jonathan called happily, as he pushed the door open. The smile on his face quickly faded when he saw me. "What's wrong?" He rushed to where I was sitting and dropped to his knees. "Is Spencer okay?" he asked.

I shook my head. "It's not Spencer. It's... we can't do this." I touched Jon's cheek with my hand and saw the hurt in his brown eyes. "I like you." He leaned into my palm.

"We can't do this because you like me?" He cocked a brow.

"Let me finish." I huffed and watched his lips twist up into a smile. "I like you too much, and I don't want something to happen to you or to Spencer. And if the Knights find out who he is or who I really am..." I bit down on my bottom lip. "We can't do this," I repeated myself.

Jon stared up at me. "I'm not going to go anywhere, sweetheart, so you can forget about that." My core clenched at his words, and I stared down at his lips, wanting to smother them with kisses. "There's this burning fire that I feel whenever I'm with the two of you that I can't describe, but I'm hoping that the two of you feel the same way." He reached up to cup my face with his strong hands. "We're keeping this under wraps until I can find a way to tell my boys about you both, understand?"

I nodded. "Yes, I understand." I closed my eyes as Jonathan leaned closer to slide his lips over mine. "We feel it, too, you know," I confessed as he stood and leaned me back against the soft mattress.

"What's that?" Jon murmured as his hard body pressed against mine.

I met his hooded eyes. "That fire." I gasped as his hand cupped my wet pussy over my panties and silently high-fived myself for wearing a dress. "Jon, we should call Spencer." I moaned as his finger slipped under the damp fabric, finding my drenched bud to flick it, and heat blossomed over my skin.

"I know, sweetheart." Jon planted kisses against my jawline before he found my mouth. "I'm not going to fuck you without him being here, even if it's via FaceTime," he assured me, and suddenly his hands and body were gone from mine. He pulled his phone from his pocket and called Spencer.

"It's about damn time," Spencer hollered when his face came into view. "Jesus Christ, I've been worried for the past two hours about you." His eyes flashed angrily as they moved between me and Jonathan. "Baby, you're okay?" he asked.

I nodded. "I'm fine," I assured him as I realized that Spencer was naked, or at least naked from the waist up. "Do you have any clothes on?" I asked before I glanced over at Jonathan, who grinned at me. "What are you two up to?" I narrowed my eyes.

"We figured since Spencer couldn't be here." Jonathan stood and started peeling off his Henley, then kicked off his boots. "We could at least have him watch. You know he likes to do that."

Spencer chuckled. "I do," he confessed.

"You planned this?" My eyes were on Jon as he unzipped his jeans, and I admired his toned arms and tight muscles. "When?" I glared at Spencer's face on the phone.

"We texted," he answered. "Take off your dress, baby." Spencer always liked to be in control, even if he wasn't here. "Jon, help her get out of that thing, would you?" He growled as I stood up so Jonathan could unzip me again, just like the other night. "Fuck, I wish I was there."

Jonathan's eyes were dark with desire. "Next time." He seemed a little more confident now.

Spencer gritted his teeth. "Damn right, and I'm going to put my hands all over you, sweetness," he promised.

White heat flared between my legs. Spencer had always been a dirty talker, but sometimes it took all my self-control not to lose it when I listened to him. I looked up at Jon as he met my heated gaze, and we both slowly moved closer.

"Make her come with your mouth," Spencer commanded. "Get between her legs to eat her cunt, Jon." I glanced at the phone to find him with his hand already wrapped around his hard length, slowly stroking himself.

I started to sit down on the bed, but then decided to lie down instead. Jonathan grabbed my hips to pull me down so that my ass was hanging off the mattress before he got down on his knees, then used his fingers to spread me open. I moaned as he slowly dragged his tongue over my clit, and I arched my hips up off the mattress. My hands went to Jonathan's hair as he did it again.

Spencer groaned. "Don't be gentle about it, either. She likes it rough. Don't you, baby?"

"Yes." I looked over at the phone and stared at Spencer as his cock jerked in his hand.

I bit my lip as he stared at me with a dark desire made my heart flutter and then looked down to watch Jonathan as he began to bring me to climax. My thighs clenched around his head as I began to lose myself in the licking. Pleasure began to wrack my body as I realized I was going to come undone already.

"Jonathan!" I cried out. Liquid fire singed my veins in a scorching heat.

I waited until my breath was back to normal before I looked back at the phone. Spencer had a big smirk on his face. "I love you," I mouthed to him, and he mouthed it back as I sat up. Jonathan was sitting on the floor, his eyes wide. "Are you okay?" I asked, touching his hair.

"I've never eaten a girl out before," he confessed and ducked his gaze away from me. "Was... Did I do it right?" he whispered.

I ran my fingers down his cheek and gripped his jaw to force him to make eye contact.

"That was perfect, Jonny." I assured him. "Now, get up on the bed so I can get you off."

I heard Spencer's moan from the phone at my words, and once again wished he were here with us. I couldn't remember the last time I touched someone without Spencer being in the room with me. The way I could feel his gaze while I did everything he told me to, the way his eyes never left mine. I glanced over at the phone, suddenly missing him, and he gave me a quick nod.

Jon stood, and I let my eyes slowly move down his chiseled chest, his defined abs, and then to his jeans, which he still had on. I reached down to pop the button and slowly began to pull down the zipper. When he started for my hand, I playfully slapped it away, shaking my head.

"No." I purred, and his eyes darkened.

I could see the outline of Jon's erection through his briefs, how it strained to break free. I tugged on his jeans to get them down his muscular thighs, before dragging them down his ankles along with his underwear. Jonathan's shaft strained upward in a thick curve, and I couldn't resist wrapping my slim fingers around it, feeling the urgent heat.

"On your knees, baby," Spencer grunted, his throaty voice sending a blaze of pleasure through my body.

I stopped to glance over at the phone, propped up on the table so Spencer could see everything. His hooded eyes, the veins in his neck, told me all I needed to know. He was holding himself back, waiting for me to bring Jon to completion before he finished himself off. I did as Spencer told me, getting down onto the dark carpet before I used my tongue to stroke the underside of Jonathan's shaft. They both groaned at the same time.

"Fuck, yes." Jon's hands found my hair twisting into a makeshift ponytail and wrapping it around his wrist. "God, that feels amazing," he murmured as I glided over his shaft in rasping strokes before taking the tip into my mouth.

I glanced up under my lashes to find Jon watching me with pure bliss written all over his beautiful face. I couldn't help but slowly take him farther inside my mouth, loving his reaction, and how his hand began to work my head up and down.

Spencer's voice had grown louder, his own climax threatening to bring Jon over the edge the longer I sucked and licked his tautness. When I looked up again, both of them were watching one another, and I couldn't help but wonder what their first time would be like. A heat like no other flared and began to burn between my legs.

Jon burst with a bone-deep growl of pleasure, his body bucking against me, and I didn't remove my mouth until I was sure he was done. I heard Spencer crying out just in time to see him splatting against his stomach in hot streams, and I once again wished he was here so I could lick it off of him, something I always enjoyed.

Jonathan touched my face, bringing my attention back to the man in the room with me. "That was amazing." He helped me to my feet and then onto the bed. "Thank you." He slid his lips over mine.

"That was hot as shit." Spencer used a towel to clean himself up before he pulled a shirt on over his head. "Baby, I'll miss you tonight." He blew me a kiss. "Next time, you two are coming here. Take care of our girl for me, Jon." He narrowed his eyes before he winked. "And, baby?" He leaned forward. "Take care of him, too, okay?" he whispered before hanging up.

Jonathan tucked a piece of hair behind my ear. "You want to sleep in one of my shirts?" he asked, leaning down to pick up my dress. "I can hang this up for you, too." He started to stand again, but I stopped him.

"Are all the Knights super sweet underneath or just you?" I teased before I took the dress from him. "You don't have to hang that up, but a shirt would be nice." I smiled as Jonathan's neck turned pink. I watched as he got up to look for a shirt, disappeared into the bathroom, and then came back with a washcloth.

I had already started to fall for Jonathan Hamden, and that could be a problem if this didn't workout. If everything was ruined before we had the chance to explain things the way we need

Chapter Eight

Jonathan

Saying goodbye to Ellie the next morning was harder than I imagined, but the best part about it was waking up to her in my bed. This was the first time that I'd woken up with someone next to me, wrapped around me so tight that they couldn't let go. Jam doesn't count because he's half of me, and we haven't shared a bed since we were in diapers. The first thing that came to my mind when I woke, with her white hair sprayed across the dark sheets, nearly scared me to death.

I could get used to this.

Unfortunately, Ellie had to be to work at Gerry's at the ass crack of dawn, and when the alarm on her phone went off at four in the morning, it was one of the worst sounds in the world. She promised to text me if she had time during her shift, but said Sunday was their busiest day of the week. Once she had showered, I kissed her until our lips were swollen and my cock hard as steel.

"Don't miss me too much." Ellie ran her thumb across my bottom lip, her green eyes the same color as the baseball field Coach Best made us run sprints on during practice.

I smirked and tugged on her ponytail. "Nah, sweetheart, wouldn't think of it," I lied before I kissed her again.

"Text Spence later. Make him feel special." Ellie grabbed my hand before she reached for the door. "The three of us will have to do something next time. It can't always be you and me, Jonny."

I didn't want that, just Ellie and myself. I wanted the whole throuple thing, and we would figure out a way to make it work.

"Will do," I promised before she disappeared from my room.

It took two seconds before I followed after her and found her already halfway down the stairs. Neither of us expected Oz to be sitting in the sitting room, his arms folded, and a pissed off look on his face. Wait, the pissed off look we were used to, but the fact that he was up, out of his room, and awake so early was a surprise.

"Where are you two going?" he grunted, hardly even looking up.

"Ellie has to work," I answered.

Ellie licked her lips nervously. "Thanks for having me, Oz. I had a lovely time." She met my gaze. "I hope that you will welcome me back again." When he waved his hand at her to dismiss her, I saw Ellie's jaw clench, and her nostrils flare like a button had been pushed.

"Thanks, buddy," I hissed and started to steer Ellie toward the kitchen so she could leave without Oz ripping her throat out. We would have words when I got back from walking her to her car.

Ellie smacked my hands away but didn't say anything until we were outside in the freezing morning air. "You're going to let him just... just treat me like I'm the help or something?" she exclaimed, her breath coming out in white puffs. "He's a real asshole."

"I can promise you that I will not let him get away with that," I assured her. "He's hurting right now. Oz had his heart broken, and even though he's never been the easiest guy to get to know or the nicest man on the planet, he's not sure what to do with himself." I heard a soft sigh escape from her mouth. "He opened up his heart only to have someone stomp on it. Pretty sure he won't be doing that again." Shit, now I felt bad for shoving my happiness in his face.

Ellie nodded. "Palmer." She touched my face.

"Palmer, yes, and he's angry at the world."

"Thanks for not letting me scream at him."

I snickered. "Trust me; Oz would have eaten you for breakfast if you had tried." I moved to pull Ellie into a hug. "I'll text Spencer," I whispered, tightening my grip. "As long as you text me when you get to work, and just let me know you got there safely."

"Will do," she promised. She unlocked her car, then climbed inside to start it.

I gripped the top of the vehicle as I brought my head inside. "Thanks for coming by last night, sweetheart. I think my friends like you, or at least everyone but Oz, but he doesn't like anyone. Don't take it personally," I teased, bringing a smile to Ellie's face. "See you soon." I grinned and stood up before shutting her door tightly behind me.

I stood there and watched Ellie drive off, honking and waving to me as she did, then turned to find Oz standing there. "Jesus, asshole." I gasped, bringing my hand up to my heart. "Don't go sneaking up on people like that, Ice. You scared the shit out of me." He looked creepy as fuck right now. "Did you even sleep at all last night? Because, honestly, you look like a cast member from *The Walking Dead*." I took in his sunken eyes and overly pasty skin. If he started walking with a limp and asking for brains, I might have to knife the guy.

"She's from Kingston." He jutted his chin at the spot Ellie's car had just evacuated.

I raised an eyebrow. "No, she's from Weston. We had this discussion last night," I reminded him. "Are you sniffing glue or something?" I started to walk past Oz, only to have him grab my arm. "Let me go," I growled, shoving him away from me.

"I'm telling you that Ellie—or should I say, Eleanor Young—is from fucking Kingston." He shoved his phone at me. "Look." He pulled up an old class photo. Sure as shit, it was Ellie from her first year of high school, dressed in what looked like a cheerleader uniform, although it was modified a bit, and sitting next to Palmer Wilson. *Holy crap*. "She was kicked out for throwing—"

"Sex parties," I finished for him.

"She told you that?"

I popped my jaw. "No, she told me her parents kicked her out." Fuck, I should not have told him that. "She also told me she got in trouble for throwing them, but not that it was here." I felt myself break out in a cold sweat. What else hadn't she or Spencer told me?

"I remember those." Oz had a gleam in his eye that sent my stomach into knots. "Don't worry, dude, I never touched your girl. But if I remember correctly, someone caught the clap, and it started to go around school. Was not fun." He chuckled, but it wasn't a laugh I liked. He was on to something, and I was worried. "Let's go inside. My balls are going to freeze and fall off." Oz started toward the house, and I had no choice but to follow after him.

I shivered, and I wasn't sure if it was from the cold or from the iceman in front of me.

***

I had cooked up a big breakfast for the Knights, with Oz breathing down my neck the entire time, and avoided questions about the next time Ellie would be coming by again from the girls. I was starting to clean up the massive amounts of pots and pans when I found Ellie's pie plate sitting in the dish drain.

"You think she did that on purpose?" Cash grinned at me as he finished off his coffee, stood up, and placed the empty cup in the sink like I hadn't just finished cleaning up after all of them. "I could take it to her if you wanted." He started to reach for the plate, but I snatched it away. "You're already madly in love with Ellie, aren't you?" Cash batted his lashes at me and cackled like a lunatic.

Brett nudged his arm. "Don't be like that, Toto." I wasn't sure why she insisted on calling Easton and Cash characters from *The Wizard of Oz*, but maybe it was because I secretly wished she had a nickname for me unless it turned out that I was the cowardly lion. "You two are super adorbs together, Jon." She leaned up to kiss my cheek. "We should double with Easton sometime. Thanks for breakfast. It was amazing, as always." She turned around to find the boss shooting daggers in our direction. "Stop." Brett pointed a finger in his direction. "I'm wearing your engagement ring on my finger."

As if she had to remind him. The thing was so big you could see it on Google maps.

"Damn right, babe." Easton stood up, and just as he went to grab Brett, she darted around him and up the stairs. You could hear her laughing as Easton chased after her, his own throaty laugh carrying back down into the kitchen.

Jameson met my gaze. "It's good to hear him like that, isn't it? He was never happy until Brett came back to Kingston." Josie hadn't shown up for breakfast, so she was either still sleeping or went home last night. She probably had enough social time with us for a while.

The sound of a chair scraping across the floor caused us both to jump, and we turned our attention to Oz. "If you two assholes are done." He grunted. "We should plan a meeting."

"For?" Lennox's brows dipped, and I felt my breakfast threaten to come back up again.

"You'll find out at the meeting, won't you?" Oz narrowed his eyes. "You all act like everything is so hunky freaking dory. Like we live in some perfect little snow globe now that Chad is gone, and my dad disappeared, but it's not. Diana is still out there, hiding, and Chad has friends who are going to come for us." He squared his shoulders.

Cash leaned back against the counter. "What time? I'll send a reminder text." He slid his phone from his back pocket.

"Two o'clock," Oz answered.

It was nearly eleven o'clock now, which would give me time to get in touch with Spencer and tell him what Oz knew about Ellie. "I'm going to go shower and rest a bit,"

I announced. "Unlike you douche canoes, I didn't get to sleep in." I tried to laugh it off, but I thought I sounded stiff and weird. I caught Lennox giving me a strange look, but I ignored her.

Once upstairs in my room, I made sure the door was locked before I texted Spencer. I didn't want to freak him out too much, but I knew that he would want to be alerted about Ellie. After all, they were a couple long before I came into the picture.

Jonathan: *Can you talk?*

Spencer: *What's up, sweetness?*

Jonathan: *Oz knows who Ellie is.*

Spencer: *How did that happen?*

Jonathan: *Okay, he doesn't exactly, but he found a picture of her freshman year with Palmer, of all people, and remembered the sex parties she used to have.*

Jonathan: *You should have told me she went to Kingston.*

Spencer: *Shit.*

Jonathan: *Shit is not the word, but it's a start.*

Spencer: *Did he say anything else? Does he know she lives with me?*

Jonathan: *Not yet, but he called a meeting for today. I don't think this is good. We're going to have to stop whatever this is between us.*

Spencer: *No.*

Jonathan: *Just until things cool down. I can't risk anything happening to the two of you.*

Spencer: *Sweetness, it's cute how you want to protect us, but we're too involved now.*

Jonathan: *Don't call me that.*

Spencer: *Admit it, you like it.*

I stared down at the phone. At the messages from Spencer. And yes, I could admit that I liked it when he called me sweetness. It did things to do me. Things I had never felt before, and if I liked being with Ellie, I could only imagine what it would be like to be with Spencer. What it would feel like to have his hands all over my skin, his lips on mine, and how his cock might make me...

I jumped as the phone began to ring in my hand, and it took a second or two for me to realize I needed to answer it.

"You ghosting me now, sweetness?" Spencer's gravelly voice caused the hairs on the back of my neck to stand up.

I shifted my erection in my pants. "No, but we can't do this. You shouldn't have called. Think of Ellie." I needed to put a wall between us.

"Don't do that."

"I'm not doing anything."

Spencer let out a short, bitter laugh. "Keep telling yourself lies, Jon, but we both know you're trying to use this as a way to convince me to back off. It's not going to work. I've been protecting Ellie for years, so I know how to take care of her. Let me do the same for you."

A warmth I never knew began to spread over my body. No one had ever said that to me before. Jameson and I had been taking care of ourselves since we were eight or nine years old, which is one of the reasons we lived here.

I swallowed down the lump in my throat. "I can't ask you to do that for me, man. There are some pretty bad people trying to hurt me, the Knights, and you don't want that."

I shouldn't be telling Spencer that, but for some reason, I trusted him.

"We're a thing now, sweetness. You don't get a say in this anymore." He sighed into the phone. "Come by later."

I shook my head even though he couldn't see me. "Not tonight. Maybe tomorrow."

"Jonathan." Spencer liked to be in control, but not when it came to the Knights' business.

"I'm sorry. I gotta go. I'll talk to you soon." I hit end and put my phone on silent just in case he decided to call me back. I considered turning it off completely, but that would send out some serious red flags to the Knights.

I needed to figure this out before I got them seriously hurt. Or worse.

Chapter Nine

Ellie

I was just getting off my shift and leaving Gerry's when I saw Brett, Lennox, and Josie walk into the building. I couldn't help but freeze the moment I saw them. Were they there for me? Did they know my secret? Or were they just there to pick up donuts for the Knights? I felt like a stalker just standing there standing there staring at them and comparing myself to how beautiful they were.

Brett was dressed in a pair of blue jeans and an oversized purple jacket that matched her hair perfectly. Once again, I was envious as hell of someone who could pull off that look because I certainly couldn't do it. I was stuck with the white hair I was blessed with, more of birthmark from what the doctors told me, and it would not hold any dye no matter how long I left it in. She was listening to something that Lennox was saying, her head tilted to the right, and her face broke into a smile that lit up her beautiful face. From the looks of it, Brett didn't have on any makeup, and she didn't need it. Her skin was flawless, her face beautiful, and I could see why Easton was so drawn to her.

Lennox wore a leather coat, leather pants, and biker boots. Her dark hair hung loose around her shoulders. I still had the feeling she didn't like me, but maybe it was more of a looking-out-for-her-friend type thing. The tattoos that you could see, mostly on her neck and hands, were on full display, and I could see some of the customers openly gawking while some muttered about how unladylike it was.

Lennox towered over her two friends who flanked her on both sides, and even if she didn't notice, she an air about her that seemed to say *I own this place.* Everyone else noticed it. The way I felt about Brett's hair was how I felt about Lennox's skin. Ideal, flawless, and everything a girl would want. She, too, wore no makeup, and I dropped my hand from my cheek the moment I realized I was touching it.

And Josie? Well, she looked like she wanted to be anywhere else but in the bakery at this very moment. Her red hair was styled the exact way it was last night, covering her scars from the world. She kept her eyes glued to her boots, possibly wishing the floor would swallow her whole. She wore Jameson's varsity jacket and jeans that looked to be three sizes too big. If Kingston thought she was no longer amongst the living, the gossip mill would be fired up now. Despite the fact that Josie was burned, she was still beautiful, and I wondered what demons were hidden inside her head.

"Ellie!" Brett exclaimed when she saw me. "Just the girl we were looking for." She rushed in my direction and pulled me into a bone-crushing hug that sucked all the air from my lungs. "I thought we had missed you." Brett pulled back to beam happily at me.

I felt my nerves taking over. "Oh, is everything okay?" I hoped that I hadn't said anything that gave me away last night, because sometimes the wine could do that to me.

Lennox raised her eyebrows. "We just wanted to come by to tell you how much we enjoyed spending time with you last night." After what she said to me last night? Lennox had made it perfectly clear that she wanted me to stay away from

Jonathan. I couldn't read her face as she turned away from me.

Brett slapped at her friend's shoulder. "Could you just be cooler about stuff?" She rolled her eyes. "We thought, you know, since you and Jon are together now"—she grinned at me—"we could hang out or something." She hooked a thumb at Lennox. "Like big mouth said, we had fun with you last night." Her smile was so wide that I thought her face might explode.

I chewed on my bottom lip. "I don't think Oz liked me much," I admitted.

Josie giggled softly before covering her mouth with her hand, then dropped her gaze back to her feet.

"Oz doesn't like anyone, El, not even me, and I'm his flesh and blood." Lennox snorted. "Can you believe you just made this one laugh?" She put her arm around Josie. "You need to hang out with us just because of that." A sincere look appeared on her perfect face. "We want to get to know you, too, because as you can tell, the Knights tend to fall pretty quickly and hard when it comes to their ladies."

Brett nodded. "We just have to fix the shit between Lennox and Cash." She moved as Lennox went to elbow her.

I wanted that. I wanted a friendship like these three seemed to have, even if Josie seemed a little off, but I could understand that. I dragged my teeth across my bottom lip. "I don't see why we couldn't do that," I told them. "We should exchange numbers so we can make plans on when I should come by."

Josie leaned over to tap her sister on the shoulder. I watched as she mouthed "Dress shopping" to Brett and then flashed a brief smile at me.

"Right!" Brett clapped her hands together. "We were going to go dress shopping." Her blue eyes lit up happily. "I can text you about that, too." She started to take out her phone and the four of us exchanged numbers just as my phone went off with text messages.

Jon: *You should have told me you were from Kingston. WTF.*

Spencer: *We need to talk when you get home.*

I felt myself grow red, and I hoped that no one saw the message. I found Lennox watching me as I looked up.

"Everything okay?" she asked, as if she knew.

I nodded. "Perfect," I lied. "What did you mean about dress shopping?" I asked, trying to change the subject.

Brett clapped her hands. "Kingston has a big dance coming up: the Winter Formal. Obviously, I'm going with Easton." She blushed as she said his name, and I wondered what it was like to be that lucky in your relationship. Not that I wasn't with Spencer, but I wasn't sure we would be with Jonathan. "You should come with Jonathan. I know he's going to ask you. And if we can get Len to go with Cash—"

"Nope." Lennox shook her head. "That ship has sailed."

Josie rolled her one eye at me. "Lies," she mouthed before she dropped her gaze again. I think I liked this girl.

Wait, did they say a dance at the school? No way. There was absolutely no way I was going to a dance at Kingston High. If I stepped foot in that school? All hell would break loose.

"I don't know." I tried to come up with an excuse, but my mind was drawing a blank.

"I know it's kind of soon," Lennox jumped in. "Think about it," she added.

I nodded. "Sure, all right. I should go, though. I'm tired. Late night." I winked. "I'll text you," I promised, and wondered if I would ever get to hang out with them again.

***

"No fucking way." Spencer shook his head when I told him about the dance. "Don't give me that look, baby. It's too dangerous. You can't go back there any time soon."

My eyebrows shot up so fast I thought they might fly off my head. "What?" I exclaimed. "Can I at least get into the house before you jump all over me about this?"

Spencer was on edge from the moment I got home, pacing and shaking his head about Ozzy knowing who he was. When I asked him to explain, he did, and I was less that happy about it.

"Sorry." Spencer moved so I could walk past him. I dropped my bag in the hallway and made my way into the kitchen to get a drink of water. "I know you like Jon; I do too, but if Oz pushes just a little more, asks around Weston..." His voice trailed off as I finished off my drink. "If something happened to you, Ellie, I would never recover." Spencer cupped my face in his big hands.

I stared up at him, my eyes taking in the worry written all over his face, and the way his brows pinched together. "That's it, then? The connection we have with him? We just forget about it?" I gripped his wrists. "It's not just about Jon for me, Spence. For the first time since I can remember, I feel like I might have real friends, girlfriends, and what if this is all for nothing? What if Oz doesn't figure out who I am?"

"You know he will. He's already dug around too much."

I knew he would, too. I knew Oz wouldn't let this rest until he knew every single thing about me, including what I had for breakfast this morning—an apple fritter, in case you were curious—and I hated that. I hated that Spencer and I couldn't be with Jonathan the way we wanted to be. I hated that I couldn't be friends with Brett, Lennox, and Josie because, more than anything, I wanted what they had.

I had never had a girlfriend I could trust like that. Someone who would have my back like they seemed to have one another's. All the fun we could have getting ready for the dance. Go shopping together, do one another's hair, makeup. And now, I probably never would.

"Hey." Spencer caught the tear that had started to fall from my right eye. "We'll find someone else." He tried to assure me, but even as I looked up into his handsome face, I knew he didn't believe it. What we felt with Jonathan was something we had only found each other.

I stepped closer and wrapped my arms around Spencer's waist, pressing my face into muscled chest.

"It's cute how you think I can't see right through your lies, baby," I whispered, breathing in his familiar scent. "It's always going to be just the two of us against the world." I wasn't sure why it felt like my world was suddenly falling apart.

"Is that such a bad thing, Ellie?" Spencer tightened his grip on me. "Isn't that what we always wanted, anyway?" His gruff voice sent shivers through my body and a pounding need between my legs.

I rested my chin against his chest to meet his heated gaze. "What if Jonathan's our missing piece?" I dared him.

Spencer's eyes flashed with want before his mouth slammed over mine. He held nothing back as his tongue slipped between my lips, his hands digging into my skin, and low, deep growls escaping his throat. I was used to Spencer being rough. We both enjoyed it like that. But there was something different about him right now. He tugged on my bottom lip, biting down hard enough that I tasted blood, and I felt his hard, thick erection pressed against my stomach right through his sweats. I slipped my hand under the elastic, only to have him suddenly pull back.

"What's wrong?"

"What if you're right? What if Jonathan is exactly what we need to complete our relationship?"

I dragged my teeth over my bottom lip. "What about Oz?" I reminded Spencer. "He's going to be digging around into my past. Then he's going to come here, and he's going to ask questions. Diana will... wait." My eyes went wide. "She won't want anything to do with the Knights." My voice came out in a hushed whispered. "She's terrified of them coming to find her after the shit she pulled at that party, when she posted those pictures and the video her skanks took..." I shuddered, not wanting to say it aloud.

Diana Monaco acted as if she ran Weston High. She had tried to blackmail Easton, and even went as far as to let him think they slept together, only it wasn't exactly like that. She got him drunk, snuck into his room, and took a few pictures. She did, however, suck his dick, and one of her minions got it all on video. Brett forgave Easton, but the rest of the Knights wanted her head on a platter. Oswald most of all, because she had the lady balls to come to his house to do what she did.

Spencer reached for my hands. "You should go to the dance with Jonathan." The look he gave me was one I knew all too well. "I could sneak in." He grinned.

"How do you expect to do that?" I really wanted to hear his answer to this one.

He leaned down so that his lips were against my ear. "We're going to go over there today and talk to him. Show him, the Knights, and everyone else just how good we are together." His lips brushed my skin.

"Are you sure? I don't know if that's such a great idea." I felt goosebumps break out as his tongue made contact.

Spencer pulled back to face me. "Trust me, Ellie. I would never let anything happen to you," he promised. A smile slid up his face as he began to unbutton my coat and dropped it on the floor. "Take off the rest of your clothes, baby," he demanded.

Heat pulsed through my body as I stripped everything off. It didn't matter how many times Spencer and I did this, it always felt like magic. I watched the way his eyes slid down my body, stopping to admire my hardened nipples before they dipped down between my legs.

"See something you like?" I whispered as we both moved together.

"Baby, you are perfect." Spencer tugged his sweats down before he pushed me back against the wall. "You want this?" He grabbed my hand and brought it down to his cock, hard and ready. "Tell me you want me." His eyes fluttered when I gripped his length.

"I always want you, Spencer."

He growled softly before he lifted one of my legs, and I instantly wrapped it around his waist. Spencer dipped his head to seal his mouth against mine before he brought my other leg up and plunged inside of me.

"Ellie." He groaned as I gripped his hair between my fingers. "God, you feel so damn good." Spencer's frantic hands dug into my hips.

"Give it to me, baby. You know how I like it," I urged.

I didn't want to think about anything else right now. Pleasure rippled through me as Spencer began to pump himself inside me, harder, faster, and I could feel the sweat break out on his skin as we moved as one.

His lips felt like fire against mine, his breath coming in quick bursts, and when I cried out in ecstasy, Spencer tumbled over the edge with me. I couldn't remember the last time I had come that fast, but I knew it was something we both needed.

I cupped his face with my hands as he helped me to my feet. "I love you," Spencer whispered. "Let's wash up and go get our man," he said.

Chapter Ten

Jonathan

I couldn't stop my right leg from shaking, no matter how many times I crossed and uncrossed my feet at the ankles. That damn thing would not stop moving.

Once.

Twice.

Three times

Still shaking.

Maybe it was the fact that everyone was late, and Oz was grinding his molars so hard I thought he was going to crack them, he was so pissed off. Oz hated tardiness like he hated everything else, and he would be sure to let everyone know when they showed up. The look in his eyes was pure murder the longer we sat there, alone, and I was pure sure the first Knight who showed up was going to get their head bitten off when they finally walked in.

"I'm going to burn this place down while they all sleep." He grunted as he looked at the time on his phone. "I get that they all have girlfriends, want to have their dicks sucked or whatever, but this is fucking important." I watched the way the vein in his neck pulsed, half expecting him to burst into flames.

I nodded. "I have a girlfriend, too, and I'm here." Although I wasn't going to be seeing her anymore, but I left that part out.

Oz bared his teeth. "I don't trust her." He reminded me for the hundredth time since I sat down. "She's up to something, in fact." He unlocked his phone. "I was going to save this for when everyone got here, but maybe you can explain this?" Oz shoved his phone at me, and I felt my stomach drop when I saw what he was asking about.

It was Ellie's Instagram account. Worse than that, it was a picture of Ellie with Spencer.

I felt myself start to break out in a cold sweat all over my body just as the sounds of laughter and footsteps began to be heard overhead, down the stairs, and suddenly everyone appeared in the finished basement.

I felt sick. Bile rose in my throat, and I swore I was going to pass out. Why didn't I think about shit like that? I should have had Ellie lock everything down. Instagram, Facebook, and probably TikTok, too. The room grew deathly quiet when everyone saw the look on Oz's face.

"Why so grim, man?" Cash flopped down on the love seat, followed by Easton, who reached up to tug on Brett's waist, so she sat down on his lap. Jameson leaned casually against the wall, without Josie, since she wasn't officially one of us yet, while Lennox sat down next to me, giving me a quick nod.

Oz's eyes were dark as night as he sat up. "Ellie's not who she claims to be." He bared his teeth. "She's with Pearson."

Easton stood up so fast he nearly knocked Brett from his lap but managed to scoop her up with one arm. "Are you fucking kidding me?" he roared while his eyes flashed with hate. Easton turned to face me. "Start talking right now." His lip curled up over his teeth.

My brain couldn't catch up with everything that was happening right now. I was pissed at myself for not thinking about shit like social media, but furious that Oz didn't come to me first. Easton looked ready to rip me to pieces, and honestly, the guy had every right to do it.

At that exact moment, the sound of squealing tires outside caused the Knights, myself included, to run up the stairs. The camera alerts on our phones were going nuts, and I had a sinking feeling I knew exactly who was outside. Easton was practically carrying Brett, and much to Lennox's squeals of protest, Cash was dragging her right behind him.

"Who the fuck is here?" Oz growled as he yanked back the curtain over the sink. "Is that Pearson? He has some serious balls showing up at my house." He started toward the door, but Easton had beat him to the punch, slamming the door against the wall so hard I swore the glass was going to scatter onto the floor.

Easton didn't bother with his coat as he sprinted across the snow-covered lawn to get to Spencer. He grabbed him by the collar and then slammed him against the hood of his car. "Thirty seconds, that's all you have. Which, honestly, is more than you deserve. I should have killed you the last time you dared to come here," he hissed.

Spencer tried to pry Easton's hands from his coat, but it was impossible. Six foot five, easily two hundred plus pounds, Easton Kennedy was solid muscle, and full of hate for everyone but us and his girl. Sometimes even us.

"Fuck you, Kennedy." His eyes moved to me, begging for help, but if I gave it to him? I was going to be the next bullseye. I had warned them about something like this happening. Why were they here?

"Don't look at her." Easton thought it was Brett that Spencer was looking at, since she was standing next to me. "I'm calling the shots here, asshole." He moved to block his view. I saw the movement in the passenger side of the car at the same time as everyone else. "Who is that, huh? Who did you bring with you?" He raised one hand to indicate one of us should check, and I knew the three of us were fucked.

Oz moved fast like a cheetah, pulling open the door to Spencer's beat up BMW, and when he dragged Ellie out, I felt my stomach drop at my feet.

"Well, well, look who it is." His face darkened. "She look familiar to you, Jon? Because if I'm not mistaken?" He dragged Ellie with him so everyone could get a closer look. "I'm pretty sure this is your girlfriend, right? Or maybe"—he shoved Ellie at Cash, who spun her around so that he could wrap his arms tightly around her waist—"maybe she's not who she claims to be?" Oz pressed his lips together in a thin, tight line. "Someone better start talking before I start putting holes through bodies instead." He lifted his shirt up enough to make sure both Spencer and Ellie saw the shiny pistol in the band of his jeans.

"What the fuck, Ellie?" Cash hissed as a gasp escaped her mouth as he ran the back of his hand down her cheek. "You seemed like such a nice, pretty girl, too." He played the role of the nice guy so well, but that was all a disguise. His blue eyes had hardened to steel. "Too bad we're not going to get to become friends after all. No free donuts and no more sweet, sweet pie." His voice was frosty as he spoke.

Spencer struggled against Easton. "Don't you hurt her, dickhead!" he shouted.

"Or what?" Easton stood him up to his feet. "Remember, you're not the one in control here, pal." He met my eyes. "What did you think you were going to get out of trying to trick Jon, huh?" He directed the question to Ellie, who was staring at me with a pleading look on her face. "Look at me, sweetheart, not him. I promise you that Jon isn't going to save you. You're in Knights territory now."

Brett touched my arm. "Jon?" Her voice was soft as she gripped my elbow. "Are you going to say something, or are you going to just stand there and watch this happen?" Her eyes told me she knew, but how? Lennox would never tell my secret, no matter how close they had gotten. She nodded as if she could read my mind, and I realized again, why she was part of the Knights.

I swallowed the lump in my throat as a cold sweat broke out on my skin.

"Wait!" I called out when I saw Oz start to move toward Spencer, his hand moving for his gun. "No one was trying to trick me into anything," I announced. "I was with both of them that night of the party. Up until that night, I thought I was gay, but now I realize that's not exactly true," I finally admitted aloud to myself and the rest of my friends.

Easton stared at me as confusion ran over his face. "Wait, you're gay or bi or whatever and you never thought to tell us?" He glanced around at the rest of the Knights. "Did you know?" he asked my brother.

"Of course I knew, man. He's my twin." Jameson nodded. "About the gay thing, not about Spencer." *Thanks for not sticking up for me, brother.*

"That's not the point, East. The point is that they are here for me." I took a small step toward where Cash still had his grimy hands all over Ellie. "Do you mind releasing her now?" I cocked a brow as he narrowed his eyes.

Cash practically threw Ellie into my arms. "You could have just been honest, dude. We're your friends, your damn family. I'm fucking insulted." He popped his jaw as Brett came over to try to calm him down, but he only shook his head at her.

I turned toward the boss, who was literally seething in my direction as Ellie clung to me. Easton narrowed his eyes. I took a deep breath, only to watch the fog of my breath come out when I released it into the frigid air.

"Can we at least talk about this?" I asked as Ellie dug her nails into my skin.

"No, we cannot." Easton's nostrils flared. "This asshole"—he paused to push his arm against Spencer's throat—"kissed my girl, thought he could put his fucking hands on her, and now what? You think you're going to ride off into the sunset like some happy threesome? Fuck right off." He started to turn around, but something inside of me snapped.

I released Ellie so that I could lunge forward to grab Easton and spin him back around. I got in one punch, which barely hit his jaw. It hurt like hell, but at least I got him before he hit me back. It sent me flying into Oz, who shoved me forward, and I face planted onto the ground. I started to get back up, only to have Cash come over to stomp down on my hand. The scream that came out of my lungs was anything but human as pain seared up my palm and through my arm.

"Are you done? Because you're... what the hell? Did you just bite me?" Cash exclaimed. He removed his foot, which is all that I wanted.

I climbed back up to my feet, swung around with my good hand, fist clenched, and popped Cash in the jaw. I watched as he stumbled back before he hit the ground just as Oz grabbed both my arms to pin them behind my back.

"Motherfucker, you are digging your own grave tonight," he hissed in my ear and squeezed the hand Cash had stepped on moments ago. "I would stop now if I were you," he warned.

Cash grinned at me with blood lining his teeth. "I did not expect that from you, Jon, so bravo for that." He spat on to the driveway. "You're lucky I don't kill you for this since it's all your fault, man, not mine. You had no business hitting me." He climbed to his feet.

"Don't you touch them," I growled.

"Or fucking what?" Oz asked. "You're a little busy at the moment."

Spencer had Ellie wrapped in his arms, and her face was buried in his chest, but the look on his face was a mixture of hatred and fear. "Don't hurt him," he whispered.

"Shut the fuck up." Easton sneered, and he took a step forward, only to have Brett put her hand on his arm.

Brett coughed nervously. "Maybe we should let them explain." She touched Easton's hand, but he shrugged her off. Now everyone was fighting, and it was my fault. I warned both of them that this was going to happen. No one was going to accept me. Or them.

"What is wrong with you? Have you all gone insane?" Lennox cried, her voice puncturing the night sky. "You're friends. No, you're more than that. You're brothers, and you're fighting like a bunch of school kids on the playground right now." Her eyes pinned behind me. "Let him go, Oswald," she demanded. Then she surprised everyone by slapping Cash across the face. "You're a fucking prick, you know that, boo?" she hissed.

"You two should probably leave before things get worse." It didn't matter what kind of chemistry I had with Ellie and Spencer. This was never going to work. I had tried to warn them.

"Jonny, we need to—"

"Did I fucking stutter?" I snarled, turning my gaze on Ellie. "Leave. Now! Before someone ends up dead!" I pointed at Spencer's car. "This was never going to work, just like I told you. There is no happy ending in this. Not for me, anyway." I felt the cage around my heart closing up again. "You were too stupid to see that because you have this nice relationship with your boyfriend that the two you seem to think is going to work with everyone else." I watched the way Spencer's body stiffened. "Newsflash, sweetheart, it's not like that for the rest of the world. Get lost before I let the Knights draw the real blood they crave." I made sure they could see me walk casually into the house and didn't turn back to see them leave.

I wasn't in my room ten minutes, nursing my swollen hand, before Easton came pounding on my door. "Let me in or I'll break it down," he warned.

"It's open," I told him. As if I would lock it when I knew he'd be coming to talk to me.

Easton walked in and chuckled nervously. "So it is." He jutted his chin at me. "Doc's on his way to take a look at that hand." He leaned against the frame. "Gay, huh?" He ran his hand through his dark hair. "Really?" He sucked his bottom lip into mouth.

I rolled my eyes. "Yes, I like dick. No, not yours, so you don't have to worry." I toed off my shoes so I could flop down on my bed to stare up at the ceiling.

"I wasn't worried about that." But something in Easton's voice told me he was lying, and when I leaned onto my good arm toward him, he had his eyes cast down to his feet. "Look, I wish you had told me. I don't want to act all weird around you now. We're friends."

I snorted. "Right. Friends. I just can't date who I want, though. Also, you might have let Oz kill me tonight if Lennox hadn't stepped in." I lay back down.

"Not Pearson, man. Anyone but him." Easton growled. "Oz was being Oz; he wouldn't have actually hurt you."

Too bad I didn't believe him.

"He didn't even want Brett. He was after me." When Easton didn't say anything, I looked up to find him staring at me. "Hard to believe? It's true. He was trying to get to me, freaked out, and kissed Brett. That's why Ellie came to me at the party, but it's too late now. I ruined any chance of a relationship with them, so I'll just mope around and be lonely with Oz. We can miserable pricks together. Maybe we can do some sort of sick suicide pact together."

Easton raked a hand through his hair again. "You think you're going to end up that miserable?" he asked, but when I didn't answer, he shook his head. "I don't care if you like dick, okay? None of us do. Just find another cock to suck, because Spencer Pearson is off limits."

"Get out."

"Jon, come on."

I pointed at the door. "Get the fuck out!" I shouted, making sure the entire house heard.

Easton didn't say another word as he shut the door behind him, and I didn't hear from anyone else the rest of the night.

Chapter Eleven

I drove faster than I ever had driven in my entire life. Not caring if I got pulled over in Kingston by a cop that was might be on the Knights payroll, not caring if I got arrested for reckless driving, because I had to get Ellie as far away from them as possible. I glanced over to find her with her legs tucked up underneath her bottom, her arms folded over chest, and her face pressed against the glass.

"Hey." My eyes moved back to the road in front of me as I slowed for the four-way intersection, not stopping for the clearly posted stop sign when I made sure no one else was coming. I reached over to touch Ellie and felt her jump as my fingers traced the skin on her cheek.

"You're not hurt, are you?" I hated that this had happened. We had only wanted to talk to them. I was fucking stupid for thinking the Knights would have listened to anything I had to say to them without using their goddamn fists. Shit, I thought Oz was actually going to hurt Jon, too.

"I'm okay."

"Are you hurt?"

Ellie sat up, dropping her feet to the floor. "I'm fine." But I heard the lie in her voice. It didn't take a genius to know that it wasn't physical pain Ellie was feeling right now.

I slammed the palm of my hand against the wheel. "Fuck!" I shouted. "I'm so sorry, baby. This was an incredibly stupid idea. I should never have taken you with me. I should have gone alone."

"You think things would have turned out better?" Her strained voice made me want to yank the car over onto the side of the road so I could gather her into my arms, but all I wanted to do was get Ellie home, where she would be safe. I knew it was only a matter of time before the Knights came looking for us. This wasn't going to be over that easily. "Spencer, if I hadn't been there, God only knows what might have happened. Jon tried, but…" Her voice cracked, and I knew without looking that she was crying.

Sure as shit, when I glanced at Ellie again, tears were pouring down her cheek. "Baby, don't do that." Reached over to touch her, but she pushed my hand away. "What, you're mad at me now?" We never fought, ever, and it hurt more than I thought.

"No, yes, I don't know!" She threw her hands up over her face as she sobbed into them.

I realized it wasn't because of me that Ellie was crying. It was for Jonathan. The three of us had something, and now it was never going to happen. I felt her pain as she let everything out, and as I rolled the car up the driveway, hit the button to open the garage, and slid my BMW inside, I wondered if the two of us would ever get over losing someone we never truly had.

"Ellie, look at me, baby." I ran my hand over her hair. "Please." I wasn't afraid to beg her if she wanted.

Ellie dropped her hands to turn her gaze up at me, her eyes rimmed with red. "I'm going back," she said softly.

I tilted my head. "I don't understand." I cupped her cheek. "You can't go back there, baby, the Knights—"

"Fuck the Knights, Spencer!" she cried. "I'm going to Kingston High, and I'm going to get Jonathan back. I'm going to win him back, win them over, and you're not going to stop me." Her nostrils flared as she dared me to tell her no.

I licked my lips as I thought about what she said. "How?" I turned my frame toward her. "How do you think you're going to just walk into that school when they run it? Cash's mother is the principal. So the second you register"—I snapped my fingers—"they will know."

"We're going to break up."

"The fuck we are."

Ellie touched my arm. "Fake break up," she assured me. "I'll beg my parents to let me move back in, and then?" She batted her lashes at me. "I'll weasel my way into their world." Ellie sighed softly. "He's right here." She tapped her heart with two fingers. "How is that possible after only knowing him for a couple of days?"

"I feel it, too, but the thought of you going back to that house makes me want to hurt someone," I whispered.

Even though I hadn't spent any time alone with Jonathan, I felt the connection. I liked him more than I had ever liked any person we had brought into our relationship, and it scared me. Not that I was ashamed of who I was, but because I knew how he was.

Ellie suddenly climbed up into my lap. "Fuck, I love you, Spencer," she whispered. "You know that, right?" Her mouth was inches from mine as she stared up at me with eyes as wide as saucers.

"More than life," I assured her. "Heaven and hell, baby, just for you."

I captured her lips, my tongue finding hers, and we sat there making out in my car, steaming up the windows like the horny teenagers that we were. Ellie had always been it for me the moment she first kissed me, but now that we both realized there was someone else involved, it scared me.

The Knights had proven tonight how much they hated me, even after one of their own had tried to jump in and help. Jonathan had told them about us, had said we were together, but that didn't stop Easton one bit, and I was afraid of what might happen if Oz found out what we were up to. I tightened my grip on Ellie, only to have her pull back to stare at me.

"You're scared." She reached up to brush a piece of hair from forehead.

I pressed our heads together. "Baby, that is the understatement of the millennium," I whispered. "You're sure you want to do this? They aren't going to want to let you back into their circle." I couldn't stress enough how hard this was going to be.

A smile pulled at her corner of Ellie's lips.

"I think I have an in," she told me, reaching over to grab her purse and pull out her phone. She held out to show me all the texts. "That would be the ones who really call the shots for the Knights." Her voice was light as she giggled. "Brett, Lennox, and"—Ellie pointed to one single text—"even Josie Silver, baby, who is supposed to be dead." She dropped the phone onto the seat. "We're doing this.

We're getting Jonathan back, we're making this work, and we're going to live happily ever after."

***

I cooked up steaks on the grill while Ellie worked on a salad and sliced up some potatoes that she tossed into the air fryer to serve on the side. Once we had everything plated and sat down at the table, I wasn't very hungry anymore. I was going to have to watch my girlfriend pack up her belongings, move back to her shitty parents' house, and pretend that we had broken up.

It made me sick to my stomach just thinking about it.

"Talk to me." Ellie cut off a small piece of meat, stabbed it with her fork, and then chewed on it while she waited for me to answer. When I didn't answer, she reached for the glass of water in front of her, took a long sip, and then leaned back in her chair.

We had spoken about this once we finally made it into the house, fucked one another silly, and then showered before we decided we should eat dinner. It was my ever empty, forever growling stomach that convinced me I should actually cook something, and since Coach Kent was big on making sure I had enough protein in my diet, steaks sounded perfect. I didn't care that it was cold as tits outside or that the weatherman had said it might snow again tomorrow. I would grill if it was ten below or a hundred and ten outside.

"You already know how I feel about this, Ellie." I poked at my uneaten meat. "Oz is going to try to break you." I finally sliced into my food. "He's going to try every single trick in the book."

"Oz is going to lose."

I took a small bite of my steak, then one of my potatoes, and made sure to chew them fully before I swallowed. "What about Easton?" He was the one I was the most worried about. The look in his eyes when he had his arm against my throat was full-blown murder. He wanted me dead because I had put my mouth on Brett. And honestly? I couldn't blame him.

"Did we not just have a conversation about this?" Ellie stood up so that she could come over to where I was sitting. "Baby, trust me." She straddled my waist.

I stared down into her emerald eyes. "You still love me, right?" I watched the way Ellie licked her lips, her fingers grazing my throat where Easton had left a small bruise. When she tangled her hands in my hair, I closed my eyes.

"How can you ask me that, Spence?" Ellie's lips slid over mine.

I shook my head. "I'm scared you might want him more."

"Look at me, baby."

I opened my eyes to meet hers.

"I love you," she assured me. "Don't ever doubt that. I'm doing this for Jon. For us and getting him back," she reminded me. "The Knights are going to realize they messed with the wrong people. They are going to wish they hadn't pushed us around." She peppered kisses against my jawline.

I reached up to tug on her ponytail. "He doesn't deserve you," I teased.

"Damn right he doesn't." Ellie started to get back up, but I kept her where she was.

"*I* don't deserve you."

"Spencer Pearson, you shouldn't say things like that."

The way she said my name like that made my stomach flip, and my dick hard. "Eleanor Young, you wreck me," I murmured before I captured her mouth with mine.

Before Ellie, before I found her and she changed me, I had never wanted to settle down with just one girl or guy, for that matter. I thought I would end up fucking everything that walked until I was an old man, but Ellie made me see things in a different light.

"Being away from you isn't going to be easy," she murmured softly. "Last night was torture, so I can't imagine what it will be like going back to my parents. At least with Jonathan, I wasn't alone." Ellie dragged a hand through my hair. "There will be rules, rules that I'm going to have to follow. I already called my mom, but now it's up to my stepfather." Her eyes hardened.

The look in her green eyes made my heart break. "You're strong, baby." I braced her head between both of my hands. "The strongest person I know."

Ellie rolled her eyes. "I doubt that." She scoffed, but a smile pulled her lips, which was what I wanted. "Promise me something."

"You don't even have to ask." I already knew what it was going to be.

Ellie dropped a kiss against my nose. "Humor me, Spencer." Her voice dripped with need, but there was something else I couldn't figure out. Fear perhaps. "Stay away from Diana. I know we're going to stage a big break up to make it look good, but don't let her put one single manicured finger on you." Her chin trembled as she spoke. "I trust you, but I don't trust her."

Chapter Twelve

Jonathan

I dragged myself to school after winter break with the rest of the Knights a couple days after the Ellie and Spencer disaster. Everyone had tried to go back to things as if nothing had happened, myself included, but it hurt more than I thought possible. I kept hoping that I would get a text from one of them, but when it never came; I finally gave up figuring that the things that they had said to me were nothing more than lies whispered in fits of passion, lust, and need.

This morning I got up, showered, dressed in a pair of blue jeans and a clean Kingston High shirt before heading downstairs to cook breakfast for everyone. I found Lennox sitting at the table, her legs crossed, her dark hair pulled back from her face, and her arms crossed over her chest.

"Uh, good morning." I saw she had already turned on the coffee. "You're up early." I bent down to grab a pan to start the eggs. "Something on your mind?" I asked.

Lennox let out a noise that sounded like a cross between a laugh and a groan. "You tell me, Jon." She sighed. "It's been three days since they came here. You look like shit, and I'm starting to think you're trying to beat Ozzy at who can look and act like the biggest dickhead in the house." Len tapped my arm as I walked around her to get to the eggs in the fridge. "You're never going to win. Oz out-dicks everyone, and ew, that sounds really gross out loud."

I cracked a couple of eggs against the side of a bowl, whisked them together, and poured them into the heated pan before I answered. "It's over." What else could I say? I knew that the moment I found out who Spencer was but somehow hoped that things could be different.

"Liar, liar, pants on fire," Lennox sang. Her chair scraped against the floor before she came around to lean against the counter next to me. The impending sounds of footsteps down the stairs caused her to roll her eyes. "Good morning, Oz." That was the end of that conversation for the foreseeable future as the rest of the Knights started to roll in behind him.

Everyone was grumbling about vacation being too short, how they hated having to go back to school. Except for Jameson. He was thrilled to be able to bring his girlfriend back with him, even if she wasn't too excited about the idea.

I finished up the eggs, bacon, and pancakes just as Cash wandered into the room, his eyes narrowed into angry slits. He hadn't spoken a word to me since I bit him, but the asshole tried to break my hand. It was fine, by the way, just a little sore, but it still pissed me off that he'd turned on me so quickly. I took pleasure in the bruise on his face and how it messed up his perfect Ken doll jawline.

Lennox helped me put everything on the table before she moved to start washing the mess I'd created. "Eat." She shoved an elbow in my direction as I tried to move toward her, and I had no other choice but to do as she told me.

I grabbed a couple pieces of bacon, a pancake, and some eggs before they were all gone, only to find there were two seats left: both on either side of Cash. I sucked it up and sat down.

"Thanks for cooking or whatever," he grumbled under his breath. I stopped to stare at him as his eyes met mine. It was unusual that Cash had stayed this mad at me for so long because he wasn't the type to hold a grudge. Ever. "What?" His blue eyes went wide.

I shook my head. "Nothing, man," I assured him.

"Are we cool?" Cash asked.

I realized that he wasn't just asking for himself as I looked around the table. Everyone was watching us. These were my friends. I loved them, and could I really let a couple of people I hardly knew get in the way of that? "We're cool." I nodded.

"Sorry about your hand." Cash reached for his coffee and drained the cup. "I can't believe you bit me like some crazy three-year-old. Not to mention this." He pointed to his face. "My beautiful, perfect face is ruined," he moaned.

I snorted. "Drama queen." I rolled my eyes. "That will heal, just like your ego," I teased. "Did I break the skin? Leave a crazy outline or anything?"

He leaned down to lift up the pant leg of his jeans. Sure enough, I had.

"You should get that tattooed."

"You wish, asshole." Cash chuckled.

"If you two are done?" Easton stood up with his plate. "We gotta bounce, or we'll be late." He put his plate in the sink along with Brett's. Once we had all cleaned up, we headed outside to the heated garage so we could make our way to school.

***

A foot hit the back of my chair in the middle of Algebra.

"Jon," Tate Bernard hissed loud enough for the entire class to hear. "Did you see that video yet?" Again, everyone could hear him, but either he didn't know how to use his inside voice, or he didn't care because he hung out with us.

Tate was not a Knight, nor would he ever be, but he was one of the people we kept around to do some of our grunt work. He had been on vacation with his family in freaking Hawaii or some shit like that, so he missed everything that had happened, but someone must have filled him in. Smack.

"Hey, Jon." Louder this time.

"Mister Bernard," our teacher, Mrs. Morgan, called out. "Is there something you would like to share with the entire class?"

"It's Knights business, ma'am, so not really," Tate answered, and I spun around to glare at him.

"I don't care what kind of business it is. Mr. Hamden, turn around. If you don't start paying attention and put your phone away, I am going to send you to see Mrs. Donovan."

I groaned silently. That wouldn't do much good either, since Mrs. Donovan was Cash and Brett's mother. My nostrils flared as I shook my head at Tate, warning him not to say a word, to keep his fat mouth shut.

"Sorry," I muttered as I turned back around in my seat. "I'm sure that whatever Tate needs to tell me can wait until class is over." I felt him poke my shoulder just as it sounded like everyone's phones started to go off.

Shit. That could not be good.

"For Pete's sake." Mrs. Morgan sighed as she glanced at the clock. "Fine, we have five minutes left, anyway." She moved to sit down.

Tate shoved his phone in my face. "Look." He pointed to the screen. "Isn't that Spencer Pearson?" I nearly ripped his arm off trying to get the phone away from him, ignoring everyone else, who was most likely watching the exact same thing. It was Spencer, and staring up at him in the still shot was Ellie. Tate hit play.

"I don't care, Ellie!" Spencer shouted as a crowd of kids surrounded them. "We're done, do you hear me?"

Ellie raised her chin. "Fine by me, jerk. You're the one who decided you wanted to chase after someone else who wasn't even interested in you. She used you to get back at Easton, anyway." Tears fill her eyes.

What was going on? They were talking about when Spencer kissed Brett? That was months ago, and from what they told me, it was only because they were trying to get to me. Right?

"Doesn't matter. I was bored with you. That's why I did it. Haven't you figured it out yet? I'm not a one-person kind of guy. I want to explore other options. Fuck as many people as I want." My stomach dropped. Was Spencer serious? That didn't sound like something he would say. Or was he lying to me the entire time?

Ellie raised her lip. "You're a bad lay, anyway." That wasn't the truth. I could see it written all over her face.

"Liar."

"Cheater."

"Whore."

The crowd gasped then, and I saw the surprise written on Ellie's face. She hadn't expected Spencer to say that. Whoever was holding the camera moved slightly, and that's when I saw her.

Diana Monaco.

The expression on her face was complacent as she tilted her head and twisted a piece of blonde hair between her fingers. Her makeup was spot on, her lips painted the perfect shade of red as she tilted her head to listen to something someone was whispering into ear. She nodded, her lips twitched into a small smile, and then she turned her face away.

Ellie took a step forward. "I hate you." She seethed.

"I want you out by tomorrow," Spencer spat back.

Ellie blinked at him. "Where am I supposed to go?" she asked.

"Go crawl back to Mommy and Daddy for all I care, but you're not welcome at my house anymore."

The video ended there, and the bell rang at the same time, signaling our class was over. I stumbled from my desk into the crowded hallway in a state of shock and came face to face with Brett, who looked exactly the way I felt.

"Are you okay?" She hooked her arm through mine, and as we made our way around the rest of our classmates, I couldn't help but wonder where Easton and Cash were. Usually Brett had one, if not the other, with her at all times.

I nodded. "I think so." I was numb, trying to wrap my head around what I had just witnessed, but I wasn't ready to share that with anyone yet.

"Jon." Brett squeezed closer to me. "You know that you can talk to me, right?" Her blue eyes were wide when I looked down at her. "I care about you, and I hope that you feel the same way about me. I won't tell them." Her lips curved up into a smile.

I tried to swallow the lump in my throat. "Of course, B." The nickname that Palmer came up with for Brett slipped out, and she flinched. "Shit, I'm sorry. I'm just..." I dropped my gaze. "I don't know what to say or think right now," I confessed.

"You really liked them." Brett untangled her arm from mine as she came to a stop in front of her locker. When I nodded, she slipped her bag down her arm, opened the door, and quickly swapped out a couple of books before she slammed the door shut. Her brows were pinched together when Brett glanced back up at me again. "I liked Ellie, too, but maybe now that they broke up—"

"No." I stopped her before she could finish the sentence, glanced around to make sure no one was within listening distance, and then dropped my voice. "It was about both of them, not just one or the other."

Easton suddenly appeared out of thin air to drop his arm around Brett's shoulder before dropping a kiss against her lips. I turned away before they could see the look on my face. I was pissed because I wanted that, I'd had that, until I was told I couldn't.

"Guess everyone has seen that video by now," Easton commented. "You think she's coming back here now that she has no other place to go?" We started walking again as the bell rang, letting us know class was going to start.

Panic gripped my mind. Why hadn't I thought of that?

"Her parents kicked her out," I reminded them as we approached my next class. "I don't think they want her back." But where else would she go? Would I end up having to see Ellie here at Kingston High?

"You okay, bro? You look like you just saw a ghost." Jameson bumped my arm as he slipped past me into the room, but I felt sick to my stomach. I wasn't sure I was going to be able to handle that.

"Jon?" Brett's voice interrupted my thoughts.

I nodded. "Right, class, I'll see you at lunch," I muttered before heading in behind my brother.

Ellie had said she hated her parents, so that couldn't actually happen. Right? Because the thought of having to see her every single day made me feel things I wasn't sure I was ready to. And what of Spencer? Did he seriously break up with Ellie that easily after he claimed she was the one? I slumped down in my seat, feeling Jameson watching me and wishing I could turn back time and go back to that party. Demand to know who they were before I even touched them, but it was far too late for that now.

Chapter Thirteen

I hadn't expected that fight to go down the way it did at school today. The words we exchanged and the mean things we said. It hurt me harder than I thought that it would, considering it wasn't even real. I spent the rest of the day with my eyes at my feet, ignoring everyone and wishing for the bell to ring so that I could go home. I didn't have anyone at school but Spencer, so it was hard to sit alone at lunch knowing everyone was talking, whispering, and judging me behind my back.

Home. I would no longer have Spencer's arms wrapped around me at night when I went to sleep, but instead would have to suffer at the hands of my stepfather. My mother would never stick up for me, so I would have to make sure to be on my best behavior while I was back there. That house would never be my home. Not to mention, no number of locks I put on the door would keep *him* out of my room at night. I shivered at the thought of what I would have to do to keep him away. The lies I would have to spin.

Spencer and I both agreed that it would be best if he wasn't around when I left. We had been together so long that one of us would end up changing their mind, try to convince me to stay, and that wasn't what we had agreed on. We had agreed to do this for Jonathan, and I was going to stick to my guns no matter how hard it was.

Once I had packed up some of my clothes—I was leaving most of my belongings here because I would be back—I looked around the oversized room that I had shared with Spencer for the past four years. I remembered the first time I woke up next to him, the smile on his face, and how happy he said he was to have me here. The night I moved in, and Spencer helped me unpack, how strange it felt that he seemed to care about me without judging. Or the day his parents had offered to pay my tuition for college when I graduated from Weston at the end of the year. My eyes filled with tears that I didn't bother to hide as I quickly hurried from the room with my sad little suitcase and stuffed it into my car before I headed back to Kingston.

The drive wasn't too long, about ten minutes, and as I pulled into the driveway, I couldn't help but feel sick to my stomach. I swore this would never happen. That I wouldn't come crawling back to this house, have to listen to his rules or deal with any of this again, but here I was running back with my tail between my legs.

"Mommy?" I cried the moment she picked up the phone.

"Sweetheart, what's wrong? You sound like you've been crying."

I paced the room. "Can I come home?" I hated even asking, but it had to be done.

"Eleanor."

"Please, Mommy, I'll do whatever I have to, whatever it takes. I'm not like that now. I just... I miss you, and things are different. Please let me come home."

The slamming of the screen door brought me back to where I was, and I saw my mother, Paige Edwards, coming toward me. I opened the door to climb out to greet her. She still looked the same, maybe a little thinner, her blonde hair piled on her head.

"Honey, you don't have to sit outside. It's freezing. Come in." She didn't smile, most likely afraid her face would crack after the last facelift she had. She didn't try to hug me or touch me in any way, but that didn't come as a surprise.

Paige Edwards had never been the motherly type.

I grabbed my bag before I started to follow her inside, glancing around to notice the new driveway that he must have put in, the fence that now ran around the back of the house, and the garage that had once been falling part had been replaced by a much bigger, nicer model.

"Where is he?" I couldn't even say his name without cringing, so I kept it off my tongue. He was not my father and would never be.

Paige hung up her coat, reached for mine, and then turned to face me. "Your father is at work, dear, but he'll be home soon. We're having lasagna for dinner tonight, since I know it's your favorite." Her thin, red lips turned up slightly.

I hadn't eaten lasagna since I left this place because it only reminded me of how much I hated it here. "That's nice, Mom." I lied between clenched teeth.

"I put some clean sheets on your bed. Your room is exactly as you left it." Paige moved to the sink where she washed and then dried her hands. "Blake and Luna will be home soon if you want to go freshen up. I picked out a dress for you. You'll find in the closet," she told me.

I knew what that meant. Go make yourself presentable. Put on a dress, wash off the makeup, and do your hair just the right way before he gets home. Because we wouldn't want to upset the great and powerful Rick Edwards after he'd had such a long day at work.

I nodded. "Of course." I gripped my suitcase in my hand as I moved toward the hallway where my room had been at the back of the house. "Thanks, Mom," I repeated before I began to walk toward what felt like my death sentence.

The door was closed when I approached, and as I slowly opened it, I felt myself take a step back. Paige hadn't been kidding when she said she had kept it exactly the same. My cheerleader pompoms were still on the shelf where I had kept them, pictures of me with my friends decorated the bulletin board by the dresser, and even the One Direction poster on the closet door still hung in the same place. I smiled to myself as I leaned forward to examine the pictures, memories coming floating back.

Palmer and me, showing off our best friend necklaces. She had one half and I the other, and they fit together to make one heart. We'd met in six grade and had instantly bonded.

Palmer and me, freshman year at our first football game, all dressed up in our cheerleader uniforms. My skirt had been let out to hang down further than everyone else, but I pretended not to care or notice. I was just happy to be allowed to do something I wanted.

Palmer and me, again, hanging out at the beach the summer before sophomore year. Both of us were dressed in the bathing suits. Palmer, of course, had on a bikini and I wore a one piece which was more modest than most girls my age would ever wear.

I had a lot of good times with her, only to have Palmer decide that she didn't want to be my friend anymore when I get kicked out of Kingston. That she was too good for me now that I went to Weston, and we couldn't be friends anymore. She said that it had nothing to do with the sex parties that I was throwing or the fact that kids from our school were having sex with one another in twos and threes.

I bumped into Spencer a couple of weeks after starting Weston, and he helped fill that empty void, but I still missed having a girlfriend to do fun things with. It was a void that I hoped Brett, Lennox, and Josie might have helped fill.

Inside the closet, I found the dress my mother was talking about. It was brown button up, which didn't surprise me, looked like it would fall to my ankles, with a round neckline and a natural waistline. I slowly pulled out to hang on the back of my door as a feeling of homesickness fell over me. Shit, what had I done? I quickly yanked my cell from my pocket to find a text waiting for me.

Spencer: *I miss you baby. I'm sorry for the things I said. You know I love you.*

Ellie: *I don't think I can do this.*

Spencer: *You can! You're the strongest person I know.*

Ellie: *I love you so much. Please don't forget about me.*

Spencer: *Never, baby, it's you and me (and hopefully Jon?) forever.*

I swallowed the lump in my throat as I began to undress to put on the horrible outfit my mother had chosen for me. These were the things I would be expected to wear now that I was here again. Clothes that covered me from neck to knee, no makeup, and my hair done up the way that he liked. Once

I had removed the jeans and sweater I had come in with, I dropped them in the hamper before I turned to look at myself in the full-length mirror.

I had sworn I would never be this girl again, but here I was. Attempting to hide from who I was, becoming someone that I didn't want to be. Tears stung my eyes as I pulled the brown fabric over my head and watched myself in the mirror. It wasn't anything that I would have chosen for myself, but then again, none of the clothes I would wear going forward would be.

A knock at the door startled me. "Come in." My voice sounded funny, like a younger, less confident version of myself.

"I just wanted to see how the dress fit," Paige told me as she stepped into the room. "Eleanor, you look lovely." Her eyes moved over my body. "Do you like it?"

I nodded. "It's perfect, Mom, thank you," I lied, not wanting to hurt her feelings.

"Would you like to help me finish getting dinner ready?"

I wouldn't, but I nodded and followed behind Paige as she led the way back into the kitchen. My feet felt like lead. I felt like I was being guided to my death. I hoped that this was going to be worth it.

My mother married my stepfather, Rick Edwards, when I was ten years old. He was the pastor of the First Baptist Church of Kingston, and even though everyone loved and adored him, I never trusted him. Beneath that happy go-lucky exterior, there was something dark and evil that no one else saw. The way his blue eyes shifted around to look at me when my mother wasn't looking or the way he tried to touch me when he didn't need to or the way he moved in closer when he was talking to me.

Rick proved my instincts correct when I was twelve years old and started menstruating. I didn't tell my mother because she had never really told me what to expect about my first period, so instead, I confided in Palmer. My best friend helped me with tampons, cramps, and what I should and shouldn't do; and before long, I was on my way to being a full-fledged woman. Until Rick found out. Some nights he left me alone, but others? He would come home, lock my door, and wouldn't leave until I wished he would just kill me.

I washed, cut up the vegetables, and placed them in a bowl, making sure to place it in the perfect spot, the way that Rick liked it. My brother and sister walked into the kitchen after washing up just as Paige put the pan of lasagna on the table. Blake was eight, and Luna was four. I was a happy to see my siblings again, but it was cut short the moment the rolls were removed from the oven and Rick walked the door. The hairs on my arm to stood up, and I couldn't help the sinking feeling that settled over me again.

"Eleanor, it's so good to have you home again." He might have hugged me if Luna hadn't stopped him by wrapping her arms around his legs.

"Daddy, you're home! I missed you," she exclaimed. Just hearing her made my heart break.

Rick smiled down at his youngest. "I missed you, too, sweetie," he assured her and patted her on the head. "Let me go wash up so we can say grace and start dinner. It's a special night with your sister home." He flashed me a wicked smile, and dread swept through me.

I had made a horrible mistake.

Chapter Fourteen

Jonathan

I shoved everything back into the box I had just emptied and rubbed the sleep from my eyes with my good hand. I felt like we had been looking for years on information about Brett's past but hadn't found anything.

We knew a little about her past. Her sister, Ruby, had taken her from Kingston, afraid of what might happen if she hadn't, and decided to raise her on her own. Her mother, Brienne Donavan, had been told she wasn't going to be able to inherit the money from her family if she had any female heirs, so she'd given up both her daughters, Ruby and Brett, seemingly without regret. But from what we had learned, that wasn't the case.

Brett seemed more willing than Cash to listen to their mother now that Ruby was gone, but that was probably because she hadn't been beaten by her stepfather like Cash had. Ruby's father, Owen Maxwell, who was Oz's father, had fled Kingston after being shot by his son, and we hadn't heard from him since. We all thought it had something to do with the fact that he had tried to have Easton killed, but no one dared to bring that up.

"Holy shit," Jameson exclaimed, causing us all to turn in his direction. He was staring down at a piece of paper in hand. "The pastor at the Baptist church."

"Pastor Rick?" Oz asked. "What about him?"

Cash snorted. "Dude, do I even want to know how you know who that is? When have you ever stepped foot in a church? You would totally burst into flames." He chuckled softly as his gaze dropped back to the paperwork in front of him.

"Ha, ha, asshole, very funny." Oz rolled his eyes. "He's buddies with my father. He's a Knight."

"He's also Ellie's stepfather," Jameson answered.

I felt myself break out in a cold sweat. "Give me that." I grabbed the papers from my brother's hands.

Sure enough, Rick Edwards had married Paige Young—now Edwards—after her husband, Ellie's father, had died in an automobile accident. Ellie had been eight when her father had died and ten when her mother remarried. I skimmed through the rest of the paperwork until I found what I was looking for.

The contract.

"Is that what I think it is?" Jameson popped over my shoulder. "Dude, it's you."

Every male Knight had a female they were supposed to marry. For Easton, it had always been Brett despite Chad trying to push Josie on him. We hadn't remembered Brett had even existed until she'd come back to Kingston last fall. We hadn't found any other contracts until right now.

"Let me see that." Easton nearly ripped the paper in half as he tore it from my hand. "Shit, bro, this is it. You were supposed to marry Ellie." His green eyes flashed with fire. "Well, I guess you were on to something there." His lips curved up into a sly smirk.

I stuck up my middle finger at him, then waved it around the room at the rest of the Knights. We were currently in the basement of the Silver house, with the girls upstairs. We hadn't wanted them to see anything they shouldn't, although Brett and Lennox had tried. Josie didn't care, or at least that's what she had told Jameson, saying she preferred to stay clear of Knight business. I couldn't say I blamed her, considering how things had turned out for her.

"Was he always a Knight, or was that something your dad worked out?" Cash asked, taking a swig of the bottle of vodka we had all been sharing before passing it to me.

I shook my head. I was already feeling too buzzed to drink any more if I wanted to be able to focus on the bombshell that had just dropped on us.

Oz made a noise that sounded like a grunt as he sat down on the floor. "I think they all grew up together like Easton's and J2's pop."

Just the mention of my dad brought my eyes over to Jameson, who widened his eyes at me.

"Wonder who I'm supposed to marry." Oz said the last word as if it was something that might turn around and bite him. "As if that would ever happen."

"What, Ozzy, you don't believe in the whole happily ever after?" Cash wrapped his arms around Oz's neck.

"Get off me, you idiot." Oz tried to shove Cash away, but that only made him hug Oz tighter. "I'm serious, dude. Don't make me hurt you."

Cash cackled. "You love me, Ice." He pressed a kiss to Oz's hair.

Oz smacked Cash in the chin with his head.

"Dude, what the hell?" Cash instantly released him, which is what Oz was probably going for.

"I warned you!" Oz jumped up.

Cash held his hand to his mouth. "Am I bleeding?" he asked us. "Am I?"

"You're being a bit dramatic. Don't you think?" I asked.

Cash scrunched his nose up at me and turned to his best friend, Easton, who rolled his eyes. "You're going to be fine," he assured him.

"At least someone loves me around here," Cash said.

"You sure you don't want to go hang out with the girls?" Jameson asked. "Your balls seem to be missing."

"You sure you don't want me to punch you *in* the balls?" Cash shot back.

I couldn't hold back the laugh that escaped my mouth, and when I started, I couldn't seem to stop. Before long, the rest of the guys joined in with me. When we finally were able to gather ourselves together, we decided we should call it a night.

"Take that." Easton pointed to the contact that had been signed by Ellie's stepfather and my father. "It might be the only copy, so we need to keep it somewhere safe."

***

I felt like a zombie as I stumbled down the stairs the next morning. Combined with the booze I had drunk last night and the information we had discovered, I hadn't sleep much once we had finally made it home. So when I finally dragged myself into the kitchen, I found everyone except my brother, who had stayed with Josie at her place last night, sitting around the table eating cereal. Just as well. I wasn't up to cooking breakfast this morning.

"Wow, you look great, Jon," Cash commented as I poured myself a cup of coffee and drank it, black. "Looking to put some hair on your chest, too?" He ducked when I went to smack the back of his head.

Lennox punched his shoulder. "Jerk," she hissed. "You okay?" she asked as she stood up. When I didn't answer, she moved closer. "You want to talk about it?" She touched my elbow lightly.

"I'm good," I lied.

"You might want to sit down," Easton announced, and when I glanced over at him, I saw the way Brett was watching me. "Babe, you're giving yourself away," the boss told her as he untucked his arm from around her shoulder.

Brett's brows dipped further. "Jon, you should really sit down." Her blue eyes were soft. "Please?" She patted the chair next to her.

"What's going on?" I asked, ignoring Brett.

"Ellie is starting Kingston today," Oz blurted, which caused the others to start shouting at him. "No need to be such pussies about it. Just rip off the Band-Aid." He smirked like a fool.

Cash averted his gaze from mine. "Mom sent me a text this morning to tell me a new student was starting. She always does that when she finds out." He glanced over at his sister. "Even when it happens to be my twin." He smiled at Brett. We all knew Brett was going to be the new girl that day but never knew she would become such a huge part of our lives.

I turned to Easton for advice. "Well?" I asked, hoping the boss man would tell me what I should do.

"This is all on you, Jon." He shook his head as he helped Brett get to her feet. "You decide how you want us to handle this." Easton took the purple coat she wore off the hook so she could put it on. "Just make sure that Spencer is truly out of her life before you put your dick in her again," He warned.

"Easton." Brett swatted at his chest. "I'm not ignoring her. She's my friend."

We all watched the dark scowl that clouded his face. "You talked to her since that day she came by here with him?" His voice was smothered in hate.

"No, but if I see her today, I'm going to make her feel welcome. Like Cash did to me the day I showed up." Brett broke out in a smile. "That goes for my girls, too, because we're a team, right?" She nodded at Lennox, who nodded back.

Easton sighed. "You're so sexy when you try to take control, Dorothy." He pulled her close, and we all turned away as he shoved his tongue down her throat.

"Dude, really?" Oz reached around them to grab his coat from the hook. "It's not like you weren't sticking it to her last night and keeping us all awake. It's like you're trying to put little Eastons inside her or something." He made a face before he opened the door to stomp outside into the cold morning air.

I followed behind him only to have Lennox grab at my elbow. "Don't shut me out, Jon," she whispered as I glanced behind me. "I'm still your best friend, even if you're mad at me."

"I'm not mad at you."

"Sure seems like you are."

I sighed as we watched Oz pull his silver Tesla out of the garage and shoot down the driveway and onto the road without checking to see if anyone was coming. He really did have a death wish.

"I'm sorry." My shoulders slumped forward. "I'm just confused."

"You need to talk to her when you see her today," Lennox told me.

I let out a short laugh. "That's easy for you to say now, but what happens when I actually see her? Come face to face with her pretty face, and I can't actually do that?" I flushed when I realized what I had just said out loud.

"You could always be a total dick to her," Easton commented as he walked by. "Look how well that worked for me." He laughed loudly when Brett protested. Would I ever get used to the happy version of Easton? Because it still seemed so strange to me.

Brett giggled. "Honestly, it's nice to have the grumpy one be soft for the sunshine one, but this isn't a romance book, Jon." She stopped to face me. "You're smarter than that, aren't you?" Her eyes searched my face.

"You two coming, or do you plan on being late today?" Easton called over his shoulder as he and Brett headed toward the garage.

Lennox and I followed behind them, but I still had no clue what I was going to do because I was even more confused than ever before.

Chapter Fifteen

I gripped my new school schedule in my right hand as I stepped from the front office and listened as the door shut quietly behind me. I felt like I was in a nightmare that I couldn't wake up from as I watched as my former classmates walk down the hallway, not paying any attention to me. It might have something to do with the dress I was forced to put on this morning along with the world's most hideous winter coat that had me sweating in under two seconds. The one that buttoned up to my neck and practically fell to my ankles.

"Ellie?"

I turned at the sound of my name to find Brett standing there watching me.

"What are you doing here?" she asked, her eyes taking in my outfit.

I could hear the false innocence in her question. I'm sure she saw the video just like everyone else. Even I had seen it because it was plastered all over Facebook, which I was now forbidden to access since my phone had been taken away from me. I now had some slower, older model that wouldn't even allow to me to add apps to it.

"Don't do that." I started to move around her, only to nearly slam right into Easton. He narrowed his eyes at me. Shit, how did I miss him? "Move," I growled. "Or I'll scream."

A smile spread across his face. "Go ahead, Ellie, try it. Don't forget who runs this place." Easton leaned down. "I'll give you a hint." His voice was cold as he spoke. "It's the Knights." He sneered while bringing his finger up to point at himself.

Brett shoved at his chest. "Stop it," \she told him. "Ellie, we're your friends. Are you okay?" She tilted her head.

"Never better," I lied. "I don't want to be late my first day back." I started to go around them, but that's when I saw Jon.

He stood with his brother, the two of them like looking like a couple of matching bookends with Lennox squeezed in between. They were dressed in tight blue jeans, long-sleeved Knights shirts, and their dark hair tousled perfectly. Why did it suddenly feel like my feet were weighted down by cement blocks?

A hand waved in front of my face, and when I focused, I realized it was Cash. "Sure, you're great." He chuckled.

"You're talking to me?" I glared up at him. "All of you? All of you want to be my friend now? Because the last time we spoke, you acted as if I had the 'Rona or something. What gives?" I was surprised at how confident I sounded, because inside, my stomach was doing backflips.

Lennox's eyes went wide. "Ellie, now isn't the time," she warned.

"You don't get to call the shots." Oz's deep voice was behind me and when his hands landed on my shoulders, I thought I would pass out from fright. "We have something we need to talk to you about, Eleanor, but we can't do that here."

I saw the way Jonathan's eyes flashed with hatred, but not at me. No, he was trying to make sure he didn't punch out his friend who was trying to scare the crap out of me and doing a pretty damn good job at it, too.

"What I need you to do is go to class, pretend everything is fine, and of course, have lunch with us. Like you're a Knight." Oz spun me around to make sure I saw the devilish smile on his handsome face. "Which, by the way, you are."

"Get your hands off her, Oz." I looked up to find Jon standing there with his eyes narrowed at his friend. "Now, before I do it for you."

Oz chuckled softly. "Sure, whatever you say." He held up his hands before he winked at me and walked off just as the bell rang, causing everyone except Jon to scatter.

I felt a hand on my elbow. "Where's your first class?" Jon's voice caused heat to spike through me.

"Wha... what?" I stared at him when he reached for my hand. The one with my schedule in it. He was still here. Wasn't he afraid of being late to class?

Jonathan carefully pried my fingers away from the schedule. "Do you remember where the computer lab is, Ellie?" His eyes had softened into pools of warm chocolate.

I snatched the paper back. "Of course I do. I'm not an idiot." I huffed.

"Did I say you were?"

I ignored him as I started down the hall, my backpack heavy against my shoulder. Only problem was that I wasn't sure that I was going in the right direction.

"Uh, sweetheart?" Jonathan called out to me. "The computer lab is that way."

When I glanced over my shoulder, he was pointing down the hall to my right. A smile tugged at his perfect lips as I met his gaze.

My nostrils flared as I peeled off my coat to hang over my arm. "I knew that," I muttered.

Jonathan winked at me. "Sure you did." He smirked.

I started to head down in the direction he just pointed, only to have him start following behind me. "What are you doing?" I hissed through clenched teeth.

"Making sure you make it to class on time."

"I'm good, thanks."

"I love the dress."

"Go away."

Jon chuckled softly. "Who picked that out?" he asked, and I felt his fingers graze the collar. Goosebumps broke out across my skin. "It does absolutely nothing for your figure, sweetheart," he murmured before his hand clamped around my arm and he spun me around to crush me against his chest. "Miss me?" Jon's dark eyes searched my face.

"Like a bad rash," I fibbed, dropping my gaze from his face.

Jonathan clucked his tongue against the roof of his month as he dropped his hold on me to tip my face up with an index finger. "Mmmmm, think you might be lying," he murmured softly before his hand snaked around to grip the back of my neck.

I stared up at him with wide eyes until the loud bang of a door caused me to jump. Who was this version of Jon right now? What happened to the shy guy I had first met?

"Mr. Hamden, are you lost? Because I don't think you have a class on this side of the school this morning." A gruff, older male voice interrupted us.

Jonathan's eyes moved behind me, but he didn't release me. Instead, I felt his grip tighten just enough to make heat pool between my legs, inside the stupid cotton granny panties my mother had picked out for me. Totally things that should not be said together at the same time.

His lip curled up into a snarl. "Not lost, sir, just making sure my girlfriend makes it to her first class." His voice was commanding. It was a side of Jon I hadn't seen before.

I liked it.

Also, girlfriend? I thought we had broken up. How was my plan working out so quickly? Or was he playing me?

Jon's eyes focused on me again. "I'll see you after your third period class, Ellie, because we have English and Chemistry together before we go to lunch." He leaned forward to slide his lips over mine before I could protest. "We'll talk about this dress later," he whispered before he turned and left me standing there watching him walk away.

***

Even though I had classes with each of the Knights except Oz, I didn't talk to any of them. They were all acting like we were best friends. As if that confrontation with Spencer had never gone down. Like they hadn't threatened to kill him or me a couple of days ago outside of Oz's house.

"Pssst, hey, Ellie." Cash's voice was loud enough to wake the dead in our English class with Jonathan. I was strategically seated in front of him like the teacher knew I was part of their little group. Which I wasn't. "What's going on with that burlap sack you're wearing?"

A few girls giggled while I sank down in my chair, hoping to disappear. I felt myself burn with embarrassment. I wasn't normally that type of girl, but then again, I was also the one who had thrown the sex parties. A few guys had already shouted that out to me when I'd walked down the hall this morning.

Cash leaned forward. "No, don't hide, because I dig it. You think they make these in tall for Len?" He snorted with laughter when she spun around to stare at him from her seat in the front row. She shot up her middle finger and rolled her eyes at me.

"Dickhead," she mouthed.

"Enough, dude," Jonathan hissed from the back. "Leave her alone."

Cash patted my shoulder. "Ellie knows I'm joking, right?"

I nodded. "Sure, right." However, I didn't think he was.

As soon as the bell rang at the end of fifth period, I tried to make a beeline out of the room, but Jonathan caught me before I could make it out the door. His arm curled around my shoulders so he could pull me close against him.

"Where do you think you're running off to?" His breath was hot against my ear.

I stared up at him. "Lunch. I'm hungry."

"Not without me, you're not."

"Hey, aren't you the sex party girl?" someone called out.

Oh, sweet baby Jesus.

Jonathan's face grew wild with rage, his eyes narrowed, and he turned to look around the hallway.

"Who said that?" he shouted. When no one answered, he let go of me. "I will repeat the question in case you didn't hear me correctly the first time." He growled deep in his chest. "Who. Said. That? Because Ellie is with me, so if you have something to say?" Jon squared his shoulders as Jameson appeared next to him. "You're going to need to go through all of us first."

I looked around, as the entire hallway grew silent as a funeral. No one dared make a sound. Or maybe they were too afraid to answer because they didn't want to find out what might happen when they confessed.

I tugged on Jon's shirt. "It's fine, honest." I tried to assure him, but I could see by the look on his face that it was far from okay.

"That's the game you want to play?" His brows dipped down. "All right, because I'll be happy to get Easton and Oz over here to help Cash, Jameson and me interrogate each of you pricks to find out who—"

One guy stepped forward. "It was me," he admitted, his cheeks red, and his blue eyes wide. "I'm the one who said it. I was just being a jerk, man. I honestly didn't know she was with a Knight. It was a joke."

Jonathan moved fast and shoved him against one of the lockers. "A joke?" he hissed. "Tell me the punchline, because I don't fucking get it."

The crowd parted as Easton appeared, his frame frightening, but not nearly as scary as Oz who was behind him, and I took a step back when he shot a glance in my direction. I wasn't afraid to admit that Oswald Maxwell absolutely scared the living hell out of me.

"Relax, Ellie, my boys got this." Cash's voice caused me to jump, and when I glanced up at him, he had the balls to wink at me before he casually threw his arm over my shoulders.

He did not just do that.

I shrugged his arm off me before I wrinkled my nose in disgust. "What do you think you're doing?"

Cash held his finger up to his lips as he grinned at me with a sparkle in his blue eyes. He was handsome, I'd give him that, but right now I wanted nothing more than to smack that smug smile right off his face.

"The big boys are talking now," he whispered and jutted his chin at me.

I suppressed a groan and folded my arms over my chest.

"Someone want to tell me what's going on here?" Easton asked. "Adam Jenkins, right?" he asked the guy who had brought up the sex parties. "What did you do?" He held up a hand when Jonathan went to answer. "Let him tell his side first."

"I made a mistake." Adam whimpered.

Easton nodded. "Oh, right, you made a mistake. What kind of a mistake did you make?" he asked, looking around before his eyes landed on me. He waved me over, but I shook my head. Easton narrowed his eyes, and when Cash began to push me forward, I had no choice but to start to walk.

"I, uh, I thought that I knew Ellie from somewhere, but I was wrong." Adam looked like he was going to pee his pants, he was so scared.

"Damn right, you were wrong." Jon's lip twisted up into a snarl. "She's a Knight, she's mine, and I want you to apologize," he demanded. "Right now."

Why did they keep saying that? I wasn't a Knight, nor had I ever been. "It's fine, Jon, let him go," I assured him, and when I met Adam's eyes, I flashed a quick smile.

"That's where you're wrong." Oz chuckled. "It's not fine. When someone messes with us, Eleanor..." He waited until I looked at him. "They have to pay. And pay, he will."

"I made a mistake!" Adam exclaimed. "I said I was sorry. I didn't know she was a Knight."

"I'm not a Knight!" I shouted. "I don't want to be, either. So let him go."

Easton leaned down, so that he was right in my face, and even if Brett was there, I don't think she could have stopped him.

"You don't have a choice in the matter." His deep voice sent shivers up my spine, and the way his eyes looked at me made me realize I never should have come back here. I looked at the rest of them, the Knights, and then sprinted down the hall as fast as I could without turning back.

Chapter Sixteen

Spencer

This was absolute hell. From the moment I woke up this morning, to the second I stepped foot into school, to right now, when I sat down with the rest of the football team. Without Ellie here, next to me, I hated everything and everyone. I couldn't text her anymore because all of a sudden, her texts weren't going through, which meant her phone was either dead or turned off.

"Dude, you look like shit."

I glared at Jimmy Roberts, the Eagles wide receiver, silencing him. "I look, feel, and am shit," I finished for him. "I don't need any of you asshats to remind me of that." I took a bite of my chicken sandwich. It tasted terrible.

"She, uh, really gone?" Scott Aarons asked.

I nodded. "Yep." I popped the p at the end as he glanced behind me.

"Too bad," Diana Monaco cooed softly as she slowly ran her hand through my hair. I swear, I felt my skin crawl. "You must be *so* lonely without Ellie here."

I didn't want Diana anywhere near me, because one, she had slept with nearly every straight male in this school, and two, I hated her, but I couldn't let her know. I had promised Ellie I wouldn't go anywhere near Diana.

I plastered a fake smile on my face before I glanced up at her. "You offering?" I hated to even pretend something like this, but right now, I had didn't have much of a choice.

Diana's eyes moved over my face, my chest, and of course, to my crotch, which wasn't even showing any sign of life, before she met my gaze again.

"Your place?" She batted her overly caked lashes.

"My parents are back." Thank God, because I wasn't about to bring Diana anywhere near the bed I shared with the love of my life. "They're kind of pissed off at me right now, you know, so if I bring home a new girl so quickly, they might get even more bent out of shape."

That was a lie. They knew nothing other than Ellie and I had a fight, she wanted some space, and had gone back to her parents' house. I didn't want to get them involved if I didn't have.

Diana dragged her teeth across her bottom lip. "You could come by my house? My parents don't care." No one got access to the Monaco house unless they were very lucky, so this was some serious luck on my part.

"How about tomorrow? I have a dinner with my parents tonight that I can't get out of."

"You sure about that?"

I nodded. "Positive."

I could, but I wouldn't. I didn't want to seem that desperate, and I needed to talk to Jonathan, even if it meant I went to his house again to do it. I might be able to get on his good graces again if could get into Diana's house.

"I'll text you the address, but plan to come by around seven, okay?" Diana blew me a kiss before she walked off, swinging her hips as she did.

The guys were all staring at me like I'd just grown a second head when I looked at them.

"What?" I asked.

"Did you just not break up with Ellie like two seconds ago, and you're already jumping into the sack with Diana?" Jimmy asked.

"Whatever." I stood up, trying to play it off like it was no big deal. "I was tied down with one chick for too long. It's time to have some fun."

I wasn't going to stick my dick anywhere near Diana. What I planned on doing was handing her over to the Knights on a big silver fucking platter so that they didn't hate me anymore.

***

Spencer: *I need to talk to you.*

    Spencer: *You can't keep ignoring me.*

    Spencer: *I have something that you want.*

    Spencer: *I have something all of you want, Jon.*

    Jonathan: *Lose my number before I block you, asshole.*

    Spencer: *Surprised you haven't already, sweetness.*

    Jonathan: *Don't call me that.*

    Spencer: *You fucking love it.*

    Jonathan: *What do you want?*

    Spencer: *Do you still want Diana Monaco? Because I have a fake date with her tomorrow night at her house.*

I stared at my phone as I waited for Jonathan to answer me back, but when the text bubble disappeared, I realized he was probably going to Easton with the information. What I wanted to ask him right now was how Ellie was, was he taking care of her, and did she miss me, but I didn't want to bring her name into this just in case he did show these texts to Easton or Oz. When my phone buzzed again, I nearly dropped it.

Unknown: *If you're lying, I'll cut your balls off and make you eat them while I make your ex watch. Not sure how you feel about eating your own balls, but I'm sure it won't be fun.*

Did Jonathan really give Easton my number without asking me first? Because that was a totally uncool and dick move right there.

Spencer: *Easton, if you wanted to see my dick, all you had to do was ask. You know I swing both ways.*

Easton: *Don't try to be funny, shit for brains. I don't like you, nor do I trust you. You have fifteen minutes to get here before I change my mind.*

Spencer: *No way am I stupid enough to come to your house again. Jon knows my address. Have him bring you here, but only you. If I see that asshole Maxwell anywhere near my house, I will personally make sure he never throws a baseball again.*

Easton: *Do you think we're scared of you?*

Spencer: *You should be.*

Easton: **middle finger emoji**

I did not peg this guy to be an emoji user, but then again you probably wouldn't expect him to put a ring on girl's finger at the age of eighteen either, so that just goes to show you shouldn't judge a book by its cover.

Spencer: *Come by after eight o'clock.*

Easton: *We're coming now, motherfucker.*

Spencer: *I'm having dinner with my parents tonight and I haven't seen them in a while. Deal with it.*

Easton: *Eat me.*

Spencer: *You'd like it too much.*

I waited for a response, but when none came, I chalked that up as a win for me.

"Knock, knock."

I turned to find my mother, Holly Pearson, smiling at me from the doorway. "Hey, Mom." I waved her in.

"You okay, sweetie?" She moved over to where I was sitting and cupped my face in her hands. With her blonde hair, dark eyes, and bright smile, my mother hardly looked old enough to have an eighteen-year-old son.

I nodded. "Sure, never better." I dropped my phone on the bed. "How are you?" I tried to change the subject.

Holly shook her head. "No, you don't." She pushed a piece of hair from my forehead. "Ellie's gone, you won't tell me what happened, and you look like someone just told you the tooth fairy wasn't real." She eased herself onto the bed next to me.

"Mom."

"Talk to me, Spencer. I'm worried."

I opened my mouth to do just that, to spill everything starting with what happened with Brett first, just as the sounds of the cameras went off alerting everyone someone was here. I jumped up, knowing exactly who it was even after I told him I was having dinner with my parents. Prick.

"Expecting someone?" Holly tilted her head. "You better not have invited a girl over already, because despite what happened between the two of you, I still love Ellie like she is my own daughter." A smile tugged at her lips as she watched me peek through the curtain to watch my father, Spencer Senior, approach the black SUV that was now parked outside.

I shook my head. "It's not a girl," I assured her.

"A guy?"

My parents knew all about me. They knew I was bisexual, and they never even batted an eye when I told them. I was lucky that way, but right now, I was watching the way Senior was speaking to Jonathan, Easton, and shit, did they bring Brett?

"Mom, I'll be right back." Grabbing my phone, I bolted down the hallway and took the steps two at a time only to come face to face with the three Knights as my father led them into the living room.

"You have a few visitors." Dad's brows lifted slightly as he turned to remove his coat. "Didn't know you were friends with the Knights these days, son." His face was blank, but his eyes told me all I needed to know.

Be careful with a side of what the hell are you doing?

I gritted my teeth. "I'm not. They just—"

"I'm friends with Ellie," Brett finished for me as she flashed a smile at Senior. "She just transferred back to Kingston, and Jon, here"—she elbowed him—"Jon and Spencer actually know one another very well. Don't you, boys?" Her smile slipped into a wicked grin as her blue eyes met my browns. What a tease.

Easton's nostrils flared. "Do you have somewhere we can talk?" he grunted while Jon made sure to keep his eyes as far away from me as possible.

"My goodness, look at you!" Holly exclaimed as she came down the stairs. "What gorgeous hair. I can only imagine how you and Ellie must look standing together," she gushed. "Spencer, invite your friends to dinner."

My shoulders dropped. "Mom, they are not my friends, and they won't be here long." I didn't want my mother getting any ideas about the Knights. Not now or not ever.

"Nonsense." Holly inched around me so that she could get a closer look. "When Spencer told me that he and Ellie broke up, I was heartbroken, but now..." She brought her right hand up to her chin to tap a finger against it lightly. "It's you, isn't it, honey?" Holly nodded at Jon, who turned a deep red.

Brett giggled as Easton slipped his arm around her waist. "I like your mom, Spencer," she teased.

"That settles it." Mom clapped her hands. "The three of you are staying for dinner. We're having a roast, which should be done in about fifteen minutes." She turned back to me. "Don't be rude, Spencer. Take their coats and then introduce us to your friends."

Jesus Christ, I had no other choice now. Once my mother dug in her heels like this, I couldn't say no.

"Coats?" I held out my hand and watched the way Easton's lip curled up in disgust. The guy totally and completely hated my guts.

"Spencer Kent Pearson!" Holly exclaimed. "You are being more than rude to your friends."

"I already told you, Mom, they aren't my friends. I hardly even know them."

"Seriously?" I dragged my eyes up to Jon, who was watching me with fire in his eyes, a dark scowl written all over his handsome face. Look who had decided to finally grow a set.

My father cleared his throat. "Holly, why don't we leave them to sort this out?" He started to escort my mother, who looked more than mortified by the way I was treating my guests, from the room.

I was simply telling her the truth. Jon made it clear he wasn't interested in having a relationship with me because of his friends. Easton wanted to slit my throat because of a mistake I made, and Brett? Well, I wasn't sure what was running through her pretty head right now.

The moment my parents were out of earshot, Easton stepped forward. "We're not staying for dinner. Talk." He pointed a finger at me while sucking his lip ring into his mouth.

"I'm going to Diana's tomorrow night." I held up my hand before anyone could jump all over me. "It's not what you think. I'm not interested. It's sort of a peace offering." I watched the way Brett stared at me. "How is she?" I couldn't help the question as it slipped from my lips. "Is she okay?"

Jonathan shook his head. "No, no way. You don't get to ask anything about Ellie. What you did... What you said to her..." He looked like he wanted to rip me apart. "How could you? What was all that shit you told me about Ellie being your soulmate?"

"That was a private conversation."

"Maybe you shouldn't have had it in front of the entire school."

Easton grunted. "Could you two do this foreplay another time? We're here about Diana."

I licked my lips nervously. "Right." They didn't know about the fight being fake. The Knights, just like everyone else, had believed it, and now Jon hated me for it. At least our plan had worked.

"The Monaco house is locked down like Fort Knox." I glanced over at Jon to find him looking at the couch. Was he remembering the last time he was here? With Ellie? How we had all cuddled up on the couch under the covers, drinking vodka laced hot chocolate. That seemed like such a long time ago.

"Yo." Easton snapped his fingers in my face. "Stop daydreaming about whatever you want to do to Jon and focus."

"Tin Man." Brett pressed a hand against his chest. "Easy, remember what we talked about?" She tilted her head to look up at him, and I watched how his face softened. Dude had it bad for her, and I regretted ever stepping on his toes.

I sighed. "Let me take your coats." I tried to sound friendly this time. "Seriously, relax, stay for dinner like my mom suggested. Her roast is out of this world amazing, and what? Why are you staring at me like that right now?" I watched the way his face darkened again.

"We are not friends, Pearson."

"Never said we were, Kennedy."

We stared at one another for what felt like forever until his lip turned up into a half smile. It was at least a step in the right direction

"Whatever," Easton growled, and then he unzipped his leather coat. "She sits next to me." He jutted his chin at Brett. "Jon sits on the other side of me with you next to him. And if you even make one comment about her, I will stab you with a butter knife right in front of your parents. Don't even fucking care."

This was going to be fun.

Chapter Seventeen

Jonathan

"So..." Mrs. Pearson flashed a big smile as she carefully placed the roast down on the table before her husband, Spencer's father, began to carve it. This was weird as hell. "How did you all meet?" Her eyes were as brown as her son's were, but they didn't have that darkness to them. Like she hadn't seen the things that Spencer had.

I dropped my gaze to my empty plate. I wasn't going to do this. I couldn't do this. It was bad enough she had somehow figured out there was something going on between Spencer and me, but now I was supposed to talk about it, like this was normal dinner conversation? I should have stayed home. I should have sent Cash instead so that I could figure out how to get Ellie to talk to me again after the fiasco that went down at school this afternoon. I suddenly realized the entire room was silent. Shit.

"You okay, Jonathan?" Brett leaned forward so I could see her face more clearly.

I pressed my lips together, ready to give her some snarky answer, until I felt Spencer's hand find mine under the table. His fingers slowly laced through mine, warm yet callused from years of football, and I didn't pull back, afraid it would draw more attention than I already had on me. His grip was strong but gentle, and when I glanced over at him, he gave a quick nod as if he knew what I was thinking.

I swallowed the lump in my throat before I opened my mouth to speak. "Sure," I lied to Brett, afraid that if I said something else, the Pearsons would see right through me.

"You're one of the Hamden twins, right?" Spencer's father had finished carving the roast, and now the plate was being passed around the table. I was far from hungry, but when Mrs. Pearson handed it to me, I took a small portion to be polite.

"Yes, sir." I nodded.

He smiled as he stabbed his fork into a potato. "None of that here. You can call me Senior, just like the rest of Spence's friends." He split the root vegetable in half with his knife before he spoke to me again. "I knew your mom in high school," he added casually.

Spencer's hand suddenly tightened around mine. "Dad." His voice was calm, but the tone had a slight warning. Did he know something he hadn't told me? I tried to pull away, but he held on.

Easton nearly spit water from his nostrils. "Excuse me?" He coughed as Brett gave his back a good smack.

"Spencer, now is not the time," Mrs. Pearson whispered, casting a glance in my direction. "Can't we get through dinner first?"

"The boy should know, Holly." Senior took a bite of his roast, chewed, swallowed, and then looked at me. "She was from Weston, lived next door to me growing up, and, until she met your father, was contracted to me."

Easton was the first one to jump from his chair as we all stared at him. "That's a goddamn lie!" he exclaimed, and I saw him reach for the piece in his waistband the same time as Senior did.

Spencer let go of my hand to get to his feet.

"Don't do that," he hissed but didn't try to touch Easton, knowing that would cause more problems we didn't need. "We can do this like civilized people, right?" He twisted his head to look at his father. "Dad, you mind explaining yourself?"

Senior tilted his head. "You boys mind sitting down? I think Easton can put the gun on the table so we can all see it, too." He pointed for effect.

"Jon?" Easton raised his chin. "What do you want to do? You want to stay here, or you want to leave? Say the word, bro."

"We need to find out about Diana," I reminded him.

"This is no longer just about her."

Easton was right. My family involved was. My mother had been from Weston, which meant Jameson and I weren't all Kingston royalty, sort of like Brett. "I'd like to know more about my mother," I answered before I sat back down.

Easton didn't say anything as he slipped his gun from his jeans and placed it on the table. Then he eased himself back into his chair and wrapped his arm around Brett's shoulder. "If you try anything—"

"I wouldn't, not with the girl here," Senior assured him, and Easton's face darkened. "Piper Hamden—well, back then she was Piper Bryant—was contracted by her parents to marry me until she met your father and ran off with him."

The happy look on Mrs. Pearson's face had disappeared, now replaced with one that looked more than just a little shell-shocked.

"By the time we found them, they were hitched, she was pregnant with you and your brother, and there was nothing my father or hers could do about it."

The hairs on the back of my neck began to rise as thoughts that I didn't want began to creep in. Did Senior have something to do with my mother's death? Did she really die giving birth to Jameson and me?

"It's a shame, really." Senior's voice interrupted my thoughts. "Piper was beautiful, full of life, and had so much potential. She never really cared too much for me, but she could have grown to love me over time."

"Excuse me." Mrs. Pearson rushed from the room and into the kitchen. Senior rose and hurried after her.

Easton shook his head. "Your dad's a dick. Talking about another woman like that with your mom sitting right next to him."

"Watch your mouth, Kennedy."

"What are you going to do, Pearson? Hit me?"

"Amongst other things."

Brett put her hand against Easton's chest and leaned forward. "Stop it," she hissed. "Both of you stop fighting." Her blues landed on me. "Do something with your man, Jon." Her lips twitched before she slid her palm up to squeeze Easton's shoulder.

"He's not my man," I objected, but when Spencer twisted to look at me, I felt my pulse quicken. I wanted him to be, but it would never happen because of the giant, tattooed elephant in the room.

Spencer looked like he was going to say something, but the sound of his parents arguing stopped him.

"You can't talk about her like that, Spencer! Not when I'm sitting next you, and with our son in the room. I'm your wife, not Piper! She's dead!"

I flinched at the cruel words and might have left the dining room if Spencer's fingers didn't slowly comb through my hair.

"Don't listen to them." His calm voice drifted through my mind. "Your mother loved you, sweetness." His breath was hot against my ear. "You know that. You told me as much."

I nodded as I fought back tears.

"Keep your voice down, Holly. The Knights are the next room! You want them hearing you?" Senior obviously didn't care if we heard him, though.

I met Easton's eyes just as he got to his feet to grab his gun. "We should bounce before this gets even uglier." I couldn't have agreed with the boss man more.

I followed behind Easton and Brett as they made their way to the living room, to the closet where we had hung our coats. Spencer stopped me before I walked out the front door.

"I'm sorry." His brows dipped. "I mean, I'm sorry that you heard that, and about you finding out about your mother and my father the way you did."

Easton was already halfway down the walkway before he realized I wasn't right behind him. "Jesus Christ," he muttered, dragging his hand over the back of his neck. "Just fucking kiss already." I heard him chuckle before I did just that.

My lips landed on Spencer's before I could chicken out, and I might have surprised him more than I surprised myself, but he gripped my jacket tight enough that I was pretty sure I heard the fabric rip. The hairs on his jaw were rough against my skin, making me want more, making me feel like Spencer was the air I needed to fill my lungs to breathe.

"More," he demanded as his tongue curled with mine, fighting for control. "I need more, Jon. Don't fucking leave me hanging." Spencer's voice dripped with desire that I felt deep in my bones, and my cock sprang to life as he pressed himself against me.

Easton's loud cough brought me back to earth. "You two can continue the tonsil hockey later. Get in the truck." I expected him to look horrified when I met his gaze, but he winked at me as if he was happy.

Seriously?

"Call me." Spencer's hand grazed my cheek.

"Oh no, you're coming too, lover boy." Easton jutted his chin toward the sleek SUV that was parked in the driveway. One of the two we usually drove everywhere. "Grab a coat and your shoes, because this ain't over."

Spencer shook his head. "I can't do that."

"There is no *can't*, Pearson. Get your shit and follow us." Easton didn't wait for a response and instead went to the truck to climb inside, where Brett was already waiting.

I watched the way Spencer's Adam's apple bobbed as he swallowed his nerves along with whatever else he was feeling at this exact moment.

"I can ride with you, if you want or whatever," I muttered.

Relief washed over his handsome face, and his features relaxed.

"Really?" His lips turned up, and his brown eyes softened.

I nodded. "Sure, why not?" I resisted the urge to slam my mouth over Spencer's again. "Go get your jacket before you freeze to death."

As Spencer disappeared into house, I casually looked over my shoulder to find Brett watching me through the window of the SUV. Her face lit up as she smiled at me before she gave me a thumbs up. I shook my head, turning away. The sound of Spencer's parents fighting drifted through the house, and I wondered if he would make it back before they caught him. It wasn't like he had done anything wrong, but I was sure they wouldn't want him running off with me like this.

"Okay." Spencer appeared in the doorway with a heavy coat wrapped around his thick shoulders and shoes on his feet. "Let's get out of here." He had a bag in his hand that he tossed over his shoulder as we both started down the steps. "I brought my school shit."

"You planning on spending the night?" I smirked as he opened the garage and revealed his BMW.

He snorted. "You inviting me to spend the night?"

He unlocked the car to slide into the driver's seat, and I climbed in next to him. Spencer started his vehicle, waited until Easton had backed out of the driveway, and then followed him. He kept his hands at ten and two, the speed right at the limit of thirty as we drove back to my place. I had never noticed how long his fingers were or just how big his hands looked until this very moment. I had always focused on Spencer's face or his perfect football player body. There wasn't anything about him that wasn't perfect now that I had the chance to look.

"Yes," I blurted out.

Spencer's lips twitched. "Yes, what, sweetness?" He kept his eyes directly on the street.

My cock plumped in my jeans at the name he insisted on calling me. I could fight him on that until we were both blue in the face, but we both knew I liked it.

"I'm inviting you to spend the night." I bit down on my bottom lip as I waited for his reaction.

"That so?" Spencer slowed the white car down as Easton stopped at the four-way intersection. He turned his head to look at me before he removed his right hand from the steering wheel. "You sure that's what you want?" He placed it on my thigh before he pressed down on the gas again. "I can go home when I know my parents are sleeping." Spencer turned into the driveway and parked the car.

"I want you here. I want you in my bed." My throat went dry with desire as he unhooked his seatbelt and cupped my face with his big hands.

Spencer leaned forward. "You have no idea how badly I want that, too, Jon," he whispered.

Chapter Eighteen

Spencer

This was not how I expected my evening to go, but here I was at the Maxwell house, and Jon had just told me he wanted me to stay the night. That he wanted me in his bed. I had no idea exactly what he meant, but I would do whatever he wanted, even it just meant a little dick-sucking.

"We should go inside." Jon started to open the door, but I grabbed his arm.

"You're sure that Oz isn't going to kill me the moment I step foot inside his house? I guess the boss has eased up on the whole murder thing, but I'm not convinced that The Iceman isn't Jeffrey Dahmer yet."

Jon chuckled. "If Easton didn't put a bullet in your head tonight, I think you're fine. Oz listens to him." He shoved the door open so that he could climb out of my car, and I grabbed my bag from the backseat so I could do the same.

As we headed toward the house, I noticed Oz, Cash, Lennox, and Jon's twin brother, Jameson, waiting by the side door for us. Easton and Brett were ahead of us, so someone must have notified them that I was coming.

"Before you say anything"—Easton pointed a finger at Oz—"we had to bring this here because shit went down that we were not expecting." He glanced back at me. "I'll let Pearson explain once we get settled inside."

Oz's face darkened. "What, I'm supposed to just let him inside the house like he's welcome here... Ow, Brett, what the fuck?" He dropped his hand to his side. "Did you just pinch me?"

"Yes," she answered. "Shut your pie hole until you know everything that happened." She pushed past him without waiting for Easton, and I couldn't help but wonder why she was sticking up for me or Jonathan, or possibly even both.

When I turned to look at Jon, his expression matched mine.

"Did that just happen?" I asked as we walked into the kitchen.

The last time I'd stepped foot in this room, it hadn't ended so well for me, and I couldn't stop the shudder that ran through my body. I'd actually believed that Easton was going to murder me in cold blood the moment he'd laid eyes on me the night of that party, and it was purely accidental that I'd had the chance to escape.

"This way." Brett motioned for us to follow her downstairs, and I made sure Jon was between us as we headed down to the basement.

I had never been down here before. The night of the New Year's party, I had spent most of the evening hiding out in my car until Ellie had texted me that she was dancing with Jonathan, and that I should get ready because she was going to try to get him upstairs.

I slowly looked around the basement. There was a giant oversized couch in front of the big screen, a love seat, and an Xbox with the multiple controllers. Giant dark pillows were arranged on the floor to sit on, and I realized that this felt like home. A place where the Knights could relax, unwind, and enjoy themselves.

Someone knocked into my shoulder, and I quickly turned. Oz limped past me with darkness in his eyes. "Getting a good look, Pearson?" he muttered before he sat down on the couch. "You might want to take it all in now while you have the chance," he added and started to remove his sneakers and socks, then rolled up his pant leg. "There, stare all you want, dick, because if you ever mutter a damn word? I'll shove my fucking prosthetic right up your ass."

"I wasn't... I mean I wouldn't..."

Oz rolled his eyes. "Sure." Doubt was written all over his over face. "Birth defect," he answered the question that was screaming through my mind. "All my friends and family know." He pushed his jeans back down. "Now you." Oz rubbed at his right thigh. "If you ever, and I mean ever, utter a word about this to anyone..."

I shook my head. "I swear." I had no clue Oz was missing his leg, or part of it, anyway. How had he managed to keep that a secret for so long? How did he have sex with girls without them knowing?

"I keep my pants on."

Did he just answer the question I was asking myself? Was he a mind reader now?

"What?" I blinked.

"You're wondering how I fuck without them knowing?" Oz's lips twisted in a freakishly cruel smile. "I keep my pants on," he said again. He lifted his chin in greeting as footsteps echoed behind me. I swung around to find the rest of the Knights, as well as Tate Barnard, joining us.

"What's he doing here?" Tate asked.

Jon squared his shoulders. "He's with me.

Tate's mouth opened, closed, and then opened again. Sort of like a fish out of water. "Like, with you, with you? I thought you were that girl with the white hair."

I was pretty sure that this guy was dumber than a box of rocks.

"I am. I'm with both of them."

Before Tate could say anything else, Easton clapped his hands together. "All right, everyone's here, minus Josie, who wasn't feeling up to it tonight." He ran his hand lightly over Brett's hair. "You text her, babe?" His voice softened as he spoke to his fiancé.

"She said she would come by tomorrow." Brett flashed a quick smile before she looked at me. "Ellie told you about Josie?"

I nodded. "Ellie told me everything that happened the night she was here." I heard a grunt from Oz. "Look, I'm not going to tell anyone, if that's what you're worried about. You can trust me."

"Trust you?" Cash let out a laugh. "Dude, you put your mouth on my sister. Who the hell do you think you were? She was Knights property." He was leaning against the banister of the stairs, his blue eyes glaring at me as if I had just run over his dog. Cash raised his brows and folded his arms over his chest, only to have his sister stop him.

"Toto, don't start," Brett warned. "We talked about this. Spencer didn't want me, remember?" Her eyes met mine, and I saw it. I saw that she believed me even if the rest of the Knights didn't. "Besides." A smile spread across her face. "Easton was busy kissing half the females at Kingston, so honestly, I had no other choice. If you want to blame anyone, you can blame me." Brett giggled softly before she covered Easton's mouth with her hand. "He's going to make me pay for that." They were sickeningly in love, and I kind of liked it. It gave me the chance to see a different side of Easton. One that only his family saw.

Easton shoved her palm away. "What in the actual hell!" He scoffed. "Not cool, babe, not cool at all." He grabbed her hand and quickly laced his fingers through hers before his cold eyes landed on me. "I hope that I don't have to remind you that what you hear today, Pearson, never gets repeated to any of your Weston buddies."

I rolled my eyes. One, I had no buddies I would even share this with, but Easton didn't need to know that, and two, he was acting as if I were a complete idiot. "I'm not stupid, Kennedy," I shot back. "I know what you all will do to me if I run my mouth." I felt Jon's hand on my arm.

Easton looked like he was going to fight me on that, but instead, his eyes swung to Jon. "Go on, tell him," he said. "Then we're going to talk about Diana, and what we're planning on doing tomorrow night, because you're going to help us get into her place." He leaned his massive body back against the couch, and Brett snuggled against him.

"Me?" Jon's brows shot up. "I have to tell him? Who found the damn papers?"

Jameson bumped Jon's shoulder. "But she belongs to the two of you."

When I looked around the room, waiting for someone to explain, Jameson threw up his hands.

"Jesus, fine. Ellie was promised to Jon," Oz announced.

I stared at him, waiting for him to crack a joke, but when he didn't, I took a step back. "I'm sorry. What was that?" My stomach clenched, and I felt like I might throw up what little of my mother's roast I'd managed to eat before we took off from the house.

Oz cackled from his chair, which almost looked like a throne. "You look like you just saw a damn ghost, Pearson." He sat forward, dropping his hands between his knees. "See, this is how is how it used to work with the Knights." Oz licked his lips as an ugly smile spread over his pale, handsome face. "Our daddies would get together so that they could decide which male would marry which female." That smile spread even bigger over his face as he leaned back to stare at me. "Ellie's stepdad, the great and wonderful Pastor Rick, signed Ellie over when she was ten years old. Right after he married her mom."

"You're lying."

"He's not."

I turned to look at Jonathan, who was holding out a few white pieces of paper. "These are copies, Spencer. We found them the other night. That's part of why we wanted to talk to you other than the whole Diana thing."

The room felt like it was spinning as I stared down at the papers Jon held out to me. This couldn't be happening. *My Ellie.* How was she supposed to marry someone else, even if it was Jon, the one guy we both agreed was the missing puzzle piece we needed?

"It's not going to happen," Jameson assured me. "The contacts are all null and void now, man. We've only found two so far. This one and Easton's."

I turned to look at Easton, who was whispering something to Brett. "It was Brett, just to answer that question," he told me. "I was supposed to marry her, and now here we are." He shrugged as if it were no big deal. "We know there's a contract for all of us. Oz, Cash, and Jameson all have them too, but we're still on the hunt for them."

Lennox made a sound from where she sat next on the arm of the chair next to her cousin. "I'm not marrying anyone. No fucking way." She stood up and pushed her raven hair over her shoulder. "Even if we weren't burning those things."

"Relax, baby." Cash winked at her, only to have Lennox roll her eyes at him.

"How can you all act so calm about this?" I blurted out. "What happens when your dad comes back, Oz? What about everyone who wants revenge for what you did to Chad?"

Easton climbed to his feet. "How the hell do you know all of that?" he roared. "And don't try to tell me it's because you were there the night Oz shot his father, because that's bullshit." He shook his head when Brett tried to calm him down.

I glanced over at Jonathan to see confusion written all over his handsome face. His brows furrowed as he tried to figure out exactly what I knew about the Knights, their background, and what they had done.

"My Uncle is a Knight."

Before I had the chance to explain myself, Oz slammed me against the floor, and his knee, assuming it wasn't the prosthetic, pressed against my stomach.

"Spill your fucking guts, asshole, before I do it for you." His eyes were as black as the midnight sky. A felt something cold pressed against my neck, and my breath caught in my throat. "J2 are the ones who are better with the blades, but I know a few tricks myself," he warned.

Jonathan was on him in a second. He wrapped his hands around Oz's throat so tight that I swear he was going to pass out.

"Let go," he hissed.

I watched Oz's face as it started to turn a shade of blue I had never seen on a human before. He gripped Jon's hands as he stumbled back from me, and Jon finally released his grip so that Oz could breathe again.

Oz began to cough and wheeze while Jon helped me to my feet.

"Are you okay?" he whispered.

"What the fuck, Jon!" Oz exclaimed as he gripped his neck. "You nearly killed me!"

Jon wrapped his arm around me as he stared down The Iceman. "He's with me, remember? Just like Josie—who tried to fucking kill Brett—is with Jameson. Don't you ever lay your hands on him again, do you hear me?" he warned.

Oz sat back down in his chair. "Explain yourself, Pearson." He waved his hand at me before he took the water Lennox handed him. "Who is your uncle?"

"Matt Maxwell."

The entire room exploded into chaos at the mention of Lennox's father's name.

Chapter Nineteen

"You're lying!"

"That's bullshit!"

Everyone was shouting and screaming at me at once. It was hard to figure out who was saying what. I surveyed the room with wide eyes, surprised that the Knights hadn't known the fact that my mother had grown up right here in Kingston before she had met and married my father. Which is why my father had been contracted to marry Piper. There was more, but I had to wait for the noise to stop.

Lennox stepped forward to speak. "How come we've never met?" Her brows furrowed together. "If we're cousins—if my father is your father's brother and buddy-buddy with Uncle Owen—why aren't we close like Ozzy and I are?" She glanced over at Oz, who was grinding his teeth so hard I thought his molars would snap in half.

"I don't think that Owen approves of my mom." I had never said those words aloud, never mind to a group of people who hated my guts. But now that I had? It made so much more sense. "My mother has pictures of us when we were babies, although she keeps them hidden away, but after that? Nothing."

"How exactly are we related?" Oz growled before he adjusted his prosthetic and stood up.

I took a deep breath. "Our mothers are sisters, but they aren't close. They had some sort of falling out." I knew they were going to ask me what happened, want to know the details, and it would hurt Lennox to know that my mother had slept with her father. From the look on Oz's face, he already knew. I had another big bomb to drop on them that I wasn't sure they knew yet.

Oz raised his chin, as if to stop me from going any further. "Maybe we should talk about the Diana thing first," he suggested.

"Are you serious?" Lennox spun around, planting her hands on her hips. "We just discovered that not only are we related to Spencer"—she hooked a thumb over her shoulder—"but he's also kind of one of us."

"No, I'm not," I assured her. I would never be a Knight.

Lennox tilted her head as she kept her back toward me. "What aren't you telling us?" she asked.

Jon reached for my hand and squeezed it lightly as if he could read my mind.

Oz cracked his neck. "I just think—"

"Oh no you don't." Lennox poked him in the chest with her perfectly manicured nail, and I swear the entire room sucked in a breath. "Spill it, dickwad. We've never kept secrets from one another, Oz, and we're not going to start doing it now." She sounded like she might be on the verge of tears.

Oz grabbed her finger. "Spencer's mother slept with your father." The words tumbled from his lips so easily that I didn't have time to prepare myself.

Lennox twisted back around. "Did you know?" I nodded. "When?" She took a step forward, only to have Oz stop her. "When did it happen, Pearson, because if you're going to tell me we're siblings, I might punch you in the sack," she hissed.

"We're not siblings," I assured her. "I don't know when. I just know it happened around the time we turned a year old. That was when our mothers stopped talking. Our moms planned their pregnancies around the same time, so we were born close together, and they were planning some giant birthday bash."

"Holy shit," Cash muttered. "I've seen pictures from that party. Brienne—uh, my mom—has a photo album from all of my parties up until I was ten, and there's this one party that we're all at from my first birthday. There was one little girl, who I learned was Brett, and one little boy, who she would never identify. Now I know why, and know I know who." He gestured around the Knights. "You really are one of us."

"No."

Easton chuckled. "Afraid are you, Pearson? Even I have to admit it."

"How come no one said anything to me?" Lennox exclaimed. "I'm not some fragile flower you had to worry about breaking into a million pieces." Her eyes filled with tears as she pushed Cash away when he tried to wrap his arms around her.

Brett moved to console her friend, whispering something that none of us could hear before she turned to face us. "Do you guys need us for anything? You can figure this Diana thing out without us girls, right?" Her eyes moved to Easton. "I'm going to take Lennox upstairs; we're going to stuff ourselves full of ice cream and talk alone."

We all watched as the two girls made their way upstairs.

I looked around the room, waiting for someone to hit me or possibly worse, but when no one did, I cleared my throat. "I'm sorry for dropping that bomb like that. I wasn't my intention to upset Lennox like that. I do have one more for you. My dad was Owen's foster brother for a very short time. That doesn't make us blood related, but my dad always called us cousins."

"Fuck you. We are anything but family." Oz flipped me the bird.

Easton held up a hand. "Relax."

"How come you never said anything before?" Jameson asked. "You could have told us that the night of Brett's homecoming party, or the night you came here with Ellie. Or even the night you kiss—er, the night Easton broke your nose," he corrected himself, but not before Easton's face darkened at the memory.

"Seems a little weird," Tate muttered, and Cash slapped the back of his head. "What?" His eyes went wide.

"Shut up," Cash told him. "No one asked for your two cents, man. You're only here for the muscle."

I ran my free hand through my hair as Jonathan turned to look at me. "It wasn't something I thought I should announce to the world, man. I mean, it's no one's business but yours. The Knights, I mean. Did you want me to announce at a party with a bunch of Kingston kids around so they could air our dirty laundry around town?"

Oz sucked his bottom lip into his mouth. "Noble," he commented. "We're going to have to figure this shit out, though. If you're a Knight"—his brows dipped—"that means you're contracted to marry someone, too."

"Bullshit," Jonathan shouted before his cheeks flushed.

I chuckled softly. "Why, sweetness, are you jealous?" I teased, only to have him turn even redder.

Cash tossed a pillow at me. "You two are too much." He laughed when I threw the pillow back at him. He caught it and tucked behind his head.

"All right." Easton rolled his eyes. "Back to the business at hand." He met my eyes. "Diana. We need you to text her, plan this damn date, and make sure we're there when it goes down. It's time she gets what she deserves."

***

After spending three hours planning with the Knights, I still wasn't going to call myself one, no matter how hard they tried to convince me I was one of them. I was now sitting with Jon in his room, and he looked more nervous than a whore in church.

"Hey." I cupped his cheek with my hand. "If you don't want to do this?" I smiled at him. "I can leave."

He shook his head. "No, I want you here. I want to do this, whatever it is," Jon assured me as he leaned into my touch. "I'm just nervous," he whispered.

"We can just lie down and cuddle."

"Yeah?"

I nodded. "Yeah." I wanted Jon in more ways than one, but if he wasn't ready, I could wait. I would wait forever if he wanted. "I know you've never been with a guy, sweetness, and if you don't want anything to happen other than a little kissing and hugging, we can just snuggle until we both fall asleep." I slid my lips over his.

Jonathan licked his lips. "It's not that I don't want you." He swallowed nervously.

"You don't have to explain anything."

I had been with my share of virgins, male and female, but there was something about Jon Hamden that was different to me. The Kingston Knights were known for their wild parties and going through girls like water; and yet here was Jon, who had never been with a girl until Ellie, and never been with a boy, until me. Or at least, I hoped I would be his first.

All on Jon's time.

I sat down on the edge of the bed while I watched Jon begin to get undressed, almost as if it were my own private strip show. He removed his long-sleeved shirt first to reveal his tight and toned biceps, which he'd developed over the past four years playing on the Kingston baseball team, his broad shoulders, and his perfectly muscular back. Jon dumped the shirt in the hamper before he popped the button on his jeans, unzipped them and slowly moved them down his hips to give me a little glimpse of his flat stomach and his thin, dark happy trail, which disappeared beneath his boxers.

"Now you're just doing that on purpose," I grumbled as he smirked at me. "Just stripping off your clothes only to keep on your underwear, flaunting that I can't have you." My cock was hard as a rock inside my pants the second I stepped foot inside Jon's room from the memories of what had happened the last time I had been here.

He chuckled softly as his neck turned red, and I watched as Jon casually ran his hand through his hair. "I'm not, honestly, I'm just..." He ducked his dark eyes to the floor. "Nervous."

I was on my feet so fast I didn't even remember moving. "Don't be." I gripped his chin between my thumb and forefinger. "It's me, Jon. You don't ever have to hide or be scared with me." Desire flooded my throat as his dark eyes met mine.

Jon nodded before his hand moved to touch my face. "You going to kiss me now, tough guy, or make me suffer?" His lips curled up into a smile that had my heart nearly bursting from my chest. I had never felt like this around another guy before.

"Thought you would never ask, sweetness."

Jon's lips opened slightly as I pressed mine against them, and I couldn't stop the low groan that escaped my throat when he gripped my shirt to pull me closer. He liked when I took control—seemed to prefer it that way—but I knew deep down he wanted to take charge, too. He was a novice, a virgin of sorts, but wanted to explore things with me he hadn't had the chance to yet. I tasted the hunger behind Jon's kiss as our tongues slicked together, his mouth hot and breathy between kisses. It would be sheer madness to let the kisses continue, because it would only lead to me to wanting more.

"I want..." Jon whispered softly.

"Tell me," I begged, as I dragged my hands through his hair. "Tell me what you want."

Jon pulled back on my bottom lip. "You, Spencer, I want you." His brown eyes were dark with molten desire.

"Are you sure? I don't want to force you into something just because we're all revved up right now. We can just get one another off."

Jon licked his lips. "I just—"

I slid my mouth over his. "Don't say anything else." I saw the look in his eyes. The uncertainty. Even though he wanted to, he was scared.

"Get on the bed," I instructed and watched as Jon did as he was told before I quickly yanked off my clothes, including my underwear. Jon still had on his, but we could easily take care of that. "Lie down, like you would if you were going to sleep, just stay over the blanket." I pointed to the pillow.

Jon scooted up the mattress, and my gaze lingered along the outline of his dick. How swollen he was, ready, and excited for what was about to happen. My own shaft strained up in a curve, waiting for relief, and I resisted the urge to wrap my hand around it, give it a little jerk. Instead, I crawled up onto the bed to join Jon and splayed myself over his warm, hard body. His hands instantly gripped my shoulders, his breath coming in shallow gasps.

"You're so eager to please me, aren't you?" I dropped wet kisses against his neck, and Jon's legs falling open. "You've always wanted to know what it was like to have a male mouth wrapped around your cock, to come inside his throat, and to feel him deep inside you." I stopped to glance up at him. His eyes were wide with anticipation.

Jon nodded. "You're the one." His husky voice caused my dick to jerk against his leg, and I knew he felt it. "What you, Ellie, and I share is like something I've never felt in my entire life. I want it. I want you both," he admitted, and my heart soared.

I lifted myself up, only to yank down his boxers. "As you wish," I told him before I dragged my tongue up his length.

"Fuck, Spencer!" Jon's hands were in my hair. "More, more of that, please." He urged me on, and when I gripped his balls, he dropped his head back against the pillow with a low moan.

I pressed my hand against his stomach and rolled my tongue over his cock. His eager sounds grew louder, but I didn't take him in my mouth, even though I knew he wanted it. I dragged my tongue across his slit. Jon's eyes rolled slightly. Then I moved so that I could align my cock with his and wrapped my hand around both of us as best I could.

Jon eased himself up to watch. "That's so fucking hot, Spencer," he hissed as he watched me jerk us together, his lids heavy with want. I leaned down and kissed him hard, only to have Jon grip the back of my neck to keep me there. "Fuck, I want... I want more."

"In time, sweetness," I promised.

I knew it was a heat-of-the-moment, pent-up thing. Jon might think he wanted me inside him now, but afterward, he might regret it. I let my finger graze his taint, then his backside, and his lids fluttered.

"Have you ever put anything in there?" I could already feel myself spiraling toward climax, my balls giving me that all too familiar feeling as I tugged our dicks together.

Jon pressed his lips together. "Mmmm... yeah," he admitted. "A couple fingers, some toys. Fuck, that feels good. Don't you stop. I think..." He reached up to grip my wrist. "I'm going to come."

The second Jon said those words, I cried out his name. He fell back, gripping the blankets, his hips bucking and grinding against the air. I watched as we both erupted in white hot passion and when I was sure he was finished, I dropped down onto the bed beside him. I knew I should go into the bathroom to get a cloth to clean us up, but my lids were so heavy with sleep I couldn't move, and before I knew it, I passed out right where I was.

Chapter Twenty

Jonathan

When my alarm went off, I reached for Spencer. He was gone, and I was alone in my bed. My brain instantly went back to what happened last night, to what he had done to me, how it had felt to have his hot, wet mouth wrapped around me, and my dick went hard in a second. But now? Now he was gone, and I was once again by myself. I pressed my nose to the pillow Spencer had slept on and caught a faint whiff of him.

It was a subtle hint of something woodsy, no doubt expensive, and all masculine. Spencer Pearson was everything I had ever wanted in a guy, but he had left without saying goodbye. It wasn't like I didn't know he was going to be gone. He had told me last night after I'd woken to find his mouth wrapped around my dick. He sucked me off, and then I returned the favor, then we talked a little about our relationship. We would need to keep it on the down low. Just until the Diana thing was over. I understood that, but that still didn't mean I wouldn't miss him.

I sat up, climbed from the bed, and dragged myself to the shower to get ready for school, knowing that tonight we had big plans in store for Diana. Ones that Easton couldn't wait to finally execute.

"You're going to her place? Her parents keep it locked up like some sort of fortress, don't they?" Easton leaned back on the couch. "How is exactly is this going to work?" His eyes moved

around the room, scanning the rest of the Knights before they landed on Spencer.

"Well..." He looked calm for someone who had just dropped that giant bomb on all of us. "Diana told me to come around seven and to text her when I was on my way, then she would give me her address. I assumed when I got there, she would let me in, then"—he waved his hand in the air—"whatever you guys want after that." He sighed softly.

Cash dropped his feet to the ground. "What were you planning on doing there? Getting a little something, something now that Ellie's gone?" His eyes glittered with something I didn't like.

"I'm not interested in Diana Monaco. I have never been, and the only reason I came to your party with her that night was because I was trying to apologize to Easton and to talk to this guy." Spencer squeezed my hand tightly.

"You've never touched her?" Cash popped his jaw. "Not even..." He raised his right hand to form a circle with his thumb and index finger before pushing the index finger of his left hand through it, making squeaking noises.

Easton slapped his hand away. "Dude, grow the fuck up," he scolded, but I saw anger flash in his eyes.

"I'm just asking." Cash leaned back and nudged Easton. "Right, best friend of mine?" They had been close since they were in diapers, and now that Brett was back, their friendship was tighter than ever.

Easton's face grew scary. "Have you put your dick in Diana?" He didn't sugarcoat it.

I yanked Spencer back down next to me as he went to stand up. "Don't," I warned. "It's a fight you'll never win, and you're sort of one of us now," I reminded him.

Spencer and Easton stared at one another for what felt like forever before Spencer spoke first. "No." His voice vibrated through his body. "She's never touched me other than a hand on my arm or back. No kisses or sex between us," he assured the boss.

Easton raised his chin. "I believe you." He looked over at Oz, who hadn't said anything. "What do you think?"

A scary look spread across Oz's face. "I think that I should go with him." He cracked his knuckles. "He can explain he's no longer single, but me?" He chuckled softly. "I'm so heartbroken over Palmer that I would just love to start courting her, and—" Oz batted his lashes. "Bygones, boys." His joker-like smile sent chills down my skin.

"What are you going to get out of this?" Spencer asked. "No offense, but I know what she did to Easton and Brett, but what is in this for you? For the rest of the guys?"

Oz's eyes moved around the room slowly as he made sure he had everyone's attention. "We're going to make sure that Diana gets what she deserves, Spence." The way he said his nickname like that came out all wrong, and I just knew that The Iceman was going to ruin Diana in ways I could not in fathom. "She came into my house; she tried to sink her claws in my friend—a man who is like a brother to me—and then?" He narrowed his eyes. "She touched him in a way she shouldn't have. As far as I'm concerned, that's rape."

"Dude." Easton held up a hand, but I could see he hadn't thought about it like that.

None of us had.

I ran the scenario through my head as I showered, dressed, and met the rest of the Knights downstairs for breakfast. They all stopped talking the moment they saw me.

"You look well rested." Cash snorted as he slapped my back.

I felt the blush start at my neck. It crept up my ears and over my cheeks. "Shut up," I muttered, which only made Cash laugh.

"No need to be embarrassed, man. We've all been there," he admitted. "The first time is always the strangest, but it gets better. A lot better."

The sound of a chair scooting back across the floor caused me to look over at Lennox. "Does it get better, Cash?" Her nostrils flared angrily. "Have you had a lot of girls in your bed since I left you?" Her voice cracked, and tears filled her big brown eyes.

"Len..." He started to get up, but she only shook her head and fled the room. "Fuck." Cash started after her, knowing he would never get past her bedroom door.

Brett flashed a smile at me. "Are you all right, Jon?" she asked and patted the chair next to her.

I eased myself into the seat, grabbed a box of cereal, not caring what kind it was, and poured it into an empty bowl.

"I feel good," I assured her. "Thanks for asking."

"So, you and Spencer are a thing? What about Ellie?" Brett pressed her lips together. "Are you going to try to get them back together?"

Shit, I hadn't even thought about that yet. "Yes." I wanted that. I wanted it to work out between all of us the way we had talked about. "You're okay with Spencer being around?"

"You really think I would stop you from being happy? That I would get in the way of true love?" Brett stood up and placed her bowl in the sink to wash it out. Then she moved to hug me. "You deserve all the happiness, Scarecrow. I wish you could see that," she whispered so only I could hear. "I'll see you at school," she promised.

Easton grinned at me as he bumped my shoulder with his fist, and the two of them left the room to head out to the garage to leave for school.

"I'm happy for you, bro." Jameson nudged me. "Josie is having a hard time with everything, and I just... I'm not sure if she'll ever be ready to come back to school. She's thinking she might just get her GED online."

I twisted my lips. "I'm sorry. I know you wanted to be able to graduate with her on your arm."

"It's not just that. I love her. I want to marry her, spend the rest of my life with, but she'll have to get out of her own head before she can do that. Fuck what everyone else thinks."

Oz nodded. "I agree with you there." He drained his coffee. "We're going to be late." He stood up.

It wasn't until I was sitting in the car with my brother that I realized that Brett hadn't called me by name, but she had given me my very own nickname. She had called me Scarecrow.

***

My eyes searched for Ellie the moment I stepped foot inside Kingston High. The texts I had sent her bounced back, which made me think she had changed her number, and I didn't like it. I couldn't remember much about Pastor Rick, only that he gave off creepy pedophile vibes. If he was buddy, buddy with Owen and he was a Knight, what else was this sicko hiding in his closet?

"Ten o'clock." Jameson elbowed my side hard enough for me to want to hit him until I saw who he was talking about.

Ellie.

She wore another ridiculous dress that started at her neck and fell straight to her ankles, but I could still imagine what was hidden beneath. This one was yellow, which reminded me of the first night we met, and her white hair was pulled up into a tight bun on head. The girl she was talking to—thank God it was a female or else I might have had to crack someone's skull—was Heidi something and in my English class last year, but I couldn't remember much else about her.

Cash chuckled. "Go make your move, lover boy, before she scatters like a field mouse," he teased and winked at me when I met his eyes.

"You're insane," I muttered but started in Ellie's direction.

Her eyes swing up to mine as I got closer, and she shook her head. "Stay right there, Jon."

"What's the fun in that, sweetheart?"

"We're over."

"We're just getting started."

Heidi spun around to see who Ellie was talking to, only to have me give her a wicked smile. "Uh, I'll just be going," she mumbled and rushed off down the hall.

"You can't be scaring my friends off like that." Ellie hugged her bag to her chest.

I leaned forward. "We're your friends," I hissed, pressing my nose against hers. "The Knights, no one else." I watched the way Ellie's nostrils flared and her jaw clenched.

"I don't want to be your friend, Jonathan." However, the way her voice wobbled told me that wasn't the truth.

I moved to cage Ellie in against the locker, my hard body covering her soft one. "Saw someone you might know last night." My lips brushed over the skin of her ear, and I felt it. The shiver that rushed over through Ellie's body at my touch. "Starts with an S and ends with an R," I whispered.

"You... you and Spencer?" Her hand suddenly clutched at my jacket. "Did you...?"

I sank my teeth into the soft lobe. "Mmmmm, not exactly, but close," I murmured, and just before she could let the moan escape from her soft, plump lips, I caught her mouth with mine.

I watched the way Ellie's eyes flew wide, her pupils dilating into a large, black orbs as our tongues slicked and rolled together, our lips fused as one. Fuck, what was it about this girl that made me want her this way? I didn't care if the entire school was watching right now.

Ellie Young was mine.

"Let me walk you to class." I pulled back as the first bell rang.

Her eyes were hooded with a need I wanted to fill. "All right, but that doesn't mean... Fuck, you know it does," she admitted, and a smile spread across her face. "You're going to tell me what happened with Spencer, right?"

I grabbed Ellie's bag, swung it over my shoulder, and curled my free arm around her neck. "Maybe," I teased before we started walking.

Chapter Twenty-One

"I'm sorry, but Oz is doing what?"

I sprang from the table where I sat next to Jon in the middle of the cafeteria, not caring that the entire room was now staring at me. My eyes flashed wildly as I waited for someone to explain, only to have Jonathan tug lightly on my hand before he pulled me into his lap.

"Don't." I pushed a hand at his chest. "You can't silence me with your mouth this time," I warned.

Brett reached over to touch my shoulder. "He's using her," she assured me, but it wasn't Oz I was so upset about going to Diana's house. It was Spencer. He had promised he would stay from that slut, and here he was, just walking right into her den of whoreness. Or whatever.

Oz tilted his head as he watched me, his black eyes trying to figure me out. "You sure that everything with you and Spencer is over? Or is there something you're not telling us?" He drummed his long fingers against the table.

"Fuck you, Oswald."

Oz's brows jumped just slightly. "Woman, name the time and place, but I don't think you could handle me." He smirked, and I felt Jonathan's body tense against my back. "Although, I wouldn't want to upset Jon boy or anything, so maybe another time." He still hadn't broken his stare, and I swear he hadn't blinked at all, like some sort of Cullen vampire.

I gritted my teeth as I refused to be the first one to look away. Why did Oz hate me so much? What had I done to him? Was he like this with Brett when she first started seeing Easton? I was going to ask her the first chance I had.

"Baby, you couldn't handle a woman like me—" Jonathan's hand clamped over my mouth, and I watched, aghast, as Oz broke into a fit of laughter.

"Don't fight with him," he warned into my ear. "I know how mean he is, and how much you want to tell him off, but you won't win." Jon's hand slipped away quickly. "Shut up." He shot at Oz, who opened his mouth to say something. "Tell Ellie your plan before I let her loose so she can do some serious damage."

Lennox leaned over to smack her cousin on the back of the head. "Stop being such a dickhead, Oz, because it's really not becoming. How do you expect some poor woman to marry you?" She brought her water up to her lips.

"Jokes on you, because I don't." Oz rubbed at the spot Lennox had just hit. His mind must have been spinning as he tried to figure out how to word this without pissing me off further. "Like the pretty purple-haired lady said, Eleanor." He said my full name like it would bother me. "I'm going to use Diana. I'm going to make her think I want to actually date her, have some sort of future with her, and then promptly rip her heart out."

It sounded like a story someone had already told me about the so-called Iceman. Only reversed.

I curled my lip. "You two would be perfect together. It's a shame you couldn't make it work. A match made in hell." I sneered.

"Ellie," Jonathan reminded me.

Tate Bernard sauntered over to the table and sat down. "What did I miss? Everyone looks super serious." His eyes landed on me. "Are you two back together? I thought you broke up? What about Pearson?" He rattled off questions without stopping.

Cash slapped the table with his hand. "Catch up, dude." He barked at Tate. "I like you, Ellie." He laughed. "I have never—and I do mean never—seen a girl give it to Oz the way you have, and that's saying something, because Len sure has tried."

Easton made a growling nose. "Can we stop the bickering for five minutes?" He shot a glance at me. "We need you to come by the house tonight, Ellie, if you can."

Fear prickled against my skull. No way was Rick going to let that happen, because he seemed to dislike the Knights even more than the Pearsons. "I don't think so." I swallowed nervously. "My parents have me on a strict schedule," I told them. "School and home during the week. Work then home on the weekend. Nothing else."

"Can you tell them you're hanging out with me?" Brett suggested. "Or Josie?"

"What, I'm not good enough?" Lennox giggled before she tossed her empty water bottle at Cash, who smacked it back in her direction.

Jonathan tightened his grip around my waist. "They know, don't they? Who Brett is, who everyone is?" His voice sounded different. Almost scared.

"I can't tell them I'm with any of you because they know everything that goes on in this town. Right now, I'm sure that someone has already told them I'm having lunch with you. That I'm sitting on Jon's lap, and that I was seen kissing him in the hallway this morning. It could be another student who might be keeping tabs on me or possibly a teacher, but someone will fill them in before I even have a chance to step in the front door. I'm sure that I'll have a speaking-to tonight, and it won't be much fun."

I remembered when they found out about the parties. How I feared for my life when Rick locked the door to my bedroom—leaving Holly in the hallway—to tell me how it was going to work if I had planned to continue living under his roof. If Spencer hadn't saved me? I shuddered at the thought of what could have been.

The table grew eerily silent as the Knights all looked around at one another, and that's when I realized Jameson was the only one who hadn't spoken. Was he too caught up in his own relationship issues to care, or was it something else? Then, without a word, Oz grabbed his trash, walked over to the garbage, and threw it away before he came back to the table.

"You're coming to stay with us."

I blinked at him in confusion. "I'm sorry... What did you say?"

"Did I stutter, woman, because I said that—"

I jumped from Jonathan's lap and flung my arms around his waist in a tight hug. I felt the way Oz's body went ridged; his arms limp against his body as if he didn't know what to do in response. He had parents, right? Did they forget to teach him what a hug was?

"I told you I liked this girl," Cash commented as the bell rang and the rest of them stood up. "I don't believe that I've ever seen Oz speechless before."

Oz pushed at my shoulder with the palm of his hand. "Woman, could you release me? I think you're killing my will to live right now. Sucking the life out of my body. Stop hugging me." His palm was still pressed against me. "Jon, a little help?"

"You did this to yourself, Ice. Now you get to reap the benefits." Jonathan chuckled. "Sweetheart, you're scaring the children. Maybe let him go?"

I looked up into Oz's large, wide eyes. "What, you don't like being hugged?" I let him go so he could step back.

"Get your shit, come to our place, and don't fight it. Either stay with Jon or you can have your own room. There is plenty of space." Oz walked off without looking back.

Jonathan took my hand. "Consider that the biggest compliment. He doesn't do that for just anyone," he assured me. "When Brett left Kingston last year, he set her up with a place, and wouldn't even tell us where she was no matter how much we begged. Cash was the worst, too, wanting to know where his best friend was, but Oz wouldn't budge."

"Does that mean he doesn't hate me or something?"

"Or something."

I rolled my eyes as we moved through the hall of crowded students. "Then why is he so mean?" I caught Oz talking to some blonde out of the corner of my eye, his body leaning against the lockers as she ran her fingers up his chest. He gave me a quick nod before he brought his attention back to her.

"It's how he copes," Jonathan answered. "Hey," He stopped to cup my head in his hands. "This is a good thing. You coming to live with us," he assured me. "After school, we'll go get your stuff."

I licked my lips nervously as I stared up into his warm eyes. "There's nothing there that I need. I didn't even take anything from Spencer's because I knew they wouldn't let me wear what I wanted or use my phone, so I left it all behind. Just the clothes on my back when I showed up."

Jon slid his lips over mine. "You're doing this then? Coming home with me?"

Shit, was I really going to just move in with him? What about Spencer? I mean, the whole point of me fake breaking up with him was so that we could all end up together.

"Yes." I nodded. "I'm coming home with you." I smiled.

***

I stayed late with the Knights after school, waiting around while they talked with Coach Best about baseball and spring training. I sat on the bleachers in the gym while the cheerleaders practiced and couldn't wait to get out of this dress. It just wasn't me.

It would never be me.

"So..." Brett flashed a big smile that lit up her entire face as she sat down on my right, and Lennox boxed me in on the left. "I heard the news." She nudged my shoulder. "You're moving in?"

I rolled my eyes. "Those guys are worse than woman." I chuckled as I looked over at Len. "You're both okay with this, right? I mean, you're not going to put Nair in my shampoo or anything, are you?" I hadn't even thought about that until this exact moment. These two wanted to be my friends before, so I hoped that nothing had changed now that I was moving into their territory.

"Are you kidding?" Brett exclaimed. "We need more estrogen in that house. Sometimes I swear I can smell dirty feet in my studio." She wrinkled her nose.

"That's Cash," Lennox teased, and Brett shot her the stink eye. "Hey, he might be your brother, but I'm the one who dated him, so I know how gross he can be. He used to go days wearing the same pair of underpants."

I couldn't help the warm feeling that began to fall over me. The feeling of belonging. Girls always seemed to hate me, keep me out, but now... Now these two wanted me to be part of their group.

Brett pinched her nose. "Lennox, ew, nasty!" she hissed, then burst into laughter. "Cash seems so clean. Tell me you're making that up," she exclaimed in between the giggles.

She shook her head. "I wish I was, but really, when he was younger? Gross-town, USA." She howled while Brett clutched her stomach as she exploded into a fit of laughter.

"What's so funny?" Cash asked as the five Knights walked up.

That only made the two of them laugh even harder and got me going with them. I couldn't picture Cash, the tall, blonde, and blue-eyed boy doing something like that. In fact, he looked like he belonged on the pages of a magazine instead of the halls of a high school, but maybe it was something that he'd grown in to.

Easton helped Brett to her feet. "Glad to see the three of you getting along so well now that you're going to be roomies and all." He seemed to have warmed up to me now that I wasn't with Spencer.

"Pussy power," I blurted out, and then the three of us started laughing all over again.

Lennox put her arm around my shoulders. "We are so keeping her around, Jon, so you better treat her right."

"As if I would do anything wrong." Jon gasped, bringing his hand up to his heart. "Ready to go, sweetheart? We're going to go home so you can get settled in your room." He smiled at me, and my stomach clenched.

I climbed up from the bleachers. "Can't wait," I told him, but there was no way I was sleeping alone. I wanted to share his bed.

I wanted to tell him tonight that Spencer and I hadn't exactly broken up.

That it was fake. All for him. To make him see the three of us belonged together.

Chapter Twenty-Two

Ellie

I looked around the room that Jon was showing me, but I hardly gave it much attention. It was nice, clean, and I *could* sleep here, but I wouldn't. I wanted to be with him. Wrapped in his arms as he spooned against me, keeping me safe. While I wrapped myself around Spencer. Or maybe Jonathan would be in the middle, his arms around me and Spencer behind him.

"So?"

I spun around to face him. "No." I shook my head.

Jonathan looked confused. "No." He sucked on his bottom lip. "I mean, there are a couple of other rooms if you want to check those out, but this one is the biggest. It has the balcony, and I thought maybe—"

"It doesn't have you."

I watched the way Jonathan blinked at me, the way his mouth moved without words, and then he broke into a smile. "You're saying you want to stay in my room? With me?" He sounded surprised, but happy.

"That's what I'm saying," I said as I took a step forward. "If that's okay with you. I wouldn't want to invade your space, so if you don't want me to be in your bed? Just say the word."

"I'd love nothing more than to share my bed with you, Ellie." He looked like he might kiss me, but the loud commotion outside in the hallway caused him to move away to the door.

"I'm not fucking dressing up. You can fuck right off," Oz barked. "You know what? Get out of my room while you're at it, too," he ordered.

The sound of a door slamming and then the low murmur of voices caused me to stick my head around Jon. Cash, Jameson, and Easton were all talking quietly to themselves right outside what I assumed was Oz's room, until they caught me watching them.

"What?" Easton narrowed his eyes. "You think you can do better, Young?"

Cash grinned at me. "I think she can, boss. We should give her a chance." He sounded like he might believe that.

"I didn't mean to eavesdrop." I blinked up at Jonathan, who looked just as confused as I did.

Jameson nodded. "No, you might be on to something. Oz was the one who suggested Ellie move in here, right? We think that it would be a good idea if he wears something other than a t-shirt and jeans tonight when he tries to impress Diana."

I raised my brows. "That's not a bad idea. She would probably appreciate her date in something other than dungarees. She's the kind of girl who likes nice things." I glanced up at Jon. "I prefer jeans myself." I assured him, thinking about how he and Spencer both filled them out perfectly.

"Fine." Easton knocked on the door. "Ice, someone here needs to talk to you."

My eyes went wide. "No, don't!" I hissed. I held up my hands and began to back up, only to have Jon stop me. Wasn't he supposed to be on my side in this?

"Didn't I tell you to fuck off?" Oz shot back.

Easton's brows dipped. "Ellie, for some reason he likes you, even if he won't admit." His voice was soft as he spoke, charming, and I saw for one second what Brett might see in him. If he didn't scare me nearly as much as Oz did.

I squared my shoulders. "I guess I can try." I wasn't sure what I was going to say to him, but as I walked over to where the Knights were standing, I felt my nerves disappear.

"Oswald." My voice sounded much stronger than I felt. "Can I talk to you for a moment?" I met Easton's gaze.

I could hear him moving around inside the room, a room I was a bit scared to step inside of, but then the lock moved, and he swung the door open. "Just you." He stood back so I could come in, and then the door slammed shut behind me. "I'm not wearing a monkey suit," Oz commented as he walked over to a giant walk-in closet. "I don't understand what the big damn deal is, Ellie." He dragged his hand through his ink-colored hair. "It's not a real date." His dark eyes landed on me. "What do you think I should do?" He almost looked nervous.

I noticed the clothes dumped on the giant king-sized bed, scattered on the floor, and then let a slow sigh. "Maybe not a suit, but what about dress slacks and a sweater?" Oz started to open his mouth to object. "Diana would want that," I told him. "A guy who's dressed nice. I know it's not who you are, but think about how you can win her over. Just so you can ruin her." I reached for a pair of dark pants. "These would work." I held them out.

Oz made a grunting noise. "This is fucking stupid," he growled and reached for the cigarette behind his ear.

"This was your idea. I also don't think you should smoke around her either."

His eyes met mine, and a smile tugged at his lips. "She'll have to deal with that now, won't she?" Oz sighed as he took the pants I suggested and hung them on the back of the door. "Oi, assholes, if you're still out there, you can piss off. Ellie's going to help me," he shouted. "Why *are* you helping me?" He turned to face me as I took in the rest of his room.

I half expected it to be painted in midnight black, but I was more than surprised to find the three walls painted a cream color while the wall that had the bed against it was painted a cool blue.

"Because you offered to help me," I told him. "And the Knights think you like me."

"Fuckers."

I giggled softly as I dug through the rest of the clothes on his bed. "Do you have any sweaters? Something that might be an intense blue?" I asked. "It will bring out the darkness of your eyes."

Oz scrunched his nose up at me. "My eyes? You think she's going to care about how my eyes look?" He balked.

"Trust me, girls notice that sort of thing," I assured him. "May I?" I jutted my chin toward the closet he was half standing in, and when he waved me in, I moved inside, trying to keep my mouth from falling open at the gigantic amount of designer clothes inside. "Did you buy all of this?" I asked, peeking over my shoulder.

Oz shook his head. "No, my mother did. She's always buying me shit while she's gone, but I never wear them. I pick out jeans and shit online or when I'm out. I usually just outgrow most of the stuff she buys and donate it."

I fingered the smooth items between my skin. "She has amazing taste," I whispered.

"In clothes," he muttered, and I wasn't sure if he was actually talking to me or not.

I pulled a few things back, admiring the Louis Vuitton, the Dolce & Gabbana that cost more than my entire car, and then saw the perfect top that would work with the pants I had found. I carefully pulled the Alexander McQueen down from the hook to hold it out in front of me, knowing that the turquoise color would be exactly would make Oswald's dark eyes pop.

"Seriously?" His brows dipped. "I'm going to look like a tool," he muttered.

I moved to hang the sweater with the pants. "Oz, you're not going to look like a tool," I assured him. "You're going to look great, I promise." When his expression darkened, I sighed. "I wouldn't lie."

"What was Spencer wearing when you met him?" Oz shoved the clothes from his bed to sit down.

I blinked at him, confused. "Spencer... this isn't about Spencer. This is about you and Diana. You want her to actually fall for you, for this, right?" I didn't want to think about Spencer or when we first met. He and I fake broke up so I could get Jonathan back.

"Don't think I don't know you still love him."

"I don't."

"Liar."

I folded my hands over my chest. "Fine, I might, but we're done." I avoided eye contact as I glanced around the room again. There were a few pictures in the corner, and as I started to walk toward where they were, I felt a hand wrap around my arm. They were pictures of Palmer and Oz, which caught me off guard.

One of Palmer sitting on his lap in her cheerleader outfit beaming at the camera. Oz was dressed in his baseball uniform, his cap on backwards, and he looked like he was attempting to smile. Another picture where Palmer was lying on Oz's bed with her hair spread out behind her, blowing a kiss at the camera. In the last one, she was smiling happily while holding a copy of a sonogram in her hand over her stomach.

"Don't touch those," Oz warned. "Those are fucking private."

When I looked up at him, his eyes weren't angry, just sad. "I'm sorry." I half expected him to dismiss me, kick me right out of his room, but instead, I watched as Oz's face completely changed.

His face, always so hard and cold, instantly crumbled at my words, and wetness leaked from his eyes. When he didn't hide, I felt my heart break for him.

"The girl that broke my heart," he confessed as he released me to sit back down on the bed. "It wasn't supposed to be like this." Oz's dark eyes shimmered with tears. "Palmer and I were just having fun, using one another until she could have the one person she really wanted. The baby thing with her was real." He paused to take a shaky breath. "I would have married her. I wanted to be a father, but Palmer wanted him. Did you know she was sleeping with Chad at the same time? She had plans on to run off with him. How could someone be so cold?"

Wasn't that exactly how he acted?

I moved between his legs, wrapped my arms around his chest, and pulled Oz against me without a second thought. His crying turned into sobs that wracked his body as he finally let himself feel what had been breaking him apart since Palmer had left him. I didn't have the answers he needed, but I could at least comfort him as best I could. When Oz had finished, he pulled back and brushed the wetness from his face.

"Black jeans and a green Henley," I said.

Oz looked confused as he stood up, towering over me, and started toward the bathroom. I noticed so far that in all the rooms I had been in—which was three now—they all had their own private bathroom. He splashed water on his face before he turned to face me again without saying anything. His usual grim expression was back on his face.

"That's what Spencer was wearing when I met him."

"You miss him?"

"All the time."

Oz nodded. "You want him back? Do you think that three of you could, I don't know, be a throuple?" He looked like he might be limping for a second as he walked back into the bedroom.

Could I trust Oz not to say anything to the rest of the Knights? I knew that they were like brothers, that they would do anything for one another, but the guy had just cried like a baby in my arms about losing a girl to me.

"Yes." I admitted. "I want that." I swallowed nervously as he leaned against the dresser.

"It would be kind of weird if, I mean, if the three of you were together or whatever, but it's not a bad thing." He smirked, and I saw a twinkle in his eyes.

I felt the smile on my face. "Really?" I asked.

Oz shrugged. "You're okay, I guess." He chuckled softly when I tossed a shirt at him, and then he smiled. Oz actually smiled, and I saw how handsome he really was with dimples that were so pronounced in both cheeks that you could probably stick your finger in there and it would get lost. "You won't... you won't tell anyone, will you? About how I cried like a pussy?" Shame mingled in his eyes.

"I would never betray you like that," I promised.

"Cross your heart?"

I did just that. "Cross my heart, Oz," I told him.

Oz coughed nervously. "So, uh, could you... like help me get ready or whatever? I need to shower, and then... I mean, if you don't mind." He flashed that smile again. If he used that smile more often, he could probably get whatever he wanted.

"I could do that. Let me just tell Jon, and maybe while you're in the shower, I'll change." I really hated this dress.

Oz's eyes widened. "No, that looks great on you, woman. You should keep it on." His face was void of any emotion until a sly smirk began to curl at his lips.

"You're an asshole, you know that, Oswald?" I swatted at his chest as he chuckled at me.

Did that mean we were friends now? Did Oz have friends other than the Knights?

"I'll be back," I assured him.

Jon was waiting for me in the hallway when I stepped back into the hallway, leaning against the wall, his phone in his hand. He slipped it into his back pocket before he spoke. "I was getting a little worried. Thought maybe Oz had finally turned into the serial killer we always knew he was," he teased, but I saw it written all over his face.

"You have nothing to be worried about," I promised as I slid my hands up his chest and locked my hands behind his neck. "Are you jealous?" I asked, pressing my body against his.

Jon nodded. "Damn straight I am, sweetheart. You're mine. Let Oz get his own girl." He tried to play it off, but I saw the confusion in his eyes.

"I'm no one else's." The lie slipped from my mouth before I could stop it, and I hoped that when I confessed everything, Jonathan wouldn't be too mad. "I told him I would help him get ready once he had finished showering." I felt his body grow tense. "Jonny." I whispered the nickname I knew he loved.

"Just so we're clear." He gripped my chin between his fingers. "You're *my* girlfriend." His lips were on mine before I could say anything word. Hot, demanding, and I gave it all right back. Our tongues folded and tangled together as if they were meant to be as I clung to his broad chest to keep from falling over. When Jon pulled back, his eyes flashed with more than just need.

"I like this version of you," I purred softly. "Do you mind if I go see if Brett might have something I could change into?

This dress is really too much." I knew anything that Lennox had would be too long.

Jon nodded. "She's in her studio, painting."

Chapter Twenty-Three

Spencer

I was nervous driving over to pick up Oz tonight. It wasn't just because I knew that he wanted to ruin Diana, but also because it almost felt, well, normal. I wished that I was there to see Jon, but I hadn't heard from him since last night, which I thought was a little odd. I took a deep breath before I raised my hand to knock on the door to the Maxwell house, only to have Easton's face appear behind the glass. He smirked at me before he unlocked it and waved me inside.

"Thanks," I muttered, stomping my snow-covered feet on to the mat. "It's cold as hell out there," I commented, trying to make conversation.

Easton raised one eyebrow. "We're not going to have the awkward weather conversation, man," he told me. "I'm still trying to wrap my head around the fact that you're a Knight, that you're dating Jonathan, and you're helping us. Let's just leave it at that. Oz will be down in a second." He started toward the basement stairs.

"Does that mean you don't want to kill me anymore?" I pushed.

Easton stopped to pin his eyes on me. Colorful ink sneaked out from beneath his Pearl Jam shirt, around his neck and wrapping his thick arms. "Not at this moment, but give it time." He grinned before running down the stairs to the furnished basement.

I wondered if I should follow him, but just as I started to move, I heard Ellie's voice, and I froze in my tracks. *What was she doing here?*

"Stop fidgeting or you'll wrinkle the sweater."

"This thing makes me itch, woman. Can't I wear something else? I swear you're doing this to torture me." Oz's voice carried down the long hallway I knew led into the formal living room.

Ellie's cheerful laughter filled the air. "We talked about this. Diana will want you dressed up, looking handsome," she teased.

Dressed up? Handsome? Was she flirting with Oz now? I balled my hands into fists as I started toward the sounds of them talking.

"What's going on here?" I snarled.

Ellie gasped as she spun around, her hands dropping from Oz's chest. "Spencer!" Her eyes went wide with surprise. She wore an oversized Knights sweatshirt and a pair of leggings that fit her perfectly, her long hair pulled up on her head. My heart ached at the sight of her.

"Pearson." Oz gave me a sly smile. "You're early." He was wearing a blue sweater and a pair of dress pants that I assumed Ellie had convinced him to put on for tonight. It was so far from what he usually wore that it might have been funny if I didn't want to rip him apart.

"Why are you here?" I hissed, ignoring Oz completely. "You're supposed... I thought you moved back in with your parents." I caught myself before I gave everything away.

Ellie glanced up at Oz before she wrung her hands together. "I moved in today. You know how *he* is." She licked her lips nervously. "Oswald told me I could stay here," she added.

"Oswald?" My brows shot up. "So you two are what, besties now or something?" I didn't like this. It wasn't just because I was jealous. It was something more. Something bigger that I couldn't put my finger on. Had they told her about the contract yet?

The smirk on Oz's face grew bigger. "What if we are, *Spence*?" He used the nickname Ellie used for me and pursed his lips. "You got a problem with that? Didn't you two break up? Aren't you with Jon now?" He made a sucking dick motion with his hand as he brought it up to his mouth.

"Knock it off!" Jonathan bellowed as he slowly descended the stairs.

The surprise on Oz's face was more than priceless. I'd be lying that I didn't want to take out my camera to take a picture, but I decided against it as Jon moved to stand between Ellie and me.

"I know being an asshole is in your veins, man, but could you for once not be one?" he said.

Oz rolled his eyes. "Nope, not ever. I think Pearson likes it when I get him all hot and bothered." He blew me a kiss.

Asshole. "This was your idea," I reminded him.

"Don't." Ellie shook her head. "Please, I don't want you to start a fight, Spencer." Her eyes pleaded with me to listen, but the way she was leaning toward Jon while her hand was laced through Oz's made my skin crawl. *Mine.* Both of them were mine.

I shook my head. "I can't do this." I turned to storm out of the living room, ready to leave and cancel this whole thing. I came to a halt when I found Cash standing in front of the door.

"You want to fight now, too?" I narrowed my eyes, wondering how long it would take before the rest of the Knights showed up if I tried to lay him out.

"No," he assured me. "I want you to do what you said you were going to do." He folded his arms over his chest. "Diana came into this house and messed with my best friend. The guy I consider to be my brother. She pretended to be Brett so she could then fuck over my sister, and that isn't something I take lightly. These people are my family, and"—Cash shrugged—"you're one of us, too."

He held up a hand when I started to object. "Deny it all you want, Spencer, but you are. Your father was born here but left because of what happened with your mother. I talked to my mother, who was more than happy to tell me as much as she could without giving away any their secrets." His eyes grew hard at the mention of his own mother. "She's so damn eager to smooth things over between us that she'll do anything I ask," he spat.

I knew things with Cash and his mother were hard. That she had pushed him away after she had to give up not only her firstborn daughter, Ruby, as well as his twin sister, Brett, just so she could keep any inheritance her parents might give her when they died. Ruby had raised Brett as her own until she had died a few months ago. I still didn't know the entire story and wasn't sure I ever would without asking, but I knew now wasn't the time.

"I need Oz to stay away from Ellie," I heard myself say.

"Why are you acting like this?" I turned to see Ellie standing with Jonathan. "We broke up," she reminded me, and the pleading in her eyes told me she hadn't had the chance to talk to Jon yet. To tell him what we had done to try to win him back. It looked like we had succeeded on both ends since I had been with him last night, and she was now living here. But without telling him the truth? It would probably ruin everything.

"I don't like him touching you. He creeps me out." I seethed. "It's not right."

Jon stared at me as if he was trying to read my mind. "What about me?" he asked.

"I trust you."

"Bor-ring." Oz pushed his way past them so he could get into the kitchen. "Now we're really going to be late, Pearson, so let's get moving." He acted like me wanting to break his face ten minutes ago hadn't happened. That I wasn't ready to slit his throat... for what? Being friends with Ellie?

Jon tucked his arm around Ellie's shoulders. "You two need to be careful." He was looking at me as he spoke. "We already know Diana has half the football team on her side."

"They're my teammates," I reminded him. "Who probably all know that I'm headed to her place tonight, too," I added, and as I looked at Ellie, I saw the hurt written all over her face. I needed to talk to her alone, but I knew that wasn't going to happen.

"We'll be fine," Oz assured everyone in the room. "Let's bounce before she changes her mind. Move, Cash, or I'll move you myself." He grabbed a coat from the hook on the wall before he headed outside, leaving me no choice but to give a quick wave and follow behind him.

****

I slowed the car down as Waze instructed me that my destination was on the right and stared up at the heavily gated house in front of me. Set back from the road, the Monaco house was lit up like a Christmas tree, with a sweeping side and front porch. I knew that Diana's parents had money, but this was beyond what I had expected.

"Shit," Oz muttered under his breath as he turned to look at me. "She's fucking loaded." As if he had to tell me what I was already thinking.

I pressed the button to roll down my window so I could announce my arrival. "Hi, Spencer." Diana's voice floated through the intercom. "Why aren't you alone? For that reason alone, I should send you packing." She sounded more pissed off than I thought she would be. I knew I should have had Oz hide in the trunk. "Who is that?" she demanded. "Is that... fuck! Are you crazy? I'm not letting Oswald Maxwell into my house."

I glared at Oz. "Diana, it's not what you think," I insisted, hoping she hadn't retreated already. "Are you still there? Please, he only wants to talk to you." I gripped the wheel with one hand as I stared at Oz. "This is your fault," I hissed once my finger was off the speaker.

"Mine?" He actually had the balls to look surprised.

"You should have gotten in the trunk... Holy shit." I gasped as the gate began to open.

"Chicks dig me." He snorted, and I wondered if maybe he was right, but then I remembered how Ellie had looked all laughing and giggling with him. I scowled at the windshield as I slid my car into park. "I don't like your girl like that," Oz insisted.

"This isn't about her."

"Ellie and I are just friends."

I resisted the urge to put my fist through his face. "Just stop," I warned as we climbed from my BMW.

Diana floated across the porch and down the stairs with her blonde hair pulled up into a bun. Her face was completely done up in makeup, and she wore some sort of fur coat—which I hoped was fake—wrapped around her slim figure. She looked ready to go to fancy ball instead of having a night at home.

"Please tell me Easton Kennedy isn't hiding in there somewhere, and"—she stopped—"since when do you hang out with the Knights, Spencer? Don't they, like, hate you or something after you kissed Brett?"

"Our moms are sisters," Oz answered for me, which caused Diana to turn her entire body to face him. That got her attention.

"Really? That is gossip I've never heard before." She tilted her face. "What do you want, Oswald? Aren't you still hung up on Palmer?" She pushed.

I saw Oz flinch at the mention of her name, but if Diana saw it, she didn't let on. "No, she meant nothing to me," he lied, but I saw the way his eyes clouded over with boredom. He never had any interest in Diana Monaco in the first place, and now he was on autopilot.

"What about you, Spence?" Diana asked as she hooked her arm through Oz's. She knew damn well I hated when she called me that because it was Ellie's nickname for me.

"I'm seeing someone." Not exactly a lie.

Diana's perfectly manicured brows dipped. "So soon?" She blinked her blue eyes at me. "That's too bad, because I thought maybe the three of us could, you know." She turned her lips up into a smile that made my stomach turn.

"No fucking way," Oz interrupted. "No offense, man, but I am not into dudes. I like pussy, tits, and ass. You're not my type." He looked horrified that Diana would even suggest a three-way.

I chuckled. "You know that we wouldn't have to touch each other, right? It could be all about Diana?" Not that I wanted to have sex with her. I had promised Ellie.

"No. Way." Oz's nostrils flared. Someone had some issues he needed to figure out.

Diana pressed a hand against his chest. "Oh, so firm," she cooed. "Relax, caveman, it can just be us. But tell me, Spencer." She turned back to me again. "Who is the lucky girl?"

I met Oz's stone face before I answered, "Jonathan Hamden."

"I'm sorry, what?" Diana gasped. "You're with a guy? I mean, that's cool. I'm not one to judge, but is that why you and Ellie broke up? Because you're gay?"

"Yes."

Oz suddenly grabbed the back of Diana's neck, tilted her head back to him and slammed his mouth over hers, letting us know that he was sick of this conversation. I glanced away, not wanting to witness whatever happened, then waited for what seemed like hours before Oz cleared his throat behind me.

"You can leave now, Pearson," he instructed.

"I think that's a great idea." Diana nodded. "I can give Oz a ride home tomorrow."

"Seriously?" I was so confused right now. "Okay, well, text me if you need anything or whatever." I gave a quick wave before I hoped back into my car, fully intending to head home until I found myself driving up to the Maxwell house.

Chapter Twenty-Four

Jonathan

Spencer: *I'm outside.*

Spencer: *Let me in.*

Spencer: *Please, sweetness.*

Jonathan: *Ellie is here. What is wrong with you? Didn't you two break up?*

Spencer: *Maybe you should ask her about the breakup.*

I glanced up from my phone to find Ellie chewing nervously on her thumbnail as she watched me.

"Spencer's here," I mentioned casually. "Why did you two break up?" I placed my phone on the table next to the bed.

"What? What did he say?" She started to climb from the bed, but I grabbed her arm. "Jonny," she whispered.

I shook my head. "Did you really break up?" I demanded, pulling her against me.

"No," Ellie whispered. "We—*I*—wanted to pretend we broke up so we could get you back. You belong with us, Jon. We're so good together. You know that." She looked terrified. "Please don't be mad. I know we shouldn't have lied to you like this, but I wouldn't be here right now if we hadn't done that," she admitted.

I released her so I could grab my phone.

"He wants to come in," I told Ellie as I read his texts again. "What's going to happen if I do that? The Knights..." I stopped when I remembered we hadn't even told Ellie she

213

was one of us yet. That she and I were supposed to be married one day.

"The Knights what?" Ellie stared at me. "What haven't you told *me*, Jon?"

Jonathan: *Why would you lie to me?*

Spencer: *Because I love you.*

I jumped from the bed, ignoring Ellie as she called after me. I ran downstairs to, I don't know, yell, scream, or kiss Spencer.

"Why, why would you say that?" I hollered into the dark, cold night.

"Because it's true," Spencer answered me as he appeared on the steps.

Without hesitation, I grabbed the back of his neck to land a punishing kiss against his mouth. We bit, sucked, and tasted one another in the velvet darkness, not caring who might catch us. Spencer's hands dug into my hair while his thick, muscled body pressed eagerly against mine. I tightened my grip on his neck, needing more.

"We should probably go inside." Heat rolled from my body as I met Spencer's eyes.

"I need you," he growled and tugged on my bottom lip. "I know you're not ready for that, but let me taste you again. Let me make you feel good, like last night." Spencer reached down to cup my more than obvious erection in his hand.

It seemed more than unusual that no one else was awake in the house as we made our way up to my room. I knew that Jameson was with Josie, and Brett and Easton had gone out for a "real date"—as she had put it. That left just Cash and Lennox, who, try as they might to pretend, still had feelings for one another. Fridays had always been filled with parties with my fellow Knights. It seemed strange not to have them up and making a shit ton of noise. I stopped to face Spencer once we reached the door.

"We haven't told Ellie yet about the contract," I whispered so she couldn't hear. "The reason she's here is because of what an asshole Rick is."

Spencer nodded. "She's safer here," he admitted. "Even safer than my house now that we know what he had planned for her."

"I have a bad feeling about this, though. She dumped the phone her parents gave her, and I don't think that's going to go over well with Pastor Rick."

Spencer's face grew dark. "It won't. When she moved in with me, they threatened to say I kidnapped her until my father got involved. Now that she's living here, under Owen's roof? I can only imagine what he might try to pull."

I sighed. "Let's not talk about that now." I moved to slide my lips over his again. "Fuck, you're really here," I murmured as he gripped my chin with his hand.

"Sweetness, you have no idea how long I've waited for this moment. The three of us?" His eyes flashed with want.

Ellie yanked the door open. "Are you two going to just make me stand here waiting?"

She was wearing one of my long-sleeved shirts that fell to her knees, and her long hair was pulled up into a ponytail her head. She looked beautiful.

"Baby." Spencer wasted no time as he grabbed her and pinned her to the wall so he could devour her with kisses.

Another man might be jealous, but not me. Not when it was Spencer. I simply shut and locked the door behind me, giving them the reunion they needed. I moved over to the bed, sat down, and waited as they whispered to one another, things they needed to share. When they were done, both Ellie and Spencer turned to look at me.

"You're not mad?" she asked, lacing her hand through Spencer's and stepping toward me.

I shook my head. "No," I assured them. "Flattered actually." My stomach flipped with butterflies.

Ellie nibbled on her bottom lip. "So, we're a threesome now? Is that what this is?" She glanced up at Spencer, her ponytail swinging around her neck. "I want that," she said, turning back to look at me. "I want you both so bad that sometimes I think I might explode."

"But you've been with us." Spencer dragged his thumb over her bottom lip.

Ellie sucked his thumb into her mouth, and my dick stirred in my pants. "I want you two together. I want to watch. I want—" She glanced back at me again. "I want Spencer to fuck you. I want to ride you while he does. God, it makes me so wet," she confessed.

Jesus Christ. Why did I suddenly feel like I couldn't breathe just thinking about that?

"You okay, sweetness?" Spencer's husky voice sent my body into overtime. "How about it? You want to try that out or what?" He wrapped an arm around Ellie's waist to pull her against his chest and used the other hand to find her nipple through the t-shirt. Her soft little moan caused my length to grow stiffer against my zipper.

I swallowed nervously as I tried to find my voice. I wanted nothing more than to be with Spencer and Ellie again. More than the last time, because I wanted Spencer to take control. Take me, fuck me, and make me come so hard I blacked out. I just...

"Hey." Ellie walked over to where I was sitting. "You don't have to do anything you're not ready to do, Jonny." Her sweet voice drifted over me. "If you're not ready for Spencer, or any penetration, we can fuck. Just you and me. You know Spencer likes to watch." Ellie ran her hand through my hair. "Jon, talk to us. You're starting to scare me, baby."

"I want you." My eyes lifted to Spencer. "I want both of you." Fuck, I was so hard my cock hurt. "I'm just—"

"Scared." Spencer finished the sentence for me. "I would never hurt you. If it ever feels uncomfortable or you don't like it? Just tell me and I'll stop," he promised.

Ellie climbed up to straddle my lap. "Baby," she murmured as she pressed a kiss against my lips. I heard the sound of Spencer's footsteps as he walked over to the bed. His hands slipped up under her shirt as Ellie's hands tugged and pulled on my hair.

"Lift up, baby," Spencer instructed. Ellie pulled back from me, lifted her arms, and I watched as he dropped the shirt on the floor. "You, too, sweetness." He jutted his chin at me while removing his own shirt.

I tossed my shirt onto the floor with theirs before I grabbed the back of Ellie's head to bring her mouth back to mine, closing my eyes. When I opened them again, Spencer had his face buried in Ellie's neck, licking and sucking at her collarbone while his fingers pulled at her nipples. Ellie gripped my shoulders and rubbed herself against me before she pulled back to cry out in pleasure.

"I need more," she begged.

Spencer grinned at me as he leaned down to take one of her nipples in his mouth. I did the same with the free one, and I thought Ellie was going to explode on contact. Her nails dug deep into my skin, and the pain only caused me to drag my teeth over the hardened bud.

"Yes!" Ellie whimpered as she continued to writhe above me. "It's not enough, Spence. I want..."

"I know what you want, baby," Spencer assured her, his hooded eyes glancing at me. He stepped back again to unbutton his pants. "You, too, Jon," he growled.

I helped Ellie sit down on the bed before I removed my jeans, and before I even had a chance to remove my boxers, Ellie's hand slipped down to grasp my shaft between her fingers. I groaned as she squeezed me, and my eyes rolled slightly.

"Baby." Spencer clucked his tongue against the roof of his mouth. "I know you're just as eager as I am to make Jonathan come, but there's plenty of time for that."

His smirk did nothing but make my already hard dick crave more. He leaned down to cage me in against the mattress one hand planted on either side of me. "You're so hard, so ready for this, aren't you, sweetness?" I let my eyes dip down his chest so that I could admire his thick muscles and the tattoo covering his abs. "Eyes up here," Spencer teased as he splayed himself over me.

Spencer's kisses were like fire when our lips met. Each flick of his tongue against mine sent a shot of electricity through my veins. His heavy, warm chest pinned me down as he spread my legs with his muscled thigh. I thought I would come right in his hand when he palmed my aching dick.

"So fucking hot," Ellie whispered. Her tongue peeked out as she licked her plump lips. "God, I want you both, but to see you two together?" Her hand slipped between her legs.

"Ellie," Spencer growled.

She only smiled. "Go back to getting each other off, baby, because I plan on enjoying the show." Her voice was heavy with lust.

"Let her watch," I encouraged before I gripped Spencer's chin to pull his face back to me. I let my fingers dance over the ink on his stomach. I had questions, but now wasn't the time.

Spencer's desire-filled eyes searched mine before he slid his lips over mine. "You sure you're ready for this?" His voice sent shivers down my spine as he stood up, only to drop down at my feet. He gripped my hard length in his hand. "Jonathan," Spencer murmured before he ran his tongue around the tip of my cock.

"Jesus." I groaned as my hips lifted up off the mattress. "More, just like that," I demanded as Spencer wrapped his mouth around me and took my length as far as he could. I didn't even recognize the sound of my voice or the sounds that I made as he took my balls in his hand and gently squeezed them.

Ellie moaned softly before she moved closer. She pinched my nipple, and her hot, wet mouth landed on mine.

She groaned softly as I repaid the favor for her, then suddenly cried out as Spencer's fingers found her aching center.

He gave a soft, sexy chuckled as he kept working both of us over. Our hands clawed at one another while our tongues wrestled together.

"You both are perfect," Spencer assured us. "Beautiful, gorgeous, and sexy." He purred as he released us to get to his feet. "Mine." He pointed at where we were on the bed. "Both of you." He reached down to pump his hard-on. "Tell me," he demanded.

I climbed up onto my knees. "Yours." I wanted to lick him. All over, but mostly I wanted to swallow his beautiful cock and make him come.

"Yours." Ellie joined me.

Spencer looked at us with pride and love written all over his face. "I'm going to fuck you now, Jon." The smirk on his face did nothing but make me want him more. "Go sit on the chaise lounge," he instructed.

I moved quickly, eager to please him and to get off at the same time. As I sat down on the lounge, I watched Spencer drop a kiss on Ellie's mouth. A smile tugged at her lips. He stopped to dig around in his pants before he pulled out his wallet. He opened it and fished out a condom.

"No." I shook my head. "You don't... I mean, unless you want to. I trust you." I swallowed nervously as Spencer turned back to face me. "You know that I've never been with anyone but the two of you," I added.

Spencer glanced over at Ellie. "What do you think, baby?" he whispered.

Ellie gave a quick nod before she jumped from the bed. I gave her body a bold sweeping gaze because, hey, I'm a guy, and she's fucking hot.

"It's what we talked about it," she answered.

Spencer sauntered over to where I sat. "If we do this—I mean, if we really do this: no protection, skin to skin. You're all in, sweetness. No fighting it or pretending it didn't happen, even if the Knights don't accept you."

"I'm all in."

Chapter Twenty-Five

Jonathan

Spencer stared down at me with smoldering eyes.

"Do you have any lube?" His voice caused anticipation to race through my veins as he cupped my face with his hands.

"Top drawer. With the condoms," I squeaked, hoping that Ellie remembered the first night they were here.

Spencer tilted his head. "Nervous, Jon?" He dragged his thumb across my bottom lip. "I promise I won't hurt you unless you ask me to." He chuckled softly as Ellie produced the black bottle from where I had told her and seemed to float over to where we were.

"I'm—" I stopped to gather my thoughts together. "I'm more ready than I've ever been," I assured them. "You two are more than I expected, but exactly what I needed in my life." I surprised myself as the truth tumbled from my mouth.

Spencer's lips curled into a smile as he released me to open the bottle. "You remember what I texted you earlier?" He squeezed a little bit of the liquid onto his finger. "Open your legs, baby. Let me in." He eased my thighs open with his clean hand, and when his index finger pressed lightly against me, followed by another, I couldn't help the moan that escaped my lips.

Ellie's eyes were wide as she watched, her fingers rolling and pulling at her nipples. I gave her a lazy grin as my own eyes rolled slightly. If I wasn't careful, I was going to combust before Spencer even had a chance to slip inside.

"Jon." Spencer's voice brought me back to him. "The text?" He started to apply the lube to himself, his hand fisting his eager dick.

I nodded. "I love you, too," I murmured as a hand wrapped around my cock. My eyes closed, and pleasure rolled over my body. "Both of you." I whimpered as I felt Spencer's head against me.

Spencer pushed my legs up. "Relax, sweetness," he uttered before he began to slide inside. "Goddamn," he growled.

I moved under him, moaning as he filled me.

"Oh, God," I cried out as he pushed all the way in and stilled.

I opened my eyes to find Spencer panting and watching me with his mouth slightly open. Ellie was still standing to the side, watching, but now she had her a hand between her legs.

"Spencer." I pinned my gaze back on him.

"If I move." His deep voice was hardly a whisper. "I'm going to come," he told me.

Ellie whimpered as she slipped her in hand in and out of her pussy, the wetness echoing through the room. "Do my boys have a problem?" She purred, bringing her hand to her lips and licking her fingers.

Jesus Christ, that was hot.

"When was the last time I fucked your ass?" Spencer asked.

Ellie sauntered closer. "It's been a few months. I can't remember the last time you took another guy in front of me." She stood up, pressing her lips against his. "I'm going to enjoy this." She told him, then turned to face me. "How does it feel, Jonny?" She started to climb up over my lap so that she was straddling me.

Was she...

"Holy shit." I groaned, as Ellie's damp, tight pussy began to engulf me. "I don't... I'm going to come if you do that," I warned.

"It's okay." Ellie squeezed herself around me, and I gripped her hips. "You're going to come a lot tonight, baby." She wrapped her arms around my neck, causing her pussy to move up my cock just as Spencer moved. I gritted my teeth.

"Kiss him, baby," Spencer instructed, gripping Ellie's ponytail in his hand. He leaned down to press a kiss against her shoulder before dragging his tongue down her back.

"I didn't say anyone could come, did I?" He narrowed his eyes as he began to slowly fuck me.

Ellie did as she was told, her plump lips finding mine as they both began to work me over. I couldn't think straight with so much stimulation. With every thrust, Spencer hit my prostate, his grunts getting louder. With every buck of Ellie's hips, they brought me closer to the best orgasm of my life.

"It's never..." Spencer's eyes met mine as he continued to pump himself inside me. "I mean, it's never ever fucking felt like this." He swore.

Ellie turned her face. "Never." She echoed his words as Spencer kissed her.

I stared at the two of them, my body growing closer to release, and realized I didn't want this with anyone else. What I had said earlier was true. I loved them. I wanted no one else. The way they watched me told me they weren't lying either. Spencer reached down to grip Ellie's hand before she pressed it against mine.

"I can't hold back anymore." Spencer's muscles went tense. "I'm going to come."

I felt him just as my own orgasm hit me, and Ellie clenched tightly around me as she came with us. Our cries of pleasure filled the room as we continued to move together like a well-oiled machine. My dick swelled and exploded as I blew into Ellie like a storm, then Spencer spilled himself into me, all three of us wanting to milk every moment of the others' pleasure before we were done.

Ellie's head dropped against my shoulder as she tried to catch her breath. Spencer was carefully easing himself from me, and that's when he let out a small chuckle.

"Next time, we fuck in the bed so we can just fall asleep in a pleasure-induced haze."

Best idea ever.

***

"What's this?" I dragged the tips of my fingers across Spencer's abs, curious about the one tattoo he had.

He smiled at me as I traced the colorful stars, not stopping me as I made sure to touch each one until I was sure he was here, in my bed, with Ellie tucked between the two of us sleeping without a care in the world.

"It's nothing, I swear." Spencer's voice was thick was slumber. "Just something stupid I did one night after a football game with the rest of the team." He chuckled as I pulled back to look at him. "Honest, we all went and got one. It's the Weston team colors, but I refused to get an eagle—you know, since that's our mascot—so we all got stars instead."

"I like it."

"I noticed."

Warmth began to spread over my body. I started to pull my hand away, only to have Spencer grab it before I had the chance. We stared at one another in silence for what felt like forever until the slamming of doors and shouting caused me to yank my hand away to jump from the bed.

"What's going on?" Ellie mumbled from the bed, pushing her hair from her face.

I yanked on my pants. "I don't know, but it doesn't sound good," I answered before I pulled my knife from the drawer I kept it in. "Keep her here," I ordered.

"I'm coming with you." Spencer sprang from the bed. "Don't fight me, sweetness, because you know I'm bigger, faster, and can kick your ass." He grinned. He wasn't wrong, and his jeans were already up over his waist.

I opened the door to my bedroom, only to find Easton standing there in his unbuttoned jeans, no shirt, and a scowl written all over his face. He dragged his hand through his hair before he started to move into my room without a word.

"What the fuck is going on?" I didn't have time to worry about what Easton would think about Spencer being here. There were cameras all over the place, so everyone already knew.

His eyes skimmed the bed, where Ellie was now sitting clutching the covers against her naked frame before he pinned them on Spencer.

"Pastor Rick is on his way over here," Easton growled. "He's not happy, doesn't seem to realize you're here, only that his stepdaughter never came home last night. He knows that she was seen with Jonathan at school yesterday." Those green eyes landed on me. "This is bad, dude," he informed me. "Ice is on his way home, and I'm sure Owen is going to have a field day when he finds out... Where the hell do you think you're going, Pearson?" he demanded as Spencer started toward the door.

"To wait for him," he shot back.

"Stop right there," Easton hissed through clenched teeth. He waited until Spencer had turned back around. "He's out for blood."

Spencer popped his jaw. "How do you know?"

Easton's nostrils flared. He really hated when people didn't understand that he was in charge. "We have our own eyes and ears out there, too." He crossed his arms over his broad chest, seemingly unconcerned that he was half-naked.

"I should get dressed," Ellie whispered, but loud enough for us to hear.

I shook my head. "No."

Ellie looked between the three of us. "It's me Rick wants. He has rules, rules that I broke, and I should confront him. Tell him I'm not part of his sick games anymore."

"Fuck him," Spencer exclaimed. "That bastard put his hands on you, Ellie! There are more of us now than of him, and he can't just march into this house thinking he's going to take you back there. I would rather die than have you under his roof again." His eyes blazed with fire.

I reached for the shirt she had on and handed it over to her. "What does that mean? He put his hands on you? Spencer, you knew about this?" I had a sick feeling I wasn't going to like the answer she gave me.

Ellie paled as her eyes went round. "I don't want to talk about that right now," she murmured, looking down at her hands.

I was going to kill Rick.

"I'm going to go make sure Brett is safe." Easton patted my shoulder. "Why don't you two finish getting dressed?" He jutted his chin out, making me realize that Spencer and I were just in our jeans. Christ, what time was it anyway? "Meet me in the kitchen in five," he added, shutting the door behind him.

When I glanced back at Ellie, she was picking at her nails and chewing so hard on her bottom lip that I thought she might draw blood.

"You know I love you," I assured her, easing myself down onto the bed. When she nodded, I continued. "Tell me what happened, because I only need one reason to gut him from throat to belly." I placed the knife on my right thigh. "Every Knight has their own thing. Jameson and I are really good with ours, so just say the word." I was itching to cut the bastard.

Spencer had finished getting dressed, and he picked up the leggings Ellie had borrowed from Brett. "When she was twelve, she got her period, and that's when it started," he answered for her.

"Say it, sweetheart." I needed to hear the words. "Whatever you tell me will not change how I feel about you," I assured her.

Ellie suddenly gripped my wrist. "He raped me, Jonny," she confessed. "It didn't matter that my mother was outside my room begging him to stop. Or that she was pregnant with my brother. He didn't care. He would come in nearly blackout drunk, blabbing on about some contract that said if I got pregnant before I was eighteen, then it would be null and void, which meant nothing to me. I would stay out late, sleep at friends, anything to stay away, but whenever I came back?" She shuddered, and her eyes grew glossy.

"How could you let her go back there, Spencer?" I roared. "He's a dead man." I jumped to my feet. "You were meant to marry me," I blurted out before I could stop myself. "That contract? The one he spoke about was something he and my father worked up. You were supposed to marry me when we graduated high school. All the Knights have one."

Spencer's mouth fell open. "Now is not the time, Jon." He looked like he wanted to hit me. Let me him try. I would knock him on his ass after finding out he let her go back into that house after being raped.

Ellie shook her head. "I don't... What are you talking about? Is that why you wanted me here? Because we're supposed to get married?" She used air quotes for supposed.

"What? Of course not. I love you," I insisted. "I love both of you." I reminded Spencer, too, just in case he forgot. "He's a Knight, too."

"Jesus Christ." Spencer groaned.

Ellie started to climb from the bed. "I can't do this now." She pulled on the leggings. "That man is coming here to force me back into his house. I was surprised the first couple of nights I was there that he didn't come for me."

"Eleanor!" Oz roared from behind my door. "Get out here. NOW! Bring those two idiot boyfriends with you, too," he added.

"Fuck off," I answered, only to hear him chuckle at my response.

Ellie pushed past Spencer and me, unlocked the door, and revealed a smirking Oz. "I'd rather be with Oswald right now," she told us. "He's not going to lie to me."

That smirk on his face grew even bigger. "Damn straight I won't, woman. I'll always tell you the truth. Which, right now, is that your asshole stepfather is outside my house, and I'm looking forward to break his face with my fist before I riddle him with bullet holes." He wrapped his arm around Ellie to bring her against his chest.

Okay, that shit wasn't cool with me.

"Back off," I warned. "This isn't your fight."

Oz growled and rolled his eyes. "Afraid it is. Come on, douches, let's go; but Jon, put some clothes on first," he added, before taking Ellie with him down the hall.

I looked at Spencer. "I don't want to talk to you right now." I seethed.

"Oz just stole our girl because you opened your mouth. You should have let the good Pastor drop that on her."

"You let her go back into that fucking house. That prick put his hands on her."

Spencer held up his hand. "I don't 'want to fight with you, sweetness. We'll have to talk about this later." He whispered.

"Trust me. We'll talk about this." I quickly finished putting on my clothes so we could meet the rest of the Knights downstairs.

Chapter Twenty-Six

Ellie

I clung to Oz as we moved downstairs, only stopping so he could shove me into his coat, and then we went outside, where we found Easton, Jameson, Cash, Brett, and Lennox standing with Rick as well as another man I didn't recognize. He was tall, with dark brown eyes and broad shoulders. He was staring at me as if he knew me.

"Dad?" Oz tightened his grip on me. "Where the hell have you been? Where's Mom?"

Owen Maxwell took a step forward. "Well, since you shot me, I've been keeping busy. That is until Rick told me that Ellie was back. Are you two...?" He waved his hand between the two of us.

"What? Fuck no," Oz shot back but didn't release me. In fact, his fingers dug even tighter into my shoulder. "She's my friend," he assured everyone.

Owen lifted his head. "Oswald, you're never friends with girls. You're a lot like I was when I was your age. You like to love 'em and leave 'em, but you never like to get to know them. Only that Wilson girl, which frankly surprised me, son, because I thought you knew better than to get attached. Especially to trash like her."

I felt Oz's body tremble against me.

"Excuse me." I spun around to face Owen. "Do you know anything about your son? Or maybe just what your little spies tell you, which would mean they are people who see him but don't actually know him."

The door slammed behind us which meant Jon and Spencer had joined us.

Owen's lip curled. "We'll get back to this conversation, Eleanor, but first, who invited Senior's son into my house?"

"He's with Ellie." Rick finally spoke. "They've been a couple for a while now, but said they broke up. Which is why I let her move back with her mother and me. Clearly the little slut lied, but I shouldn't be surprised, since she's just like her mother."

"Don't you talk about Ellie like that." Spencer sneered.

Owen was still staring at Jonathan and Spencer, his eyes narrowed into angry slits. "You two fucking one another?" He dropped his chin. "I always knew Jon wasn't right in the head, but I didn't know Spencer Junior was the same way."

"Jon, don't!" Spencer shouted, but suddenly Jonathan rushed past me and knocked Owen to the ground.

"You can't talk about them like that." He pressed the knife against Owen's throat. "Do you hear me?" he warned. "They belong to me, and you don't call the shots around here anymore."

I heard the cock of a gun, looking up to find Easton holding it up to Rick. "I wouldn't." He shook his head. "Stay right there, Pastor, unless you want to join your first wife." He kept his arm wrapped around Brett.

"I invite you into my home, take you in as my own, Jonathan, and *this* is how you repay me?" Owen's eyes were wide but oddly calm as he managed to keep his voice firm. "How would your mother react to this, huh, boy?"

"You never invited me here. That was all Oz." Jon pressed the blade down enough so that a sliver of blood appeared.

"You don't get to speak about my mother, asshole, not now, not ever." His knee dug into Owen's chest.

Oz let go of me so that he could go to Jon and his father.

"Bro." He touched his shoulder. "If anyone gets to kill him, don't you think it should be me?" He tilted his head as if they were having a silent conversation.

Jonathan looked like he wanted to argue, but instead stood up, grabbed my hand, and pulled me over to where Spencer stood. "Fuck you," he spat.

Owen stood up, lifting his hand to the cut against his neck. "You'd better kill me tonight, boys, or else you're going to regret it. I'll make sure you're all six feet under by the morning light," he promised.

Cash stepped forward. "Is that what you want?" He lifted the hem of his shirt. I didn't have to look to know he had to have a gun, too. Was this what the Knights did? Played with guns and knives when they weren't playing baseball or fucking?

"Easy." Easton's calm voice surprised me.

I felt like I was going to throw up, but the Knights made all of this seem so normal.

"You, the good Pastor Rick." He waved the gun so that my stepfather moved closer to Owen. "Did you call Owen to make sure he would show up, knowing that Ellie wasn't going to go anywhere with you? She's not, you know"—he glanced at me for a moment—"going with you. She's staying here. With us, with Spencer and Jon, and there is nothing you can do about it," Easton promised.

Rick's eyes darkened. "You think that contract is going to stand now?"

"We don't give a rat's ass about your contracts, Pastor," Jameson chimed in. "You think that's what this is about? We plan on finding the rest of them so we can drench them in gasoline," he hissed.

Rick looked around at the Knights, including Spencer, before he locked eyes with Owen. "Isn't that what this is about?" He continued to stare at the older Maxwell, waiting for help, but when none came, he bared his teeth. "That was on him—on Chad, Max, Ralph and Lee." I felt Jon bristle at the mention of his father's name. "I didn't want any part of that."

"Bullshit!" Owen exclaimed. "You were the one who pushed for that contract, saying it would be the perfect pairing. It was Ralph who didn't want the contract. He never wanted any of them but went along with it because of the elders."

"Mention my father's name again, and I'll blow both your brains out." Easton's face had grown so scary that I almost didn't recognize him. "Dorothy, take the other girls inside." He pressed a kiss against her hair. "This might get bad, and I don't want any of you to see it."

But I had questions. So many questions that I wanted answers to.

"Why the contracts?" I pushed Jon and Spencer's hands away when they tried to pull me back. "What is the big damn deal? Why force your children into a marriage that you knew isn't going to work? I know my mother wasn't your first choice, but you did it because my father... No." Tears pooled in my eyes. "Did you kill him?"

"Baby, now isn't a good time." Spencer brought his hands up to my shoulders, but I shook him off.

"I want answers!"

We were always told that my father, Edward Young, had died in a car accident, but what if it hadn't been an accident? What if Rick had done something to the car just so that he could be with my mother and marry me off to Jonathan, just like the so-called elders wanted.

"Answer the question." Oz had his gun pressed right against his own father's temple. He lifted his hand to wiggle his fingers at me. "Eleanor," he said my name when I didn't do what he wanted.

Owen's lips curled. "Two isn't enough for you? You have to go after my son, too, is that it? What kind of slut—"

Oz smacked him in the head with the butt of his gun, and we all watched as he dropped to the pavement, completely knocked out.

"Jesus Christ!" Rick looked around at us. "That's your father, boy, and I suggest you start showing the man the respect he deserves."

Oz gripped my hand as I moved to take it, and then cocked the pistol to point it at my stepfather.

"I would watch what you say, Pastor, or you're next. He might be my father by blood, but he doesn't deserve my respect." His voice was full of venom as he wrapped an arm around me.

"Have you touched Luna yet?" I couldn't help but ask, although I figured he hadn't since she was so young.

Rick paled. "What kind of a question is that? I would never hurt my own daughter."

"But it's okay to rape your stepdaughter, hoping she would get pregnant?"

"It worked, didn't it?"

The silence that followed was nearly deafening as everyone stared at me, looked back at Rick, and back at me again. Oz's arm seemed to get heaver the longer no one spoke, and I felt like I might go mad from the lack of sound. Just the wind and my own heavy breathing filled my ears.

"Ellie." Jonathan spoke first, his voice soft and calming. "Did he impregnate you?" When I didn't answer, I heard him speaking to Spencer in low tones I couldn't make out.

Rick looked more than pleased with himself at ruining everything I'd tried to hide from Jonathan and my new friends. "You never told him." He smirked, pushing his tongue against the inside of his mouth. "My, my, Ellie, you kept that secret deep, didn't you?"

Rage flashed through me like fire. "I hate you," I hissed. "You made me give up my baby and pretend she was my sister. Act like I didn't carry her for nine months at fourteen years old and then pretend like she wasn't mine. MINE! My own flesh and blood. She calls my mother mommy, thinks I'm just her cool older sister, and it breaks my heart every single minute of every day," I shouted into the night.

"Say the word," Cash spoke up. "We'll take care of this bastard for you, Ellie," he promised.

Easton nodded. "No skin off my back," he added.

"Been too long since I drew blood." Jameson grinned.

I untangled myself from Oz. "He's too good for that." I poked my finger against Rick's chest. "He deserves to suffer. Look over his shoulder every single minute, wondering if today is the day. Will the Knights come for me? Will they kill me today? Or maybe tomorrow?" I let out a laugh that sounded manic. "Maybe I should cut your balls and dick off." I looked back at Jonathan. "You mind if I borrow your knife, baby, because that way I know my daughter is safe."

"What? You wouldn't," Rick insisted.

I turned back with a smile on my face. "Wouldn't I?" I asked as I felt Jon press the handle of his blade into my hand.

The sound of Owen stirring brought our attention away from Rick, and before we realized it, he had shot down the driveway into the darkness. I met Spencer's eyes as he stared wide-eyed at me, while Oz dropped down to face his father.

"How are you feeling, Pops?" He gripped Owen's chin to jerk his face toward his. "Hurts, right?" He twisted his lips into a smile. "It's going to hurt so much worse, though. For everything you've done. To Mom. To me. To my friends. Payback is going to be a real bitch."

Owen glared at his only son. "You're going to kill me now, is that it?" He tried to stand, but Oz pushed him back down.

"Death would be too good for you." Oz stood up. "Everybody, saddle up, because we're going to the cabin," he announced.

I found myself standing there with Spencer, Lennox, and Brett as the Knights began to move back into the house. Was I supposed to go with them? What was this cabin they were talking about?

"Ellie." I turned to sound of my name to find Easton watching me from the door. "You say the word, and we'll go to his house. Drag him out, kicking and screaming." He let the door slam behind him as he disappeared inside without waiting for my response.

I locked eyes with Spencer just as Brett gripped my arm. "We should probably go inside, try to get some sleep," she suggested.

I pinned my eyes on hers. "Sleep? I don't think I can sleep right now."

"Me either," Spencer agreed.

"You should probably go with them." Lennox nudged Spencer. "You're part of this now, and they're going to want all the help they can get."

Obnoxious laughing from a few inches away from us brought our attention back to Owen, who was still trying to get to his feet. There was blood seeping down his head where Oz had hit him with the gun, and he didn't look too good.

"You think you're going to get away with this? Right now, Rick is already notifying the elder Knights what happened, and there will be no hiding. No running. You're dead. All of you," he threatened.

"I'd shut your trap if I were you," Easton warned as he grabbed Owen's hands to keep them behind his back. "You killed my father, you tried to kill me, and now you're threatening my girl." He caught the handcuffs that Jameson tossed in his direction. "My friends. Man, I thought you were smarter than that." He tsked softly.

"Get him into the SUV," Oz ordered before he met my gaze. "Lock the doors and make sure you turn on the alarm system. Brett and Len both know the code, but it's time you learned it, too." He turned away as I wrapped my arms around myself.

"Come on." Lennox nudged my shoulder. "Let them do their thing." She reached for the door behind us, and we followed her inside.

Chapter Twenty-Seven

Spencer

I shouldn't be here right now. I didn't belong in this vehicle while Owen Maxwell was in the back with his hands and feet handcuffed together. Right before they shoved him into the SUV, Cash shoved something into his mouth to keep Owen quiet.

My stomach clenched, and I clutched my thigh with my hand as I tried to keep myself from screaming about how insane this was.

This wasn't who I was. I wasn't a killer or a kidnapper, and I certainly did not want to be a fucking Kingston Knight if it meant doing either of those two things. I was a normal eighteen-year-old boy with hopes of graduating high school, marrying his girl, and settling down with their boyfriend in a nice house where they could live some sort of normal life.

Nothing about this was normal.

"Hey." Jon's voice interrupted my thoughts as the shiny SUV cruised down the dark roads of Kingston. "You all right? You haven't said anything. We need to finish that conversation we started back at the house." He tried to pry my hand from my thigh, but I only dug in harder.

"Are you serious right now?" I hissed. "Oswald was ready to kill his father, and you're asking if I'm all right." I pinned my gaze on him. "I am pretty fucking far from all right," I told him.

"You pussying out, Pearson?" Oz asked from the driver's seat in front of us, where he held the steering wheel in a death grip.

My lip curled up in disgust. "If not wanting to commit murder or be an accessory to murder means I'm pussying out, then yes." I yanked my arm away when Jonathan tried to take my hand again. "Don't touch me," I warned.

"Well shit." Cash turned around from the front seat. "You two having a lovers' spat?"

Jonathan leaned forward. "When you fix whatever the fuck you did with Lennox? Then you can talk to me about me, my boyfriend, and whatever problems we might or might not be having." His voice was a low rumble.

"So touchy." Cash tried to laugh it off, but his eyes gave him away. Hurt mixed with confusion, and possibly shame filled his blues as he turned his massive body back around.

I leaned as far as I could against the door. "I didn't sign up for this," I told Jonathan.

"Are you breaking up with me?" Jon exclaimed.

I caught Oz shaking his head as he raked his hand through his hair.

"No," I whispered, hoping he would bring his voice down a few octaves. "I'm just saying..."

"I heard what you said," Jon assured me. "But you knew who I was when you came to me, Spencer. You pursued me. I told you this was a bad idea, but you didn't listen. You made me fall in love with you, with Ellie, and the idea of the three of us together, so you can't just back out now because you're scared."

My nostrils flared as I watched him, thoughts flying through my head. With only one thing that I knew firsthand, Jonathan Hamden was no one's doormat. When I opened my mouth to tell him something, anything, I realized the SUV was slowing down, and we were now approaching a cabin nestled into the woods. It was covered in snow and hidden by the trees. I had heard the rumors about the Maxwell cabin, but up until a few seconds ago, I had thought that was all they were. Rumors.

"If you want to leave, go on." Oz shifted the truck into park. "You won't be allowed back into my house or our lives again. Which means you stay away from Jon and Ellie. If you open your mouth to speak about anything we told you?" He opened the driver's side door to climb out. "I'll kill you myself," he promised with a wink and a smirk. "Let's fucking go, boys!" he hollered.

I found Jonathan watching with me a look I couldn't read before he followed behind the rest of the Knights, not giving me the chance to assure him that I wasn't going to leave. As I heaved myself from the SUV, I heard them pulling out Owen, laughing and talking as if this was something they did every single day.

"It isn't always like this." Easton's voice caused my back to go rod straight. "Most of the time we're just regular guys who play ball, sleep with our girls, have fun. It's just sometimes..." He moved, so that he was in front of me. "Sometimes we have to take charge of our lives because our parents thought they should make that decision for us." His eyes narrowed. "You understand what I'm saying?" He patted my shoulder. "Make your decision, Pearson, because I could use you on my side." Easton nodded before he moved to help the rest of the Knights.

I watched as they started to move Owen across the snowy driveway. He struggled in their grip, and they moved together, not saying a word, hauling him up onto the porch. I could go. Now would be my chance. I could walk away now, and not have to worry about the Knights ever again. But that would mean leaving the two people I loved most in the world, and I knew I couldn't live without them.

I shot across the snow, up the steps, and to the porch just as Oz opened the front door. His icy gaze landed on me as he turned back to move his father into the cabin, and I saw the way his lips twitched. Jameson, Cash, and Easton all gave me a curt nod before I managed to finally look at the boy who had stolen my heart.

"You couldn't get rid of me if you tried, sweetness," I promised.

Jon didn't say anything as we moved Owen into the house, through the kitchen and living room, and finally stopped at another locked door, which I assumed led down to the basement. As we stopped so Oz could unlock the door, I gave a quick look around the hallway. Five rooms were wide open as well as the bathroom, and as I brought my attention back to the task at hand, I wondered who actually owned this place.

I noticed the stairs were new as we slowly moved Owen down into the basement. They looked recently updated, painted, and possibly reinforced in the past couple of months. It was on the tip of my tongue to ask why, but instead, I followed the Knights as they dragged Oswald's father down the steps, across the room, and dropped him against the basement wall.

"Tie him up," Oz instructed as he turned back to face me. "This cabin has been in my family for years, Pearson." He smirked. "Built by my great-grandfather, an elder Knight, for this reason alone. To keep, torture, and murder someone if we had to." He swung back around as J2 closed the shackles on his father. "Isn't that right, *Daddy*?" Oz sneered as he took a step forward. "How many people have you killed here?" He brought his leg back so he could kick Owen in the stomach. "I know of a few, but I'm sure there are plenty more I'm not even aware of. It's good to be king, isn't it?" He started to raise his leg again, only to have Jameson stop him.

"Hey, we have plenty of time for that." He tried to pull Oz back away from his father. "We just got him here." He looked around the room at the rest of us. "We should go upstairs." Jameson jutted his chin.

Oz coughed and then spat it out in Owen's face. "Don't get too comfortable. I'll be back."

I followed Jonathan back up the stairs, and when he reached his arm back, wiggling his fingers at me, I took his hand, squeezing it tightly. I still felt uneasy, but something in the back of my mind was telling me this was the only way.

"Sit." Easton pointed his finger at everyone as we moved into the overcrowded living room with the overstuffed sectional couch. "Anyone want a drink?" he called over his shoulder as he moved toward the liquor cabinet. "I know I need something stronger than beer right now, and I don't care that it's nearly six in the morning. Sleep isn't happening any time soon. We're not going anywhere until we figure out what we're going to do about Owen, and…" He brought the glass of brown liquid up to his mouth. "We need to find out who the mole is."

My brows shot up. "It's not fucking me. I swear to God." I held up my hands only to have Jon push them down.

"We know, Spencer. Relax," Cash assured me, standing up to get himself a glass of what I assumed was whiskey. "We think it's someone at school." He tipped his head back to shoot back the booze before he did another.

Relief flooded my body as I let out a slow breath. "Any ideas?" I could probably use a sip of that whiskey right about now.

Oz stood up. "I have one theory," he announced as he grabbed the bottle of whiskey, brought it up to his mouth, and took a swig. He wiped his lips with the back of his hand. "Tate."

"Bernard?" Jonathan's leg pressed against mine. "I don't think it's him." He looked around the room.

Oz nodded. "Think about it." He folded his arms across his chest as he spoke. "He's not a Knight, nor will he ever be, but he wants to be included. We let him into our group to do grunt work, the shit stuff, and to watch over Brett while she was gone because someone had to do it at night while we had other things to worry about."

Easton looked like he might rip something apart with his bare hands. "He took an oath." He seethed.

"Don't think that matters, boss." Jameson threw in his two cents. "He could have taken that oath, crossed his fingers, and lied to us, and we wouldn't have known otherwise. He wanted Brett, and when she blew him off, he wasn't too happy about it."

I felt confused. "Someone want to fill me in?" I asked, as Cash cracked his knuckles.

"Tate likes to throw these lame parties on Green Road over by the school," he answered for me. "We went there the night he was harassing Brett, before Easton got his head out of his ass and realized how perfect they were for one another. Her lady balls are big." He snickered.

"Huge," Easton added. "I wanted to push his nose through his skull for that, but I let it go. After we taught him a lesson." He lifted his arms. "We brought the fucker here, to torture, maim, whatever, and instead, we fucking let him go because my girl wanted that."

Oz snorted. "Of course." He rolled his eyes.

"Hey, man, whatever Brett wants she gets, and you, of all people, know exactly what that means," Easton snarled. "Don't act like you weren't all goo-goo over Palmer, and don't try to threaten me either because I dared to bring up her name. Man the fuck up."

Oz bristled. "Says the guy who was nearly blackout drunk the entire time Brett was gone because he couldn't stomach the idea of being without her," he snarled.

"True love."

"Fuck off."

"Okay, okay." I stood up. "I get it. You let Tate go for Brett, and now he's telling your secrets. How many does he know?" I pushed up the sleeves of my shirt.

"Not as much as you, but enough to get us in some serious trouble." Cash brought his left foot up to rest on his right thigh. "Most of the cops are on our payroll, thanks to Oz's dad here, but not all of them are dirty. The ones who aren't are the ones we need to worry about."

I chewed on my lip. "I don't think it's Tate. Think about it. He was on vacation, right?" I was trying to be helpful. Jon pulled on my hand so that I sat back down.

"Shit." Jameson nodded. "Then who else would stab us in the back?"

"We have some digging to do." Easton clapped his hands together. "We need to find out exactly who is doing this, because everyone at Kingston wants to either be a Knight or fuck one. Why is he different? Owen can wait. He's not going anywhere."

We all filed out of the cabin and back to the SUV that was parked outside just as the sun started to come up. My entire body was screaming at me to go home, go to bed, and forget about this. But the dark-haired boy sitting next to me, drawing circles with his thumb against my palm, was a very compelling reason to stay.

Chapter Twenty-Eight

Brett, Lennox, and I were too riled up to sleep once the boys left, so at Brett's suggestion, we tossed a bunch of pillows and blankets onto the floor of the family room, trying to keep each other company. I knew I didn't want to sleep alone, and I figured they felt the same way, so it was a good excuse to turn on some Netflix before we all passed out on the floor.

I woke up first, turned off the television, and headed upstairs before I remembered I was supposed to work at Gerry's this morning. When I glanced at the clock, I saw it was nearly noon. I'd probably had lost my job. What I was going to do now? I loved that job, even if it wasn't much. It gave me the chance to learn how to bake things I hadn't before, and the people were nice, too. It certainly wasn't my dream job, but it was something.

After I brushed my teeth and took a quick shower, I changed into another pair of leggings and one of Jon's oversized shirts, then headed into the kitchen. My empty stomach rumbled, and I realized I'd missed breakfast and lunch. I began to dig around in the cabinets, looking for items I could use to make French toast casserole, and once I had it all thrown together, I popped it into the oven to wait.

"Making yourself comfortable?"

I jumped at the sound of the voice behind me and let out a nervous giggle. "Oz, you scared the shit out of me," I told him. He had big, dark circles under his eyes from the lack

"

of sleep and looked exhausted. "Where is everyone else?" I asked.

"On their way." He moved around the kitchen island to get closer. "Do you really have a daughter with that man?" Oz tilted his head to the right.

Hot tears pricked my eyes. "I don't want to talk about it." I turned away, but Oz caught my wrist and pulled me back against him.

"You love her," he whispered. "You find yourself thinking about her constantly, even though there isn't anything you can do about it. She's your flesh, your blood, and you would kill for her if you had to."

I raised my eyes to his. "Yes." I nodded. "If it came down to it, I would give my life for her," I confessed.

"Do you trust me?"

"One hundred percent."

Oz released me so he could reach into his back pocket and pulled out his wallet. He rifled through it for a second before he pulled out what looked like a piece of paper. "I got this in an email a couple of days ago," he confessed.

It was a printout of sonogram.

"No doubt it's from Palmer, which means she lied to me," he growled. "Although, why should I be surprised?" Oz laughed bitterly. "It's a girl."

"How do... oh," I said as he flipped it over to show me the message printed on the bottom. "What are you going to do?"

The sound of the rest of the Knights coming into the house startled us. He grabbed the picture from my hand and shoved it back into his wallet. He raised his index finger to his lips to keep his secret.

"What smells so good, woman?" His voice, his body language, his everything changed the moment they stepped into the room. He was a completely different person when they were around.

"Did you make what I think you did?" Spencer engulfed me in a warm, tight hug. "It smells amazing, baby." He kissed the top of my forehead before Jonathan moved in to do the same.

"Whatever it is, I hope there's enough for everyone," Jameson announced as he dropped into one of the chairs. "All I want to do right now is stuff my face before I sleep for the next ten days."

Jon wrapped his arm around my chest, and he pulled my back against his chest. "No time for that, bro, remember?"

"Where's Brett?" Easton sounded distressed. "She's not upstairs and isn't answering her texts." He looked ready to snap someone in half.

I pointed to the stairs that led to the family room. "Relax, Caveman, she's downstairs sleeping. Probably didn't even hear your text."

Relief flooded his face before he hurried downstairs. We all heard Brett's squeal of laughter, followed by Easton's laugh.

"All good." I smiled at the other five Knights.

"So much for sleeping in." Lennox dragged her feet across the floor and pushed her hand through her raven hair. "I'm going to shower."

Cash took a step forward. "Can I talk to you for a second?" he blurted out before she waved him off. "Len, this is serious."

"As serious as my foot in your ass, Cash, so leave me the fuck alone," she called back to him.

Cash sighed heavily as he sat down next to Jameson. "Chicks," he mumbled before he remembered I was in the room. "Sorry, Ellie." He flashed a quick smile.

"Anyone want to tell me what happened while you were gone?" I untangled myself from Jonathan so I could check on the food in the oven. When no one answered, I turned back around to fold my arms over my chest. "Don't all talk at once or anything."

Spencer patted an empty chair. "You might want to sit down, baby," he told me.

I shook my head. "I'd rather stand."

Easton gave a quick nod as he and Brett appeared at the top of the steps.

"Fine." Oz opened the fridge to dig out the orange juice, popped the top, and then drank straight from the container before he wiped his mouth. "We found out that our mole is Heidi Morgan. She is being paid by your stepfather to watch you."

I sat down in the chair before my legs gave out. "What... why... how?" I couldn't form a complete sentence.

"We did some digging, as we've learned it's the only way to find out the truth these days," Easton answered. "My father has tons of paperwork at his garage, which will be mine when I graduate high school, and we know there is more at Josie's place."

Where was Josie, anyway? I felt like I hadn't seen her forever.

I swallowed the lump in my throat. "Is that why she was trying so hard to be my friend?"

"Seems that way," Oz nodded. "She doesn't really have a lot of friends around the school, mostly a loner, but she goes to church with her parents on Sunday, and we figure that's how good old Pastor Rick hit her up." His eyes hardened around the edges. "We never even thought it would be someone we didn't have contact with."

My mouth fell open. "What did he offer her?" I exclaimed.

Jameson raised his right hand to rub his fingers together. "Money talks, Ellie, and it seems Rick was willing to pay big bucks for information about you. He knows all about you, Jon, and Spencer. Don't ask me—shit!" He shot out of his chair. "Have you checked this place for bugs or cameras?"

The Knights exploded into a rage of confusion and yelling just as the oven's timer went off to inform me that my brunch was ready. I grabbed two potholders so that I could remove it safely and placed it on the divot on the counter. Their voices got louder and louder, but it was nearly impossible to understand what they were saying. I moved to grab some plates from the cabinet, as well as silverware, and then turned back around to the mass commotion.

"Hey!" Oz shouted as he tried to get everyone's attention. "Oi, assholes, we're not going to get anything sorted out with everyone screaming and yelling about nonsense!" The kitchen suddenly grew quiet. "Now, Eleanor was kind enough to make us something to eat, so I suggest we all fill our pie holes and try to discuss this like normal human beings." He winked at me.

Spencer got up to help me place the casserole on the table, while Jonathan helped with the silverware and plates. Everyone started to dig into the food while I grabbed glasses, and then everyone was able to get their own drinks.

"You holding up okay?" Jon's fingers grazed my hand as I sat down. "You're taking this all in stride, baby." He broke off a piece of the casserole on his plate before he took a bite. "Shit, this is fucking fantastic!" he announced once he had finished chewing and swallowing.

I flashed a big smile. "Thanks. It was my father's recipe," I told him. "I'm all right, Jonny. Just... this whole thing seems crazy." I looked around the table of Knights. "Why is this all happening?" I watched Spencer's brows dip slightly. "What? Is there something else?"

His brown eyes slid over to Easton, who gave a quick nod. "Baby, we think Rick had your father killed." My fork dropped to my plate. "We found some documents that said he was supposed to marry your mother—that whole contract bullshit—and it looks like Paige married your father instead." He reached for my hand, but I shook my head.

"No, what? No." I gasped as I tried to wrap my head around it. "What kind of a monster does something like that?" That was a question I already knew the answer to without anyone telling me. "We have to stop him. He's going to do something horrible to my mother or Luna or... We can't let him!" I jumped from my chair, and Spencer and Jonathan joined me.

"Easy." Jonathan's voice was calm as he spoke. "We've already got an eye out."

I balked at him. "Who? Heidi could be anywhere."

"Don't worry about Heidi, baby, relax," Spencer assured me. "I got a couple of my guys on it."

I swallowed nervously. "Footballers from Weston want to help the Knights?" I didn't feel right about this.

"It's not a Knights or Eagles thing. They want to help *you*."

My eyes zeroed in on Spencer. "What if he touches Luna?" I whispered as fear ripped through my body.

"I can fucking promise you that no one is going to hurt your daughter, Eleanor," Oz assured me. "If they even touch one hair on her head? I'll kill them with my own bare hands."

I felt Spencer's muscles tense as he pinned his gaze on Oz. "We all will," he growled, but there was something he wasn't saying. Was he still jealous that we were friends? Because I wasn't interested in Oz in any other way.

"I think I need to go lie down," I muttered before I rushed upstairs to Jonathan's room. He and Spencer were right behind me. "Please, just don't," I begged as I flopped onto my back on the bed. "This is all too much for one person to handle. My stepfather killed my dad. This contract thing!" I dragged the palm of my hand down my face. "I was supposed to work today, and I forgot to set my alarm," I muttered before I met their eyes.

Jon dug his teeth into his bottom lip. "You don't need to work, sweetheart. We'll take care of you." He looked at Spencer, who nodded in agreement.

"We'll be your sugar daddies, baby. No problem." A smile tugged at Spencer's mouth.

I dropped my hand to my stomach. "It wasn't the money. I mean, that was nice. But it was more about getting the chance to bake the donuts and learn new things." I eased myself onto my side. "You know how much that means to me."

Jon moved to sit down on the end of the mattress. "You can always bake here. Cook whatever, whenever you want. This is your house now, too, Ellie. I'm sure that Cash would happily sample the goods, too." He patted my thigh. "Whatever you need, or might want, will never be a problem. If you want to take baking classes to learn more, you can do that, too."

"Who is going to pay for that?" I sat up to stare first at Jon, and then at Spencer.

"We are." Spencer sat down next to Jonathan. "I'm going to move in here once I graduate, and we're all going to be together."

I pulled my legs up to my chest before I wrapped my arms around them. "You talked about this? Without me?" I ping-ponged my gaze between the two of them.

"We didn't think you'd mind." Jon reached for Spencer's hand. "We had a lot to do while we were going through that paperwork, and so we discussed a lot of things. You being one of them, since you're the piece that holds us together, sweetheart." He gazed lovingly at Spencer.

I scooted over to rest my head on Jon's shoulder. "At least I have the two of you to lean on when my world is falling apart," I whispered.

Chapter Twenty-Nine

The three of us spent the rest of the day in bed until the boys passed out from exhaustion. Then I left them there, cuddled up together, after taking a picture to save as my background on my phone. I made my way down the hall in the eerily silent house. The rest of the Knights must have ordered pizza, because when I stepped into the kitchen, I found a couple of boxes. One had a few pieces left, which I happily ate. Then I went into the basement to see if anyone was awake.

"There she is!" Cash exclaimed, pausing their Xbox game. "Was kind of hoping you and Jon were going to make dinner with dessert today, but we went with pizza instead." He grinned at me, and Oz slapped his arm. "What? I'm being honest."

I smiled as I sat down on the couch. "My guys are sleeping now. I'm honestly surprised to find you two awake. Do you sleep at all?" I asked.

Oz nodded. "I'm one of those types who only needs a few hours." He stood up, and as he walked over to where I was sitting, I noticed the prosthetic leg. "Get that look off your face, woman." He dropped his arm over the back of the couch above my shoulders. "It was a birth defect," he told me.

"I didn't see anything."

"Don't lie to me, Eleanor. I don't like it. You're not like everyone else."

I stared at Oz's side profile, the way he gritted his teeth. His narrowed eyes told me that he was pissed at me.

"I'm sorry." I chewed on my bottom lip. "I mean, I'm sorry if I offended you by staring."

"It's no big deal, really, just be honest, like you usually are around me. You're my friend, and I don't want you to think you have to hide or protect me." He ruffled my hair. "It's never held me back."

I smiled as Oz pinned his dark eyes on me. "I don't think that anyone or thing could, Oswald." I chuckled as he rolled his eyes. "Everyone else sleeping?" I asked.

"Easton took Brett to bed, so that means anything but sleeping for them. Jameson went to go see how Josie was. She's been acting stranger than normal." Cash stretched his arms over his head. "Lennox is in her room with the door locked, and she won't come out." He twisted around to face us.

"I was going to find out when they wanted to go shopping for the dance." I was planning to bring my own date, since I was a Kingston student, and meet my other date there. I didn't care what the rest of the school thought anymore.

Cash tilted his head. "Dance?" He looked confused.

"The Winter Formal, idiot." Oz threw a pillow at his friend, who propped it against his back as he leaned against the love seat. "You're going with Jon and Spencer." He winked at me. "Guess I'll have to suck it up and ask Diana."

"I have to..." Cash was on his feet. "I need to talk to Len." He gave a quick wave before he hurried up the stairs.

Oz patted my arm. "He's still crazy about my cousin," he told me.

"Can I ask what happened?" I hadn't had the nerve to talk to Lennox about it, but I was curious about her relationship with Cash. He seemed like the nicest one of the Knights, and that was saying something, since I was in love with one—or was it two now?—and another was sort of my best friend.

Oz made a clucking noise with his tongue. "Lennox kissed someone else. That's all I'm going to tell you, woman, because it's not any of my business. She won't talk about it or Cash, only to say that she made a mistake and wishes she could take it back. If you want the truth, you're going to have to ask Len yourself, but don't expect her to be too forthcoming. I don't think she's told Brett the whole truth, and they're best friends."

I couldn't imagine what Lennox must have gone through to feel that that was her only way out. "Maybe when I feel like she won't bite my head off." I leaned my head against Oz's shoulder and closed my eyes.

***

Spencer

"Come here, sweetness." I kept my hand wrapped around my length. "Sit on my cock." I watched the way Jon's eyes grew dark with want. When he started toward the bed, I yanked the covers back all the way. "You're not too sore, are you?" I asked, as he licked his lips.

Jon shook his head. "No." He quickly yanked his shirt up over his head.

"Grab the lube," I instructed. He removed his sweats next. "Cover my dick in it."

My cock jerked at the thought of Jon touching me. I watched with hooded eyes as he flipped off the top, squirted some onto his hand, and began to slowly stroke me.

"Fuck, that's it." I groaned as Jon tightened his grip. "Come here." I curled my finger. "Kiss me," I whispered.

Jon's lips slammed against mine, rough and hard. He continued to jerk me with one hand while the other curled into my hair. His tongue met mine as he opened his mouth, and he let out a whimper when I reached between his legs to stroke his hard length.

"Spencer," he murmured my name as I pulled back.

"Ride me." I wrapped my hand around his to stop him from jerking me. "Think about how good it will feel." I felt my body break out in goosebumps at the thought. "Hand me the lube so I can make sure it won't hurt." I took the bottle when Jon handed it to me. "Just a little, since you coated me pretty well." I ran the tip of my finger against his backside, and he groaned at my touch. I eased a finger inside and watched Jon's eyes roll when I added a second.

He grabbed my wrist. "Don't, it's too much." His brown eyes were full of desire.

"You're ready to come already?" I dragged my teeth over my bottom lip. "We can't have that, Jonny, we're just getting started," I teased.

Jon released my hand to climb up onto the bed. He straddled my waist, reached down to grab my cock, and pressed it against himself.

"You know I'm going to explode the second you're inside me." He slowly began to ease himself down. "Shit," he muttered and pressed his eyes together tightly. "Baby, it's too good. I'm not going to last." Jon panted.

"Easy." I cupped his cheek as pleasure pulsed through my body. "Take it slow." I commented as I gripped the back of Jon's neck to bring his face closer to mine. I peppered kisses against his lips as he began to move above me, my eyes never leaving his face.

Jon arched his back and pulled out of my grasp. "I need..."

"Whatever you need, sweetness, take it."

"Need to come."

I groaned. "Not yet, Jon, hold on."

His eyes closed, and he began to really move. His arms flew behind him to grasp my thighs as he slid up and down my cock. His own cock moved with every one of his movements, and I couldn't stop myself from wrapping my hand around it.

"Fuck, Spencer, don't..." Jon's eyes flew open as I applied pressure. "It feels so good." He began to move his hips faster as I bucked my own. I released his dick so I could reach back to grip his ass and spread his cheeks.

"You like that, don't you?" I watched Jon's hooded lids flutter and his eyes roll back. "Want more?" I asked, and he nodded. "Look at me, Jonathan," I growled.

When his eyes opened, they were on fire. Jon reached above me to grab the headboard. "More, always more." He slid his lips over mine.

I ran my palms lightly over his ass before I slapped both cheeks just to hear the soft whimper Jon let out. Then I gripped his hips to press him further down.

"Fuck me until you come," I demanded.

Jon's hips arched back at my words and then he began to rock his body.

"Spencer," he whispered my name as he moved.

Heat exploded over my body as he rode me. His eyes never strayed from mine as we moved together, our cries of pleasure filling the room. He began to move hard and fast, jackhammering toward a desperate climax.

I let out a loud shout before I blew into Jon like a hurricane, just as I felt him tense above me with a violent eruption. His hot seed sprayed over my stomach and chest before he finally shuttered to a stop.

"You okay, sweetness?" I smiled as his heavy eyes met mine.

"I think that I died and went to heaven," he teased before slumping down next to me. "Jesus, that was amazing," he murmured into the pillow.

Jon sat up as I climbed from the bed. "Spencer?" He blinked in confusion.

"Just going to get a cloth to wash up with. I'll be right back," I assured him before I stepped into the bathroom.

I quickly cleaned myself up before I grabbed another one for Jonathan. When I moved back into the bedroom, he was snoring quietly on the bed. I smiled to myself as I slowly ran the cloth over his shaft, cleaned up his balls and ass, then his hands before I disposed the cloth in the hamper. I pressed my lips against Jon's forehead as I climbed back into the bed with him.

Jon's arms instantly wrapped around my waist, and he pressed his face into my chest. "I love you." His voice was soft when he spoke. "You and Ellie, I can't imagine myself without you both." He raised his head to look at me.

"I know." I brushed a piece of dark hair out of his eyes. "I love you, too," I answered. "I would do anything for you and Ellie. I want you to know that." I felt my stomach clench at the thought of anything happening to either of them.

Jon went tense against me. "Nothing is going to happen," he hissed. "I would kill someone, anyone, who tried to hurt you." His eyes narrowed.

"Easy, sweetness." I felt my lips turn up slightly.

"We should probably get up." Jon sighed as he began to untangle himself from me and the blankets. "Make sure Ellie is okay. Although, she's probably with Oz." He rolled his eyes.

"You trust him?" I sat up as Jon began to put back on the clothes he had shed so quickly for me.

He tugged his shirt down over his thick chest and nodded. "I do. He might be mean as hell, and probably a little crazy, but Oz is not going to hurt Ellie. He likes her, and that's saying a lot."

"As a friend."

Jon smiled. "Oz isn't after Ellie like that. He's still hurt from the whole Palmer disaster, and besides"—he sat back down on the mattress—"Oz isn't the kind of guy to steal his friend's girl. You're one of us now, remember? He wouldn't do that." He patted my hand.

I let out a slow sigh, then moved to get up. "I wouldn't call us friends, Jon. But as long he doesn't hurt her..." I shrugged when he shook his head. "Ellie's special," I reminded him.

"Don't I know it?" He chuckled. "Come on, baby, let's go check on our girl and get something to eat." He pinned his eyes on me for a second before he broke out into a huge grin. "Something substantial." He winked.

Once I changed into a fresh pair of clothes, I followed Jon out into the hallway. We found Cash sleeping in front of Lennox's room with his head resting against the door and his arms wrapped around himself.

"Be right back," Jon whispered, and I watched as he moved to one of the doors to reveal a cabinet. He dug out a blanket and draped it over Cash's body. He reached for my hand as we moved down the hall and the stairs.

"Are you here to make dinner?" Easton asked as we stepped into the kitchen. "We're starving and all the pizza is gone." He jutted his chin at Brett, who only giggled.

"We're perfectly capable of making our own food, Tin Man. Leave the poor men alone. They just woke up." Brett slapped at Easton's arm playfully. *Not exactly, but what they didn't know...* "Ellie's downstairs if you're looking for her. But, boys—" She stopped us before we headed down into the family room. "Just remember, they are only friends." She flashed a smile.

"Oz," I muttered before we took the stairs two at a time, only to skid to a stop to take in the sight before us.

Ellie had her head against Oz's shoulder with his arm around her. They were both sharing a blanket, although Ellie seemed to be hogging most of it, and they were passed out cold. As much as I wanted to be angry about the situation, seeing the so-called Iceman like this was something altogether weird. And kind of nice, if I were being honest.

Oz lifted the hand behind Ellie to flip me the bird. "Take a picture, turds. It will last longer," he snarled as he opened his eyes. "You get a good look? Want to hit me now because I'm friends with your girl?" He tucked the rest of the blanket around Ellie's body before he climbed to his feet.

"It's cool, man," I assured him.

Oz's dark eyes narrowed as he looked between Jon and me. "What's going on? Something feels off about this exchange." He grunted before his lips curled into a smile. "You two fucking in my house?"

Jon squeezed my hand. "You have a problem with that?" he demanded.

Oz waved his hand in the air. "No, I just wanted to know if the maids were going to have to work extra hard to get the semen from your sheets. Don't want them breaking in half or anything. Relax, man, I don't care if you like dick." He clamped a hand over my shoulder. "You hurt either one of them, Pearson, and I'll break your legs," he warned before he went upstairs.

"He hates me," I reminded Jon as we both sat down next to Ellie, one on each side.

"He doesn't," Ellie muttered before she broke into a smile. "He's just being protective."

I snorted. "He can eat me. I would never—" I stopped as Jon leaned across Ellie to kiss me. "What was that for?" I asked.

Ellie sighed softly. "God, you two are so sexy. Did you fuck while I was gone? Did I miss the fun?" She eyed us with desire in her eyes.

"Nothing we can't recreate later, sweetheart," Jon promised as he slid his mouth over hers. "Why don't you go shower while I whip up something to eat? It sounds like we missed dinner, and I fear the natives are getting restless."

Ellie wrapped an arm around me, then one around Jon, bringing us both closer. "Promise, boys?" she asked as we both pressed our lips to hers.

"Promise," we answered.

Chapter Thirty

Jonathan

Spencer and I set out to make dinner while Ellie was showering. He seemed to know his way around a kitchen nearly as well as I did, so it was fun to have someone else to cook with since Jameson had been MIA for a bit. Easton and Brett kept us company at the kitchen table while Spencer dug out the pots and pans so I could figure out what we had in the house that I could throw together.

"I have all the ingredients for meatloaf," I announced, grabbing the ground beef, eggs, and cheese from the fridge. I made a mental note that I needed put together a grocery order and to find out what Ellie and Spencer might like to have in the house.

"Sounds good to me." Cash grinned as he waltzed into the room. "You guys all walked right past me sleeping on the floor but didn't think you should wake me? I have the neck cramp from hell right now." He made a point of bringing his hand up to grip the back of his neck. "Anyone want to volunteer to give me a massage? I'm a cheap date." He wiggled his brows, and everyone groaned.

Brett smacked at his arm. "You could, I don't know, start dating again, Toto." She tilted her head as she raised her brows at her brother.

"Not going to happen, cupcake." He blew off the thought. "Lennox still loves me. She'll come around." He sounded more sure of himself than I would be.

"In your dreams." We all turned to see Lennox standing in the doorway. "We broke up, Cash, and I think it's a great idea. You should start dating, so maybe you could stop stalking me." She looked exhausted.

Cash's nostrils flared. "You'd like that, wouldn't you, Lenny?" He shot out of his chair so fast it might have fallen to the ground if Brett hadn't caught it. "So you would have an excuse to fuck the entire football team. Or maybe you want them, plus the rest of the baseball team, too? Is that it?" A deep growl vibrated from his chest. "I. Love. You." He pointed a finger at her. "You're the one who cheated one me. You're the one who decided what we had wasn't worth holding on to or fixing. I never gave up on you, and I'm not planning on doing that now."

"Easy, Cash." Easton pressed a hand against his friend's chest. "You're going to pop a blood vessel if you keep getting angry like that." He wrapped his arm around Cash's shoulders. "Let's talk." He maneuvered them away from Lennox.

Cash nodded. "Yeah, okay, I can do that, man." He nodded in agreement and let Easton direct him to the family room.

Lennox looked close to tears as she sat down across from Brett. "I don't know what to do," she whispered.

I quickly rinsed my hands off and gave a quick look to Spencer, who nodded as if he could read my mind. "Len," I touched her shoulder. "Do you want to be with him?" When she shrugged, I sat down next to her. "Do you still love him?" I wasn't sure if it was my place to ask.

"Yes," she confessed. "I've always loved him, even when we were in diapers and didn't know what that even meant. I royally fucked this up." She bit her bottom lip as her chin quivered. "He's never going to forgive me."

Brett reached across the table to take Lennox's hand. "I have never seen Cash look at another girl, babe, and you know that. He's the most loyal person I've ever met, and that's saying something." She squeezed Len's hand. "He's hurt, but he doesn't hate you."

Lennox grabbed a napkin from the holder to dab at her eyes. "I made a big mistake instead of telling him the truth. I pushed away the man I loved because I was scared." She dropped her gaze.

"Tell him," I urged. "Tell Cash exactly what you just said. Put him out of his misery. Fix this."

Lennox shook her head. "I couldn't. It's been too long, and I just…"

"You just what, Lenny?" Cash interrupted. "All I want is for you to talk to me. Let me understand what made you do what you did. I'm not asking you to marry me." His shoulders slumped forward as Easton moved around him. "I know." He held up his hand when Easton opened his mouth. "I'll give you your space," Cash told her. "All the space you need until you're ready."

"What if I'm never ready?" Lennox asked as she looked down at the napkin in her hands.

Cash made a strange noise and shook his head. "I can't fucking do this right now." He hurried out of the room, and Brett quickly followed.

"Jesus," Spencer whispered as he opened the oven to put the meatloaf inside. He removed the potholders before he moved to my side. "I love you," he murmured before his lips met mine.

Easton cleared his throat. "Get a room," he teased, but I could see the hurt in his eyes for his friend. I felt it, too, and if that were me? If Ellie and Spencer hadn't decided I was worth it, I might be the one who needed the comforting.

Spencer's fingers grazed my chin. "You want to make something to go with the meatloaf?" His soft voice sent shivers up my spine. "A side salad, maybe?" His brown eyes met mine.

"I think that would work." I nodded. "Maybe some potatoes if we have them." I started to stand up, but Spencer stopped me.

"Relax; I'll take care of it."

Easton drummed his fingers on the countertop before he eased his giant frame into the chair next to me. "You, uh, happy?" His brows dipped as he searched my face. "I mean, they're it for you, right?" His eyes swung over to where Spencer was washing off the potatoes.

"Yes." A smile spread across my face. "Yes, to both of those questions. I hope that you can accept that."

Easton shook his head. "I'm sorry for trying to tell you who you could love." He twisted his lips to the left nervously. "I had no right to do that, and I don't give a shit who you're with it. You know that, right?" I nodded for Easton to continue. "Love is love, Jon, and I'm happy for you." He dropped his gaze to his hands.

"Thank you, boss." I caught the grin on Spencer's face as he placed the potatoes in the microwave. "I appreciate that," I said.

Easton raised his eyes back to me. "We're good?" he asked as Spencer moved back to my side.

"We're more than good," I assured him.

Spencer chuckled. "Does that mean you no longer want to break my face?" he teased.

"Don't make me change my mind, Pearson." Easton grunted before he let out a laugh. "Just think of this as my peace offering, since my boy is in love with you. Plus..." He shrugged. "When you're ready to accept the fact that you're a Knight, we'll handle it." He stood up. "I'm going to check on my woman," he told us before ambling down the hall.

Spencer let out a whistle. "That was not on my list of things I ever thought would happen in my lifetime." He reached for my hand.

"Well..." I moved to press my lips against his neck and inhaled his spicy scent. "Easton can be a good guy when he wants to be." I could get lost in this boy without even thinking twice about it.

Spencer pulled my head up to look at him and cupped my cheeks with his large hands. "I could get used to this." He slid his mouth over mine. "Waking up with you and Ellie by my side. Making you come every night, listening to the sounds you both make when you reach orgasm, the sounds of you sleeping," Spencer nipped at my bottom lip. "The way you both have this damn hold on me that wants me to just keep you safe," he murmured.

"Me, too," I whispered as I caught movement out of the corner of my eye. "Ellie?" I pinned my gaze on her. "Are you all right? You look like you just saw a ghost."

Spencer spun around. "Baby, what's wrong?" He quickly got to his feet.

Tears filled her green eyes. "I called my mother." She dropped to her knees, and the tears fell. "He... he took Luna," she whispered.

"That motherfucker!" I growled.

Spencer grabbed Ellie and pulled her back up onto her feet. "Ellie, it's okay." He pushed the hair from her eyes. "Rick is only doing this to get our attention. He wouldn't hurt her. He knows better than that," he assured her.

I shot out of the kitchen as fast I could, taking the stairs two at a time. "Oz!" I shouted as I slapped my hands against his door. "Easton!" I called his name, too, because every single Knight needed to be in on this.

"What?" Oz growled, his nostrils flaring. "Is the house on fire? Because if it's not—" I shoved my foot in the door before he could close it and ignored the pain that pierced my body. "Move, Jon," he warned.

I pushed back. "Rick took Luna," I told him.

His eyes darkened, and his face grew angrier.

"He can't seriously be that stupid," Oz hissed.

"He's that stupid."

Easton stumbled into the room with Brett, Cash, Lennox, Spencer, and Ellie right behind him. "Is everything all right," he asked as he moved so everyone could get into the room.

"Make yourselves comfortable, Christ," Oz grumbled under his breath.

I spun around. "Tell them, sweetheart. Tell them what you told us."

She clung to Spencer, her eyes filled with fear and sadness, and I realized that she was terrified. Not just because of what Rick had done, but about what he might do.

"He took my daughter." Her voice was hardly a whisper. "He took Luna, and I'm scared if I don't do what he tells me to do, he'll do to her what he did to me." Tears began slipping down her cheeks. "She's four years old, just a baby, and if he..." A sob escaped Ellie's mouth as she buried her face into Spencer's chest.

"What does he want? And don't tell me it's you, because that's not happening," I snarled.

Ellie's sad eyes met mine. "You... you need to let Owen go," she uttered. "If you release him, he said he would give Luna back to me."

"He can fuck right off, because there's no way," Oz barked.

Cash squeezed through the mass of Knights. "Maybe she's right. I mean, what are our plans for your father, man. Are we going to kill him?"

"We haven't gotten that far. Everything has been happening so fast we haven't figured out our actual plan," Easton answered.

"If we let Owen go"—Oz took a step back—"he'll kill us instead. He might act like he won't, that he loves me, blah, blah, blah, but when we're not looking?" He slapped his hands together. "Easton will be the first one he puts a target on, and he'll make sure to leave me for last, so I can see all my friends and family die." Oz blinked back tears, and my stomach dropped. "I can't do that to you." He looked around the crowded room.

Ellie untangled herself from Spencer so she could wrap her arms around Oz, which didn't surprise me. What surprised me more was when he returned the affection.

"I wouldn't want that, Oswald," she assured him.

"Then what are we supposed to do?" Brett asked. "We can't just sit here and let this happen."

"I say we go downstairs, eat dinner, and figure this shit out," Spencer spoke up. "Obviously he didn't go too far, because he's still got church and the town to worry about, and if he disappears like that, people will start to talk."

I nodded in agreement. "I think that's a great idea, sweetheart," I told him.

We all began to move slowly toward the door, and that's when I noticed Lennox holding Cash's hand. When I met her gaze, she simply shook her head at me, but I saw the blush creep up her neck. I had so many questions right now.

Chapter Thirty-One

I stared at the plate of food in front of me but couldn't bring myself to eat anything. Everything seemed to be happening so fast that it was a blur. How could my stepfather be so horrible? Luna was his daughter, yet he would use her to get to me. Why? Why was I so damn important that he had to ruin everything I loved to just to get me back under his thumb?

"Baby." Spencer's deep voice drifted through my ears. "You need to eat. Just a little bit." He dragged my plate closer, but I only shook my head. "You're going to be useless if you pass out from hunger," he teased, but it didn't bring a smile to my face.

Jon's hand found mine under the table. "He's right, sweetheart. Just a few bites, then we'll leave you alone."

I picked up the fork with my free hand and pushed the meat around my plate.

"I can't," I whispered. "I can't eat while she's with him. I keep thinking about all the horrible things he did to me, and I was ten years older than Luna." Tears blinded me. "I will die if he hurts her." I blinked, and the tears began to fall down my cheeks.

"Ellie," Lennox said loudly. "You're only letting him win if you don't take care of yourself. We already have people trying to find him, and—" Her eyes rolled to Oz. "I have it on good authority that someone has their eyes on Heidi, and she might just lead us to where we need to go. But we can't leave unless you eat." Her look pleaded me to do what they asked, but it looked like there was something else hidden behind her dark browns.

I stabbed my dinner with the fork and brought it to my mouth. "Is it true?" I locked my gaze on Oswald as I took the tiniest of bites.

"Oi, it's true." He nodded. "Thanks to some of the Kingston footballers who decided they wanted to help us." Oz smirked as he wiped his mouth with his napkin. "Think they're a little jealous we're using the Weston boys, so they were more than happy to jump in." He got up and carried his plate to the sink. "Eat, woman, or you're staying here," he grumbled.

I took another small bite. I should feel safe right now, but I didn't. I had my guys flanking my side, my best friend making sure we had all the help we needed, and the support of the Weston and Kingston footballers. So why did I feel so alone?

"If I eat any more, I'm going to throw up." I pushed the plate away.

Jon met Spencer's stare. "It's fine," he murmured.

"It's more than enough," Spencer added. "We'll bring along some snacks in case you change your mind about food." He and Jon squeezed me between them. "Everything is going to work out fine, baby girl. Just you wait and see. The Knights know exactly what they're doing."

It made me wonder just how many times they'd had to hurt, maim, or kill someone to fix whatever their families had messed up in the past.

Easton grabbed his half-empty plate as well as Brett's before he climbed to his feet.

"Everyone finish up, because we have a lot of work ahead of us," he announced. "First, we're going to stop to pay Owen a little visit, and then we're going check on our new friend Heidi. And after that?" He leveled his serious face on me. "We're getting your daughter back." He paused for a moment. "Has anyone been able to get a hold of Jameson? He's not answering my calls or texts. I even tried Josie, but she must have a new number." Easton scanned the room.

"He said he was on his way," Jonathan answered. "I told him we needed him STAT, but that was nearly an hour ago." He chewed nervously on his bottom lip. "Maybe we should swing by the Silver place first?"

Easton moved his head in agreement. "Sounds perfect." He swung his arm around Brett's shoulders. "Make sure you change into some warm and comfortable clothes. It's going to be another long night."

***

I sat in the back of the SUV with Spencer and Jon while Oz drove. Lennox sat in the passenger's seat, staring out the window. I had questions for her, mostly about Cash, but also about what she had hinted at over dinner and what she hadn't said aloud. We followed the other SUV that carried Easton, Brett, and Cash as we made our way to Josie's place, which was black as night when we pulled up.

"Weird," Oz muttered as he opened the door to climb out of the vehicle. "You and you." He pointed at my boys. "Girls stay here."

Jon kissed my left check. "Lock the door, sweetheart."

"I second that." Spencer's lips brushed the other side as Brett climbed into the front seat next to Lennox.

I watched as they both disappeared toward the house with the rest of the Knights and turned my attention to girls in the front.

"Is this bad?" I asked. "I mean, you know Josie and Jameson better than I do, but is this like him?" I had no idea what to think.

"There was a time when Jam was hiding a few things." Brett answered first. "He was seeing Josie behind Easton's back while they were still contracted to one another. Not that East was faithful to my sister, but Jameson loved her. He let her drug me. But since then, he's tried desperately to make up for it. I forgave both of them because I know that love can make you do crazy shit.

"Josie wasn't sure what she wanted until the explosion that made her look the way she does now. She realized that Easton wasn't the right one for her, since he wasn't going to give me up, and she changed. She goes to therapy, we talk—or rather, I do all the talking—but it's getting easier." She flashed a quick smile. "I want a relationship with my sister, and she wants one, too."

"But this isn't like either of them. Jameson would at least respond to Easton unless something was seriously wrong," Lennox said.

I opened my mouth to ask Lennox about what she meant at dinner when all of a sudden a giant floodlight came on outside where we sat parked. A gasp escaped my mouth as fear rolled through my body. I needed to be strong, but right now I felt anything but.

Brett reached back to touch my shoulder. "Relax, the guys are inside." She jutted her chin toward the house. "See?"

The Silver house was now lit up like a Christmas tree.

"I'm not usually this jumpy. I'm just..."

"Scared?" Lennox finished for more. "It is fucking scary as hell, Ellie, but you've already been through so much." Her brows dipped. "I finally told Cash the reason why I did what I did to him. Why I left when everything started to fall apart between us."

Brett's jaw dropped. "You haven't even told me that." She sounded hurt.

A loud commotion brought the attention away from Lennox. The guys were suddenly running out of the house, waving their arms in the air. "Shit." I started to open the door, but someone slammed it shut.

Jonathan stood outside the SUV, but I couldn't hear what he was saying. Was this vehicle soundproof? He was gesturing at the house, as he spoke to his brother, and both of them looked white as a ghost.

"Does anyone have any clue what might be wrong?" Brett pressed her lips together. "I should text Josie again. Maybe she'll respond this time." She reached for her phone as Easton yanked the front door open.

"Out," he growled at his fiancé. "We have to get the fuck out of here."

Brett looked confused. "Easton, what's going on?" It took him one second to wrap an arm around Brett's waist so that he could haul her out of the vehicle. I watched as her legs flared around. "Put me down!" she screamed.

Oz took her place as the right-side door opened. Spencer climbed in, looking pale as a ghost.

"What happened?" Lennox spun around. "Someone has to tell us what happened because this is bullshit!"

"Len." Oz shook his head as their eyes met. "It's bad."

The sound of Jameson crying out caused me to jump, since Oz's door was still open.

"Is Josie... Is she okay?" I asked.

Jonathan looked like he was feeling everything that his twin was feeling, and it made my heart break for him. He tried to pull Jameson into a hug, only to have him shove him away.

"You don't know." Jameson shook his head. "She's my world, bro, and I can't be without her. You have to understand what that feels like."

Jon took a step forward. "She's sick, Jam. She needs help. If you really love her, then let us do this for her." He wrapped his arms around his brother and pulled him into a hug while Jameson let his arms hang to his side.

Jameson's face crumpled as another car sped up the driveway, just as it looked like he might give into Jonathan's embrace. Instead, he shoved at his chest and dashed away to greet whoever had arrived. Jon chased right after him.

"Dorothy, you can't go in there!" Easton shouted as he sprinted after Brett, who was now headed toward the house.

I met Lennox's wide eyes. "What the fuck?" I mouthed before I turned to Spencer. "Tell me." I poked his arm with my finger.

"Josie slit her wrists tonight," he answered.

Lennox jumped from the car before anyone had a chance to stop her, leaving the door wide open. She might have made it if Cash hadn't caught her and dragged her back kicking and screaming.

"Let go of me!" she hissed. "Josie is my friend!" She shook her head. "I hate you, Cash." She spun around to glare at her cousin. "You, too, asshole." Lennox shoved at Oz who only shook his head.

"Say all the terrible things you want, Lenny, but you are not going into that damn house." His nostrils flared. "Do you understand me?" His face clouded over with anger. "What do you think you're going to do when you go in there, huh, boo? You think you're going to waltz in there and save her? I got some news for you. That girl is way beyond saving," he snarled.

I felt all the blood drain from my face as heard Spencer's words repeatedly in my brain. *Josie slit her wrists.* Was Josie dead? Was she bleeding out inside that house right now? Why hadn't Jameson called someone, anyone, to help her? I gripped Spencer's hand tightly as I tried not to freak out.

"Doc's taking care of it," Oz answered like he was reading my mind.

I met his eyes. "Who?" I asked as I noticed an ambulance pulling up without the lights or sirens.

"Our doctor." Cash pointed a finger at Lennox. "Stay in the fucking truck, Len," he warned before he stomped over to the ambulance just as the back doors open and two EMTs jumped out.

Lennox quietly shut her door before she locked it and slumped down in her seat.

"Fucking asshole," she muttered, causing Oz to snicker. "You, too, Oz. I've had my fill with you Knights. As soon we graduate, I'm outta here," she promised.

Oz leaned forward so that his face was right next to hers. "You try that, Len." He made a clucking noise with his tongue. "See how far you get before he drags you back here by your hair." He bared his teeth before he stood back up. "I'll be back," he promised before he shut the door.

"Spence," I whispered. "Is she dead?"

"No, baby, she's alive." However, something in his voice caused the hairs on the back of my neck to stand up. Spencer pressed his lips to my hair. "She's going to be all right."

The three of us watched in horror as the EMTs who had gone into the house came back out carrying a lifeless Josie on a stretcher while Brett followed behind them with her head down. Easton was right next to her, trying to calm her down, but she looked pretty shaken up. Brett slapped his hands away when he tried to touch her, then she fell into his arms.

My heart stuttered in my chest as Jameson dropped to his knees, his mouth open and tears streaming down his face before Jon helped him back up again. This time, his brother didn't fight him when he wrapped an arm around his shoulders.

"God almighty," Lennox whispered.

It was all over in seconds, then Brett and Jameson climbed into the back with Josie while the other three took a few minutes to talk to Doc. Then Easton and Cash hurried off to their truck while Oz and Jonathan jogged back to ours.

"Anyone want to go to the hospital?" He turned to look at Spencer and me before his gaze landed on Lennox.

She nodded. "I do."

"Me, too," I answered. I knew Rick wasn't going to hurt our daughter, at least not without an audience. "Go, Oswald, this is important." I waved my hands at him before he started the SUV and hauled ass after the ambulance.

Chapter Thirty-Two

I had never seen my brother this upset before. *Ever.* He was inconsolable as we were told that we couldn't see Josie, not even Brett or Cash were allowed, and he was damn near impossible when I tried to calm him down. I had only seen him cry three times in our lifetime together, and this was the third.

"I need... Jon, I need to be with her. She's scared. She's going to wake up confused and think that I left her when I told her I wouldn't." Jameson's voice was hoarse. "I promised Josie I wouldn't leave her side, and now I look like a damn liar." He wiped at the wetness on his face.

I squeezed his bicep. "Josie isn't well, Jam." I hated to be the one to tell him that, although I'm sure Jameson already figured it out, but he had to calm down before he made himself sick; and then where he be?

"I know!" he cried as fresh tears spilled from his eyes. "I've been telling her for days now that she needs to go back to therapy because this isn't working. Someone who isn't me or her friends needs to talk to her and make her see she's not the horrible monster that she believes she is."

Jameson grabbed a tissue from the box next him and blew his nose. "Josie promised me. She swore on her father's grave that she would, but..." His voice trailed off.

Brett moved over to squat down next to Jameson's feet. "Talk to me, Lion." Her thick, rich voice was soothing as she spoke. "Josie isn't well." Her blue eyes were wide. "You love her, right?" When Jameson nodded, Brett continued. "She needs to get better; I don't think that is going to happen with just you or me or Cash." She placed both hands on his knees.

"What do you mean? Are you saying we're not good enough?" His eyes shifted around nervously. "I would never hurt her, Brett. I love her!" Jameson slapped a hand over his heart. "She's everything to me, and I need her as much as she needs me."

Brett's eyes began to water. "Jam, all I'm saying is that she needs help—professional help—that none of us are qualified to give her." She bit down on her bottom lip.

"Brett's right, bro," I said.

Jameson shook his head. "I can't just leave her here." He pressed his lips together. "I told her I would never do that. That I wouldn't put her in a hospital because it would kill her."

"If you don't, she's going to kill herself for real next time." Easton's hand landed on his shoulder. "Brett isn't saying that you just abandon your girl. She's just telling you that she needs help we simply can't provide. You can visit, you can talk on the phone, and when she's ready to come home?" His green eyes shifted to his girlfriend. "She can come stay with us."

Jameson swung around. "You mean that?" He sounded like he was five again, the time our father told us we could get a puppy for our birthday. A promise he never kept.

"Absolutely," Oz agreed. "She's more than welcome, and there is more than enough room. Not that she'll need her own one, of course, since she'll be with you, but the option is always there."

Jameson grabbed my hand. "You... you think I should do this, Jon?" He sniffed as he looked at me for approval. It felt so weird to be on this end when I was always the one looking up to him.

"Tell Josie I did it." Brett stood up. "Tell her I was the one who had her admitted if you're afraid she'll push you away."

Jameson shook his head. "Brett, no. I can't do that to you."

"Lion, please," she insisted.

"Thank you," he whispered.

Brett moved around the chairs to get to Easton, and I pinned my eyes on my guy, who was currently holding *our* girl. Spencer looked unsure of himself, but it was the look on Ellie's face that scared me most of all. She looked terrified. I started to climb from my chair, but Jameson stopped me.

"I'm sorry I haven't been around for you like I should have been lately." He glanced over at Spencer and Ellie. "You're all right? They're taking care of you?" His eyes filled with guilt.

I smiled. "I'm great, Jam. I love them," I admitted. "They are exactly what was missing from my life." Truer words had never been spoken, or at least not by me.

Jameson's lips tilted up. "I'm glad, bro, because you deserve it. You're the better half of us, and don't you ever forget it." He winced as spoke.

"I love you," I assured him. "No matter what, after everything, you've always looked out for me. I don't know if I've ever thanked you for that, but I am now."

"I'll always have your back, little brother," Jameson teased. "Go sit with your girl and your man. They look a little nervous." He tried to laugh, but it came out all wrong.

I squeezed his wrist. "You're sure?"

"Go on. I'll be fine." He was lying, but I didn't want to wait to talk to them anymore.

When I stood up, so did my brother, and he hugged me tight against his chest. When I met his eyes, the brown ones that were identical to mine, I saw the horror he had witnessed behind them. Then his mask was back.

"I love you, too, Jonny. Now go." Jameson slapped my arm.

My feet felt like they weighed a million pounds as I moved over to Spencer and Ellie, who both looked absolutely relieved to see me.

"Hey," I smiled down at them.

The sound of yelling caused me to spin back around to find Jameson, Brett, and Cash all screaming at top volume at a doctor who looked like she wanted to be anywhere but here.

"You're all going to need to calm down," the doctor ordered. "Or we'll have you removed from the building."

Brett's mouth clamped shut as she looked at Easton and Cash for help.

Cash stepped forward first with his all-American boy smile on his face. "What do we have to do, to, uh, get in to see our sister?" His voice was flirty. "We really just want to talk to her and make sure she's all right, Doctor"—he picked up the nametag she wore—"Moore."

I fully expected us to be booted, but instead, Dr. Moore's cheeks flushed pink, and she ducked her eyes away. "If you hadn't freaked out on me like that, I would be able to tell you. The doctor has Miss Silver sedated at the moment, so if you go in there—and that's a big *if*—she's going to be sleeping. We do have more questions about what happened, since she was pretty out of it when they brought her in."

"I can tell you," Jameson offered. "Josie's my wife."

My jaw dropped. Did he just say wife?

"Jam, that's cute." Cash rolled his eyes. "But we're her relatives... I'm sorry, but why do you look so serious?"

Jameson nodded. "We, uh, we sort of eloped." He gave me a sheepish smile.

That brought on a completely new round of screaming and yelling. I could see by the look on the good doctor's face that she wanted the floor to open up and swallow her whole. Brett and Cash were snapping at Jameson, pointing fingers at him, trying to get answers while everyone else in the hospital stared.

"SHUT THE FUCK UP!" Easton cried loud enough to wake the dead. Everyone immediately stopped talking. "Jesus Christ, that's better. I can't think with all this commotion going on," he growled. "Is it true?" He narrowed his eyes at my twin. "You're actually married?"

Jam nodded. "I can show you the marriage license." He started to open his phone, but Easton pushed his hand away.

"No, man, you're good," he assured him. "You're the husband, so you get to see Josie first." He glanced at his fiancé. "Babe, you're closer to Josie than Cash, so you can go next, and then"—Easton patted his friend's shoulder—"you go."

Brett touched Cash's hand. "Can we go together? We're her siblings. She would want that." She squeezed his fingers.

Dr. Moore nodded. "I'll see what I can do, but any more outbursts like that and you're all going to permanently banned from here. I don't care who you are or how much money your families have donated to the hospital." She looked exhausted as she glared at us. "You come with me," she instructed Jameson.

***

By the time we made it back to the house, it was nearly time to go to school. We all agreed that we should skip today, and maybe the next few days, since we had so much going on.

Jameson had stayed back at the hospital with his wife—that sounded strange to say—and even though Brett had wanted to do the same, Easton managed to convince her to come home. Ellie and Spencer were unusually quiet on the way, and it wasn't until we were all sitting in my room that I finally had a chance to talk to them.

"Spill it," I demanded as I stripped off my clothes to put on some sweats and a shirt. "You two have hardly said one single word since the hospital, and that is unlike you. If you want out? I need to know." I felt my pulse quicken at the thought.

Ellie shook her head. "Jonny, we're not going anywhere. I'm just in shock." She swallowed nervously. "Everything has happened so fast, and I'm just scared."

"That about sums it up." Spencer nodded. "You have to understand that this is all new to me, to Ellie, and we love you—hell, I even like the Knights a bit—but we've just had so much shit dumped on us these past couple of days." He placed his hand on Ellie's thigh and squeezed.

"I get that." I licked my lips. "It's fucking crazy, right? You find out you're a Knight, and then we find out that I'm contracted to Ellie, and all of this just feels like too much." I dropped to my knees. "I love you. I love you both, and I want you in my life. I don't think I can do any of this without you," I whispered as I buried my face in my hands.

"It's okay." Ellie's voice was music in my ears as her arms wrapped around me. "We're not going anywhere," she promised.

I looked up to find Spencer nodding his head as he crouched down to our level.

"Hey." He cupped my face with his big, warm hands. "We're not leaving you, sweetness," he reassured me. "I don't know why you keep thinking that, but we're here. You're stuck with us."

Ellie flashed a brief smile. "We love you, Jonathan." She pressed her lips to my forehead. "I'm scared as hell about my daughter, Rick, and Josie, but I would never put that over my feelings for you." She glanced up at Spencer, who nodded in agreement.

"I'm sorry," I whispered.

"Don't do that." Spencer moved to sit down on the floor as I did the same. Ellie moved to my right, so that I was in between them. "You never have to say you're sorry because of something you can't control or something you didn't do. Do you understand?" he growled.

"Okay," I answered.

Ellie's hand found mine. "We should try to get some rest. From what Easton said earlier, I think we're going to need it."

Spencer grabbed my other hand. "I think that's a great idea. No funny business, just sleep." He tugged my arm as he stood back up.

My lips curled into a half smile. "No funny business?" I teased.

"You up for some funny business, Jonny?" Ellie's hands slid up my legs before she yanked down my sweats. "Mmmm, looks like it to me," she purred softly.

I couldn't stop the moan that escaped my throat as Ellie's mouth found my cock. "Fuck." I couldn't even think straight now, but at least it shut out my overthinking for the time being.

"Let's get you out of this shirt, too." Spencer helped me remove my top before his lips found mine.

Then we lost ourselves in each other.

Chapter Thirty-Three

We probably didn't get as much rest as we needed, but the sex was more than enough to relax me, and by the looks of Ellie and Jon, they weren't too bad off themselves. I woke first to find them both cuddled against me, and it made my heart swell with happiness. Despite everything, we were a team.

I hated to leave them since it was more than comfortable, but I wanted to try to talk with the other Knights before they woke. I managed to not wake either one of them, showered, and dressed quickly before I headed downstairs.

"You're up early." Oz grunted from the kitchen table. He had a half-empty cup of coffee in front of him. "Sit." He kicked the chair next to him out with his foot.

I eased myself down into the chair as Oz had instructed. "Everyone else still sleeping?" I asked.

Oz shrugged. "Depends on who you're asking about. Cash and East went for a run to work out some stress. Len and Brett are still in bed." He leaned closer. "Assuming that's where Eleanor and Jon are?" He chuckled as I got back to my feet. "Did I scare you off already, Pearson?" His voice sounded like he was teasing, but I knew better.

"No." I grabbed a mug from the cabinet to pour myself some coffee. I took a sip and let it run through my veins. "I needed this first," I answered before I sat back down. "What's the deal with my father?" I raised an eyebrow as Oz sat back.

He folded his arms across his chest. "What do you mean?" he snarled. "You think he's up to something?"

"I know he is."

Oz smirked. "You're almost worse than I am," he pointed out. "You just don't have your old man tied up in his cabin until you decide what to do with him." He reached for his cup.

I snorted. "We all can't be a stone-cold asshole, man." I watched the way his lip turned up at the corner.

"Touché." Oz raised his mug. "Your father, do you think that he knew about Eleanor, about the contract, and that was why he was more than happy to let her come stay with you? For the two of you to be together so she wouldn't end up with Jon?"

"I never thought of that." I shook my head. "He always treated her like she was the daughter he never had. He never raised his voice and made sure that Ellie always had everything she wanted. Told her to ask if she needed anything and..." A quick picture flashed through my brain.

Oz jumped from his chair. "What, what is it?" He wrapped his fingers tightly around my arm. "Talk to me, Spencer, because right now you look like you just saw a ghost," he hissed.

"I just remembered something that happened right before Eleanor moved into our house." I blinked in confusion.

"Senior, you can't be serious." Uncle Owen threw his head back, laughing. "You honestly think we're going to let Eleanor live in this house? With you? Let you raise her like she was your damn kid?" he roared.

"It's not like I would put my hands on her." Senior scoffed.

Rick's hands curled into fists, but he kept them at his side. "She's mine," he hissed.

"She's your stepdaughter!" Senior reminded them. "She's just a child, and she needs someone to protect her." He took a step back. "What have you done?" His brows shot up so fast they looked like they might fly from his head. "You haven't touched her, have you?" Senior's nostrils flared.

Owen slowly turned to look at Rick. "You swore that you wouldn't," he reminded the pastor. "You said she was safe in your home until the time was right, and you promised you wouldn't do anything to hurt her because you loved her mother." He grabbed him by the collar. "What did you do?"

I stared at Oz as the anger rolled from his body. "That memory just came out of nowhere. They caught me right after that, so I didn't hear anything else," I admitted.

"They knew." Oz stared at me with wide eyes. "They fucking knew Rick raped her, impregnated her, and they didn't do a thing to stop it." He moved to grab his coat from the rack by the door.

"Where are you going?" I shouldn't have asked because I already knew the answer to that question.

A wicked smile spread across Oz's face. "I'm going to kill my father," he announced. "And then? Then I'm going to kill yours." He tilted his head as he stared at me with fire in his eyes. "What, you want to come with me?"

"Yes." I nodded. "She's my girlfriend, and I've loved her for years. If those bastards knew what Rick was doing, or had done, and didn't do anything to stop it?" I stood up. "Then I

want to be there when the light disappears from their eyes."
I popped my jaw.

***

Oz didn't say much on the way to the cabin, just kept his hands mostly at ten and two while he pushed his Tesla to go faster. I might have been worried if I didn't know why he was doing this.

Because of Ellie.

We shared a common interest, loved her in our own way, and Oz simply wanted to take care of the problem before it got out of hand.

"You, uh, mind if I turn on the radio?" His deep voice caught me off guard, and I turned to look at him in the dark. Oz's jaw was set in a firm, hard line that looked almost painful. "What?" He glanced at me for a second. "You checking me out or something? Because I'm not like that."

I raised my hand. "Dude, relax." I chuckled. Why was it the straight alpha guys always thought I wanted a piece of their dick? Not that Oz wasn't hot, but he was so not my type. Too many daddy issues. "Put on whatever you want. It's your car." I motioned to the giant screen of controls.

Oz grunted something, then pressed a few buttons on the tablet. Classic rock began to filter from the speakers.

"Sorry," he muttered.

"For?"

"Being an asshole and thinking you might be checking me out."

I smirked. "Man, you know that I've never even looked at you in that light. No offense." I watched the way his eyes narrowed. "Now you're offended that I don't find you attractive?" I snorted with laughter when Oz gave me the middle finger. "Noted," I told him.

Oz moved his hand back to the wheel without saying another word. He was absolutely *not* my type, but if he had ever made a move? I would have had a go at him. He would probably scar me for life, but that would be fine by me.

"What's so funny?" He interrupted my thoughts again.

"What?" I hadn't realized I had made any noise.

Oz made a sound that was between a groan and a sigh. "You were laughing. I was wondering what was so damn funny?" He slowed the car down as we approached the driveway to the cabin. "I've been with a guy before," he blurted out.

I stared at Oz as if he'd just told me he had two dicks. "I'm sorry. What did you say?" I asked.

"What, like you're special because you like guys and girls?" Oz smirked. "It's not a big deal. It was a onetime thing," he assured me as he parked his Tesla. "Just thought you might like to know."

I blinked a couple of times, trying to make sure I'd heard Oz right. "You're trying to bond with me now? Because you had sex with a dude? Is that what this?"

Oz threw his head back and let out a belly laugh before he answered. "No, Pearson, that's not what I'm doing. I was drunk. I was with a chick, and the guy was into it, too. I sucked him off while I fucked the girl. End of story. You tell anyone about it, and I'll deny this entire conversation ever happened. Let's talk about something else." He unbuckled his seatbelt.

I had so many questions right now. This was not the way I had thought this night was going to go.

"What's the deal with Diana?"

Oz shook his head. "She's nothing but a hole for me. Trust me when I tell you that cunt will get what she deserves," he assured me. "She's a bit clingy, but that's the fun in this whole thing. She's already texted me ten times today, and I haven't responded once. Left her on read."

"That's a bit—I don't know—rude, isn't it?" I wasn't Diana's biggest fan, but I wouldn't string her along like he was.

Oz eased the car into park before he twisted his large form toward mine. "You suddenly grow a conscience?" His dark eyes searched my face to the point where it made me uncomfortable.

"No," I assured him, but it still bothered me.

Diana was a person, too, and maybe we were being a little hard on her.

"Good." Oz opened the door of the silver vehicle. "Let's go get this over with now that you're done asking me about Diana, who, by the way, was more than happy to suck my cock before I fucked her. She's using me probably as much as I'm using her. Thinking she can hang with the Knights now or something, which is never going to fucking happen."

He climbed from the silver Tesla, and I had no choice but to follow behind him. His long legs moved fast, and it almost felt like he was running toward the cabin.

"Look, Pearson." Oz suddenly spun around to point a finger at me. "I have a few things I need to clear up with my father, things that happened to me when I was younger," he warned. "I don't want you to be surprised when you hear what I'm going to say. Just so you're prepared."

Something in his face made me pause for a moment. What had happened to Oz that he was telling me? Clearly, we both had daddy issues. I was learning so much about the Knights.

"Do what you have to," I told him.

"Oh, believe me, I plan to." Oz unlocked the door and flipped on the light. "We're both going to get answers, then shut him up." He left footprints of snow as he walked across the floor. "Guess this place will be mine, too, just like the house." He glanced over his shoulder at me. "Your dad ever been here?"

I twisted my lips to the side. "Not that I'm aware of, but he kept that shit to himself most of the time after I caught them. Sure, Uncle Owen came by the house, but there was never any talk of whatever I walked in on that night."

I listened to the sound of the basement door being opened just as a thought came to me. "You're sure we shouldn't wait? Maybe get the other guys here before you go all cray on him?"

"You think I needed Easton's permission to kill my own father?" Oz shot back. "Do you think he ever asked me before he went and saved Brett from Chad? Or asked if it was okay to kill him? Because he never did." He pulled the door open.

I didn't say another word as we moved down the stairs, into the damp and very cold basement. Oz flipped on the light, and Owen glared at us with hatred in his eyes. His lips turned into a sneer when he spotted me.

"What's this?" Owen struggled to square his shoulders. "You hanging out with him now?"

Oz pulled the Glock from his back pocket. "You have a problem with your brother's kid, Dad?" He released the safety. "The cousin I never knew about until a few days ago because you kept yet one more fucking secret from me."

"You've been talking, boy?" Owen glared at me with dark eyes. "Telling secrets you have no business telling?" He pulled on the chains around his wrists. "That bitch had it coming."

Oz slapped the gun against his cheek. "Speak of her like that again, and we'll have a bigger fucking problem."

Owen only laughed, a deep, horrifying sound that sent chills up and down my spine. "What, you two tag-teaming her now?" He taunted his son.

The sound of the gun hitting his father's other cheek echoed throughout the basement. "What did I say about Eleanor, old man?" He shot a look at me. "Ellie is my friend, nothing more."

"Right, like she can keep her legs closed."

I lunged forward only to have Oz stop me. "Watch your mouth," I warned him.

"I don't have to listen to you, Junior. Your father isn't here to protect you, and—"

The sound of the gun going off just missing his ear caused him to rear back.

"The fuck, Oswald! You nearly shot me!" Owen exclaimed with wide, frightened eyes.

Oz moved so that his nose was pressed right against Owen's, the gun pointed at his chest. "Next time, I won't miss," he promised. "What do you know about Rick and Ellie's father?" he demanded.

A sneer appeared on Owen's face. "You know, don't you?" He pursed his lips. "He knocked her up because he didn't want her to marry Jonathan, but I think you figured that out already." He leveled his gaze on me. "If you, Junior, hadn't stepped in his way, who knows what else might have happened?" He chuckled softly. "If you had read the entire contract, there's a clause that states if the female is impregnated before said marriage occurs"—Owen dragged his eyes to the ceiling and back to me again—"it becomes null and void. It's written on every one of them. Most of the time it can be ignored, but not when they're as young as she was."

"Fuck you!" I blurted out as he continued to watch me. "Where is he? He took Luna." I didn't care about their damn contracts or revenge anymore. I wanted to save Ellie's daughter before something horrible happened.

When Owen continued to just stare at me with a crazy look on his face, Oz moved close enough to press the gun to the side of his father's temple. "Answer the damn question, *Dad,*" he growled.

"You boys, always so dramatic," he scolded, but a look of fear passed through his eyes. "Fine, fine. Pastor Rick has a room in the basement of the church. He turned it into some sort of safe place and odds are, that's where she is." Owen raised his chin. "Good luck, fellas, because you'll never save her in time."

The roar of the gunshot caused me to jump in surprise, and it drowned out the rest of what Owen might have said. I stared in horror as I realized Oz had shot his father right in the stomach.

"That," Oz growled. "Is for all the times you let your friends have their way with me while you pretended not to notice." His voice sounded a million miles away as the gun rang out again, and I turned away so I couldn't see where it hit. "That is for ruining my life." I felt him grip my wrist. "And this, this is for mom." Oz emptied the rest of the bullets into his father, his fingers digging into my skin.

When the gunshots stopped, I turned to find blood, brain matter, and... I wasn't exactly sure what that was... splattered all over the floor and wall behind Owen. When I glanced at Oz, I noticed he was drenched in it from head to toe. Bile filled my throat, and I wrenched my hand away from his.

"Fucking prick, that's the last time you hurt me," Oz muttered, and for a second, I wondered if he realized I was in the room. "Dude, if you're going to throw up, use that bucket over here." He pointed to the right.

I grabbed the orange *Home Depot* bucket, but nothing but dry heaves shook my body. "Jesus Christ." I wiped at my mouth. "You actually killed him." I blinked at Oz in surprise.

Oz nodded. "That's what I came here for, Pearson. After everything he did to me, to the Knights, my mother... I should have done it sooner, but whatever." He wiped the blood from his lips with the back of his hand, leaving a smeared mess behind. "Gotta say, that felt better than I thought."

He reached into his pocket to pull out his cell. "Guess I better call in reinforcements, because we have a big mess to clean up."

Chapter Thirty-Four

Jonathan

The cabin was eerily quiet as I walked down the stairs to the basement behind Easton, Cash, and Tate. My brother was still at the hospital with his wife, and we had somehow convinced the other three girls to stay back at the house. I think Ellie was more than happy to not make this trip, although she was still worried about her daughter. Neither one of us had realized that Spencer was missing until I climbed from the bed.

The scene in front of me looked like something out of a horror movie. Blood and what I could only assume was brain matter were splattered on the wall behind where Owen had been. My eyes moved around the room, and I saw his body face down on the floor. Oz called Easton and told him that the rest of the Knights were needed at the cabin immediately, and now we knew why.

"What the fuck, Ice." Easton ran his hand through his dark hair. "Really?"

Oz shrugged. "The guy was a piece of shit. He had it coming."

He acted as if he hadn't just killed his own father, and why was Spencer with him? I thought they hated one another.

As if he could read my mind, Spencer took a step toward me. "You look like you have questions," he murmured. "I can explain." He dropped his eyes to his feet.

"Hey." I tucked a finger under Spencer's chin to force him to look at me. "You think I'm mad?" I tilted my head as he brought a hand to my wrist.

Spencer nodded. "You look mad, sweetness." He swallowed hard, and I watched his Adam's apple bob with the movement.

"Not mad," I told him before I slid my lips over his. "More like worried, you know?" I glanced over to where Easton stood, whispering in hushed tones with Cash, Oz, and Tate. "Come on." I jerked my chin toward the other guys. "Let's find out the plan."

"The plan"—Easton spoke up—"is to clean up this damn mess Oz made. Has anyone heard anything about Heidi?" His brows dipped when no one answered. "Don't all speak at once or anything."

Cash raised his hand. "I texted the guys we have watching her, but she hasn't left the house. I wonder if she knows that we're onto her."

"How?" Oz demanded.

I noticed he had cleaned the blood off his face, but now it was smeared over his chin, and it made him look more evil than usual.

Cash shook his head. "I don't know, but..." He stopped when we heard the sound of tires outside and the slamming of a car door. That sent us flying up the stairs to intercept whoever was here before they came down into the basement. Imagine our surprise when Lennox burst through the front door.

"They're gone!" she exclaimed as she brushed her dark hair from her eyes. "I was taking a shower, and we were going to go grab something to eat, but they were both gone by the time I was finished. It's all my fault that Brett and Ellie snuck out on me!" A sob caught in her throat as she dropped to the floor.

Cash rushed to her side. "It's okay," he assured her as he glanced around the room. "Do you know where they went?" He cupped her face in his hands.

"Brett texted me that they thought they knew where Rick was. Where he was hiding with Luna."

"Fuck!" Easton exclaimed. "I swear to God, if something happens to Brett, I will make that son of a bitch suffer." He spun around to glare at Oz. "You are cleaning up this mess. Tate can stay here and help." He pointed a finger at him. "You killed the old man without thinking about the repercussions, so you're going to be the one to take care of it."

He pushed past Spencer on his way to the porch, then let out a whistle and raised his hand to snap his fingers. "The rest of you are with me. That includes you, too, Pearson. Ice dug his own grave with this one." Easton stomped out the door.

"Why do I have to help? I didn't fucking kill anyone," Tate grumbled.

"Because I fucking said so, Bernard, that's why," Easton called from upstairs.

I caught the brief look between Spencer and Oz before he turned to me. "You have something you need to tell me?" I raised an eyebrow at him, but he just shook his head.

Cash helped Lennox to her feet, but when he tried to wrap an arm around her shoulders, she shrugged him off.

"Stop it, Cash," she hissed.

"I wasn't doing anything."

"You were, and it's not happening. I'm fine now." She yanked her hair up into a ponytail, pulled the elastic off her wrist, and twisted it tightly. "I don't need anyone to take care of me," Lennox reminded him.

Cash's face fell before he stood up to his full height and squared his shoulders. "You know what, Len?" He raised his lip into a snarl. "I'm done." He waved his hands. "Done with you treating me like I did something wrong, like I'm not good enough for you."

"Fine." She rolled her eyes.

"Fine," Cash repeated before he followed Easton.

I touched Spencer's shoulder. "We should, uh, probably get moving." His eyes were wide, and he didn't say anything as he moved to leave the room. Nor did he say a word as we walked out into the cold air to find Easton sitting in the truck with the music so loud it might blow out the windows. Cash climbed into the passenger's seat, and Lennox climbed in next to me but kept her gaze on her hands, which she placed in her lap.

"Finally. Christ, I thought I was going to have to come get you," he shouted as he turned down the radio. "Put on your seatbelts because there is no way I'm obeying the speed limit."

***

Easton wasn't kidding about speeding. It felt like he was trying to win the Daytona 500. He didn't even bother to slow down for stop signs, corners, or lights as he headed toward the church. The entire time, Spencer had my hand in a death grip that hurt enough for me to finally pry his fingers off me.

"You're fucking petrified," I whispered as he met my eyes. His dark browns were wide with fright. "Baby, it's okay. You're with me," I assured him.

"He killed him. He just put the gun to his head and pulled the trigger like it was nothing." His eyes filled with tears before they spilled out.

"Shit, is he freaking out?" Cash asked from the front. "East, slow down," he added.

Easton gripped the wheel tighter. "I'm not slowing down, and I'm sure those two don't want me to either. Our girls are in danger, man, and I will never forgive myself if something happens to them." He glanced at me in the rearview mirror.

"Baby." I ran the back of my hand over Spencer's cheek to bring his attention back to me. "You're safe," I reminded him.

Spencer blinked at me. "Jonathan." The way he said my name caused goosebumps to break out all over my skin.

I opened my mouth to respond just as Easton pulled the SUV into the church parking lot, slammed on the brakes, and put the vehicle into park. I leaned forward to slide my lips over Spencer's just as Easton and Cash jumped from the truck.

"Let's go."

I followed my friends into the dark night with Spencer behind me.

"The basement," Lennox announced, causing Spencer to jump.

Easton moved fast, but stealthy, toward the church, causing the rest of us to run to keep up with him. He turned to look at us, drawing his finger to lips to make sure we kept quiet. Then we moved up the steps, opened the doors, and stepped into the empty church.

A strange feeling crept over me as I glanced down the aisle and let my eyes wander over the empty pews. Easton nodded his head toward the door that was to my right before he reached for the handle and pulled it open.

"Sweetness." Spencer's hot breath was in my ear as he reached for my hand. "I don't think that I can do this."

I gripped his fingers tightly. "You can," I assured him.

His brown eyes were full of fear when I turned to look at him.

"You are one of the bravest people I know, Spencer. You stepped in the Maxwell house knowing that Easton would kill you on sight, but you didn't give two shits, did you? You wanted me, you came for me, and you made me realize that I'm worth it," I told him.

His face softened, and his eyes lit up. "I love you."

The sound of screaming cut him off, and we all raced downstairs without a second into the darkened room.

"Shit, where's the light?" Cash hissed as someone knocked into me.

"I can't see anything," Lennox whispered loudly just as the lights came on.

Right across from us stood Rick with a wicked grin on his face. "It's nice of the Knights to finally show up. I was starting to think you forgot about us."

He moved to reveal Ellie and Brett, tied back-to-back on chairs with tape covering their mouths. But more than that, Heidi Morgan was leaning casually against the wall, her arms on her slim hips and a smirk on her pretty lips.

"You," Easton growled. "Why are you involved in this? What does Rick have on you?"

She simply rolled her eyes. "You stupid boys, never paying attention to the simple girls, only the beautiful ones." Heidi made a silhouette motion with her hands. "You never noticed me. No matter how hard I tried."

"That's what this is about? Because we never looked at you the way you wanted?" Easton's hands balled into fists at his side. "You're dead." His body vibrated with hate.

Heidi covered her mouth with her hand as she giggled. "You don't hurt girls," she said casually.

"But I do," Lennox promised. "I will have no problem pulling every single strand of hair from your head." Heidi's eyes went wide. "You can count on it."

"Let them go." I stepped forward just as Rick raised the gun in his right hand. Spencer's grip tightened around mine.

Rick chuckled softly as he brought the gun to his chin level. "You Knights, just assuming that everyone is going to listen to you, do whatever you want." He rolled his eyes. "Silly, really, but what do I know?" He smirked. "Oh, wait." He knocked on the wall.

The door behind him opened. You could have heard a pin drop when Spencer Senior walked into the room.

"Dad?" Spencer sound surprised.

Senior shrugged. "Sorry, son, but I tried to warn you that the Knights were bad news." He glanced over at the pastor, Heidi, Ellie, and Brett, then back at his son. "You should have listened," he told him.

"You," Easton snapped. "You're the one who is really in charge." He popped his jaw. "If you let them go, let me have Heidi, I promise I'll kill you quickly."

Senior made a finger gun. "Bingo, boy." He winked. "I'm not letting anyone go tonight, Easton. Too bad about your daddy, though. Never did what he was told, and maybe if he had listened..." Senior shrugged his shoulders.

"You son of a bitch!" Easton sprang forward and might have gotten to Senior if Rick hadn't had that gun.

The sound was deafening when it went off, and Lennox screamed in horror as Easton dropped to the ground. Cash stopped halfway like a game of red light, green light, before he ended up in the same position as his best friend.

"What is the deal with these Kennedy boys, Pastor?" Senior clucked his tongue off the roof of his mouth. "Always thinking they're some sort of God." He laughed.

Blood began to seep out onto the floor beneath Easton. I looked up at Spencer and noticed his skin had turned ghost white. His entire body had begun to tremble before he released my hand and sank to the floor.

"You always were such a pussy, son." Senior sighed loudly. "Never had the guts that I did at your age, but I supposed that might have something to do with your mother. She always babied you too much, let you date who you wanted, and even though you were doing so well with

Ellie here"—he waved his hand in the air—"You had to go bring home a Knight."

Spencer had buried his face in his hands and begun to rock back and forth.

"Disgusting." He tsked.

"You're a monster," I snapped. "How dare you talk about your son like that?" I wanted to smash his face in. "What kind of a father you are you, anyway?"

Rick chuckled at my comment. "Like you know anything about having a father."

It was meant to provoke me, but I wasn't going to take the bait.

"Like *you* know about being one?" I didn't even flinch when Rick turned the gun on me. "You raped your step-daughter, got her pregnant, and made her own child believe she was her older sister."

Rick clicked back the safety again. "Keep talking, Jon-boy; it will give me a reason to kill you like I did your friend."

I took a step forward, but Spencer beat me to him, jumping from the ground to knock into Ellie's stepfather. Before Senior had a chance to intervene I yanked the knife from my back pocket and aimed it at his right thigh before I let it go. He went down faster than I thought his pants quickly turning a deep red.

Everyone watched in horror as Spencer and Rick struggled with the gun before it slid across the floor, and one of them kicked it across the room toward Cash. Lennox quickly grabbed it and let off one shot. Both Spencer and the pastor stopped in their tracks.

"Dare me, motherfuckers, because if you kill my best friend's boyfriend, I will end you," She promised. Her hand wasn't even shaking as she waved the gun at Senior. "You, untie them," Lennox insisted. "Cash, you can move now, baby. Go check on Easton. As for you, Heidi..."

Her eyes narrowed eyes just as she put a bullet into Heidi's leg. Heidi screamed.

Cash dropped down next to Easton. "You're okay, boss," he assured him, rolling him onto his side.

"Cash." His voice was weak, but he was alive, thank God. "Where's my girl?" His eyes rolled back slightly.

"She's right here, buddy." He smiled nervously.

"Tin Man!" Brett exclaimed the second her mouth was free.

Easton tried to get up. "Babe." He planted both hands on the floor but couldn't raise himself onto his knees.

"Easy, big guy." Cash patted his arm. "Cupcake, get over here." He started getting up so Brett could move into his spot.

Ellie threw herself at Spencer, plastering kisses all over his face, her arms wrapped tightly around his waist. "Baby, I thought I would never see you again," she cried as she clung to him. "You were so brave to do that. Stupid, but brave."

"I couldn't let anyone hurt you, Ellie," he murmured.

"Cash, tie them up," Lennox instructed as the sound of feet overhead caused us all to look up above us.

A hand wrapped around mine, and Ellie's scent invaded my senses. "Jonny." I turned to look down at her. "You saved me." She grabbed me as if she might fall over just as Spencer came up on my left to wrap his arms around both of us.

"Everyone okay down here?" Oz's voice boomed through the stairwell as he made his way downstairs. "Ho-lee shit." He whistled as he looked around the room. But it wasn't Oz that I was staring at it. It was the man standing directly behind him.

My father.

Chapter Thirty-Five

"Dad?" Jon sounded confused. "What... what are you doing here?" He untangled himself from Spencer and me so he could move closer.

Lee Hamden looked so much like his twin sons it was scary. He had brown hair that held no traces of silver and dark eyes that seemed to take in everything. He was tall, not as tall as Easton, who was a giant, but he was a few inches taller than his son. Lee was handsome for a man I figured to be in his forties, and I might have mistaken him for Jonathan and Jameson's older brother if I hadn't known better.

The older Hamden moved around Oz to get closer to his son. "Your brother called me." His eyes traveled around the room. "He told me he needed my help, but it didn't say anything about this." He stopped to take a deep breath. "I had no idea that all this... this shit was going on." Lee narrowed his eyes.

Jonathan raced over to his father to embrace him. "I've missed you," he told him.

Lee pulled back to grip Jon's face. "I'm sorry, son." He pressed his lips into a thin line. "For not being the father you needed in your life, for not being there when you needed me. We'll talk about it more later, but right now, we need to clean up this mess." He tilted his head. "Someone notify Doc about Easton?"

"I did," Cash told him.

"Good." Lee backed away from Jon. "Now we can deal with these two." He pointed at Rick and Senior, who were watching, wide-eyed, from where Cash had tied them up. Heidi was holding her weeping wound muttering nonsense as tear spilled down her cheeks.

"You really fucked this up, didn't you, Pastor?" He took a step closer. "Didn't I tell you to stay away from my sons? To let things happen the way they were supposed to happen, and if Ellie and Jonathan met, fell in love, whatever, then so be it. Yet, you couldn't keep your dirty hands off your own stepdaughter, could you?" His nostrils flared.

Rick sounded like he was trying to say something, but it all came out muffled. We heard the sound of a siren just as another car pulled into the parking lot. I suddenly craved Spencer's warmth, and when he wrapped his arms around me without even saying anything, it felt like he could read my mind.

"That's Doc," Cash announced. "He said he was going to call the paramedics, which by the obvious noise outside, they're here, too." He was standing next to Lennox. The gun was still in her hand, but now rested at her side.

"Anyone here?" a deep voice called out, and then it sounded like someone was coming down the steps. "Jesus Christ," the man I recognized as Doc grumbled. "You kids can't seem to stay out of trouble, can you?" He squatted down next to Easton. "You went and got yourself shot again," Doc commented.

Easton made a grunting noise in his throat. "Think... it just... grazed me." He panted and gritted his teeth.

"Don't talk." Brett clutched at Easton's arm. "Just relax," she told him.

"Nothing to worry about, dear," Doc assured her. "He's right about the grazing thing." He felt around Easton's body. "Looks like it hit him here." He tapped his shoulder. "So it looks a lot worse than it is. We'll patch him up in no time." Doc stood up as the EMTs scrambled down the stairs. "You think you're going to need me here, Lee?"

Jon's dad shook his head. "You can go, Andrew. I'll be fine."

"Let go of me!" Easton shouted as the EMTs began to assess him. "Brett, where are you? I need you." He reached out his hand for his fiancé.

Brett gripped it tightly. "I'm right here, Tin Man. I'm not leaving your side," she promised.

"She can go with Mr. Kennedy," Andrew—I finally knew the good doctor's name—spoke up before there were any problems. "She's family." He winked at Brett, who flashed him a grateful smile.

Lee suddenly pinned his eyes on me. "Where's your daughter, Eleanor?"

"I... don't know." I swallowed nervously as I spoke with Jonathan's father for the first time. "I thought—"

"She's with your mother!" Rick cut me off before I had the chance to finish. The piece of cloth that Cash had shoved into his mouth now sat on his chest.

Lennox smacked him in the back of the head. "No one was talking to you, asshole," she snarled. "You hurt her? Your own kid?" she asked.

"That's none of your business, slut... OW!" Rick cried out in pain when Cash gripped the back of his hair and yanked his head backward to look up at him.

Cash leaned over to press his face close to Rick's. "Talk to her again like that, dickwad, and I'll break your neck with my bare hands."

"All right, all right." Lee clapped his hands. "Now that Easton is being taken care of—" He glanced over at where I stood with his son and Spencer before turning his attention back to Rick and Senior again. "You're both done." Rick started to open his mouth, but Lee held up his hand. "Too late to apologize, *friend*. You've made one too many messes, and I honestly don't want to clean them up anymore." Lee waved Oz over. "Mr. Maxwell will take care of things. He's good at that."

Senior began to thrash in the chair despite the knife wound from Jon, and I felt Spencer grow stiff next to me. Wait, were they actually going to kill them? Despite everything, Senior had been like a father to me, and I couldn't stand here and let something like this happen to him.

"Wait!" Spencer beat me to it. "That's my dad, sir. Don't I have a say in this?" He looked close to tears.

Lee sighed softly. "For reasons I will never understand, Spencer, you love him. He's done horrible things that you aren't even aware of. I'm not sure why Ralph ever left him in charge, but those two had a friendship I wasn't privy to when I was your age. Owen, on the other hand, was always insanely jealous, wanting to be the boss and trying to one-up everyone. The things he did..." His voice trailed off. "Sorry, we're talking about your father now." Lee let out a long breath. "You think I should spare him? Even after all the things he's done. The killing, lying, cheating, stealing... You're okay with that?" He tilted his head.

"I... I don't... I don't know," Spencer cried. "Jon, what do you think I should do?" His brows dipped together.

"Let the bastard fry, Pearson." We all turned to stare at Oz. "He was planning on murdering your girlfriend along with Brett before we showed up. He's done nothing but talk shit about you to my father for years, and never once were we introduced like proper family. We could have been friends sooner." He licked his lips. "He slept with my mother while cheating on yours. He ordered Easton's father killed because he wanted to control everything. He was going to kill your girlfriend and your boyfriend tonight without even thinking about it. Does that sound like father material to you?"

I stared up at him wide-eyed. "How do you know all this?" I demanded.

"While I was cleaning up my mess, I cleaned out my father's pockets and found his wallet. Inside there was the password for his phone, the dumb boomer," Oz said smugly. "His phone has all the information we need." He folded his arms over his chest. "Who I'm supposed to marry, as well as Cash, Jameson, and you."

"Oswald," Lee warned. "Now is not the time."

He held up his hand. "Sorry, sir." He nodded at him.

Spencer shook his head. "I'm supposed to marry someone? I thought that was a Knight thing." He looked between Jon and me. "Who is it?" he demanded.

Lee took a step forward. "You don't want to do this now," he said. "There is a time and place for this conversation."

"I want to know now!" Spencer exclaimed before he spun around to stare at his father. "Who the hell do you think you are, huh? Trying to plan my life before I even knew who I am? I'm bisexual, Dad, that's not a horrible thing. I'm in love with Ellie and Jonathan, so how does that work into your twisted little games?" His nostrils flared.

Senior shook his head, staring at his son. He still had the white cloth shoved into his mouth.

"Let him talk." Oz sneered. "Let's hear with that the asshole has to say." He raised his brows.

Lee looked around the basement at everyone before his eyes landed on Spencer. "Is that what you want? To hear it from his mouth so that it will seem real to you?"

"Yes, please," Spencer answered.

Lee moved swiftly and quickly yanked the gag out of Senior's mouth. "You have the room, Pearson. Your son wants some answers." He stayed where he stood.

"You were never going to marrying Ellie," Senior growled with narrowed eyes. "You've been contracted to Diana Monaco since the day you could walk," he spat. "She knows because her big-mouthed father told her, but that's how it's going to go."

I gasped. "Like hell it will. She's a first-class skank," I told him. "The only people that Spencer is going to marry will be Jonathan and me. That slut is never touching my man."

"I think all of your plans are going to go up in smoke."

"What does that mean?" Ellie demanded.

Spencer squared his shoulders before he turned to face us. "You need to get out of here."

I shook my head. "Nice try, but we're not leaving without you." I gripped Jon's hand tightly.

"I'm serious, baby. If you don't leave now, something bad is going to happen," he promised.

"What are you talking about?" Cash asked.

Spencer was as white as a ghost. "That explosion at the castle, the one that nearly killed Josie?" he whispered. "That was my father."

"Boom!" Senior laughed maniacally. "You might want to listen to my son, guys and gals, because this place is scheduled to go up like the Fourth of July any second now."

Mass confusion broke out in the basement as we all headed for the stairs and tried to get out. I felt Jon's hand slip away from mine as I followed behind Cash and Oz, while I heard Lennox yelling behind me.

"Wait," I cried as we hit the dark cool air. "Where are Spencer and Jon?" I was able to locate everyone, including Lee, but my guys were missing. "I have to go back in there." I started toward the church, but Oz grabbed me around the waist.

"Can't let you do that, Eleanor." He pulled me up against his broad chest. "You go back in there, you might die, and I couldn't live with myself if that happened."

I struggled in his arms. "Let me go," I pleaded. "Oswald, they might end up dead—"

My voice faded out as soon as the church exploded in flames. I was thrown off my feet and flew across the lawn, landing in pile of snow with soft plop. I was on my feet in a heartbeat ready to make a beeline back to the church when Oz grabbed me, shoved me down, and used himself as a shield when the second explosion went off.

Chapter Thirty-Six

Everything hurt. My muscles, my bones, my brain.

It felt like my lungs were on fire as I tried to suck air in through my mouth, and I wondered just how bad this situation really was.

I knew where I was before I even opened my eyes. The antiseptic smell that invaded my nostrils, the slow beep of my heart rate on the monitor, and the hushed murmurs of the staff as they walked past my room.

I was in the hospital.

The last thing I remembered was being in the basement of the church right before everything seemed to explode at once.

"Holy shit!" My voice was a hoarse whisper as my lids flew up.

I tried to pull back the scratchy blue blanket wrapped around my body, but pain seared through my shoulder and chest.

"Jonny!" Ellie rushed toward me and stopped right next to the hospital bed. "I should get someone." She turned to leave, but I cupped her elbow. Her green eyes were filled with exhaustion and worry.

I licked my dry lips before I spoke. "Spencer." I sounded nothing like myself.

"He's okay," she assured me before she pulled back the curtain to the bed next to me to reveal Spencer was sleeping. "I had to fight like hell to get you two in the same room." Her pink lips turned up around the edges. "I have Doc to thank for that." She reached for my hand. "I should get someone."

When I swallowed, it felt like razors in my throat. "Luna," I croaked out.

"She's safe."

"Where?"

Ellie squeezed my hand. "She's home." I must have looked confused, because she tilted her head. "Our home, the Maxwell house."

I closed my eyes just for a moment, and when I opened them again, the room was dark. My brain was so foggy that for a split second, I forgot where I was until I glanced to the right.

Spencer.

His face was turned toward me, but he was fast asleep. They probably had him on the same drugs they'd pumped me full of. It made me feel loopy, like a floating balloon. In the dim of the hallway lights, Spencer's lids fluttered, reacting to whatever he might be dreaming about. I hoped it was something good. I could make out a jagged cut on his cheek, but that was the only damage to his perfection that I could see at this moment.

"Are you awake, baby?" Ellie's voice filtered across the room before she appeared at the end of my bed. "Good stuff, huh?" She slowly moved toward my side. "You broke your collarbone as well as a couple of ribs, but you're going to be all right. The healing process will take a while."

My dick jerked beneath the rough blanket as she dragged the back of her hand over my cheek.

I grabbed her wrist. "How is he?" I jutted my chin at Spencer. What about Cash and Oz? Easton had been shot, but Doc assured us he would be all right. "My dad?" I barked out as my memories started to hit me.

"Spencer is going to be okay."

"The guys?"

Ellie ran her hand through my hair. "Can you scoot over?"

Her eyes glittered in the dark as I made room. She carefully pulled back the blanket before she slowly eased herself onto the bed next to me. Her fruity scent was a welcome home, blocking out the horrible one inside this room.

"The Knights are recuperating." Ellie's voice was gentle as her hand smoothed down the blue-checkered gown wrapped around my chest. "Oz has a broken nose, a broken collarbone, and a fractured ankle." She pressed her warm lips against the skin on my neck. "He covered me with his own body when the second explosion hit. Saved my life, or so I was told." She stopped to look me in the eyes. "Cash and Lennox have a little bruising on their bodies from when the place went up, but somehow managed nothing more."

I could see her face crumbling. "What aren't you telling me?" I grabbed her hand from my chest to lace our fingers together.

"Senior, Rick, and Heidi are all dead."

"Jesus Christ." I hissed as dread filled my body.

Ellie nodded. "Spencer... He has a couple of broken ribs and some bruising and burns on his legs. But"—she turned her head toward our boyfriend—"he didn't take the news so well... about his father." Ellie met my eyes again. "He's on some sedatives now because he kept screaming."

"Don't talk about me like I'm not here." Spencer's mouth sounded like it was full of marbles.

"Baby, go back to sleep," Ellie told him. "You're dreaming again." She pressed her lips together. My brows dipped as I opened my mouth, but she shook her head. "He needs to rest," she whispered.

I glanced over at Spencer before I spoke again. "How is Easton?" I suddenly felt like I couldn't keep my eyes open.

"He's fine. He was discharged this morning. They wanted to keep in longer, but he threatened to walk out."

I smirked. "Sounds like the boss to me." I wanted to hold Ellie, but my body seemed to have a mind of its own. "Love you," I heard myself mutter before I drifted off again.

***

"Rise and shine, little bro." Jameson's voice was close to my ear. "You would think you would wake up to see your own twin," he teased.

I popped open one eye. Ellie was gone, as was Spencer. "Where are they?"

"Relax." Jameson sat down on the bed Spencer had been in. "Your boy is having some x-rays done, and your girl went with him." He tilted his head. "I tried to convince them you needed a new brain, but they wouldn't listen." He snickered.

I raised my hand to flip him the bird. "How's Josie?" I asked.

Jameson dropped his chin and slowly ran his hand through his hair. "Uh, she's okay," he mumbled under his breath.

"She won't see you." Jam nodded at my statement. "Shit, man, I'm sorry."

"Not your fault, Jon," Jameson assured me. "I try to visit every day, but I'm always turned away. It sucks, though, that Josie, my wife, wants nothing to do with me." His voice shook. "I've been writing her letters in hopes that she'll finally reach out to me. She's probably throwing them out before she even reads them."

I wished I could comfort him right now. Wrap my arms around him like when we were kids and hiding from the thunder and rain.

"She'll come around," I said. "She loves you; she's just frustrated and hurting right now." I had no idea if that was the truth or not, but I hoped it sounded convincing.

"Right." Jam nodded.

"Looks who's awake!" Ellie's soft voice filled the room as she walked in. Jameson stood to give her a brief a hug before she moved to slide her lips over mine.

"It's too crowded in here," Spencer complained as the nurse pushed his wheelchair over to the bed. "Leave me here. I want to be near Jonathan. I'll be fine," he growled as he kept his dark eyes on me.

The dark-haired nurse nodded. "Just let me know when you need help to get into your bed," he said before disappearing out of the room.

Spencer touched my arm. "Hey, sweetness." His brown eyes searched my face.

"Hey," I managed to answer him. "You holding up all right?" I relished in the way his hand squeezed my forearm before he found my hand.

"Tip top shape." He winked, but if he was trying to sound funny, it wasn't going to work. His eyes told me everything he wouldn't.

Jameson coughed. "I should go. Let the three of you catch up."

"No, stay." Spencer waved his free hand around. "You're family now, man." The comment sounded off.

Ellie shook her head. "Spence." She bit her lip.

Spencer closed his eyes. "My father is fucking dead, Ellie. I have a right to be upset. My mother is already planning on selling the house, so she can leave Kingston, and I'm left with so many unanswered questions."

"You don't have to take it out on Jameson," I spat. "He didn't kill your father."

Spencer turned to glare at me. "No shit. My father managed that all on his own." He popped his jaw before he dropped his gaze. "I'm sorry. This entire thing has me so fucked up." When he looked back up, tears shimmered in his brown eyes.

"Baby." Ellie moved to wrap her arms lightly around him.

I itched to do the same.

My brother touched my shoulder. "I know," he told me and bent down to hug me. "I love you, Jon." He shouldn't be the one comforting me right now. "I'll talk to you later." He patted my arm, gave a brief wave to Ellie and Spencer, then walked out of the room.

"He told you about Josie." Ellie was watching me when I looked back at her and Spencer. "Sad, but I think that she's going to be okay."

"Have you spoken to her?"

Ellie nodded. "She'll see me and Cash, but she's pretty pissed at her husband and sister. God, that sounds so weird to say. Husband." She pressed her lips into Spencer's hair.

"And the letters?" *Please tell me she is reading them.*

"She's read them."

Relief flooded my body for Jameson. He needed her like, well, like I needed Ellie and Spencer.

"Jon." I glanced over at Spencer. "My mom packed up all my shit, and the rest of Ellie's. It's already at the Maxwell house. I hope that's all right." He kept his eyes down. "Oz didn't care and said if I needed my own room, he'd get me one," he added.

"I want nothing more than for the two of you to live with me," I assured him. "You won't need your own room, Spencer, unless you want it. We'll need a bigger bed, though." I winked.

Ellie gave me a big smile. "How do you feel about being a dad?" When my eyes nearly popped out, she giggled, and her cheeks flush pink. "To Luna. She's excited to meet you. She has so many questions right now. I don't think she really understands that I'm her mommy yet." The happiness vanished from her face. "All this time..." Ellie's big eyes filled with tears.

"Hey." I reached over to run my fingers down her arm.

"I'm all right." She said. "My daughter is finally with me, and Rick is gone." She pressed another kiss to Spencer's head. "I have the two of you." Ellie stepped closer to me.

Spencer nodded. "You two are all I have now," he murmured before he dragged his gaze to me. "My family." He sniffed.

"That's not true, man." Cash's voice filled the room. "Nice to see you two both up and awake for once." He casually leaned against the doorframe.

Spencer's eyes went wide as his mouth dropped open. "How did you escape unharmed?" He was as confused as I was.

"Don't know, dude, but I'm not complaining. Needed to protect my girl, you know, and I wanted to make sure she was safe. I thought I would wake up in hell with Satan as my new best friend, but turns out I got real fucking lucky." Cash folded his arms over his chest.

"How is Len?" Ellie spoke before I could.

Cash dragged his teeth over his bottom lip. "Pissed at me. Hates the world." He tried to make a joke of it, but his eyes gave him away.

"So, the same?" I chuckled. "Good to see you, man." I meant it, too.

Spencer raised his arm. "Can I ask a question?" he asked.

"Shoot." Cash gave him finger guns, which caused Ellie and me to groan. "You fucking love me. Knock it off." He laughed.

Spencer glanced at me before he spoke. "What did you mean when you walked in? About Ellie and Jon not being all I had." He sounded hopeful.

"You're going to make me say it?" Cash asked. "Fine, whatever. You, Pearson, are a Knight. You have your two baes, of course, but you also have me, Easton, Jameson, and Oz. Not to mention Brett and Lennox. The crown will always reign for the Knights, and you are one of us." He glanced up at the ceiling. "We found the proof, too, which"—he paused—"we'll share with you once you're on your feet again."

"No." Spencer grunted. "Tell me now."

Chapter Thirty-Seven

My dad was dead.

Spencer Pearson, Senior. The man who loved me so much when I was born that he gave me his name. The man I used to follow around, begging him to take me to work with him. The man I idolized because he seemed to have it all. The one who taught me how to ride a bike, drive a car, use a gun—

Was dead.

At first, I wished that I was dead, too. It wasn't that I felt guilty about his death, because it wasn't my fault. It was *his* fault. The fire, the explosion, that shit was all on my old man. But wasn't he trying to do all of this for me?

"I can't tell you now." Cash sighed and stood up to his full height.

Guy was fine as all hell, broad shoulders, that tan he continuously wore even in the middle of winter, and those eyes. Blue as the morning sky, perfectly shaped, and dancing with laughter only he could seem to find. Square jaw covered in a dusting of blonde scruff and plump, pink lips that would make anyone, myself included, weak in the knees.

Good to know my dick was still working, even when my whole world was falling down around me.

I shifted in the uncomfortable wheelchair. "Is it Easton?" My brows dipped when he nodded. "Shit." I felt anger nip at my brain. "Can't you just, I don't know, text him or something? This is my life we're talking about." I felt sick to my stomach.

"Baby, you want me to get the nurse? You look exhausted." Ellie's voice drifted over me. She brushed the hair back from my forehead before she pressed her lips to my skin. Damn, all the blood in my body was rushing to my cock again.

"I'm fine." My eyes flew open. "I'm serious, Cash. If I'm your family now, I deserve to know the truth about my own." I didn't mean to sound as angry as I did, but I couldn't help it.

Cash grimaced. "Don't do this to me, man." He pleaded with me.

Maybe it was the look on my face, or he felt bad for me, because he eased himself down into one of the plastic chairs.

"Fine, but if the boss man says anything, you tell him your father told you. Got it?" he hissed.

"Yeah, sure, whatever." I waved my hand in the air.

Cash dropped his shoulders so he could lean his elbows on his knees. "You already know he was crazy for power. He was controlling everything once Ralph Kennedy died; he was the one who convinced Chad to kill him. He made Easton's father convince him they were friends, best friends, but every time Ralph made a move or did something, Senior was right there to stab him in the back." His words sent shivers up my spine. "You were originally supposed to marry Brett, because you're who her father, Chad, wanted. Diana is not part of the Knights at all, but your father dug his heels in and somehow convinced everyone that she was proper for you. When you two got married, you would inherit her fortune, which is well over a billion. That's billion, with a b." He twisted his lips as he waited for my reaction.

"Holy shit." Jonathan wheezed.

I felt like I might pass out. "I'm not... I won't... I would never..." I tried to swallow the lump in my throat, but it only seemed to get worse.

Ellie ran her hand through my hair. "No one is saying you have to do anything, Spence." She wrapped her arms around my neck. "I love you." Her lips brushed my skin as she spoke.

Jon reached his hand out toward me. "You're with us, baby. We're not going anywhere," he murmured as I linked our fingers together. "I think that's enough, Cash." His voice dripped with anger.

"No!" I objected as Cash stood up. "There's more, right? What aren't you telling me?" What could be worse than what I had just learned?

Cash gritted his teeth. "Your mom slept with Owen," he spat.

"We all know that." Jon reminded him.

"Right, well..." Cash's eyes were full of guilt. "It was just a onetime thing, but she did it just to piss off your father. Seems he had a side piece, too." He grimaced.

I bit down on my lip so hard that I tasted copper as I waited for the next shoe to drop. Was I secretly Oz's brother? Or was Lennox my sister?

"It's not what you're thinking," Cash answered, as if he could read my mind. "Well, there was a baby..."

I groaned. "This just keeps getting worse. Was Senior even my father?" I whispered.

Cash looked surprised. "Uh, yeah, man. You don't need a DNA test for that. You look just like he did at your age. No, your mom got pregnant, was planning on leaving your father because she didn't want to deal with the Knights anymore, and she sort of had an accident."

"Sort of had an accident? What the hell does that even mean?"

He nodded. "There was a bad storm going on outside. She had packed all of her belongings in a suitcase and was headed out of town. She wasn't even leaving him for Owen, but had plans to get out of Kingston, raise you and the baby together; she just had to stop to pick you up."

I tried to brace myself for whatever Cash was going to tell me next, but it didn't work.

"Her brakes failed." He ducked his eyes to his bright white sneakers. "The baby and your mom"—Cash met my gaze—"both died on impact."

"What?" Ellie, Jon, and I all shouted together.

"My mom isn't dead," I insisted. "She's..." Wait, was the woman I thought was my mother... not? I tried to rack my brain to remember something, anything, that might tell me otherwise. My parents didn't have wedding photos. My mother said her parents died before I was born. No cousins that I was aware of until recently, Oswald and Lennox. My parents had always made it seem like Owen didn't have children, which I knew wasn't true because they'd talked about Oz all the time.

Jonathan squeezed my hand. "Say something, Spencer," he pleaded.

"Who was the woman pretending to be my mother? Was her name really Holly, or did she just take over my mother's life? Was Tina really her sister? Fuck!" I exclaimed and heard my voice bounce around the room. "My whole life was a fucking lie," I whispered.

Cash looked horrified for a split second before his face grew dark. "You're not saying anything I haven't lived through myself, bro." He bared his teeth before his muscles relaxed into a friendlier tone. "Look, I'm sorry, but you asked."

"Who. Is. She?" I asked again.

"Just some woman your father met while traveling the world. He wasn't really a nurse, you have to know that." Cash's brows shot up.

I closed my eyes. "Some woman? Just some woman?" I wanted to disappear.

"She looked enough like your mother that people didn't really question it. Senior had your real mother—the real Holly—buried, told no one about the baby or accident, and brought the fake one home. You were just a baby, hardly even walking yet, and that is the real reason Tina stopped speaking to your father. Not because of the affair or the pregnancy, but because he lied about what happened." Cash's soft voice did nothing to calm me.

Ellie moved around to face me. "I think that's enough." She cupped my head with her small hands. "Baby, this is too much, too soon. You were in an explosion, you almost died, and you don't need to get any more upset than you already are." Tears filled her eyes.

"Too bad, baby, because I am." My nostrils flared. "You don't get to decide anything right now, Ellie, because this is my fucking life."

Her face turned white. "Really, Spencer? You think I don't know anything about what bullshit families are? My stepfather killed my dad and then raped me. He took my virginity, planted his seed inside me, and I ended up pregnant at fourteen. Did I mention he raped me?" Ellie sucked her bottom lip into her mouth, and her chin trembled. "So don't talk to *me* about family drama without *thinking* about that." She turned away so I couldn't see her, but the way her shoulders shook told me all I needed to know.

"Ellie." I ran my hand down her back. "Baby, I'm sorry." I was, too. I was a horrible, terrible person who didn't want to see his girl or guy hurting.

Ellie shook her head, and I watched the way her white hair bounced in her ponytail. "We're in a fight right now," she insisted.

I noticed how Cash tried to look anywhere but in my direction, and when I met Jon's heated gaze, a sob escaped my throat.

"Don't hate me," I begged. "You two are all I have left, and I just... in the moment, didn't think when I spoke." Hot tears burned my eyes. "I love you. I love you both so much, and if you push me away, I will never survive."

Ellie spun around. "You stupid, stupid boy." She peppered kisses all over my face as Jon tugged on my hand. "I'm mad, but I could never hate you," she promised.

"Spencer." Jon's voice brought my attention away from the Goddess in front of me, and to the God at my right. "It hurts me to see you two like this. I love you, too, and I would never leave you." His cheeks flamed pink as he snuck a look at Cash, who chuckled softly.

"You confessing your love for me in front of your friends now?" I grinned, despite everything.

Cash coughed. "I'm your friend, too, Pearson." He stood up. "That's enough for today. Easton will have my balls if he finds out I told you any of this. Remember..."

"Lee told me," I finished for him. "Hey, where is he, anyway?" I realized I hadn't even thought to ask that. I'd just made sure he wasn't dead.

Cash pursed his lips. "Gone." He grimaced.

"Gone? How can he be gone? He was in the explosion with us. How can he be gone?" Did he leave again without saying goodbye to his son or making sure I was alive?

"You said he was okay," Jon reminded Ellie.

Cash answered for her. "He was supposed to come here in the ambulance, but..." He made a face I couldn't figure out. "Doc swears he has no idea what happened, but they made a stop on the way, and Lee disappeared."

"I need to lie down," I told Ellie, who pressed the button for a nurse. "Cash..." I wasn't sure what I was supposed to say to him. He told me what I wanted, but also told me things I had never even thought I would hear in my life.

Cash climbed to his feet. "Sure, no problem." He zipped up his coat. "Sorry to be the one to drop all the bad news on you." He gave a little wave of his fingers and disappeared from the room.

***

They let Jon out a week after the accident, and I was discharged a few hours later. Accident, ha, it was no accident, but that's what the fire marshal declared, and everyone went along with it. Someone must have paid them a lot of money to come up with that, because that was two explosions in the past six months, and no one has batted an eye at it.

It left no doubt in my mind that the Knights ran this town. Now I was one of them.

"Spencer!" Luna came flying at me the moment I stepped into the house. She glanced up at Cash with big eyes—he was the one who had picked me up today because everyone else was busy—and then she broke into a big grin. Her little hands were covered in pink paint, and her blonde hair, not as white as her mother's, but close, was pulled back in two pigtails.

I smiled at her as I stopped to rest. My ribs felt like they were going to explode, and I was pretty sure I'd lost all feeling in my legs, but I was just happy to be out of the hospital.

"Hey, sweetie, what have you been doing?" I noticed the paint droplets on her face and shirt.

"Auntie Brett is teaching me to paint," Luna gushed.

I glanced over at where Easton sat on the couch. He simply shrugged his shoulders as if it was no big deal.

"That's great, Luna," I told her before I dropped onto the couch. "You like living here?"

"I have my very own room." Luna climbed up on the cushion between us. "It's like, big. It's purple, my favorite color." If the smile on her face got any bigger, I was afraid her cheeks would burst.

Easton chuckled. "Brett gave up the room she was using to paint in, but not before little Luna here saw all the paint, canvases, and easels. She insisted someone teach her how to paint, and Brett was more than happy to oblige." He looked, well, happy for maybe the first time I had known him. "Luna, why don't you go find Brett and ask her to teach you how to draw."

Luna's eyes went wide before she hugged me, stopped to give Easton a high-five, and dashed up the stairs, calling out Brett's name.

"She's pretty great," Easton commented.

My brows dip. "You want babies with your girl, Kennedy?"

"Hell yes, of course. I want a ton of little Eastons and Bretts running around." He laughed when my eyes went wide. "She's fucking *it* for me. I don't have to explain that to you. I knew the moment I saw Brett that I wanted her in every way possible. Only I had to act like the asshole first," he teased. "We think little Luna has a crush on Cash," he added.

My head spun around to stare at Cash, who grinned at me. "What can I say? The ladies love me." He chuckled softly before he leaned against the wall. "She's adorable as all hell. I like having her around. We play dolls together. I let her do my hair. It's fun." He winked.

"We've never had a child in the house before," Easton told me.

This was too much for me to handle. Everything was happening so fast, and I just needed a second to catch my breath.

"Pearson, you all right?" Easton leaned forward.

"There you are!" Ellie cried as she walked down the stairs. "I'm sorry that I couldn't be there when you left the hospital, baby." She hurried down to see me.

I nodded. "Sure, I get it. Jon needed you." I didn't mean to sound angry when I spoke.

"Don't do that." Ellie's voice was low as she met my eyes. "You think I'm picking him, is that it?" She gritted her teeth.

"Didn't say that."

"You didn't have to, Spencer; I can see the hurt written all over your face."

I popped my jaw as Easton slowly climbed to his feet. "Come on, dude. Let's go check on Oz." He jerked his head in the direction of the stairs.

I continued to stare at the door in front of me until Ellie gripped my chin and turned my face toward her.

"Baby," she whispered before sliding her lips over mine. "Talk to me." She pushed. "I love you. *We* love you."

"I needed you," I confessed. "I needed both of you." I felt stupid admitting that. I wasn't a child anymore.

"Come with me." Ellie tugged on my arm. "Come see Jon." She stood up and waited for me to do the same.

I moved slowly behind her, wishing I didn't feel like an invalid, or so helpless. My ribs hurt with every step, making me feel like I couldn't breathe. When Ellie stopped outside Jonathan's bedroom, she knocked once before she opened the door.

He looked like some sort of prince lying in the middle of the oversized bed. I realized it was new—maybe an Alaskan King King—and that it would hold all three of us comfortably now. Jon didn't have a shirt on. His bare shoulders sent lust through my veins, and I was thankful that the covers were tucked in around his chest. His dark hair was damp as if he had just washed up, and when he opened his eyes and saw me, a smile broke out on his rugged face.

"Hey baby," Jon wheezed. "Welcome home," he whispered.

I moved as fast as I could to get to him—the hell with my ribs—and sat down on the mattress.

"Hey yourself, sweetness." I brushed the hair from his forehead before I pressed my lips against his warm skin. I was an asshole of the grandest kind. "How are you?" I noticed the few cuts on his face were practically healed, though his eyes looked glossy—he was probably on medication.

"Better now that you're here," Jon said with a sloppy smile. "Love you," he confessed, and his eyes fluttered.

I glanced up at Ellie, who had hearts in her eyes. "He's in a lot of pain," she told me. "His shoulder is bad. He might need surgery, but Doc wants to wait to see on that." Her expression hardened. "It's why I needed to stay with him, Spencer, because he's—"

I didn't let her finish, but instead got up and covered her mouth with mine.

"Don't," I whispered. "I'm sorry. You did the right thing," I assured her before shouting came from down the hall.

"Get bent!" Oz exclaimed. "You two need to stop fussing over me like I'm broken. I'm not fucking broken! Get out of my room before I kick your asses out of my house."

Something slammed against the wall, and a moment later, Luna ran down the hall toward the sound.

I started toward the door.

"Wait." Ellie cupped my elbow with the palm of her hand. "He adores Luna. And she loves him."

I tilted my head. "Say that again?"

Ellie broke into an easy smile. "Oz has spent hours with Luna since he got home just reading to her. It's the cutest thing." I could tell she was dead serious. She glanced behind her at Jon, who was sleeping again. "You'll see." Ellie tugged on my arm and guided me out the door.

Chapter Thirty-Eight

Maybe it was the fact that he was going to be a father himself or maybe it was just because he wasn't the asshole he wanted everyone to think he was, but Oz took to Luna like a fish to water. The moment he saw my daughter, it was love at first sight, and I haven't had to worry about her since she officially moved into the house.

"Ozzy." The way Luna said his name made Spencer stop dead in his tracks. It sounded more like Ah-Zee. "'Gain, Oz, 'gain!" she cried happily, and I knew exactly what she wanted.

Oz chuckled happily. "You sure, sweet pea? I think you know this story by heart now. Maybe you should read it to me."

Luna's cheerful giggles rang out. "No, silly. I can't read." She laughed again.

"What are you now? Forty? Fifty?"

"I'm this many now."

I knew Luna was holding up her chubby little hand with four fingers when she answered him, and when I turned to meet Spencer's eyes, I saw the complete and total shock on his face.

"I told you," I whispered, taking his hand. "True love." I winked. "Not like some creepy Jacob and Esme *Twilight* shit," I said quickly. "More like he's the big brother she's going to need when she gets older."

Spencer's lips turned up into a slight smile before he tugged me down the hall so he could peek into the room. Luna was tucked in next to Oz, while her little hands gripped one side of *The Wizard of Oz*. She looked up at him with big green eyes before he booped her nose. He didn't seem to care or notice that she was still covered in paint.

"Oi, I know you're there." He grunted before looking up. "Pearson." His entire face was a mixture of colors, mostly black and blue, but there was red mixed in for good measure. His eyes were bruised from his broken nose, but his spirits seemed different when he was around Luna.

Luna clapped her hands. "Mama, Spencer, Ozzy is reading to me."

Would I ever get used to her calling me Mom? It made my heart ache with something I had never felt before.

"I can see that." Spencer jutted his chin out. "Don't let us stop you."

Fuck off, Oz mouthed, batting his lashes. "How are you?" he asked before closing the book. "Sweetie, why don't you go wash up. I'll read to you after dinner. I need to talk to your mom and Spencer."

Luna rolled her eyes. "Fine." She huffed, but before she climbed off the bed, she pressed her lips against Oz's cheek. "Love you."

"Love you more," Oz assured her.

Once Luna had left the room, after stopping to hug Spencer and me, we shut the door to talk in private.

"I need to thank you." Spencer dragged his hand through his hair and gripped the back of his neck.

Oz's brows shot up. "For?" He looked between the two of us.

Spencer sighed before he sat down on one of the oversized chairs. "For saving Ellie's life," he answered. "If it wasn't for you, she might not be here right now."

"Pffff." Oz waved a hand in the air and winced. "It's nothing, so don't go making a big deal out of it." He grunted.

"No, man," Spencer told him. "If you hadn't used your own body as a shield? We'd be having a much different conversation right now. So, thank you."

I felt warmth spread over my body. "Look at you two, bonding and shit," I teased them before I dropped a kiss into Spencer's hair.

"Woman, it's not like we're going to be holding hands and skipping through the meadows or anything." Oz grunted, but I saw the way his lips turned up slightly. "You're welcome, Spencer." He gave a curt nod of his head.

Spencer squeezed my hand. "You hear that, baby? He called me by my first name." A smile spread across his face. "I think he's thawing."

"*He* is right here, so don't talk about me like that." Oz scowled as he stared Spencer down.

"Admit it. You like me," Spencer teased.

Oz bared his teeth. "You can fuck right off." He rolled his eyes. "You're one of us. You're my family, and that's all." He held up his hand. "If you say one more thing about it, I will slit your throat while you sleep." He met my eyes. "Eleanor, can you get me something to drink?"

Oz dropped his gaze. I knew how much he hated being stuck in this room. Hated the idea of sharing one with Jon even more after I suggested it as a way for them to keep one another company. Maybe I should suggest that again.

"Sure." I walked over to the small fridge that Cash had installed, pulled out a bottle of water, and opened it before I handed it to him. "You need anything else? Sponge bath?" I teased.

Spencer's eyes flew open, and Oz let out a bark of laughter. "Relax, man, she's kidding," he assured his cousin. "Diana's coming over. She said she would help me with whatever I needed." Oz wiggled his brows.

"Diana Monaco? Is coming here? Are you crazy?"

"We've talked about this, Eleanor."

I gritted my teeth. "She's bad news," I reminded him for the millionth time.

He swore to me it wasn't serious, he was only screwing her the way she deserved, but I wondered if it was because he was so lonely. I had my guys, Easton had Brett, Jameson was wrapped up with Josie, and hell, even Cash had Lennox—whether she wanted to admit it or not.

"Do I look worried?" Oz asked, and he looked anything but. His porcelain skin looked as cold as his tone, and even that bothered me. "Don't worry about me, woman, worry about your boys. Go take care of them. Send your little in before I get too busy." He winked.

I moved to press a kiss against Oz's forehead. "Be careful, Ice," I reminded him as Spencer opened the door to leave. I turned back to meet Oz's eyes again. "Brett and Easton know she's coming over?" I asked.

"Don't you worry your pretty head about them, Eleanor. This is my house," Oz reminded me. "I'll handle them when the time comes." He reached for his phone on the table next to him.

I shook my head. "It's your funeral," I warned as I shut the door behind us.

***

"You have got to be kidding me!" Brett sounded pissed. I don't think I had ever heard her like that before. She was usually so bubbly and friendly.

"Keep your voice down, B, the entire house can hear you," Oz snapped back.

"Don't fucking call me that, Oz," she warned. "I don't care if she was your girlfriend; Palmer stabbed me in the back just like she did to you. That nickname is off limits. Now you expect me to just let that cunt in this house?"

"I might win the screwed-over-best award from Palmer," Oz insisted.

I glanced up at Spencer as he chuckled softly. We had been cuddled up on the lounger, listening to them bicker for a few minutes now, and I was surprised Jon hadn't woken up yet. Those must be some serious painkillers.

"You do realize she tried to sleep with my fiancé, but pretended to be me so she could suck his dick, right?" Brett reminded him.

"Uh, duh. I saw the video, just like everyone else," Oz answered.

"Video?" I mouthed to Spencer, who shook his head. "There's a video?"

Spencer nodded. "Remember the night of the Christmas party? The one I made sure you were far away from?" The sound of his voice vibrated against my chest as he spoke.

He placed his phone down on the lounger just as we both saw the headlights from the window. I immediately climbed to my feet with Spencer right behind me.

"How do you think this is going to go?" I asked.

"Badly," Jonathan rasped, and when we turned to look at him, he grimaced. "You think I can sleep with all this noise going on?" He started to adjust himself against the pillows.

I reached over to help him. "We can give you something else. Doc said..."

"No." Jonathan shook his head. "I don't want any more medication. I'm sick of sleeping." He held his hand out toward Spencer, who took it. "I don't want to miss any more time with the two of you." He squeezed both our hands.

"We have the rest of our lives, sweetness," Spencer whispered before he slid his lips over Jon's. "The three of us against the world," he murmured as Jon tugged on my hand.

I moved closer. "I second that." I moaned softly as my lips connected with Jon's, and Spencer's tongue licked at mine.

Jon growled as the kiss lengthened, but we all jumped when we heard the sound of a door slam.

"Bet that's Len getting ready to throw punches." He chuckled softly, and then clamped his eyes shut. "As much as I want to keep kissing you, it's only going to leave me wanting more, and we all know that isn't possible right now." He gritted his teeth. "Maybe I should take an Advil."

"I got you, baby." I hurried to grab the pill bottle from his dresser. "We have plenty of time," I assured him, handing Jon the medicine and some water.

"Exactly." Spencer nodded his head. "We're not going anywhere," he told Jon as we both watched him pop the pills into his mouth and drain the entire bottle of water.

A smile tugged at Jon's lips. "Never enough time with you two," he murmured. "I can't wait to see you both naked again. Love you," he teased before he drifted off to sleep again.

I couldn't help the happiness that began to spread through my body as Spencer wrapped his arms around me. I really felt like I was home.

Until the sound of the doorbell ran through the house.

"Shit," Spencer muttered. "Do you think we should stay here?"

"Oh, I'm going to want to see this in person." I grabbed at his hand so we could go downstairs for the main event.

Brett was standing in the living room, her arms crossed over her chest, and glaring daggers at Diana, who stood in the doorway. Easton had his arm wrapped around Brett's shoulders, his own glare of death on his face, and all Diana did was smile. Her lips were a shade of hooker-red.

"No hard feelings, right?" She batted her long lashes as she began to remove her coat. When neither one of them spoke, she rolled her eyes. "Can't we be adults? I'm dating Oz now. You're going to have to get used to seeing me here." Diana pursed her lips right as her blue eyes landed on me. "Ellie." She almost sounded surprised as she took a step forward.

Brett held up a hand. "I don't think so," she hissed. "You're not welcome here, bitch."

"Oz invited me." Diana was stilling starting at me, like she didn't know I was going to be here.

"I live here, too, Diana, and we don't want you here," Brett pushed. "Go home before I have Lennox hold you down so I can finish what I started. You know, like the night you crashed yet another party you weren't invited to." She trembled with anger.

Diana finally broke my gaze. "I'm sorry," she blurted. "For that, for ruining your party, and doing what I did. It was uncalled for."

"You put your mouth on my fiancé's dick. You don't get to say sorry, and I will never forgive you."

Diana's brows shot up. "You two are engaged?" She looked between Kingston's power couple. "Congratulations." She looked like she regretted coming here.

"You need to leave." Easton finally spoke, but the way he did sent chills downs my spine. I felt Spencer tighten his grip on my hand.

"That is enough!" Oswald shouted, and we all turned to see him sitting in a wheelchair at the top of the stairs with Cash right behind him. I noticed he had made sure to put his prosthetic on along with shoes, so Diana didn't notice.

"Diana is welcome in this house. You don't have to like it, but she's my guest. You will be polite like I was when all your significant others started showing up." He bared his teeth. "Come on, baby, get that hot ass up here."

I was pretty sure I was going to lose my lunch.

"Let's go." I practically dragged Spencer into the kitchen as Diana made her way up to Oz. "That was something."

"It's fucked up," Easton answered as he stopped in the doorway behind Brett. "That bitch had better watch herself or she's leaving here in a body bag." He wrapped his hand around Brett's ponytail and tugged her face up toward his. "I fucking love you, Dorothy." He brought his lips down to hers.

Wow, Spencer mouthed to me, and I couldn't stop the giggle that escaped my throat.

"Sorry." I held up a hand when Brett turned back to look at me.

"I hate her," she hissed. "I hate having her in this house, knowing what she did. How she lied, and... fuck." Her blue eyes filled with tears, and she buried her face against Easton's chest. He easily wrapped his arms around Brett to hold her close.

"He's only doing this to get back at her. To make her pay," I reminded everyone.

Easton popped his jaw. "He'd better do it soon or I'll take care of her myself."

Epilogue

Jonathan

"We're late."

"That's your biggest concern, sweetness, that we're late? Not the fact that I was buried balls' deep inside you thirty minutes ago while you fucked our girl?"

I felt my stomach clench at Spencer's words. That was the reason we were late to the dance in the first place. He took one look at me in my dress slacks before he yanked them down and wrapped his mouth around my cock. It hadn't taken long after Ellie had walked out of the bathroom, fresh from her shower, before the three of us had forgotten about the winter formal.

Ellie's hand slipped into mine as we stood in the doorway of the Kingston High gym. "Nervous?" Her soft voice brought my attention back to the task at hand.

I was scared out of my damn mind right now. We should have walked in with the rest of the Knights. Maybe this was a horrible idea, and everyone at Kingston was going to run me out of town. This would be me officially coming out.

"Hey." I felt the pads of Spencer's fingers dance across my cheek before he turned my face toward him. "Say the word, and we'll leave. We don't have to do this now or ever if you're not comfortable." His brown eyes searched mine. "You're okay," He reminded me.

My guy. Spencer Pearson had been through so much in the past six weeks, yet right now, he was being strong for me. After everything that happened, losing his father, finding out the woman he thought was his mother wasn't actually his mother, Spencer had spiraled into a bit of depression until my sister-in-law convinced him to try therapy.

I might not ever get used to calling Josie that, but I was thankful for her help.

Spencer might not fully understand the lies his family had buried, but he was starting to realize that none of it was his fault. My brother wasn't here tonight because Josie was keeping her distance from him now that she was back home. He didn't like it and said he was trying to win back her trust.

Spencer was still watching me with concern written all over his handsome face. "Did we lose you?" he asked.

I could see Easton dancing with Brett, both of them smiling at one another like they were the only two people in the world, while "Shivers" by Ed Sheeran drowned out the sound of the rest of our classmates. They looked so incredibly happy, so in love and I realized how desperately I wanted that right now.

"Baby, I think he's freaking out. With everything that happened, it's probably too soon." Spencer leaned across me toward Ellie. "Maybe we should go."

I dropped Ellie's hand so I could grip the back of Spencer's head, then I slammed my lips over his. The low moan that escaped his throat before he grasped my shoulders made all the blood rush between my legs as our tongues slicked and swirled together.

"I'm not freaking out," I whispered, nipping jaw. "I love you," I added before I grabbed Ellie to crush her against my chest. "And you, sweetheart, I love you, too." I leaned down to take her warm, welcoming lips with mine.

"Is this what I'm going to have to watch all night?" Oz's deep voice caused me to chuckle softly. "The three of you making out like you don't do enough of that at home?" His ankle wasn't healing properly, which was causing him to use the wheelchair more than he liked. He tried to act like he didn't care, but since he wasn't able to do a lot of things, he was more bitter than ever.

Ellie rolled her eyes. "Not our fault you're dating the Anti-Christ, Oswald, and had to come stag to the dance."

We all refused to welcome Diana Monaco into our fold. Even if he was just using her just to break her heart. Brett hadn't spoken to Oz since the first night Diana came to the house, and I think he was actually starting to get worried about it.

"Save a dance for me." Oz held out his hand. "Come on, come on, you spend every single moment with these two idiots. The least you can do is spent a few minutes with your best friend tonight." He waited for her answer.

Ellie moved closer to Spencer and me. "I'm here with my guys tonight. I don't think... Wait, did you just call me your best friend?" I watched the way her eyes went wide at his words.

He nodded. "I did, woman, because it's the truth. I love you like a sister, and that means I would die for you if I had to. I almost did," he reminded us.

"Oswald." Ellie practically jumped into his lap to hug him, and the smile on Oz's face was one none of us saw often. "You're an asshole," she said as she wrapped her arms around his neck.

Oz held her tightly before he pulled back. "Oi, that's nothing I've never been told before, Eleanor." He glanced up at Spencer and me. "You're going to make them jealous." He chuckled.

"Nothing to be jealous about, man," I assured him. "She's our girl." I gripped Spencer's hand tightly in mine. "She's in our bed every night, screaming our names, but if it makes you happy to think we're jealous, by all means." I grinned at the way Oz flipped me the bird. I had no doubt he would never change.

Spencer let out a deep, throaty laugh. "Exactly my thoughts, sweetness. But you can have the first dance if you want since you're so hard up and all, Oz."

A month ago, Spencer never would have spoken to Oz like that, but now? I was happy my boyfriend got along with one of my best friends the way he did. They enjoyed playing Xbox games together, fighting over the remote for the television, and poking at one another to the point I thought someone—Oz most likely—would start throwing punches, but they always ended up laughing and acting as if nothing had happened.

"Fuck you." Oz pointed a finger at Spencer. "And fuck you, too, Jon." He started to roll the wheelchair away. "Maybe I'll just keep Eleanor to myself tonight," he called back over his shoulder.

"He wouldn't?" Spencer's brows dipped.

I smirked. "He can try, but you damn well know she's going to come back to us," I reminded him. "You want to go dance with me?"

"I thought you'd never ask."

As we moved out onto the dancefloor, I caught Lennox standing off to the side with her arms folded over her chest. Cash was in front of her, no doubt trying to get her to dance, but Lennox was having none of it. I wanted nothing more than the two of them to work things out, but if Cash kept pushing the way he was, it would never happen.

I slipped my hands up Spencer's chest so I could hook them around his neck. "You know everyone's watching us," I commented.

"They all think you're with Ellie."

"They know I'm with you right now, too."

Spencer dragged his thumb across my bottom lip. "Damn right, sweetness."

He caught my lips with his, and I closed my eyes to relish in his mouth. The way he took control of me, making me feel like it was just the two of us in the crowded gymnasium.

"Wait, wait!" Ellie suddenly squeezed in between us. "I told Oz he was going to have to wait for me. I couldn't let you two suck face without me." She wrapped one arm around me and one arm around Spencer. "I need to be with my men." She sighed happily.

When the slow song ended, I heard a giggle from Lennox as Oz did a wheelie with her in his lap around the dancefloor, and then I caught Cash spinning Brett around as Easton looked on. He narrowed his eyes just before he grabbed Ellie out from between Spencer and me, the both of them kicking up their heels to "Bang, Bang" by Jessie J, Ariana Grande, and Nicki Minaj.

"Did that just happen?" Spencer blinked at me while a smile spread across his face.

I nodded. "Pretty sure it did." I pulled him closer, feeling happier in my life for the first time in a long time. I just wish it didn't have to end.

Book Four Coming Soon

A Note from Sundae

Every single time I dive back into the Knights world, I feel like I'm coming home, because that's what they are to me. *Home.* Kingston is literally the town I grew up in with a few minor changes, and even though I wasn't a huge fan of being there when I was growing up, I can look back on my years there with a smile on my face. Especially all the Saturday morning Gerry's runs picking out the best donuts.

When I first introduced Spencer in *Piece of Cake,* I did not intend to bring him back for something bigger, but then I thought *what if...* What if he is the one Jon ends up with? The one he falls for, and Jon was who Spencer was after all along, not Brett? I feel like Ellie was the perfect piece to fit them both together. Not mention to put Oz in his place, because we know he needs that.

Writing the epilogue for this was **HARD!** I had so many ideas spinning around inside my head, only I wasn't sure if I wanted to go in that direction. I needed Jon to get his happily ever after, at least until the next round of nonsense rolls around for the Knights. I also hate saying goodbye when I've been in their world for so long.

I can tell you that Oz's book is next in the series. I feel like he's been getting meaner and darker with each book, so I'm ready to write his story now. Especially after he killed his father. I've already started taking notes. When they talk to me, they talk to me, and I can't let them rest.

Whatever questions you might still have, I promise they will be answered. Diana, Oz's mother, Palmer, and anything else you can think of.

Acknowledgments

Katie at Kay Kemp Book Polishing— thank you, thank you, **THANK YOU** for taking me on with three weeks to go before the release of this book. To quote Titanic, something I do often, you saved me. In every way that a person can be saved.

My husband— **my ride or freaking die.** Without you none of this would possible. Thank you for supporting me, trusting me, and talking me down from the ledges. I love you more than life.

My readers— without you I wouldn't be able to continue to do what I love. Your continued support does not go unnoticed.

Laura (@messing_with_books on IG)— again, your beautiful edits and love for my work overwhelms me. Everyone says Cash is their favorite Knight but just so everyone knows? Cash is yours.

Stephanie— you are the Nikki to my Tommy, the Lennox to my Brett. Meet you at the halfway point, bestie.

My friends and family— some of you may not read my books (mom, you probably still don't understand what MMF means which is perfectly okay), but you still share my teasers on FB and I love you for it. Thank you!

About the Author

Sundae Leighton writes romance novels that are sweet with a dark twist. She got her start writing fan-fiction with her friends in school, but didn't take the plunge to publish her first book (Picture Perfect) until 2020. Born and raised in Connecticut, where she currently resides with her husband and their cats. She sometimes scares herself when she writes things darker than intended, considers coffee the nectar of the Gods, and once ran the NYC marathon (OK - half marathon). When she isn't writing down what the voices in her head tell her to, she likes watching murder shows, NASCAR, and reading romance books with lots of angst.

You can keep in touch with Sundae at sundaeleighton.com and find her on most social media platforms.

Read more at https://sundaeleighton.com.